PANDEMONIUM

WORLD FALLEN

SUSANNA STROM

Visit my website at www.susannastrom.com
https://www.facebook.com/Susanna-Strom-Author-101447404809167/

Developmental Editor: Christina Trevaskis
www.bookmatchmaker.com

Interior Designer: Jovana Shirley
Unforeseen Editing, www.unforeseenediting.com

Proofreader: Brittany Meyer-Strom
brittanymedits@gmail.com

Cover Designer: Lori Jackson Design
www.lorijacksondesign.com

Photography: Wander Aguiar Photography
www.wanderbookclub.com

Model: Zack Salaun

ISBN ebook: 978-1-7348292-0-4
ISBN paperback: 978-1-7348292-1-1

The Saving Setora series, by Raven Dark and Petra Knox, is mentioned with the kind permission of the authors

Published by Cougar Creek Publishing LLC

AUTHOR'S NOTE

Every romance novel explores the power of love, human connection, and hope to make the world a better place. Some romance novels are set in a lighthearted, rom-com world. Others take place against a grim backdrop. Whatever the setting or circumstances, romance novels assure the reader of the possibility of a happy-ever-after.

I wrote Pandemonium in the summer of 2019. When my editor and I finished working on it in September, we decided to postpone publication until I wrote its sequel, Maelstrom. We planned to include a pre-order link for the second book at the end of the first. As I was finishing Maelstrom in late March of 2020, real-life events caught up with the fictional flu pandemic described in my novels.

Pandemonium and Maelstrom were in no way inspired by the Covid-19 virus. The timing is entirely coincidental.

I thought long and hard about how to proceed. I spent almost a year writing a story and creating a world and characters that I'm proud of and that I love. Some readers will choose to keep any story that reminds them of grim reality at arm's length. I understand and respect that choice. Other readers will welcome a story where characters struggle with and overcome a dire situation, finding the love, hope and connections that romance novels promise. For those readers, I decided to move forward with publication.

ONE

Kenzie

I slicked my wet hair back from my face and grabbed the towel that I'd slung over the shower curtain rod. A shadow fell across the plastic curtain. I glanced down at the three-inch gap between the bottom of the waterproof fabric and the floor. Bare feet—the toenails painted a bright apple green—shambled past the shower stall.

Jeez. At 3 a.m. on a Sunday morning, I'd figured I was alone in the big, communal bathroom. Whoever walked by was ignoring the unspoken rules of dorm life, not to mention common sense. You didn't sneak up on somebody in the middle of the night. You called out "Coming through" or "Hi" so you wouldn't startle them or look like a creeper. And nobody in their right mind walked across a public bathroom with bare feet. Hadn't they heard of foot fungus?

Muttering to myself, I wrapped the towel around my body.

The overhead lights flicked off and plunged the room into semidarkness. Only a narrow shaft of light from the hallway pierced the gloom. Stumbling backward on the slippery tiles, I almost fell out of my flip-flops. I groped for the walls, my heart thumping in my chest.

"Hey! Turn the lights back on."

Most people would have apologized and flipped the switch. Not my mystery intruder. She shuffled down the hall, leaving me alone in the dark.

"Thanks, asshole." She was probably the same type of joker who swiped my towel midshower during my first week in the dorm. Swathed in the flimsy shower curtain, I'd done my own version of the walk of shame back to my room.

That was bad. This was worse.

Squeezing my eyelids shut, I leaned back against the wall and sucked in a calming breath. Okay. If I waited a minute or two for my eyes to adjust, I should be able to navigate my way to the door, then out into the well-lit hallway. No need to freak out; I'd crossed this bathroom at least a thousand times. I counted backward from sixty, opened my lids, and swept aside the shower curtain.

Eyes on the prize.

The hallway light beckoned. I kept my gaze laser-focused on it, ignoring the shadows that hovered in my peripheral vision as I stumbled toward the open door. I stuck my head into the hall and looked in both directions. Green-toenail girl was nowhere in sight.

I marched down the long corridor, past a dozen dark, silent rooms. Lights flickered from the TV lounge. I paused in the doorway. One of those 1950s alien invasion movies that Uncle Mel and I used to watch played on the big screen. Smiling at the memory, I stepped into the room and scanned the sofas and chairs for signs of life. The place appeared empty.

Just last week the perky resident assistant had sent out a memo reminding people to turn off the big TV when they were done watching it, part of the university's green initiatives. I sighed. If Janie found the TV on when she made her rounds in the morning, she'd probably issue another flurry of memos. Picking up the remote from a table, I clicked off the television and turned to head back to my room.

Somebody groaned, and I jumped backward. Who was that? My gaze darted around the room, finally landing on a figure sprawled across a sofa. Guess I should have looked more closely instead of dismissing the lump as a pile of pillows.

"Hi," I called out.

Another groan.

With halting steps, I approached the sofa. Long, curly red hair spilled across a cushion and partially obscured her face. It had to be

Rachel what's-her-name from down the hall. One night last month, I found her at 2 a.m.—key in hand and reeking of tequila—passed out in the hallway outside her door.

"Hey, Rachel. You need help getting to your room?"

She mumbled her response, the words lost behind the tangle of hair.

"You okay?" I leaned over and brushed the hair back from her pale face. Her eyes fluttered open, and she squinted up at me. Her lips parted and she burped, spewing out a rancid cloud of rum-tainted vapor.

"Shit!" I staggered backward, lifting a corner of the towel to hold over my nose.

Rachel's chest hitched and she retched.

"No, you don't." I rolled her on her side, jammed a pillow behind her back, then pulled a small wastebasket close to the sofa, positioning it next to her head.

I was willing to play good Samaritan to keep the girl from choking if she puked, but if she was dead drunk, there was no way I could carry her back to her room. She'd have to sleep it off in the TV lounge.

"You want some water?" I offered.

"Huh-uh." She shook her head, then raised a hand to her temple, groaning again. I bet the rum was giving her one hell of a headache.

"You sure? How about an aspirin?"

"Wanna sleep," she slurred.

My conscience clear, I kept watch over her for another few minutes, until her dry heaves subsided, and she drifted off to sleep.

First the green-toenail girl and now Rachel; I don't usually see this much excitement in the middle of the night.

Must be a full moon.

I yawned. The fatigue that I'd been holding at bay for hours finally caught up with me. With heavy eyelids, I trudged back toward my bed, hesitating only when I passed Jenna and Lauren's room. Their door stood open a few inches. I stretched out a hand to close it. Somebody coughed inside the room, and I reconsidered. Maybe they left it open on purpose. Maybe they wanted fresh air. In that case, not my business.

Back in my room, I tore off the towel and climbed into bed. If I slept for three hours, I'd have plenty of time to finish my paper before Ali got back tomorrow. No, let's go crazy. Make it four hours. Four blissful hours of uninterrupted slumber. Then I'd roll out of bed, guzzle coffee, and finish the damned paper. Smiling to myself, I set an alarm and burrowed into my pillow.

When 7:15 came around, it took all my willpower not to shut off the alarm and go back to sleep. Grumbling, but resolute, I warmed water in the microwave and made a cup of instant coffee. Not my favorite, but caffeine was caffeine, and once it hit my system, I went back to work.

Ali burst into our dorm room, throwing the door open with such force that it struck the wall and rattled the framed poster. I jerked upright from my cross-legged position on my bed and pulled out my earbuds. What was she doing back so early? I wasn't expecting her until evening.

Ali met my startled gaze.

"If the governor declares a state of emergency and orders us to shelter in place, I'm not going to be stuck in the fucking dorm." She dumped her backpack on her bed, scattering books, papers, and pens over the rumpled quilt.

Ali slid her tablet into the empty pack. Her gaze swept over the room, pausing on her desk. She unplugged the charger and stuffed it into the pack, then retrieved her toiletry bag from her nightstand and packed it, too. She dashed across the room and threw open the door to her wardrobe.

"Jake's grabbing his stuff. He'll be here in five minutes." She glanced at me from over her shoulder, her hands busy pulling shirts off the hangers. "You need to come back to Boise with us. Mom likes you. We have plenty of room. It won't be a problem if you stay with my family."

She shoved the clothes into her backpack before turning to me.

"Kenzie, get your shit together so we can get out of here."

I stared at her, shaking my head. "What's going on? You make it sound like the world's coming to an end."

Ali threw her hands in the air. "Hello? The flu?"

I shrugged. Some crud was making the rounds of the campus. On Monday, a few people were hacking into tissues, and there were a scattering of empty seats in normally full lecture halls. By Friday morning, nearly three quarters of the students had missed my international marketing class. It was either a particularly nasty bug, or people were jumping at any excuse to take off early for the weekend.

No taking off for me. Procrastination inevitably bit you in the ass, and I was so late starting my big paper on the business culture of India that I had no choice but to unplug and buckle down to work. At least it had given me a legitimate excuse to miss the party at Jake's place last night.

"I can't go to Boise. I've got a paper to finish."

"Forget your paper. Campus alert sent a message an hour ago. Classes have been canceled for the next two weeks."

"No. That's impossible."

"The flu," Ali repeated. "Haven't you been watching the news? Or checking texts?" Her gaze swept the room. "Where's your phone?"

I pointed at my nightstand drawer. "Powered off. And I turned off internet access on my laptop, so I could finish the paper without any distractions."

"Of all the times to go radio silent! You haven't been online? Or talked to anybody since Friday?"

"Nope." I nodded at the mini fridge. "I've been holed up, eating yogurt and leftover Thai food since Friday night."

"Well...crap." Ali perched on the edge of my bed and grasped my hand, her hazel eyes uncharacteristically serious. "Listen. It's bad. The flu outbreak has exploded over the weekend."

"Gone viral?" I drawled.

"Shut up! This is serious."

"Okay."

I loved Ali, but she was a drama queen, lurching between joy and despair over the most inane stuff. One day she was giddy with excitement at the birth of some celebrity's baby. The next, she was donning black and declaring "Love is dead" when a famous power couple broke up. Maybe the flu outbreak was getting scary, but this was probably a case of Ali being Ali.

"The Centers for Disease Control is calling it the worst pandemic in history."

That *had* to be an exaggeration. Worse than the bubonic plague? Worse than the Spanish flu? Could the world possibly have gone to shit in the two days that I'd been out of the loop?

"I read the news last week," I said slowly. "A new flu virus came out of nowhere. Outbreaks around the world and in every state. Followed by the typical advice. Wash your hands. Cover your cough. Stay home if you're sick. Blah-blah-blah."

"No! There's nothing blah-blah-blah about it. Lots of people are dying," Ali said. "Not just old people or people with weak immune systems. Hospitals are swamped. There's no point in even trying to go to an emergency room." Her eyes widened and she continued in a low, urgent voice. "Yesterday, the news reports said that most of the people who get sick, die. We're talking super-high mortality rate. And there are stories that sometimes, before they die, some people get violent and attack their families or hospital personnel."

There was no bigger fan of zombie apocalypse entertainment than Ali, and this sounded like something right out of one of her favorite shows. How many times had I rolled my eyes while she and Jake debated the best weapon for dealing with the reanimated dead, or what foods they'd stockpile in their imaginary apocalyptic retreat?

Her icy fingers tightened their grip on my hand, and the dusting of freckles across her nose and cheekbones stood out against her pale skin. She might have been obsessed with pop culture, but Ali was no flake, and my best friend never lied to me.

What the hell was going on? The first trickle of fear crawled up my spine.

"Have you seen anything odd going on in the dorm?" she asked.

I thought about it. "It's been quiet. I think a lot of people bugged out for the weekend. I heard people moving around in the halls Friday evening and Saturday morning. I left the room to take a shower last night…." I frowned, remembering. "I don't know if I'd call it odd exactly, but a girl turned off the lights when I was in the shower and she didn't turn them back on, even after I yelled. Rachel was passed out drunk in the TV lounge. Lauren and Jenna are still here. Their door was open a crack, and I heard coughing."

"Kenzie, I'm not kidding. We need to get out of here. Coughing is a symptom, and this flu is super contagious. They say the governor plans to declare a state of emergency and a quarantine. She's going to order everybody to shelter in place. Shut down the airports and public transportation. We don't want to be trapped with people who are already sick. Especially not when they might go ape-shit and attack people."

Unreal. I heard the words Ali was saying, but I couldn't wrap my head around their meaning, couldn't make sense of a world turned topsy-turvy. Worst pandemic in history. Quarantine. Homicidal flu patients.

Ali jumped up and pulled me to my feet.

"Jake's going to be here any minute. Pack what you need. We have to get out of here."

I nodded numbly. If the flu was half as contagious as Ali claimed, it made sense to get away from other people. And the dorm was the last place I'd want to be stuck in if the shit hit the fan. But Boise? I'd begged off accompanying Ali home for Christmas break, but had given in and gone to Boise for Easter. Huge mistake.

I pulled my suitcase out from under my bed and followed Ali's example, throwing my phone, a charger, and my toiletry bag into the case. I grabbed a couple pairs of jeans and some yoga pants, a few T-shirts and sweaters, my favorite boots, PJs, underwear, and socks.

What else? What would I need while I waited to see if the world was falling apart?

Ibuprofen. Tampons. Body lotion. Lip balm. What if we lost power? I pulled a few paperbacks from our small bookshelf and a blank spiral notebook and a couple of pens from a desk drawer.

"You want to grab some water?" I suggested, angling my head at the mini fridge.

"Good idea." Ali took out four bottles of water and crammed them into her pack.

My gaze fell on the small, hand-cranked emergency radio my cousin Miles had given me for Christmas. The box sat unopened on the floor of my wardrobe. I had intended to take it to Goodwill or to sell it on Craig's List. Only my oddball prepper cousin would think an emergency radio an appropriate gift for a twenty-one-year-old college student. I can't remember the last time we lost power. Portland is nowhere near tornado alley, and we rarely see snowstorms, but Miles had solemnly told me that I needed to *be ready*. I shook my head. Maybe there was something to Miles's paranoia after all. I wedged the radio into a corner of my suitcase.

The door swung open, and Jake rushed into the room. "It's getting crazy out there." Nodding at me, he wrapped his arms around Ali. "I thought I'd fill up the tank before we hit the road, but the line at the gas station went around the block. I decided not to wait."

"Do we have enough gas to make it to Boise?" Ali asked.

"We should. I went back to my apartment, jimmied the lock on the maintenance shed and took the two five-gallon gas cans they keep for the leaf blower. They're mostly full, so we should be okay."

Ali pulled back to look into his face. "You stole gas?"

"Yeah, ladybug. I did. The cops are too busy to come after me, so no worries there. And if I didn't take the gas, somebody else would've. Just glad I thought of it first. Nothing is going to stop us from making it home."

Ali's face crumpled, tears welling up in her eyes.

"Dammit," she said, furiously wiping away the tears. "I feel like the biggest baby ever, but I just want to go home. I want my mom and dad."

"We'll be there this evening," Jake promised. He glanced at me. "You about ready, Kenzie?"

I stared at him, at a loss for words. Everything was happening too fast, my orderly, predictable world unraveling from one moment to the next. Ten minutes ago, all my attention was focused on my business paper, and now I was supposed to be fleeing from a pandemic?

A soft rapping on the door caught my attention. The door cracked open, and a tall man with dark blond hair leaned into the room, his broad shoulders blocking the light from the hall. Well, crap. Here was the very last person I wanted to see.

Kyle's gaze skirted over my face, lingering for just a moment before settling on Ali and Jake. "We need to get moving."

The appearance of my ex snapped me out of my distracted state. I threw an accusing glance at Ali, who shrugged apologetically.

"Kyle's riding with us to Boise."

Of course he was. Jake and Kyle were lifelong best friends, growing up in the same gated community overlooking the Boise River as Ali. Their families belonged to the same country club and even shared a vacation house in Maui. It made perfect sense for them to travel together. Only I was the odd man out.

I shut my suitcase and hefted it from the bed.

"Let me take that," Kyle said, reaching for the suitcase. My stomach clenched. When he wanted to, Kyle could be a perfect gentleman. Too bad he was a chicken shit who couldn't stand up to his mommy.

The case was heavy, but I'd be damned if I'd accept help from Kyle. My lips curved into an icy smile. "I can fend for myself, remember?"

"Don't be stubborn. Let me carry it."

"I got it," I said between clenched teeth.

"Cut it out, you two," Jake said. "It'll be a long ride to Boise if you guys can't be civil."

Kyle's face assumed an air of offended innocence. "I've got no problem with Kenzie."

Right. It was all me. I didn't know how to behave, and if you didn't believe that, ask his mother. Or his sister. That clinched it. There was no way I'd be stuck in a car with my ex, even if the world was going to hell.

Besides, I couldn't ditch Miles.

"I won't be riding with you to Boise," I said slowly. "I have family in town, remember?"

"Oh, no!" Ali glared at me. "You mean the weirdo?"

I ignored her. "Jake, can you drop me off at my cousin's? He lives in southeast, just off 82nd. It shouldn't be too far out of the way."

"Seriously?" Ali protested.

"Yes. I want to be with family, too. Miles might be a little different, but at least there's an upside to his obsessions. You've read his blog. He's stockpiled food and water. He's got guns. I can't think of a safer place to be."

If you'd told me just a few days ago that I'd be arguing in favor of hunkering down with Miles, I'd have laughed in your face. I loved my cousin, but our lives had veered off in different directions. While Miles ranted on his blog about government conspiracies, my focus was strictly on getting good-enough grades to keep my scholarship and to earn the international finance degree that would help me land a decent job. I was preparing for life as an upstanding, tax-paying citizen, while Miles was getting ready for Armageddon. Who would have thought he was on to something?

No. I shook my head, rejecting that thought. I was getting way ahead of myself. When this flu burned itself out, things would return to normal. It might be scary for a while, but order and law would prevail. Until then, I might as well ride out the storm in the safety of my cousin's fortress.

"Please, Jake?"

"Okay," he agreed, frowning.

Ali punched him on the arm. "You can't leave her with the weirdo."

"I'll be fine," I said firmly.

"Not a good plan." Kyle tilted his head and fixed me with one of his *I-know-best* expressions.

"Nobody asked you."

"Enough already. We don't have time for this," Jake said. "We can talk more in the truck." He swung Ali's backpack over his shoulder and took her hand. Following them, I snagged my cross-body bag from my nightstand and slung it over my neck. At least my suitcase had rollers, so I wouldn't have to carry it downstairs.

Once in the corridor, I paused, wrinkling my nose. What was that smell? I caught the scent of something sickly sweet, a mixture of urine and something else I couldn't identify. In the background, the central air conditioner hummed, but the air circulation wasn't enough to overcome the whiff of putrescence that tainted the atmosphere.

The hall usually thrummed with activity, even on a Sunday morning. Doors opening and closing. Voices. Music coming from the rooms. Now, an eerie silence reigned.

I stared at the closed doors, my scalp prickling with atavistic dread. Every horror movie I'd ever seen popped into my head, and my imagination spun images of what lay beyond the doors.

I trotted to catch up with Ali and Jake, then paused outside Jenna and Lauren's room. The door still stood ajar. I couldn't leave without checking on them.

"Hold up a minute. I need to see if they're here."

I pressed my palm against the door and drew in a shallow breath, summoning the nerve to enter the dark room. I shook my head, trying to dispel the image of the clueless girl in every slasher movie who just had to check out the sound she heard in the basement.

"I got this." Kyle appeared beside me and laid his palm next to mine, the platinum and diamond band ring he'd inherited from his grandfather glinting on his thumb. He pushed, and the door swung open.

He took a few steps into the room, and I followed him, my heart beginning to race. With the blinds pulled and the lights off, the room was bathed in darkness. Only a narrow ribbon of light from the hallway cut through the blackness. I clenched my fists when my hands started to tremble.

It took a moment for my eyes to adjust. At first, I saw only the outline of a dark shape stretched out on Lauren's bed. My throat constricted. I stumbled sideways and trod on something soft, something that yielded to the pressure of my foot.

No! No! No! I started to fall, but strong hands caught me and hauled me to my feet.

Breathless, I clung to Kyle's forearms while I regained my balance. After a moment, he nodded, then extracted himself from my grip. He stepped over the shape on the carpet and fumbled at the lamp on the nightstand. A click, and light spilled across the room, illuminating a nightmarish scene.

Lauren lay still on her bed, a pillow pressed over her face. She was wearing her favorite pink unicorn T-shirt. Tendrils of her long, dark hair had escaped the pillow and lay plastered against the sheets. Kyle lifted the pillow, then glanced at me.

"She's dead. You don't want to look."

"Okay," I agreed, my irritation with him forgotten.

His gaze fell to the rug by my feet. I had deliberately avoided looking down, not wanting to see whatever slumped on the carpet, but when Kyle turned his eyes to the form, my own followed.

Jenna. Of course, it was Jenna. She sprawled on her side, her back arched, her face contorted in agony.

I stared at her, my mind blank, unable to process the image. My friends were dead. While I'd been curled up on my bed, listening to music, writing my paper, and eating leftover Pad Thai, Jenna and Lauren had grown sicker and sicker and had finally died.

No, wait. That was wrong. Jenna had pressed a pillow against Lauren's face, suffocating her best friend.

Jesus. My stomach lurched.

"I'm gonna puke."

Kyle grabbed my hand and pulled me into the hall. I leaned against a wall and bent over double, gasping for air while I fought the nausea.

"They're dead," Kyle said. "It looks like one of them killed the other."

Before Jake or Ali could reply, something thumped against the door across the hall. I straightened and stared at the closed door. The knob twisted back and forth as someone sought to exit the room.

"Should we see if they need help?" Ali asked hesitantly.

"If they're sick, there's nothing we can do. And if they're violent..." Jake's voice trailed off.

"Out," Kyle said. "We're getting out of here. Now."

An hour ago, I would have argued with Kyle on principle. We're decent people, and decent people do the right thing. They step up. They help. And honestly, disagreeing with Kyle had become second nature since our ugly split, but under the circumstances, all I wanted to do was nod my head in agreement and flee.

The knob turned, the latch clicked, and the door slowly opened.

TWO

Kenzie

"Hello?" A tall, slim girl whose name I couldn't recall clung to the door frame, wavering unsteadily on her feet. Lank, sweat-drenched blond hair fell to her shoulders. Fever had scalded her cheeks and cracked her parched lips. She peered at us through sunken, bloodshot eyes. She was barefoot, and apple-green polish adorned her toenails.

The knot in my stomach wound even tighter. The girl I'd blamed for turning off the lights—for leaving me in the dark—had been wandering around in a flu-induced stupor.

Who's the asshole now?

"Have you seen my dad?" she rasped. "He said he was coming to pick me up."

"Shit," Ali said under her breath.

Afraid that softhearted Ali might approach the girl, I grabbed her wrist to hold her back, shaking my head when she turned imploring eyes on me.

"No," I mouthed. After what I had seen in Jenna and Lauren's room, I knew we didn't dare get close to a flu victim.

"Hi there." At the sound of his voice, the girl turned her head and fixed her tremulous gaze on Kyle. "You should lie down and wait for your dad. Save your strength." His tone was gentle, persuasive. He exchanged glances with Jake. "We need to go."

Jake nodded.

The girl lifted a hand to her temple. "My head hurts."

"Hold on," I said, seizing on her words. I dropped to my knees and zipped open my suitcase, then pawed through the items I'd hastily packed until I found the bottle of Ibuprofen. I dumped three pills into my palm, then handed the bottle to Jake. "Miles has lots, so take this, but give me a bottle of water from Ali's pack."

Jake shrugged off the backpack, extracted a bottle of water, and handed it to me.

The girl's glazed eyes had followed our movements. At the sight of the water, she swayed, taking a lurching step toward me.

I held up a hand. "No. Stop."

She paused.

"Jesus, Kenzie. We have to get out of here," Kyle warned.

"Wait!" I hissed. Turning back to the girl, I softened my voice and assumed a cajoling tone, as if I were talking to a small child.

"See." I held up the water and the pills. "I'm going to set these down right here." I pointed to the floor by my feet. "After we leave you'll pick them up. You'll take the pills, drink the water, and then you'll go lie down in your room."

It wasn't much, a woefully inadequate response to the dire situation. No painkiller could halt the progression of the virus that was ravaging her body, but maybe the pills would take the edge off her pain. And maybe that would allow me to live with myself after hightailing it away from someone in need.

She frowned, swaying. "Have you seen my dad? He's supposed to pick me up."

Kyle seized my arm and hauled me to my feet, his eyes hard and his jaw clenched. "Move, or I'll throw you over my shoulder and carry you out of here."

"Fine." I jerked my arm out of his grasp, but didn't complain when he took my suitcase. Kyle was stronger than me, and it was ridiculous to argue when we had to make a fast retreat.

With a final, regret-filled glance at the sick girl, I whirled and followed the others as we sprinted down the hall.

By unspoken consensus, we bypassed the elevator and hurried down the stairwell to the ground floor. We'd all seen too many horror movies with victims trapped in an elevator. I sure didn't want to be stuck in one if the power cut out, or worse, watch the doors slide open only to find myself cornered by a crazed, end-stage flu sufferer.

We burst out the lobby door and exited the building, and I blinked against the bright, incongruous sunlight. I hadn't stepped outside since Friday and half-expected the campus to look different, as if nature would accommodate the new deadly reality by painting the world in dour shades of black and gray. Instead, I entered a balmy, sun-drenched landscape that reminded me of a basket of Easter eggs. A few puffy clouds dotted the blue sky. Pink and purple rhododendrons, peonies and iris bloomed in the neat flower beds that ringed the campus buildings.

I inhaled deeply. After the stale atmosphere of the dorm, the air smelled wonderfully fresh and clean. Impossible to reconcile this beautiful late spring day with a life-threatening pandemic, until my gaze fell on Jake's black pickup.

Ignoring the school's parking restrictions, Jake had pulled his truck up to the curb in front of the dorm, occupying a space reserved for buses. On any ordinary day, he'd be ticketed and towed within minutes. The problem today wasn't campus security. No. The problem was the burly, dark-haired man hefting one of the five-gallon gas cans out of Jake's truck bed.

Somebody was stealing our gas? Had the rule of law already given way to every man for himself?

Jake and Kyle dropped our luggage and took off at a run.

"Stay with our stuff," I ordered Ali, pointing at the abandoned suitcase and backpack. I chased after Jake and Kyle, my hand fumbling inside my purse. There. My fingers closed around a small cylinder attached to my key fob.

I skidded to a stop next to the pickup. Kyle and Jake stood on opposite sides of the truck bed, blocking the man's escape. The man tightened his grip on the gas can's handle, his expression apologetic, but resolute.

"I don't want any trouble," he said. "I'll take one can and leave the other for you."

Jake snorted. "If you don't want trouble, you should keep your hands off other people's property."

"Put it down and walk away," Kyle added, his voice deadly calm and full of menace. He rolled his shoulders and cracked his neck, the classic signal for *I'm-getting-ready-to-whoop-ass*. Where had he learned that? The movies? To the best of my knowledge, Kyle had never been in a fight, although years on the fencing team had left him lean and fit. Under the right circumstances, I supposed, he could hold his own.

"Sorry. No." The stranger deposited the gas can at his feet and planted his hands on his hips. His gaze swung between Kyle and Jake, as if daring them to make a move.

"Hey!" I shouted, trying to get the men's attention.

They ignored me, seemingly intent on their macho posturing.

"Hey," I repeated, and they finally turned their eyes toward me. I held up the small, pink canister, flipped the lid up, and positioned my thumb on the trigger.

"Hot pepper spray." I swallowed and willed my voice not to tremble. In my whole life, I'd never threatened anyone, never dreamed I'd need to. "Drop the gas."

He frowned at me, uncertainty sketched across his features.

"Come on, man," I urged. "You want to spend the next couple of hours curled up in a ball, crying like a baby? Back off, or I hit the trigger."

"Okay." The man raised his palms, signaling his surrender. "Okay. You win."

I flicked the fingers of my left hand, gesturing at him to skedaddle. Balancing one hand on the railing, he vaulted from the truck bed. With his palms still held high, he backed away for a few paces, then whirled and ran up the street.

Kyle and Jake stared at me in stunned silence. I snapped shut the lid on the pepper spray and tucked it back into my purse. My hands were shaking, probably from adrenaline, so I shoved them in my pockets to hide the evidence of my agitation. I wanted to collapse against the side of the truck. Instead, I stood up straighter. Affecting a false nonchalance, I shrugged and offered a bright smile.

"Let's go."

Ali approached, dragging both the suitcase and her backpack.

"Where did you get pepper spray?" she demanded, red faced and out of breath, whether from exertion or excitement I couldn't tell.

"Birthday present from Miles last year."

"Should have known." She rolled her eyes.

"We gotta hurry." Jake threw the suitcase and backpack onto one side of the back seat, then wedged the gas cans into the space on the floor. Kyle and Jake's packs were already in the back. With the luggage taking up more than half of the seat, I practically had to sit on Kyle's lap.

Once we were all belted in, Jake pulled the truck away from the curb.

I'd suspected that the campus would be empty, devoid of activity, and that we were the last students jumping ship before things got worse, but our thief wasn't the only other person still on the grounds. Dozens of people rushed between the dorms and cars waiting on the street. The teaching assistant from my marketing class slammed his trunk shut as we drove past. I waved, but he ignored my greeting.

We wended our way across the campus to the exit and then proceeded down a quiet residential street for a few blocks. As we approached the commercial district, traffic picked up.

"See the line for gas?" Jake asked.

I peered out the window. Sure enough, a row of cars hugged the curb, blocking the parking lane, waiting for their turn at the pumps. Pumping your own gas was illegal in Oregon. I'd imagined people would be honking and shouting, but it was an orderly line, cars inching forward as the harried attendants rushed to fill their tanks.

"When the stations run out, how long till you think people will be fighting over gas?" Kyle asked.

"Seriously? They already are," Ali reminded him.

The car rolled to a stop at the next intersection. I don't know why I was surprised that the traffic lights still worked. Maybe in my mind they symbolized life as usual, tokens of an ordinary, predictable world. But now, the world was anything but ordinary and predictable.

While we waited for the traffic light to change to green, I glanced at my favorite Ethiopian restaurant on the corner of the intersection. The lights were off, and a closed sign hung on the glass door. No surprise there. The restaurant was always closed on Sundays. What caught my eye was the two men sprawled under the awning that hung over the door.

Homeless people often slept under the protective awnings of restaurants and shops, but the cops always rousted them in the morning, well before the street came alive with activity. They should have been long gone by now.

I squinted and leaned closer to the window, studying the men. One sat upright against the door, his head cocked unnaturally to the side, his mouth wide open. Blood ran from his nose, covering his lips and chin. I turned my eyes to his companion. At first, I'd assumed that the man was curled up on his side, asleep. Wrong. The man lay face down, his nose and mouth pressed into the concrete. Some dark substance stained the concrete around his head. More blood. He'd either bled out through his nose, or his companion had bashed his head against the sidewalk.

Bile rose in my throat. Homicidal flu mania. If I hadn't seen it with my own eyes—twice—I never would have believed that such a thing was possible.

"Are those guys dead?" Ali asked, her voice rising shrilly.

Jake squeezed her shoulder. "Don't look, ladybug."

Don't look. Pretend it wasn't happening. That was Jake's solution for a world devolving into violence?

The light turned green, and Jake hit the gas hard. The truck launched through the intersection with so much force that I bounced against Kyle. My chin struck his shoulder, and I bit my tongue.

"Ow!" I rubbed my jaw, wrinkling my nose as I tasted blood.

"You okay?" Concern creased Kyle's brow. He reached out to touch my face then seemed to think better of it, withdrawing his hand without making contact.

I nodded. "I'm okay. Thanks."

"Take it easy," Kyle called to the front. "You're knocking us around back here."

"Sorry." Jake eased off the gas pedal.

The pickup turned a corner, and I spied the small, family-run market where I frequently bought Russian pastries. Mr. Dmytryshyn, the owner, and one of his sons-in-law were outside nailing sheets of plywood over the store's windows. Somebody had painted CLOSED on the plywood, the paint still so fresh that it dripped from the letters, sending rivulets of color snaking across the wood.

"Aren't they jumping the gun?" Jake asked. "You'd think they'd want to make as many sales as possible before the governor shuts down the stores."

You couldn't visit the market without hearing about Mr. Dmytryshyn's three daughters and eleven grandchildren. The last time I stopped by to pick up a slice of his wife's famous honey cake, the proud grandpa had shown me pictures of his grandson in his Little League uniform. Family meant everything to Mr. Dmytryshyn.

"They probably decided they'll need the supplies for themselves," I answered. "And they probably don't want to run the risk of a customer coughing on them and infecting the family."

"If they're just closing down now, bet they're already infected," Jake replied.

"He's right. Bet we've all been exposed," Ali said.

That was a sobering thought. As the car passed the store, I craned my neck to watch the son-in-law hold a stepladder as the elderly shopkeeper began to pound nails along the top edge of the plywood. *Keep them safe.* I sent a silent plea to the universe before they disappeared from sight.

I leaned forward. "Any word from your parents? Are they all right?"

"The phone lines have been jammed, but Mom got a call through early this morning. So far, so good. None of our parents have come down with it, but they want us to come home."

Kyle twisted in the seat to face me, his gray eyes serious. "Will you change your mind and come with us? I get that you're mad at me, but that's no reason to choose your cousin's crappy shack over Ali's big, comfortable house. Use your head. Come with us to Boise."

This conversation was going south fast. Dormant anger flared to new life.

"You know, Kyle, some of us belong in a mansion, and some of us belong in a crappy shack. You can't fight nature, isn't that what your mom says?"

"My mom? What are you—"

"Jake." I spoke over Kyle's protests. "You're getting closer. We'll be at his place in less than five minutes."

"Kenzie, please," Ali begged.

"No." My voice was firm. "I need to be where I belong, and I belong with my cousin."

"Can you at least call him to tell him you're coming?"

"I'll try."

I pulled my phone from my bag and punched in Miles's number. Miles never picked up, but he'd listen to a message if I got through.

"All circuits are busy," a mechanical voice intoned. "Please try your call again later."

Ali raised her brows in a wordless question.

I shook my head. "All circuits are busy."

"What are we supposed to do?" Kyle demanded. "Drop you at his door and hope he lets you in?"

"As if she'd make it as far as the weirdo's door," Ali scoffed.

Ali had seen Miles's place last winter. I'd called to check on him, only to discover that he'd been diagnosed with pneumonia. I decided to bring him some chicken soup from my favorite deli. Since Kyle was busy, and I didn't have a car, Ali borrowed Jake's truck and gave me a ride. My cousin's over-the-top security system and waiting outside the locked gate for permission to enter *the compound* had freaked Ali out. Miles thanked me for the soup, but refused to make eye contact with Ali.

"What do you mean?" Jake asked.

"Miles has a perimeter fence with a locked gate." I answered before Ali could say anything else snarky about my cousin. "Nobody gets on the property unless he lets them in."

"Seriously?"

I shrugged. "Under the circumstances I'd call it a good thing."

Kyle was silent for a moment, his expression a battlefield of conflicting emotions. He sucked in a breath, then exhaled.

"How's this for a compromise. If your cousin lets you in, we'll go on our way knowing you're in a safe place. But if he doesn't let you in—maybe he isn't home, or maybe he's too sick to answer the door—then you come with us. We're not leaving you alone on the street."

"Sure," I agreed.

No risk in placating Kyle with the promise. Miles rarely left home, and with a real live disaster unfurling around us, I was certain that he was hunkered down in his fortress. He was home, and when he saw me at the gate, my cousin would let me in.

"Good enough." Kyle nodded.

I leaned forward. "Jake, take the next right. Go eight blocks, then take a left."

"Got it."

We rode in silence for the minutes it took Jake to navigate the distance. Ali kept glancing back over her shoulder at me, but she kept her thoughts to herself. As he turned onto my cousin's street, Jake slowed the truck and examined the 1930s bungalows that lined the street. Once a tidy, working class neighborhood, whose homes and yards reflected pride of ownership, renters had replaced homeowners, and the place had gone downhill since Miles was a child.

"Fourth house on the left."

Jake pulled the truck up in front of Miles's house, craning his neck to look at my cousin's fortress. Only the leafy canopies of the apple and pear trees Miles had planted in his front yard and the gray shingle roof were visible. A chain-link fence woven with vinyl privacy slats blocked the view from the road. Instead of a standard chain-link gate, a sliding corrugated metal door controlled access to the front yard. An intercom and keypad were attached to one of the heavy posts that flanked the door.

I opened the truck door and hopped down onto the sidewalk. Two steps put me at my cousin's gate. Kyle, Jake, and Ali followed me. Before I could press the intercom button, Ali grabbed my hand.

"Are you sure?" she asked.

"Yeah." I pointed at Miles's mailbox, the name M. Dunwitty spelled out with peel-and-stick letters. "See. M. Dunwitty. I'm home."

My lame attempt at humor did nothing to lighten her mood.

"Kenzie." She shook her head reproachfully. "This isn't a joke."

"I know." I squeezed Ali's hand in return.

Her distraught expression tugged at my heart. She loved me, and I knew that she just wanted me to be safe. Was I doing the right thing? Abandoning Ali in order to avoid Kyle felt like an immature, knee jerk response to the situation.

I glanced at Kyle. If I had to, I could put up with him for the duration of the drive to Boise. It wasn't too late to change my mind.

My gaze returned to the locked metal gate. An image of Miles as a boy filtered up from my memory, his earnest face screwed up with concentration as he filled in the lines of one of those paint-by-numbers kits he had loved so much.

"You have to stay in the lines to do it right," he had warned me. A cautious, lonely boy had grown into a cautious, lonely man. If I went to Boise with Ali, my cousin would be alone to face whatever was coming.

"You have Jake and your family. Miles only has me. I want to be with him." It was true. I hugged her. "Besides, in a couple of weeks everything will be back to normal, and we'll be arguing over whether to order Thai or Mexican food while we're cramming for finals."

Ali released me and stepped back. "You better be right."

"We're not leaving until he lets you in," Kyle reminded me.

I nodded.

Jake tilted his head, studying the top of the fence. "Is that razor wire?" A double row of razor wire, partially obscured by vines, angled into the yard from the top rail of the fence. "That can't be legal."

"The city's not likely to do anything about it unless somebody complains," I explained. "And nobody's complained."

A clicking sound drew our attention to a camera perched atop a tall post just inside the yard. The camera rotated until the lens was pointed at us.

"Say hello to Miles," I instructed, waving at the camera. Kyle scowled, while Jake raised a hand to the camera.

I pushed the intercom button. "Miles, my friends are on their way to Boise, and I asked them to drop me off here. Let me in, please."

For a long moment nothing happened, and I squirmed. I'd feel like a fool if after pitching a fit and demanding to be brought to his doorstep, Miles wouldn't let me in. Finally, with a clank and a mechanical whirring from some mechanism inside the heavy posts, the metal door began to slide open.

Kyle handed me my suitcase.

"Thank you." I extended my hand for an awkward handshake. Now was the time to be mature, to be civil, but it was an oddly formal way to part with a man I'd once been crazy about and who now just made me crazy. "Be safe, Kyle." I turned to Ali and Jake. "And you two, take care of each other. Love you, Ali. I'll see you soon."

We hugged. Ali sobbed and buried her face in Jake's shoulder.

"See you, Kenzie," Jake said, leading Ali to the truck.

Kyle hesitated for a moment, studying my face, frustration and unhappiness clearly dancing across his handsome features.

"Bye, Kyle," I said firmly, then I turned my back on him.

The truck engine roared to life behind me as I watched the door slowly slide open. Tears stung my eyes. I refused to allow myself to turn around for a final glimpse of my friends.

When the door had opened wide enough to allow me access to the yard, I picked up the suitcase and stepped through the opening.

PANDEMONIUM

I heard the truck pull away from the curb and the metal door rattling in its tracks as it reversed course and began to close.

The door clicked shut, sealing off the outside world.

THREE

Kenzie

Miles liked to call his place an urban homestead. The description was apt. Instead of grass and flower beds, two fruit trees dominated the front yard, their spent blossoms littering the ground beneath their branches. Raised vegetable beds hugged the perimeter and spilled into the back yard, where he'd installed a generator and built a small chicken coop. Sturdy cement posts—formed around rebar that Miles had pounded into the ground—were spaced every three feet along the front fence line.

"So nobody can drive a car through the fence and breach the compound," Miles had told me once.

I made my way across the concrete pavers that led to his front porch, the security camera rotating to follow my progress. As I drew near the porch, the front door swung open and Miles stepped outside.

A shaft of sunlight gilded his light brown hair, the shade identical to my own. Silent, he watched me narrow the distance between us, his eyes the same pewter gray I saw when I looked in a mirror.

I halted a few paces away from him. His blank expression showed neither welcome nor displeasure. Had I made a mistake? I was descending on him uninvited at a time when his paranoia must be jacked up. Our similar coloring marked us as family, but that didn't mean he'd willingly share his fortress with me.

"Hi, Miles. Thanks for letting me in."

He nodded and held open the door. "It's good that you came. You'll be safe here."

I released a deep breath and climbed onto the porch. Miles didn't like to be touched, so I kept my arms by my side, resisting the urge to hug him. I followed him through the front room and waited patiently while he turned the three deadbolts that secured the entrance to the house. Blackout shades covered the picture windows, blocking out the sun's rays, but an overhead fixture illuminated the room.

The room looked exactly as it did the last time I visited. Miles had relegated Aunt Debbie's sofa, coffee table, and china hutch to the attic. Uncle Mel's beat-up recliner and old TV were all that remained of the family furnishings.

Two long, folding tables, covered with monitors and communication equipment, formed an L along the front and side wall. *The command center*, Miles called it.

Months ago, he'd tried to explain his ham radio setup—his base station—to me. He pointed out the transceiver and tried to tell me about wavelengths, but the techno-babble went right over my head. Hanging on the wall above his computer was a map of the world, dotted with colored thumbtacks. A split-screen monitor displayed the feed from his four exterior security cameras. An old, rolling desk chair sat in front of the monitor.

The chair's wheels had gouged grooves into the hardwood floor when Miles scooted back and forth from one end of the table to the other. I winced. Aunt Debbie would pitch a fit if she could see the damage.

I glanced back at the door, then frowned. A shotgun hung from a pair of metal hooks screwed to the wall. That was new. Miles had weapons, but he usually kept them out of sight.

Trying to appear nonchalant, I stepped farther into the room and peeked through the arched opening into the kitchen. Sure enough, another shotgun was hanging by the back door. My gaze returned to the command center. A handgun lay within reach of the keyboard.

I lifted my eyes to my cousin's face and found Miles watching me. So much for stealthy observation.

"Why all the guns, Miles?" I asked, keeping my tone even.

"Haven't you been following the news?"

"Not so much. I've been busy working on a paper. My friends said the flu has turned into a pandemic and the governor might declare a state of emergency. We decided to get out of the dorm." I hesitated a moment before continuing. "I hope you don't mind that I just showed up on your doorstep."

"No. I don't mind. We're family, and Mom always said family sticks together."

"Thanks, Miles, I appreciate it...but...what were you saying about the guns?"

"We'll need to defend ourselves. Violence is inevitable."

"I don't understand."

"This flu was no accident. The Centers for Disease Control has stockpiled body bags in a warehouse near the Atlanta airport. I can show you pictures. Obviously, they knew the virus was coming." Miles was becoming agitated, his words tumbling over each other.

My stomach clenched and old, familiar stress twisted my guts. If only Aunt Debbie were here to deal with this. "How could the CDC know the flu was coming?"

"Because they created it!" His eyes glittered with excitement. "I thought at first that the CDC was in cahoots with the pharmaceutical companies. Engineering and disseminating a virus, then taking out a patent on the strain, so they could make a fortune from the cure."

Oh, man. The CDC created the killer flu? I kept my face blank, careful not to reveal the tension churning in my belly. "You said *at first* you thought it was the CDC working with pharmaceutical companies. What do you think now?"

"Well, I haven't absolutely rejected that possibility, but now I think it more likely that the CDC is acting under instructions from the president."

"Why would the president want to create a virus that kills so many people?"

Miles snorted. "Because a devastating pandemic would allow the president to declare martial law and to shut down all the checks and balances on his power. Oh, he'd *say* he was calling out the troops to prevent looting, to maintain law and order, but it would all be part of his plan to seize absolute power."

Oh my God. Miles had hopped aboard the crazy train, and if I didn't play my cards right, I'd be riding along as an unwilling passenger.

I held up my hands. "Let me get this straight. You're saying that the CDC invented the virus. *Maybe* they're working with pharmaceutical companies, or *maybe* they're working with the president. But Miles, have you considered the possibility that the flu occurred naturally? That a virus mutated into a new, deadly form of flu?"

Miles shook his head, vehemently rejecting my idea. "Hardly likely. Not with all the evidence to the contrary. But let's say you're right, that the flu occurred *naturally*." He emphasized the word with air quotes. "Doesn't make a bit of difference. The outcome is the same. Millions die. The economy falters. Civil order breaks down. So whether it's from soldiers who've been ordered to seize everybody's weapons, or from people who want to take what we have, it's on us to protect ourselves. And my guns are our best defense."

He spoke with such matter-of-fact certainty that I got chills. Was Miles spinning paranoid delusions, or was society really on the brink of chaos?

"I hear you." It was too much to take in, and there was no need to rile him with further discussion. Time to beat a retreat. "I need to use the bathroom."

Miles nodded, took a seat at his command center, and slipped headphones over his ears. He flipped a switch and fiddled with a button on his tuner. I studied the back of his head for a long moment, at a loss for what to do.

Finally, I followed the short hallway to the bathroom.

I sensed Aunt Debbie's comforting presence in the powder blue room. Miles had installed bars over the window, no doubt to keep out intruders, but the daisy print curtains she'd sewn still hung over the glass. The butterfly soap dish and toothbrush holder she loved perched on the back of the sink. On top of the toilet tank, Miles kept a spare roll of toilet paper in the ridiculous, yellow toilet paper roll cover she'd crocheted. I felt her everywhere in the room. I sank onto the edge of the tub.

What do I do, Aunt Debbie? I rubbed my eyes.

After my dad ran off with a waitress when I was five and depression consumed my mom, my aunt and uncle had stepped up to take care of me. I spent most weekends with them. Aunt Debbie taught me how to bake a pie. Uncle Mel escorted me to my Girl Scout father-daughter dance. I owed them so much. Now that they were gone, I had to repay that debt.

I pulled my phone from my purse and stared at the screen. Ali and the guys had left, what, fifteen minutes ago? If I texted and asked, they wouldn't hesitate to turn around and come back for me. If I told them that Miles had planted guns by every door, and that he was ranting about the flu being a CDC plot to kill people, nothing would stop them from driving back and whisking me away to safety.

And then what? I'd be in Boise, a guest in Ali's home. No matter how gracious her parents, I'd feel like an intruder, another mouth to feed, another person to worry about. Kyle's proximity would be a constant reminder of our ugly breakup.

And what about Miles?

"My boy has a good heart, but no common sense," Uncle Mel used to say. "He needs somebody to help keep his head screwed on straight."

I'd watched Aunt Debbie talk him down when he got worked up, cajole him back into seeing reason. I couldn't abandon him to fend for himself, not when he was spiraling out of control and I might be able to help. Could I?

Leave it in the hands of fate. Try the text. If you get through, you're supposed to go to Boise. If you don't, you're meant to stay with Miles.

Screw that.

I shoved the phone back in my purse, then stood. Pausing at the sink, I washed my hands and splashed water on my face. I'd be safe here. No matter what, Miles would never hurt me. He might hurt somebody he saw as a threat, but not me. My job now was to make sure that Miles was safe, too, that he stayed on the right side of rational.

I held my breath, then slowly exhaled. Okay. I nodded at my reflection in the medicine cabinet mirror. I could do this.

FOUR

Kenzie

Pasting a pleasant expression on my face, I walked back into the living room and stood by Miles's side, waiting for him to notice me. After a moment, he pulled off the headphones and turned around in his chair.

Miles got cranky when he missed a meal. "Have you had anything to eat today? I'm hungry. Maybe I could make us something."

Miles stroked his chin. "We should eat the perishables first. I bought cheese and lunch meat last week. You can make sandwiches. Bread's in the breadbox on the counter." He started to put the headphones back over his ears, then paused. "You might want to sniff the ham to make sure it's still good."

Swell. Sniffing sketchy pork.

"No problem." I smiled.

I cleared a space on the kitchen table so I could slap together two sandwiches. The ham passed muster, thankfully. Spicy brown mustard on the sandwiches. No mayo. Miles hated mayonnaise and wouldn't have it in the house. I found an unopened gallon of milk in the refrigerator and the last two clean glasses in the cupboard. After arranging our plates and glasses on a tray, I carried lunch to the living room.

I placed the tray on the table, then grabbed a sandwich and settled on the recliner, balancing my plate on my lap. Miles picked up his sandwich and swiveled around to face me. We ate in silence for a few minutes.

"It's good you opened the milk," Miles said between bites. "We need to drink it before we lose power. I have cases of powdered milk in storage, but the fresh stuff tastes better."

Electricity was an essential utility. Keeping the lights on—and the refrigerators humming—*had* to be a top priority for the authorities. "You don't really think we're going to lose power, do you?"

Miles shrugged. "No question about it. People are going to die without turning off their TVs and lights, so the drain on the electrical system will continue. There won't be enough workers left to mind the power grid. Sooner rather than later, it will shut down, and the city will go dark."

Dark? Crap. I swallowed hard and set my plate on the floor, my appetite gone. "We can't know how bad it's going to get. Maybe the worst is over."

He rolled his eyes and pointed over his shoulder at his ham radio. "I've been talking to people around the country, around the world. I know exactly how bad it's going to get. The press is hiding the truth from us."

"So you're saying the press is in cahoots with the CDC and the president?" Good lord. Hadn't Miles been listening to the news for the last couple of years?

"Yes. Millions of people have already died, and the press isn't reporting it."

He was ramping up again. With Miles—as Aunt Debbie used to say—*distraction* was the better part of valor.

"You said you have cases of powdered milk in storage. Just how much food do you have put away?"

"Enough," he said simply. "You need to get familiar with our supplies. Later on I'll show you the pantry and explain the security system."

"That sounds like a good idea."

"And we need to find a place for you to sleep. I took the furniture out of Mom and Dad's room, so I could use the space to store water. We can move a dresser back down from the attic and put a cot in there for you."

"Okay. Thanks. It would be nice to have my own space." Miles yawned, and I took a closer look at his face. Purplish smudges discolored the skin under his eyes and uncharacteristic lines bracketed his mouth. "Speaking of sleep, you look tired, Miles. When's the last time you slept?"

If hunger made Miles irritable, sleep deprivation triggered all of his worst impulses.

He held up a hand, counting off on his fingers. "I've been up listening to reports since Thursday morning."

"Miles!" I exclaimed. "You've been awake for more than seventy-two hours?"

"Can't be helped. I need to monitor channels and keep my eye on the surveillance cameras. Stay on top of what's going on."

No wonder he was on edge. Fatigue, hunger, and real-world events combined with his default paranoia to create a toxic mental stew. Aunt Debbie always said that Miles made his worst decisions when he was tired.

I leaned toward him. "You need to sleep."

He shook his head, vigorously protesting the suggestion. "No. Not yet. I'll take another pill and I'll be fine."

"What kind of pill?" As far as I knew, Miles had refused every prescription suggested by his doctors.

"Chad, one of the high school kids up the street, has a prescription for Adderall. He sells me the pills for $10 a pop."

Great. Miles refused medication while under a doctor's supervision, but he was willing to take black-market stimulants.

I tried another tack. "You said I'd be safe here. I'm counting on you. You can't be at your best if you're dragging ass and taking stimulants to stay awake."

Miles frowned, rocking back and forth, a sure sign that he was working out some inner conflict. I waited in silence. There was no point in trying to rush Miles. He had to follow whatever process allowed him to reach a decision.

"All right," he said at last. "I function better if I'm rested, and I promise I will sleep, but not yet. I'm waiting to hear from friends in Indiana and Florida." He pointed at his ham radio. "After I talk to them, I'll take a nap."

That was probably as good a concession as Miles could make.

"I'll watch the surveillance feeds while you're sleeping, if that helps. You've got coffee, I presume."

The query elicited a reproachful frown from Miles. Of course he had stockpiled coffee. I thought caffeine was his drug of choice, until I learned about the stimulants. If I had to be stuck in a doomsday retreat, at least it came with a bountiful supply of good coffee beans.

"And maybe, while you wait to hear from your friends, I can set up my bedroom," I suggested.

"Good idea. Let's get the dresser down from the attic, then you can put your things away."

The attic was accessed through a hatch in the hallway ceiling. Miles pulled down a rickety, wooden ladder, and we ascended into the dusty attic. We quickly spied Aunt Debbie's old bird's-eye-maple dresser, and the two of us managed to manhandle it back down the ladder and carry it into the master bedroom. Miles climbed back into the attic to fetch a folding cot and a table lamp. That accomplished, he returned to his station at the command center and left me to set up my new room.

First things first, I opened the cot and smelled the blanket and sheets. A musty odor assaulted my nostrils.

I stuck my head out the door. "Miles, I need to wash the bedding. You want me to do your sheets at the same time? Who knows how long we'll be able to use the washer and dryer."

"Good idea," he agreed. When I took a step toward his bedroom, intending to strip his bed, he hopped up and rushed toward his room, blocking the door. "No, I got it."

Odd. What didn't Miles want me to see in his bedroom?

He appeared a minute later, his dirty bedsheets balled up in his hands.

He hesitated. "If you don't mind, I'd prefer that you not go into my room."

"Sure." What else could I say?

He passed the sheets to me, then took up his position in front of his computer.

Uncle Mel had enclosed the back porch and converted it into a laundry room. I carried the bedding through the kitchen to the laundry room and started a load of wash. I paused on my way back to my room, examining the kitchen.

Dirty dishes covered the countertops and filled the sink. In a half-assed attempt at maintaining order, Miles had squirted dish soap into the sink and filled it with water. The water was cold now, with a few bubbles and a rust-colored scum floating on the surface. Gross. An empty jar of peanut butter sat open on the small kitchen table, a fly crawling along its rim. Bet the floor hadn't been swept in a week.

What happened to my ordinarily tidy cousin? I sighed. Apparently, Miles had given up both sleeping *and* picking up after himself.

I spent the next hour restoring order to the room. Just as I dumped a dustpan full of debris into the garbage can, the washing machine signaled the end of the cycle. I advanced the wash to the dryer, then returned to my new bedroom to empty my suitcase.

The afternoon passed uneventfully. I unpacked my belongings into the dresser and made up my bed. The small room was crowded. Only the sunny-yellow paint—Aunt Debbie's favorite color—kept the room from feeling claustrophobic. The cot and dresser were jammed together along one wall, with the lamp atop the dresser. A tall, double row of five-gallon water containers filled the opposite wall, forty-eight in total. The water bottles protruded several feet into the room, leaving a narrow corridor between the bottles and my bed. If an earthquake struck, they'd topple onto my cot. Of course, the risk of an earthquake was the least of my worries.

I wanted to hear Ali's voice, to confirm that their drive to Boise was going smoothly, to reassure her that I was fine. I pulled up my contact list and punched her number. The now familiar "All circuits are busy" sounded in my ear. I tried to watch national and local news on my phone, but couldn't get a stable connection. It took forever to load, then played for only a few seconds before freezing. I glanced toward the living room. Maybe I could catch the news on the small television in the front room. And risk inciting another antipress tirade? Nah, not worth it.

Muttering to myself, I kicked my pillow across the room and sent it sailing to the top row of water bottles. Well, wasn't that a mature outburst? By squeezing between the rows of bottles and balancing on my tiptoes, I managed to retrieve the pillow, then threw it back on the cot.

What now?

I'd promised to monitor the security feed while Miles slept. If I settled into bed and read for awhile, I might relax enough to nap before pulling an all-nighter. I cozied up with one of my favorite romance novels. My lack of sleep caught up with me and I drifted off, trusting that Miles would wake me after his friends contacted him.

A soft rapping on the door awakened me.

"Mackenzie?"

"I'm here." I sat up, swung my legs over the cot, and fumbled on the dresser for my phone. I checked the time. 7:42 p.m. I rubbed my eyes, trying to erase the last vestiges of sleep.

"I heard from my friend in Florida," he called through the door.

"One sec." I thrust my legs into my yoga pants and hiked them up over my hips. "Okay. I'm decent."

Miles popped his head into the room. "The power is out in Orlando. He's hearing reports of looting. The central police station is on fire."

I shook my head in disbelief. I'd clung to the notion that eventually everything would be fine. We might tiptoe up to the precipice, might even peek over the edge, but somehow we'd back away from disaster, and the world would right itself. Some people would die—I'd witnessed that myself—but the center would hold. It was hard to reconcile that optimism with the image of a police station in flames.

"Did your friend say what he's going to do?"

"Yes. He's going to hang tight for now, but if things go south, his car is gassed up, and he'll head for his grandpa's place."

"How about your other friend, the one in Indiana?" I asked, following Miles back into the front room.

He shook his head, worry clouding his face. "Nothing."

In the perverse logic of our new reality, where assumptions were flipped on their heads, it shouldn't be surprising that words, too, could take on new meaning. Nothing could mean anything. Maybe his friend had fled to safety. Maybe his radio equipment had malfunctioned. Maybe he'd come down with the flu. Maybe he was dead.

I had no comfort to offer Miles, so I simply nodded.

"Probably doesn't make sense to wait up to hear from your friend," I said gently, avoiding the obvious. "You promised you'd sleep."

Miles struggled to answer, reluctance writ large across his face. I didn't push. He'd come around. He'd made a promise, and Miles knew that promises were sacred.

"All right," he said at last.

"Good." I injected a false, positive enthusiasm into my voice.

"Please don't touch my computer or radio equipment while I'm sleeping."

"Okay."

Well, crap. I'd hoped to try to go online while Miles was asleep. Why didn't he want me to touch his computer? Did he think I'd break it? That I'd snoop? Could he tell if I did?

"Just keep your eyes on the surveillance feed."

"I will. I'm going to make myself a cup of coffee, grab my phone, then I'll be all set."

"I'll see you in a couple of hours." He hesitated, hovering in the arched entry to the hall. "Wake me if anything happens."

"Go to bed, Miles. I'll be fine."

He turned and walked toward the bathroom. After a few minutes, the toilet flushed and water ran in the sink, then the door to Miles's room opened and closed, followed by a series of metallic clicks. I cocked my head, frowning. He had a deadbolt on his bedroom door. Maybe it made sense to secure his door if he were alone in the house, but why do it when I was here? Habit? Didn't he trust me? Who knew.

I ground beans and brewed a cup of French-press coffee, retrieved my phone and settled into the old recliner. I'd downloaded the final *Saving Setora* novel a few days ago and had been saving it as a reward for finishing my term paper. With the university closed and my paper on hold, there was no reason to postpone reading it, no need to delay gratification. I could use a good distraction now, and nothing would distract me more than losing myself in the world of Setora and her bad-boy bikers. I clicked on the e-reader app and snuggled down in the recliner.

At first, I glanced up every few minutes to check the security monitor, a pointless exercise if ever there was one. After all, a tall chain-link fence topped with razor wire encircled the entire property. The only way in or out was through the locked, sliding metal gate I'd used to enter the yard. Moreover, Miles's reputation as the neighborhood weirdo should discourage anyone from trespassing. And didn't people have better things to do right now than breaking and entering? Still, I'd given my word, so whenever I thought of it, I checked the monitor.

Around midnight, I got up to use the bathroom, pausing afterwards to press my ear to Miles's door. Soft snores assured me that sleep had claimed my cousin. Good. After being awake for three days, he'd been operating at a significant sleep deficit. Lack of sleep was as dangerous as hunger for Miles. Nothing could induce me to roust him from his slumber.

I turned off the overhead fixture and switched on the floor lamp in the corner. The old-fashioned filament bulb cast an insipid pool of light over the chair, leaving most of the room in darkness. After a quick glance at the security monitor, I clambered back onto the recliner, curling on my side with my phone clutched in one hand.

Raindrops tapped a staccato rhythm on the roof, a sound that always made me feel chilly. I snagged the crocheted afghan from the back of the chair and tucked it over my legs and chest. Warm and cozy, I touched the screen of my phone and once again was drawn in to an enticing fantasy.

Setora rode on the back of Steel's bike, her arms wrapped around his waist, her cheek resting against his powerful back as she inhaled the scent of leather and man.

Smiling at the image, I closed my eyes and drew in a deep breath.

I jerked awake, my cheek plastered by drool to the padded arm of the Naugahyde recliner. Shuddering, I peeled my cheek away from the faux leather, then sat up. I scrubbed at my face with my sleeve while I glanced around the room.

Crap! I wasn't supposed to fall asleep. If Miles woke up and found me snoozing in the chair, he'd never again trust me to keep an eye on things while he rested. My phone had slipped from my hand down onto the floor when I drifted off. I retrieved it and checked the time. Almost 1:30.

A long night stretched ahead of me. "Coffee," I groaned.

As I took my first stumbling steps toward the kitchen, my gaze fell upon the security monitor. I froze. Miles had installed top-of-the-line, hi-def security cameras that could pick up detailed images in low light. Three of the video feeds displayed views of the empty front and side yards. The fourth feed revealed a dark shape near the fence in the backyard.

What the hell? I leaned toward the monitor, my mouth hanging open.

The form approached the house and consolidated into the image of a tall man striding toward the back door. Even in the dim porch light, I saw that he was wearing a vest covered with patches, the kind worn by Setora's bikers.

Maybe I was dreaming, a nightmare inspired by the novel? My sleep-addled brain clutched at the possibility until I slapped my face, testing the theory.

Shit! He was still there, walking purposefully toward the kitchen door.

My head swung frantically from side to side as I searched for inspiration. I couldn't wake Miles. I'd be asking for trouble if I startled him from a dead sleep.

I glanced at the shotguns hanging near the doors. Who was I kidding? I had never touched a gun and had no idea how to use one. While I fumbled with it, trying to figure out if it had a safety that needed to be disengaged, he could be through the door and on me.

Maybe I could hide, run to the basement or climb into the attic. And leave sleeping Miles at his mercy.

Dammit, no.

The pepper spray.

I almost tripped over my stockinged feet as I bolted toward my bedroom. I grabbed the canister and rushed toward the kitchen, pausing only to glance at the monitor. The stranger was mere feet from the back door.

With only seconds to spare, I slid to a stop by the refrigerator. Pressing my back to the refrigerator, out of sight of the door, I flipped the lid up on the canister and placed my thumb on the spray button.

My heart hammered so loudly that I could barely hear the lock click and doorknob rattle before the stranger stepped into the room.

I whirled to face him, my arm extended, the pepper spray's nozzle pointing at his face.

In the dim light that spilled from the living room, I saw a huge, imposing figure, with rain-slicked hair falling to his shoulders. I must have startled him. His eyes grew wide, and he jerked back involuntarily, pausing for a crucial half second before he leapt at me.

I held my breath and blasted the pepper spray.

FIVE

Kenzie

He was supposed to collapse to the floor, incapacitated and howling with pain from the caustic spray. Instead, the stranger lunged, capturing my shoulders in a powerful grip before slamming me against the opposite wall.

My head bounced off the surface, and the air exploded from my lungs. He leaned into me, pinning my body from knee to chest. I gasped and tried to suck in a breath, but he pressed against me so heavily that I couldn't inhale.

What was happening? Why hadn't he gone down?

"Drop it," he growled.

He reached out with one hand and slapped at the light switch on the wall. When the overhead fixture flickered into life, I stared up at him, my eyes wide. I'd hurt him, no question about that. He blinked against the corrosive spray that coated his face and dripped down his neck, his eyes red and watering, his skin inflamed.

Instead of driving him to his knees, I'd provoked him. Poked the bear with a sharp stick.

Shit. I had no Plan B. I shivered, both from cold and dread.

He'd been out in the rain. His dark T-shirt clung like a second skin to his sculpted chest, and his jeans were soaked. My yoga pants and tee leeched the moisture, chilling me and raising goosebumps across my flesh.

I'd removed my bra before my nap. Now, only two thin layers of cotton separated my breasts from his torso. My nipples peaked from the damp cold. It took all my willpower not to glance down at the embarrassingly perky points. Instead, I fixed my eyes on his shoulder. My heart sank. The embroidered patches stitched on the shoulder of his leather vest confirmed my earlier suspicions. The Janissaries Portland.

Way to go, Kenzie. Pissed off a freaking biker.

His right forearm dug into my throat, and his left hand clamped my wrist. He jammed a finger into the sensitive spot at the base of my thumb.

"Drop it," he rasped in my ear.

I turned my head and saw that I was still holding the pepper spray. He had to be compressing a nerve because my hand was going numb; I could barely feel my fingers.

I nodded jerkily, twitching my hand to release my grip on the canister. It fell. He caught it and stuffed it into a vest pocket.

"Good girl," he breathed. "Now, how about you tell me who the fuck you are and what you're doing here?"

"Get off me," I gasped, pushing against his chest and struggling to fill my lungs with air.

He didn't budge. "Answer the fucking question."

Who was *I*, and what was *I* doing here? That was rich, coming from a man who'd just broken into Miles's house.

Wait... I frowned. The stranger hadn't broken into the place. The back door had been locked, and I remember hearing a click when a key turned in the deadbolt. Why did this man have a key to the door?

He squinted at me through angry, red-rimmed eyes.

I decided not to poke the bear again. "I'm Miles's cousin," I choked out.

He shifted his weight, allowing me to inhale, but my breasts were still smashed against his chest.

It was his turn to frown. "You're cousin Mackenzie?"

If he was aware of cousin Mackenzie, he was no stranger to Miles.

"Only Miles calls me that. My friends call me Kenzie." My voice shook. It was hard to maintain any composure when pinned against the wall by an irate biker.

"Yeah?" He swiped at his cheek, glowered at his sticky fingertips, then wiped the mess on his jeans while shooting me a dirty look. "Guess that means I'll be calling you Mac."

Not in this life. I wasn't about to share my name with a truck or a knife. Under the circumstances, I wasn't stupid enough to say it out loud, but my displeasure must have been obvious.

He offered a smug smile. "You always pepper spray your cousin's friends...*Mac*?"

Charming.

I drew in a lungful of air and found my voice. "Only when they burst in uninvited in the middle of the night."

At least he wasn't a looter. And he called Miles a friend. He still intimidated me, but my panic had ratcheted down a notch. I squirmed against him, drawing his attention to our joined chests.

"Do you mind?" I huffed.

He leaned closer, and I caught a whiff of his scent, a mixture of leather, engine exhaust, and clean, masculine sweat overlaid with the acrid bite of pepper spray.

"Not at all...*Mac*." He stepped back. Before I could breathe a sigh of relief, he shrugged out of his vest and pulled his shirt over his head, revealing a chest corded with heavy muscles and a pierced right nipple.

Why was this man stripping?

"What do you think you're doing?" I hissed.

"Gotta rinse this shit off," he said. He wheeled and headed into the living room, on his way to the bathroom shower, I realized.

"Hold on." I chased after him and seized his arm.

He glanced at my hand and raised a brow, smirking. "Want something, Mac? Maybe feeling a little dirty? If you're looking to join me in the shower, I'm game."

I gritted my teeth and rolled my eyes, then tugged him back into the kitchen. "Yes, I want something. I want Miles to stay asleep, and the shower might wake him. He's been up for more than three days."

The stranger's expression sobered, and his voice lost its mocking edge. I'd swear he looked genuinely concerned.

"That's not good. Miles decompensates when he's sleep deprived."

Wait. What? Suddenly the biker was talking like a psych major?

"It's the flu," I said. "He sees conspiracies everywhere."

"Afraid of that," he said, raking a hand through his dark hair. "That's why I came over. Just got back into town and wanted to check on Miles before I turned in."

"Who are you?" I demanded, unable to make heads or tails of this man claiming to be my cousin's friend.

"Don't come around much, do you?"

My face heated. I'd neglected Miles since my breakup with Kyle. For the past few months, I'd pulled misery over my head like a blanket and had wallowed in anger and self-pity. Oh, I'd called a couple of times a month to check in on Miles, but I hadn't taken the time or trouble to come see him. Jesus. I'd been selfish and pathetic.

"I haven't been around nearly enough," I admitted, shame twisting in my guts.

He was quiet for a long moment, and I shifted uncomfortably under his piercing scrutiny.

"Lemme get this shit off my skin," he said at last. "Then we'll talk."

He opened the back door and the window over the kitchen sink, allowing fresh air into the room, then he twisted the faucet. He ran his fingers through the stream of water, testing the temperature.

"I'll get you a towel," I offered and tiptoed to the bathroom to fetch one.

By the time I returned to the kitchen the stranger was bent over the sink, scrubbing his face, hair, and chest with liquid dish soap. A tattoo of the Janissaries logo covered much of his back in an intricate, colorful design.

Despite my love for hot-biker romances, I'd never spoken to a member of a motorcycle club. Fantasy is one thing, reality another, and I generally steered clear of anything or anybody that might derail my life plans.

Speculation ran rife in Portland about what the Janissaries were up to, and none of it was good. Drugs. Gunrunning. Prostitution. The trifecta of criminal behavior.

Until now, the closest I'd come to a real biker had been when I'd followed a man wearing a Janissary vest up the cereal aisle at the grocery store. I'd pretended to examine the granola options while surreptitiously eyeing the embroidered patch on his vest. He caught me in the act, flashed a smile, and said hello. I blushed, sputtered, and fled. Typical Kenzie suave.

The stranger finished washing up and toweled off his hair and face. I caught a glimpse of another inked symbol on his left forearm, this one all black.

"Wanna sit?" He gestured to the small kitchen table.

I sat and folded my hands on my lap. He turned around the maple chair opposite me and straddled it, resting his forearms on the chair back. The position allowed me a closer look at his tattoo, a skull wearing a beret surrounded by the words "Death Before Dishonor."

"Name's Ripper," he said, interrupting my examination of his tattoo.

I raised startled eyes to his face.

"Ripper? Like Jack the Ripper?"

He shrugged, his expression bland.

Was he messing with me? I glanced at the vest he'd tossed on the table. A patch on the right shoulder spelled out Ripper, clear as day. An irresistible impulse seized me, and I spoke before I could think better of it.

"Then I guess you won't mind if I call you Jack? Jack. Mac. We rhyme."

He tilted his head and offered a reproachful scowl. "Miles never told me you're a comedian."

"Miles never told me word one about you. Who are you...*Jack*? And how do you know Miles?"

He ignored the dig. "Bought the house behind Miles a few months ago. Was a bargain. Most people don't wanna buy next door to a man who surrounds his yard with razor wire. Didn't bother me. Live and let live is my motto. A couple of weeks after I moved in, my dog Hector dug a hole under the fence and came home with a chicken in his mouth."

"Your dog killed one of Miles's chickens?" I could only imagine how Miles would react to this breach of his compound.

"Yeah. I got a case of beer and rang the buzzer at his gate. Planned to apologize and to pay for the chicken. To offer to help him patch up the hole along the fence."

"I bet he was upset about the chicken."

"Thought he would be, especially after what the neighbors said about him, but he was cool with it."

"Miles was cool with it?" This boggled my mind. Miles lived to defend his property.

"He said it hadn't occurred to him that an intruder would go under his fence, and he got excited by the prospect of 'fortifying the perimeter.'" From the way Ripper said it, I knew he was quoting Miles.

Maybe Miles's reaction made sense, after all. He was never happier than when he could devote all his time and attention to a new project.

"I know something about security, and my dog started it, so I offered to help him. We pounded metal stakes into the ground every twelve inches along the property line."

My gaze swept over Ripper's chiseled chest, shoulders, and arms. It was easy to imagine him swinging a mallet, driving metal stakes into packed soil. Hot and sweaty work.

"And you ended up drinking the beer," I guessed.

"Yeah." He smiled. "Miles told me he doesn't touch alcohol, but offered to keep the beer in his fridge, so I'd have something to drink when I come over."

"That doesn't explain how you got in the yard tonight."

"Couple of weeks ago, we put a gate between our yards, so I wouldn't have to go the long way around every time I stop by. And he gave me keys to the house."

Unbelievable. Miles never opened up to strangers, yet he'd invited this big, scary biker into his life, into his fortress. "Miles must really trust you," I observed.

"Like I said, we're friends. Your cousin's got his quirks, but he's a good kid. I think he's lonely and could use a friend."

That was a knife to my heart. I squeezed my eyes shut and dropped my head. "I've been such a selfish shit."

"Yeah? Then do better."

I jerked, startled by his matter-of-fact exhortation. Kyle would have told me that I was a good person and hadn't really done anything wrong. He would have soothed my conscience, placated me, and tried to make me feel better about myself. Not Ripper. It was a shock, but I appreciated his clear-eyed lack of sympathy. I'd rather be told that I could mess up and make amends than be offered a false assurance that I hadn't done anything wrong.

I met his eyes. "I will."

He nodded. "Good."

The silence between us stretched out, morphing from companionable to awkward. I cleared my throat and pointed to his arm. "Is that another club tattoo?"

"Nah. Got this when I was in the army."

"You served?" I couldn't keep the note of incredulity from my voice. The only thing I'd assumed Ripper had served was time.

"75th Ranger Regiment, Second Battalion."

I knew as much about the military as I did about guns—just this side of diddlysquat—but I'd heard of the Rangers.

"The Army Rangers?" I marveled aloud. "That's almost as good as being a Navy SEAL, isn't it?"

From his expression, you'd have thought I called his grandma a skank.

"Mac, you shouldn't offer an opinion about things you know nothing about."

Yeah. Now that I thought about it, maybe my comment had been unintentionally insulting.

"I'm sorry. You're right. Let me try that again. An Army Ranger. That's impressive. Thank you for your service."

My gaze fell to his motorcycle club vest as I spoke. It was hard to reconcile the two roles, Army Ranger and outlaw biker. American hero and probable criminal. Damnedest career trajectory ever. I couldn't leave it alone.

"So...is that common? I mean, to go from the army into a motorcycle club? Have many of your—" I halted, at a loss for words. If I said *brothers*, a term I'd learned from my biker romances, he might ask how I knew to use the word. No way would I confess to reading novels about fictional, over-sexed, alpha-male bikers. Not to the real deal. I started again. "Have many of your *fellows* also served?"

Fellows. I winced as soon as I said it. Could I have picked a lamer, more prissy word?

"You might be surprised." Ripper's shoulders shook, as if he were suppressing a laugh. He cocked his head and despite being bloodshot, his brown eyes sparkled. "Tell me, Mac. Everything you know about MCs, you learned from that damned TV series, right?"

That was perilously close to the truth. "I have no idea what you're talking about," I lied.

"Yeah, you do." He leaned across the table and seized my chin. "You like bad boys. You got all hot and bothered by what's his name, that blondie all the girls were swooning over."

I jerked my chin from his grasp. "I've only seen a couple of episodes of that show, and I can assure you that it inspired no bad-boy fantasies in me." Nothing but the truth there. The fantasies came from novels.

"Right." Ripper smirked, leaned back, and crossed his arms over his chest.

"What do you do?" I asked, trying to steer the conversation toward safer grounds. "When you're not at your club or helping Miles pound stakes in the ground."

"Custom-built bikes. Bought the place behind Miles because the previous owner was a mechanic, and the garage is twice as big as the house."

"A lot of room for your toy boys," I observed. Oh, shit. "That came out backwards." Heat suffused my cheeks, and I fought the urge to hide my face in my palms.

"Keep my toy boys in the attic," Ripper quipped. "But did you seriously just call my bikes boy toys?"

Batting a thousand today, wasn't I? Didn't miss a single opportunity to give offense.

I shrugged and deflected. "Maybe my brain got scrambled when you smacked my head on the wall."

"Maybe you shoulda thought twice before blasting a man in the face with pepper spray."

We locked eyes. Despite the accusatory tone of our banter, our mutual gaze held no hostility. I still had reservations about Ripper. He was probably a criminal, but the man clearly cared about Miles and had stepped up to watch out for him.

"Can we start over?" I suggested. "Listen, if I had any idea who you were, I wouldn't have pepper sprayed you. And I assume that you didn't intend to scare me to death by walking into the house. We were victims of bad timing and a lack of information."

"Not a victim of anything, Mac. And you'll be better off if you refuse to think of yourself as one."

What the hell. When Kyle and I split up, he told me I had a victim complex. Did I give off some long-suffering martyr vibe? Crap, I hoped not. That was my mother's thing, not mine. No. Ripper had simply placed too much importance on my innocent choice of words.

"There's a shitstorm coming our way," Ripper continued. "It's gonna get ugly, and you'll have to suck it up and be strong if you wanna survive."

"It's already ugly," I said. "I saw four bodies on my way here, and when a man tried to steal our gas, I scared him off with my pepper spray." What's that saying? Fake it till you make it? "I'm not a wuss," I met his eyes. "I'm not useless. No matter what, I intend to survive. And I'm going to make sure that Miles survives, too."

Ripper studied me, his gaze appraising. "You know how to shoot?"

"Not yet."

"All right. First lesson tomorrow." He yawned, then stood and picked up his shirt and vest. "I'm beat. Gonna head home and crash for a few hours. Tell Miles I'll be over in the afternoon."

"Okay."

He took a step toward the door, then turned back to face me. "Pleasure to meet you...Mac." He extended his hand.

Long, strong fingers imprisoned mine. The muscles in his forearm flexed as he squeezed my hand. It was the confident handshake of a man who knew how to take care of business, a firm grip that promised protection in a world that was descending into chaos. For a crazy moment, I clung to his hand, unable to relinquish that illusion of safety. Then I remembered that I'd just declared that I'm not a wuss. Not helpless. Not a victim.

I surrendered Ripper's hand and smiled. "Pleasure to meet you, too. I'll see you tomorrow...Jack."

"Smartass," he said under his breath. "Lock the door after me."

I turned the deadbolt and watched Ripper's retreating figure until he disappeared through the gate in the fence.

There were still a lot of hours to burn through until morning. I didn't trust myself to stay awake if I returned to the recliner. I boiled water, filled the French press with coffee, and left it to steep while I fetched my phone from the front room. Coffee in hand, I sat at the kitchen table, and lost myself once again in Setora's world. Only this time, when I imagined myself riding on the back of a bike, the man I clung to had shoulder-length brown hair and piercing brown eyes. And he wore a vest emblazoned with Janissaries Portland.

SIX

Ripper

It was quiet. Too fucking quiet. I cocked my head and held my breath, straining to hear any sounds coming through the front door of Jethro's house, but—nothing. No muffled voices. No TV. No footsteps. No signs of life. Nada. Window shades blocked the view from the front porch into the house, so I couldn't see squat.

The unnatural silence made the skin on the back of my neck prickle, a warning signal from my hind brain. I reached automatically for the Colt 1911 in my shoulder holster, then stilled my hand before my fingers touched the Pachmayr grip.

Whatever enemy waited for me inside the house couldn't be dispatched with a bullet.

I rattled the knob. Locked, of course. My prez was no fool, and only a fool would leave his home open to all comers. No help for it, but hey, at least the door was wood and not metal.

I stepped back, shifted my weight to my left foot, then kicked hard, the tread of my boot striking the weak spot above the knob. The wood splintered. One more kick, and I was in.

I flipped on an overhead light and scanned the room. Hard to tell at first if anything was wrong. Jethro was a slob, and since his old lady had dumped his ass last year, there was nobody to pick up after him. The empty beer cans and pizza boxes could have been piling up on the floor of his living room for weeks. I checked out the kitchen and bathroom, but again—nothing.

Pausing outside his bedroom, I wrinkled my nose, smelling piss and sweat, but not the sickly sweet stink of decomposition.

Jethro might be alive, but he had to be out of it if the racket I made kicking down his front door hadn't roused him. Still, no point in taking a chance. Couldn't risk startling him and facing the business end of his Glock.

I pounded my fist on the door. "Prez, it's Ripper."

No response.

"I'm coming in."

The hinges creaked as I stepped into the room, then recoiled. Jesus Christ, it reeked. I gagged and pressed my nose into the crook of my elbow. Yeah, Jethro had to be here. Only a disease-riddled human body could produce that noxious stench.

The shades were drawn, but morning light filtered into the room from the slits between blind and window frame. Spying Jethro stretched out across his bed, I dropped my arm and drew a shallow breath.

"Prez?"

When he didn't stir, I clicked on the small lamp on his nightstand. Jethro groaned and twisted his face away from the light.

"Sorry, man." I switched off the lamp. My eyes adjusted to the dim light, and I studied his sprawled figure.

His eyelids fluttered, as if he were struggling to escape from some no man's land between consciousness and unconsciousness. He gasped for air like a winded animal, his chest rising and falling at an alarming rate. Mottled red blotches stained his cheeks, and his sweat-soaked hair clung to his skull.

I hesitated for a second before touching his shoulder. This shit had to be contagious—who was I kidding, it was a fucking plague—but like as not, I'd already been exposed. Didn't know if this flu spread from direct contact or breathing it in, but either way, I was likely screwed.

I'd dealt with half a dozen people while riding back from Seattle yesterday. The kid behind the counter at the quickie mart where I'd stopped for gas had wiped his runny nose on his arm before handing me my change. And the waitress at the diner where I stopped for dinner—the one who apologized for slow service because a cook and two waitresses had called in sick—kept sniffing and clearing her throat.

I'm not a fatalist by nature. If there's a way out of a jam, I'll find it. But a man's gotta accept reality. I'd already been exposed, and I was either gonna fall sick, or I wasn't.

My fingers closed on Jethro's shoulder. "Prez, wake up."

He grunted a protest.

"Come on, man. Open your eyes."

He mumbled something unintelligible. I was about to shake his shoulder when his eyes snapped open, and he lifted his head from the pillow.

"Ripper?" he croaked.

"Yeah. It's me."

His head fell back on the pillow, as if the effort of holding it up was too much for him. Jethro was built like a tank. I'd seen the man bench-press 300 pounds. Watching him strain to keep his head up was unreal. He licked his lips, and I saw fuzzy white spots on the tip of his tongue.

"You thirsty?" I asked.

"Yeah."

I grabbed the empty glass from his nightstand and headed toward his kitchen. After filling the glass at the tap, I opened his fridge and pulled out a sports drink. I carried the drinks back to his bedside and held both up.

"Got water and Gatorade. You look dehydrated. The electrolytes in the Gatorade might do you good."

"Okay." His voice was a weak rasp, nothing like his usual booming bellow.

"Lemme help." I averted my eyes from the contents of the bucket on the floor next to the head of the bed, carefully avoiding kicking it over as I slipped an arm under Jethro's head and lifted him up so he wouldn't choke on the liquid. He managed three small sips before frowning and pushing the drink away.

"What can I do?" I placed the drink within reach on his bedside table.

"Fuck if I know." His eyes were glassy, and he spoke with an obvious effort. "My head is killing me."

I fetched three aspirin from the bathroom medicine cabinet and held the glass of water to Jethro's lips so he could swallow. He nodded his thanks.

"You been to the club?" He shoved his lank hair away from his eyes. With his hollow cheeks and sunken eyes, Jethro looked like he had aged ten years in the past few days.

I fixed my gaze on the floor so he wouldn't read the concern in my eyes.

"First thing this morning. About twenty brothers decided to hole up there with their old ladies and kids. Hauled in food and water. They got the gate locked and the building buttoned up tight. Some of the men decided to ride out the epidemic at home, or at least that was the last word from them. Hard to tell what's happening now with the phones down. Several of the men never reported in, so..." I trailed off, reluctant to state the obvious. "Chimney stopped by while I was at the club. Said he's taking his family to his dad's cabin at Lost Dog Lake."

"You see Reno?"

"Nah, he wasn't there. Why?"

"I started to feel like shit Saturday afternoon. Too dizzy and too sick to ride, so I had the prospect drive me home from the club." He cleared his throat and reached out a shaky hand for the glass of water. After a sip he continued. "The kid stepped up. Fussed over me like an old woman. Even tried to feed me a can of soup. He spent the night on my couch. When the phone lines jammed up yesterday, I sent him to the club to check things out. He never made it back."

"Reno wouldn't bail on you." I frowned, lifting my eyes to his face.

"No, he wouldn't. Something happened to him."

"Not just Reno. Something's happened to a shitload of people."

Nothing but the truth there. When I'd left town on Saturday, the city was quieter than usual, and a couple of businesses were unexpectedly dark. Nothing too far out of the ordinary. By Monday morning the world had tipped on its axis, and the familiar, laid-back Portland landscape had begun to morph into something alien.

Boarded up storefronts dotted every block. Saw two men prying the boards off a pharmacy window and another man emerge from the building carrying a shotgun. Only a handful of cars crossed my path. Looked like most people had either already abandoned the city or had decided to stay put. I saw a man bashing in the window of a sedan—crammed to the ceiling with suitcases and boxes—whose driver had been stupid enough to stop at a red light. The assailant had glared at me then looked away when he spied my cut. Probably figured I was packing. Damn right I was packing.

The homeless encampments I passed were eerily quiet, the ever-present panhandlers nowhere in sight until I passed a scruffy young man sprawled on a sidewalk, a sign that read "GOTTA BE HONEST I'M JONESING FOR A TACO" on the ground next to him. Counted seven additional bodies before I made it to the club.

"It's bad out there," Jethro concluded, interrupting my train of thought.

"Yeah."

We lapsed into silence. After a long moment, I glanced at Jethro, half expecting him to have fallen back asleep, but he was awake and watching me with hooded eyes.

"Gonna ask you to do something for me," he said, straining to rise up on his elbow.

"Anything, prez."

"If everything goes to hell, if I don't make it, I want you to ride to Grants Pass and make sure my old lady's all right. I haven't been able to get through to Sara. Shit, maybe she's still too pissed to talk to me, but maybe she's sick or in trouble. Will you do that, Ripper? Will you promise to check on her for me?"

The long speech drained him and he collapsed against the pillow.

"Of course I will, but don't you give up, man. You still might beat this thing, then you can check on her yourself. No way Sara will stay mad if you ride into town like a hero come to rescue his woman."

I was spinning a fantasy, and we both knew it.

Jethro's lips twisted in a rueful smile. "You heard of anybody who beat this thing? Nah. It is what it is, brother."

I opened my mouth to protest, then snapped it shut. False hope was a cruel lie, and Jethro deserved better. Everything pointed to the flu being a death sentence. I seized his clammy hand and squeezed, offering him the only assurance that mattered. "Rest easy, prez. If things go to hell, I promise to go to Grants Pass and find Sara."

He sighed. "Good. Good."

"What else can I do for you? You want me to fix you something to eat?" I glanced at the sodden tangle of sheets on his bed. "You be more comfortable if I put clean sheets on your bed?"

Jethro laughed, a sound that changed into a ragged cough. "I got no appetite, and there's no point in changing the sheets."

"How about I pull up a chair and hang for a while?"

"I don't need a babysitter, Ripper. And if the rumors are true, it wouldn't be smart for anybody to be by my side at the end. Tell you what. Leave a couple of bottles of Gatorade and some pain pills on the table here. Make sure my Glock is in reach. Then I want you to go."

"All right." Hated like hell to walk away from Jethro when he was in such a state. Felt like I was abandoning a brother in need, but I had to respect his wishes.

I dumped out the bucket and placed it back on the floor before fetching the drinks and pain pills. On the off chance he woke up hungry, I put a box of crackers next to the aspirin. I found his Glock on top of a dresser and tucked it under the pillow on the far side of the bed.

Jethro watched me through heavy-lidded eyes, sleep already rushing to reclaim him.

When I was finished, Jethro rallied his energy and spoke again. "What are you gonna do? You gonna go back to the club, or are you gonna hang tight at your place?"

I'd been considering that question all morning. My first impulse was to make a stand with my brothers, but truth was they didn't really need me. They had weapons and experienced men to use them, but a finite amount of food and water. I might end up a drain on their resources, assuming I didn't get sick, of course. Besides, plenty of men had opted to hole up at their homes with their families.

I kept thinking about Miles and his cousin Mac. Despite all his preparations and security precautions, Miles didn't have a clue how the real world worked. He'd be an easy mark for predators. I oughta know. Couldn't leave the kid to fend for himself.

And Mac? I turn my back and the only thing between her and danger would be a pink canister of pepper spray. Could I live with that?

I shook my head. Socrates said "Know thyself." World might be coming to an end, shit hitting the fan six ways to Sunday, but I couldn't pretend that altruism was the only thing on my mind. Jacked off before I fell asleep last night, imagining Mac's long legs wrapped around my waist while I pounded into her.

Yeah, I'm a fucking white knight.

"Ripper?" Jethro's voice interrupted my thoughts.

I pulled my head out of my ass. "I got people at home I need to watch out for."

Jethro nodded, reaching out to clasp my hand. "See you on the other side, brother."

SEVEN

Kenzie

"You need to see this," I called to Miles.

He stuck his head out of the bathroom door, wiping shaving cream from his chin. "What?"

"Something's happening on the news," I motioned for him to join me.

For the past hour, while I waited for Miles to wake up, I'd been scrolling through the local stations on Uncle Mel's old TV. Convinced that cable companies could spy on him through their equipment, Miles had canceled his parents' cable plan, but a converter box allowed him to watch local channels. So far today, instead of the regular morning programming, the local stations were showing reruns of court TV and game shows. Now, a little past 10 a.m., a live camera zoomed in on an empty news desk.

A dark-haired young woman walked across the stage and took a seat behind the desk, an unfamiliar face against the newsroom's familiar backdrop of the Portland cityscape and Mt. Hood. Clearing her throat, she addressed the camera. "Good morning."

Miles shuffled into the living room. "Who's that?"

"Shhh." I patted his chair seat, then pointed to the travel mug of hot coffee waiting for Miles on his desk.

My fingers were wrapped around what had to be my tenth cup of coffee. Even though I'd been awake most of the night, so much caffeine was buzzing through my veins that I felt like tap dancing across the house.

"Your regular newscasters are unavailable today, and we're operating with a skeleton crew," the young woman said. "I'm Jessica Ortiz, a production assistant for the midday news team. This is my first time on camera, so I hope you'll bear with me. Let's get to the news."

She cleared her throat and read aloud from a piece of paper. "The World Health Organization and the Centers for Disease Control have confirmed sustained human-to-human transmission of a new and virulent influenza virus. According to all reports, this virus has an unpredictable incubation period, is extremely contagious, and has an exceptionally high mortality rate. We're expecting an announcement from the president and FEMA concerning a national response to the pandemic, but at seven this morning the governor of Oregon declared a state public health emergency."

I glanced at Miles, and he nodded.

"In order to minimize transmission of the flu virus, she's ordered the immediate shutdown of all public transportation, government offices, schools. Retail businesses, including grocery stores and pharmacies, must shutter by 8 o'clock this evening. After that time, only police and fire department vehicles are authorized to be on the roads. Everyone is asked to shelter in place."

She dropped the paper onto the desk and looked into the camera. "If there's another announcement from the governor, the president, or FEMA, we will break into programming. Until then take care, stay safe, and may merciful God watch over us all."

"Just what I expected." Miles took a long sip of coffee.

Miles might not be surprised, but I was. Despite all the signs to the contrary, I'd clung to the hope that things would somehow sort themselves out. The CDC would announce a cure, or the flu would fizzle out. Reality had smashed that fantasy into smithereens. And hearing a stand-in newscaster pray for divine intervention—in secular Portland—brought home how much our familiar world was slipping away.

"What are we supposed to do now?" My eyes widened as I pondered a question more rhetorical than sincere.

"After breakfast I'll give you a tour and show you all the supplies I've stockpiled." Miles, as always, was literal in his reply.

"Aren't you scared?"

I could have kicked myself as soon as the question escaped my lips. Miles didn't like to answer questions about his feelings, especially questions that implied he should feel a certain way. He told me once he felt put on the spot by them, like a student taking a pop quiz he hadn't studied for.

He squirmed, frowning. "We're prepared. No matter what happens out there." He waved a hand, indicating the outside world. "We'll be safe in here. You don't need to be scared."

On his face I saw the hesitant, tentative expression he'd worn as a child when he thought he'd made a mistake or said the wrong thing.

Guilt welled up in my chest. If Miles could rise to the occasion, so could I, dammit. I couldn't afford to panic or whine or feel sorry for myself just because my life had upended. Everybody's life had upended.

"You're right." I jumped to my feet. "We're going to be okay. You made sure of that. Now, how about we take advantage of the electricity while we still have it and make a hot breakfast? I can scramble some eggs while you make toast."

We prepared the food and took seats at the small kitchen table, the same table where I'd sat with Ripper the night before.

"I met your friend last night," I said, spreading marmalade on a slice of toast. "Ripper came over to talk to you."

Miles collapsed back in his chair.

"Stupid. Stupid." He thumped his palm on his forehead. "I should have told you my neighbor has a key to the gate."

"Hey." I leaned forward and smiled, tapping on the table to get his attention. "Not a problem. We introduced ourselves. It's all good."

A sanitized version of the truth, at best, but Miles didn't need to know that I'd been so terrified that I'd pepper-sprayed his friend, or that a furious Ripper had pinned me to a wall.

"He said to tell you that he'll be over this afternoon after he runs some errands," I added.

"Okay." He frowned. "But the governor said nobody is supposed to be on the roads."

"The governor said people shouldn't be on the roads after 8. Besides, your friend doesn't strike me as the kind of man who'd stay put just because the governor told him to."

Miles considered that for a moment. Rule breaking always made him uncomfortable.

"You're right," he conceded.

What an odd pair of friends they were, an outlaw biker and a hermit who was a stickler for the rules. I shook my head and took a bite of my toast.

After we finished breakfast, Miles announced that we'd start our tour in the back yard.

"The vegetable beds and chickens will supply us with fresh food." He pointed to the roof. "Solar panels, to augment our energy supply." He pointed next to a neatly stacked pile of firewood under a blue tarp. "Kindling and logs for the wood stove. The shed in the corner of the yard holds propane tanks for the gas grill and gasoline for the generator. I've got a solar oven, too. It's slow, but it'll let us bake bread when the electricity goes off."

"Impressive," I murmured.

"Most of the supplies are in the basement," Miles said, leading the way back into the house.

I followed him inside, then stopped dead in my tracks when he opened the door to the basement and flipped a light switch. Miles glanced back over his shoulder. I willed myself to take a step, but my feet were rooted in place.

"There's nothing down there that will hurt you." He was quoting Aunt Debbie, who hadn't believed in indulging childish fears.

The basement had creeped me out ever since I was a child, and I'd dreaded the times she would ask me to fetch a jar of canned food from its musty confines.

"I know there's nothing to be scared of." I laughed shakily. "You'd think I would have outgrown this a long time ago, wouldn't you?"

"Yes," he agreed. The social niceties often eluded Miles, and it wouldn't occur to him to make it easier for me with a tactful expression of understanding.

Miles jogged down the stairs. I straightened my back, determined to follow at his heels. Instead, I halted on the top step, gaping in amazement.

The dark and dusty cellar that had haunted my childhood was no more. Back then, a single bulb had illuminated the well-worn stairs, leaving the basement a pool of darkness as I reluctantly descended, gliding my hand along the stair rail, taking tentative steps toward that ominous gloom. I always held my breath, straining to hear whispers or scampering feet.

Maybe I was an over-imaginative child, maybe I'd watched too many scary movies, but I was positive something evil waited for me down there. And I'd been certain that inevitably, one of the times when I reached the bottom of the stairs and stretched out a quivering hand to switch on the main light, something would grab me.

Miles had no such qualms and had actually set up a card table in a corner of the basement, a quiet retreat where he could work on puzzles in peace.

Now, bright light flooded the basement from a bank of overhead lights, banishing any menacing shadows. I took a few steps down and paused again, gripping the new, heavy handrail as I bounced on the balls of my feet. Miles had replaced the creaky 1940s-era stairs with rock solid boards, treads that wouldn't buckle under the weight of all the stuff he had hauled in.

My head swiveled from side to side as I took in the changes. Substantial metal shelving units—crammed full of supplies—lined three walls, the fourth was stacked floor to ceiling with the same large water containers that filled my bedroom. A row of shelves extended into the center of the room, creating additional storage.

Miles wasn't kidding. He was prepared for the apocalypse. And now I knew what he'd done with the settlement money he received after Aunt Debbie and Uncle Mel's car accident.

Miles motioned impatiently for me to follow him down. "I had an electrician rewire the place, then had it waterproofed and improved the ventilation."

Excitement animated his features. I recognized that look. Miles was about to launch into a long-winded explanation of a subject he found fascinating. But this time, instead of zoning out while he droned on about ham radio networks or something equally tedious, I was eager to hear what he had to say.

"What do you need to ride out the flu pandemic? What do you need when the shit hits the fan?" he asked.

Miles didn't use crude language. He must have found that phrase on a prepper website, or maybe he learned it from Ripper.

"You need food," he answered his own question. "Water. Shelter. Heat. Light. First aid supplies. Trade goods. Weapons. Energy. Sanitation supplies. We have it all covered."

He pointed to the shelves that hugged the right wall. "Canned foods. Fruits, vegetables, meats, soups, etc. Most of the cans are pop top, but there are manual can openers in a box on the top shelf there. See those big, plastic storage containers?"

"Yes." I nodded at the neatly stacked containers that filled the center aisle of shelves.

"Each one is lined with mylar, and they hold grains, dried beans, oats, rice, pasta, dehydrated fruit, and powdered milk. Oxygen absorbers keep the dry food dry and bacteria free. We have sugar, honey, salt, condiments, and spices. Yeast. Baking powder. Oils. Peanut butter. The canned goods go bad after a couple of years, so I also bought freeze-dried food that can last for twenty years. And I laid in a supply of MREs—that's meals ready to eat—in the bug-out section."

Holy shit. It was one thing to know that Miles was obsessed with prepping. I always thought of it as a more or less harmless pursuit. It was another thing entirely to be confronted with a wall of carefully organized emergency foods.

"How long will all of this last us?" I asked.

"For three people?" He focused his eyes on the ceiling and his lips moved while he did mental calculations. "At two thousand calories per day, per person, our supplies should last close to three years."

"Wow."

He walked to the next shelf. "Soap. Laundry detergent."

"Wait," I interrupted. "How do we do laundry if the power goes out?"

"*When* the power goes out." He emphasized the first word. "I have a hand-crank washing machine that can do five pounds of clothes at a time. If it's sunny, we can hang the clothes to dry on Mom's clothesline in the back yard. If it's raining, we'll use a drying rack in the house."

"Okay." My head was swimming.

"Sanitation will be very important moving forward. We have to avoid bacteria and infections." He pointed at the next shelf. "Cleaning supplies. Garbage bags. Bleach. Baby wipes so we can clean ourselves up without using too much water. Toilet paper."

"Why do you have bags of cat litter next to the bleach?"

"When the sewer system fails, we'll make toilets by lining buckets with heavy plastic bags filled with cat litter."

"Huh." I frowned, trying to imagine myself squatting over a bucket filled with kitty litter.

"Toiletries are on the next shelf, shampoo, toothpaste, etc. First aid supplies, too. Extra blankets and towels. Extra clothes. And over here, we have luxury goods we could use for trade. After the stores have all been looted, people will still want alcohol, cigarettes, and chocolate."

"You've thought of everything," I marveled, admiring the neat rows of scotch, tequila, and vodka, and the vacuum-sealed cartons of cigarettes and candy bars.

"Yes. I believe I have," Miles agreed before moving on. "This final shelf holds bug-out supplies, things we'll need if for any reason we have to flee the compound. The backpacks are filled with MREs, protein bars, a few pouches of water, portable water filtration kits, mylar thermal blankets, flint matches, antiseptic wipes. Sleeping bags and a tent are on the lower shelf. What we carry would depend on whether we're on foot or in a car."

"I'm blown away," I said, turning around to survey the room. "When you said you were prepared for anything, I had no idea what that meant."

He shrugged. "Lots of people are prepping. It's easy to find the information online."

"Maybe, but it's not so easy to actually follow through. I'm impressed. You've done an outstanding job, Miles."

Miles ducked his head and scuffed his shoe on the cement floor, a small smile on his lips.

"I saw the shotguns by the doors," I said. "Where do you store your other weapons?"

I got to confess, the idea of Miles holding a loaded gun freaked me out. When agitated, he acted impulsively, dancing a fine line between a reasonable or unreasonable reaction to whatever pushed his buttons. Nobody in such a state of mind should have a weapon. Of course, Miles had a reputation in the neighborhood as a doomsday prepper. If the shit really did hit the fan, his well-fortified and well-stocked compound would be a target for looters. Looters, or worse.

Crap. Was I living in a world where the notion of Miles with a gun made any kind of sense?

And what about Ripper? A week ago he would have set off all the warning klaxons in my brain. Fictional bad boys might leave me hot and flustered, but I knew better than to hook up with one in real life. Still—despite his tough exterior—he seemed to genuinely care about my cousin. Strength and competence clung to Ripper like a second skin, invaluable assets in any crisis. Could I count on him to help me manage Miles in this crazy new reality?

Was I living in a world where relying on an outlaw biker seemed like a good idea?

"I store the weapons in my bedroom, not down here," Miles said, interrupting my train of thought.

"What kinds of weapons are we talking about?"

He hesitated. "The kind that will allow us to defend the compound and ourselves."

"Vague much, Miles? Just what do you have in your bedroom?" I tried to keep my tone light and jocular, although his reluctance to spill the details concerned me. "You aren't hiding a black market rocket launcher, are you?"

"Ripper knows what I have," Miles said after a long silence. "He made me buy a gun safe."

"And you don't want to tell me what's in the gun safe?"

Miles rocked on his heels, his brow creased while he considered his answer. Maybe it would be smart to back off, to change the subject, to mitigate his obvious discomfort, but I couldn't let it go.

"Come on, Miles. Don't I have a right to know if I'm sleeping ten feet away from a bazooka? You have something in there that might go boom in the night?"

He frowned. "Ripper told me not to tell anybody what we keep in the gun safe."

"We?" What the hell. "Is Ripper storing stuff in your safe?"

Miles nodded.

"Do you know what it is?"

"No. He keeps a locked case on the top shelf. He told me not to touch it."

All the news stories and rumors about what the Janissaries were up too came crashing into my mind. Gun running. Drug dealing. Murder. Ripper was a proud member of what the authorities considered a criminal enterprise. Yeah, he was strong and confident, and I was drawn to that strength, but he was also dangerous. Maybe I'd been a little too willing to overlook that.

Just what was Ripper storing in my naive cousin's safe?

EIGHT

Kenzie

I startled awake, squirming as a wet, warm tongue scraped across my cheek. Hot breath tickled my ear, and a heavy weight pressed me into the mattress.

"Get off," I shrieked, flailing against the unknown intruder.

The overhead light clicked on. Turning my head, I spied Ripper leaning nonchalantly against the door frame, a mug of coffee in his hand.

I turned back to the beast straddling my body, squinting up at a black and tan muzzle hovering inches above my face. Eager brown eyes gazed down at me before a wet tongue dragged across my chin and lips. I sputtered and swiveled my face, wiping the slobber onto my pillow.

"Did you sic your dog on me?" I demanded indignantly, as Ripper took a long sip of his coffee.

"It's after two in the afternoon," Ripper said. "Too late to be sleeping in. I sent him to wake you up."

"Seriously, I think he tried to French me." I scrubbed my hand across my mouth.

"He's just happy to see you. Mac, meet Hector."

Hector tilted his head and angled his ears back, a friendly expression on his furry face. My heart melted. I always wanted a dog when I was growing up, but Mom said no, claiming they were too much trouble and too expensive.

"I haven't spent much time around dogs." I wriggled into a sitting position. "Is it okay if I pet him?"

Ripper set his coffee cup on the dresser and squatted down next to the cot.

"Are you afraid of dogs?" he asked in a low voice.

"No. Not afraid, just unfamiliar with them."

"All right." Ripper placed his right palm on the back of my hand and entwined our fingers. I held my breath as the most gorgeous man I'd ever met pulled my hand toward his dog, the muscles of his tanned forearm flexing with the movement. "Hector likes to be touched on his chest, shoulders, and the back of his neck. Reach in from the side, not over the top of his head when you pet him."

Our hands were locked together as he directed my fingers to stroke first Hector's chest, then his shoulders. When Hector leaned into my touch, I smiled.

"Who's a pretty boy?" I cooed. "Who's a pretty, pretty boy?"

I felt Ripper's shoulders shake as he laughed softly. "Don't go emasculating my dog," he warned. "No sparkly collars. No ribbons. No dumb-ass outfits."

"Time to join the 21st century." I slanted my eyes at him, deliberately focusing on the notch at the base of his throat. "Some of the manliest men wear sparkly collars."

"Not on your life," he growled.

I raised my brows "Keep an open mind, that's all that I'm saying. You might surprise yourself."

His fingers tightened on mine, not enough to hurt, but enough to make a point. "Don't give a rat's ass what anybody else does. I don't judge, but I know myself. Like Polonius said, 'This above all, to thine own self be true.'"

"You've read Hamlet?" I sputtered. Crap. Once again I spoke without thinking.

"Because a dumb biker can't read Shakespeare? You an intellectual snob, Mac? Now who needs to drop their preconceived notions and join the 21st century?" Ripper released my hand and stood. "You gotta get out of bed. We were supposed to shoot yesterday and you flaked on me."

My cheeks heated as both accusations hit home.

"Sorry, no insult intended," I said. "And I didn't flake yesterday. I'd been up all night. My head was spinning, and my hands were shaking from too much coffee."

Did my excuse sound as lame to his ears as it did to mine? I had been buzzed on caffeine, but that wasn't the only reason I'd postponed our lesson.

"I don't buy it." Ripper dismissed my explanation. "You telling me you bailed because you'd drunk too much coffee? Nah. Doesn't pass the sniff test. If you don't want to do it, you don't want to do it, but don't waste my time. This is your last chance. If you're serious about wanting to learn how to shoot, we'll do it today."

"I am serious," I insisted, swinging my legs over the edge of my bed. Even if I wasn't sure that I should trust Ripper, I needed to learn how to handle a gun. If we ever had to defend ourselves, I'd be more likely than Miles to keep a cool head. "Listen, I need to take a shower and eat before we start."

"All right. I'll be back by four to pick you up."

"Pick me up? Aren't we going to set up a target in the back yard?"

"Nope. Can't have you shooting through the fence and accidentally hitting somebody. We'll go to an indoor shooting range nearby."

"I guess that makes sense. But, will we get in trouble for being on the road?"

He raised his brows, his eyes dancing with amusement.

"What's that look for?" I demanded. "It's not a dumb question. The governor ordered everybody to stay home. Aren't you worried about being pulled over by a cop?"

A grin split his face. "Let me worry about the cops, Mac."

I shrugged. "Have it your way, tough guy."

"Come on, Hector." Ripper patted his leg. The German shepherd hopped off my cot and followed his master through the door. "Ass in gear, Mac," Ripper called over his shoulder.

"Yes, Dad," I mumbled under my breath.

I gathered up clean clothes, my toiletry bag, and my phone and headed toward the shower. I passed Miles, who was sitting at his desk, his back to me. Headphones covered his ears, and he fiddled with the knobs on his ham radio, oblivious to my presence.

Sitting on the edge of the tub, I tried to send a text to Ali, but the progress bar stopped before the message went through. It took about seven hours to drive from Portland to Boise. With any luck, my friends had arrived home Sunday evening and were now safe behind the locked gates of their upscale community. I just wish I knew for sure that they made it home.

After taking a shower and getting dressed, I ate a cup of lemon yogurt and a slice of toast. I was finishing my second cup of coffee when Ripper strode through the kitchen door, Hector at his heels.

"Hi, sweetie." I held out a hand toward my new friend, who trotted over and sniffed my legs.

"You ready?" Ripper asked.

"One sec." I quickly washed my hands, then washed and rinsed my cup and plate and stacked them in the dish drainer. I shrugged on the hoodie I'd hung on the back of my chair. "Okay, I'm ready."

Ripper stepped into the living room and halted by my cousin's side, waiting quietly until Miles noticed him. Smart. He knew better than to tap Miles on the shoulder and startle him.

Miles pulled off the headset. "Hey, Ripper."

"Hey, Miles. Listen, Mackenzie and I are going out for a few hours. I'm taking her to the shooting range. Hector will stay with you."

"But it's dangerous outside, and the governor said to stay at home." Miles spun his chair to look at me, his brows drawn together. "I don't want her to go."

"Mackenzie will be all right. We'll stay clear of people, and if anybody comes at us, I'll protect her." Ripper's voice was calm and reassuring. "Always keep my promises, don't I?"

Miles wrapped his arms around his waist and rocked back and forth while he considered the question. When he stopped, he glanced at Ripper's face, meeting his eyes for a fleeting second. "Yes. You always keep your promises."

Ripper nodded. "And you'll hold down the fort while we're gone." That was a surprisingly old-fashioned phrase, something Uncle Mel might have said, but the quaint expression seemed to comfort Miles and give him purpose.

He sat up straight. "I'll watch the security feeds and keep trying to contact my friends around the country."

"Good. It's a plan. Hector, stay with Miles." The dog obediently sprawled on the floor by my cousin's chair.

"Bye, Miles," I said, but the headset was already over his ears, his back was turned, and he didn't reply.

I followed Ripper through the kitchen and across the yard, staring at his broad back when he paused to unlock the gate.

Ripper was good with Miles, but was it because they were friends, or because he had something to gain from the relationship? I didn't want to be a cynic, to doubt my cousin's ability to make a friend or to distrust Ripper's motives, but I couldn't shake loose my nagging questions.

Was he hiding something for the club that he didn't want the police to find? Crack? Meth? A gun that could be traced back to some crime? Was Ripper a charming criminal taking advantage of a lonely young man?

"Earth to Mac." A voice pierced my reverie. I glanced up to find Ripper examining me, his forehead wrinkled, his hands on his hips. "Something on your mind?"

Nothing I was prepared to talk about. I fixed my eyes on the ground and shook my head. "No. Everything is fine."

He grunted derisively, but to my relief, he let it drop before leading me across his tidy backyard and through a door into his huge garage. The walls were lined with workbenches and shelves full of tools and other things I assumed he needed to work on custom-built bikes. Chrome pipes and fenders were neatly arranged on shelves. An engine hung from a t-shaped engine stand. A dozen bikes occupied one bay, in various states of completion.

"Which one do you ride?" I asked.

"That one." He pointed to a black and chrome motorcycle. "A 1977 Shovelhead Lowrider."

I nodded as if his words meant something to me and stepped closer to admire it. "I like the paint job on this tear-drop-shaped thing at the top."

He cleared his throat. "You mean the gas tank?"

"Yeah." I flashed him a bright smile. "The gas tank. It's *sparkly*." I infused the word with faux enthusiasm.

He scowled, but his lips twitched. "Smartass."

Ripper pushed a button, and the garage door rolled open. He opened a cupboard, pulled out a matte black helmet, and handed it to me. "This will do. Put it on."

I turned it around in my hands. It was shaped like a bowl with a rolled rim and looked darkly familiar.

"I don't want to wear this," I said after a long moment.

"Afraid you'll muss your hair?" He sighed heavily. "I'm not taking you on the road without a helmet, so put it on." When I hesitated, he snatched it from my hands and reached over to place it on my head.

I stepped back. "I don't care about my hair. What kind of a ninny do you think I am? I don't want to wear a helmet that makes me look like a Nazi."

That stopped him in his tracks. He dropped his arms. "What?"

"My grandpa fought in Italy during World War II. He hated the Nazis, and this looks like a Nazi helmet. Don't you have something else?"

Ripper blew out a long breath and shoved a hand through his hair. "It's a German-style helmet, but wearing it doesn't mean you're a Nazi sympathizer. I fucking hate Nazis, too. My grandpa was in the Sixth Armored Division during World War II. They liberated Buchenwald. He told me the concentration camp was the worst thing he'd ever seen."

Even though I disliked the thing, I felt a bit ridiculous for making such a big deal over it. A flu virus was sweeping around the world, and I was complaining about a helmet? "If you don't have a different one, it's fine, I'll wear it."

"Nah. I got something else." He dug around in the cupboard and handed me a white, retro-style helmet. "Don't want to offend your Nazi-hating sensibilities."

"Thanks. That's much better. I'd rather look like Speed Racer than a Nazi storm trooper any day."

"Speed Racer, huh?" Ripper snorted. He stepped close, so close that I could scent the same mixture of leather and exhaust that I detected the night we met. "Let's make sure it fits right."

With both hands, he smoothed my hair back from my brow, then his fingers caught my chin and tilted my face up, a surprisingly intimate gesture. We locked eyes. My breath caught in my throat, and for one absurd moment I thought that he was going to kiss me.

He grinned, as if reading my thoughts, and I felt my cheeks flush. Of course, he wasn't planning to kiss me. We barely knew each other. Even though he looked the part, with his leather vest and tattoos, this was real life, not a scene from one of my motorcycle club romances.

Ripper took the helmet from my hands, slipped it over my head, and adjusted the strap under my chin. He grabbed the back of the helmet and yanked hard, as if trying to pull it forward off my head.

"What are you doing?" I protested.

"Wanna make sure it's not too big. So you won't get hurt if something goes wrong."

Wanna make sure it's not too big. No. No. No. My over-heated imagination went straight to the gutter, and a blush scalded my cheeks.

What the hell was wrong with me?

His lips quirked. "The helmet, Mac. Wanna make sure it fits."

I nodded, trying to gather up the tattered shreds of my dignity. "So, what's the verdict?"

"It's fine. Should stay in place in an accident."

"That's good."

"You ever been on the back of a bike?"

Only in my dreams, but I couldn't say that out loud, could I?

I shook my head. "No."

"All right." He pushed his Harley onto the driveway, put down the kickstand, closed the garage door, then stood next to the handlebars on the left side of the bike. "Come here." He curled his fingers and motioned me over to stand in front of him. "When we ride, I'll mount first, then you put your left foot on this peg." He pointed to a small, metal protrusion. "You'll hold onto my shoulders and swing your right leg over the bike."

"Got it," I said.

"Want you to practice mounting."

Mounting. Why did every word out of his mouth strike me as a sexual innuendo? I deliberately bit my cheek, the pain squashing the impulse to giggle like a juvenile preteen. No man had ever made me this flustered, reducing me to a jumble of conflicting impulses. I wanted to both keep my distance because I wasn't sure I could trust him and to trace the outline of his stubbled jaw. This wasn't like me. I really needed to get a grip.

Focus. He wanted me to practice mounting the bike. I waited for him to climb on the bike, but when he didn't, I frowned. "You're not in the right position. You're standing up, and you're facing me."

"Doesn't matter. Wanna be able to catch you if you lose your balance. Hold onto me while you step on the peg and swing your leg over."

"Okay." I splayed my hands across his chest and felt the muscles tense when I touched him. Leaning into him, I wobbled a bit when I shifted my weight onto the small metal footrest. Ripper wrapped a hand around my elbow to stabilize me while I threw my right leg over the bike.

"Good. Now dismount," he said.

I climbed off the bike. We repeated the process a couple more times, until Ripper was certain that I'd found my balance.

"I think I got it." I gazed up at him while I awaited further instructions.

"Need to go over a few more things," he said. "Keep both feet on the pegs. I put my feet down at stops. You don't. The exhaust pipes are hot and could burn you, so keep your legs away from the pipes. You with me so far?"

"Yes."

"Good. You're going to wrap your arms low around my waist and press your knees against my thighs," he continued. "The bike accelerates and brakes hard, so you have to hold on."

I swallowed at the prospect of wrapping my legs around his body. "Got it."

"Don't move around while we're riding. You might upset my balance. The bike has to lean when we go around curves. Don't freak out. We're not tipping over, so don't try to compensate by leaning the other way."

I nodded. "Don't wiggle. Don't lean against the turn."

"Last thing. If you need to get my attention, do this." He reached down and tapped my thigh, his hand stroking up and down my leg.

"All right." Goosebumps erupted across my shoulders and arms when I felt the heat of his palm through the denim fabric of my jeans.

He squeezed my thigh, then straightened up and folded his arms across his chest, his head tilted to one side as he studied me.

I shifted uncomfortably under his silent scrutiny and focused my eyes on the Ranger tattoo on his forearm. My gaze traveled from the dusting of dark hairs on the tattoo, up over the curved muscles of his bicep, and across the black T-shirt that clung to his chest, before settling on the embroidered patches on his leather vest. Janissaries. Portland. 1 %. Ripper. Patches that proclaimed his loyalty to an outlaw motorcycle club.

Damn it. I frowned, my brow furrowing. Why was I reacting so intensely to a man I didn't know if I could trust?

"You having second thoughts about learning to shoot?"

"No. Absolutely not," I said firmly. At least I was certain of *that.*

"All right. Let's go."

He put the German-style helmet on his head, swung onto the bike and started the engine. I jumped at the sound, much louder than I expected.

Balancing my hands on his shoulders, I climbed on behind him. Despite all Ripper's warnings, I startled when his bike accelerated up the street. I tightened my hold on his waist. To my surprise, he laid a hand over my mine and squeezed reassuringly before gripping the handlebar again.

The engine roared louder than I anticipated, and its vibration jarred my legs and butt. I pressed my cheek against Ripper's back and closed my eyes for a moment, giving myself time to adjust to the new sensations before I took note of my surroundings.

It felt good to hold on to him, to relax and catch my breath while somebody who knew what he was doing took the lead. I intended to learn how to kick ass—I had no choice—but I savored the moment.

If only I were certain that I could trust him. Dammit. I wanted to trust him.

After a few minutes, I opened my eyes and gazed around at the world outside the safety of the compound.

The bike glided along quiet, sun-dappled neighborhood streets. Dogwood and rhododendron blossoms stirred in the late afternoon breeze. It was a glorious late-spring day, until you looked closely.

A blue sedan had taken out a fence and crashed into a mailbox. A man's body hunched over the steering wheel. Had he waited too long to flee the city, spurred into action as symptoms of the virus got worse, only to succumb within blocks of his home? I'd never know, and my imagination was running wild.

On one block, an elderly woman had toppled sideways on her porch swing, apparently choosing to meet death within sight of her garden. A Steller's jay pecked at a wire suet feeder hanging from the porch rafters. Birds ate through a block of suet in three or four days. Aunt Debbie used to complain about the expense, although that didn't stop her from buying it. The old woman must have refilled the wire feeder mere days ago, never guessing that her world was about to come crashing to a halt.

Nobody saw this coming. Within a handful of days, everything went haywire.

I squeezed my eyes shut and buried my face in Ripper's vest, as if blocking out the images could spare me the horror.

Fifteen minutes after we left the compound we pulled into the parking lot of the shooting range, a windowless, one-story gray building with a gabled roof. If I glanced at it from the road, I might assume it was a small neighborhood church.

"How are we going to get in? Isn't it locked?" I asked as we dismounted.

"I'm a member, and it has a card-lock entry system. Getting in is no problem. Besides, I served with the owner's son. If the old man's here, he knows I'm a friend."

Ripper removed a case from a saddlebag on the bike and held it up. "For you."

We entered the building and crossed through a small lobby to the shooting range, a long, deep room with the numbers one through ten painted on the back wall. Under each number, the white silhouette of a man's head and torso was attached to the wall. A bright yellow line, painted on the floor, ran from wall to wall at our feet.

"Fifty feet from the yellow line to the target," Ripper explained when he saw me looking around the room. "First things first. You ever handle a pistol?"

"No." Dad and Uncle Mel went deer hunting every fall when I was little, but otherwise we weren't a family of gun owners. On top of that, hunting was strictly a boys club thing, and it never would have occurred to them to include me.

"All right. Basic safety rules before we get started. Treat all guns as if they're loaded. Don't point at anything you don't intend to hit. And keep your finger off the trigger until you're ready to shoot."

"Makes sense," I said, committing the rules to memory.

"You're gonna wear goggles and earmuffs once you go live fire, but before that I'll teach you how to stand, how to grip, and how to line up sights."

"All right." I swallowed the lump in my throat. Shit was getting real.

Ripper cocked his head, his eyebrows furrowing. "Have you seen or heard a handgun fire?"

"Only on TV."

He considered that for a moment. "Change of plans." He reached into his vest and pulled his gun from his shoulder holster. "I carry a Colt 1911 45 ACP. I'm gonna shoot the target. I want you to see how the gun behaves in my hands. Hear what it sounds like. See what the brass—that's the spent bullet casings—does while I fire."

He narrowed his eyes, studying my face.

"Hold out your hands, palms up," he ordered. When I complied, he placed his Colt across my palms. "Feel what it's like to hold a pistol. Don't worry. The safety's on."

I held my breath. It was the first time I'd touched a gun, and as much as I wanted to learn how to defend myself, holding a weapon felt totally unnatural. The metal was cool against my skin, and it was heavier than I expected as I hefted the weight.

The full force of what I was doing, the responsibility I was taking on, crashed through me. If I were careless, if I did something stupid, I could really hurt somebody.

"Breathe," Ripper said. "You got this."

"Yeah." I lifted my gaze from the gun and met his brown eyes. "Yeah, I do." I couldn't afford to be squeamish or second guess myself. I would mold myself into whatever this new world required.

Maybe he sensed my resolve. Maybe he saw me in a new light. Something ineffable passed between Ripper and me then, and something new flickered into life. I felt the force of his regard. My heartbeat quickened.

Tall, built, and dangerous, he was the bad boy from my fantasies come to life, but it wasn't simply his looks or aura that sent my pulse racing. What was it Ripper had said? *To thine own self be true.* The truth was that I was drawn to an unapologetic alpha male who took care of the people he considered his own. His brothers in the club. Miles. Maybe even me.

I was floating in a sea of contradictory, incongruous impulses. Could I both kick ass and take comfort from the presence of a strong man? Maybe. Assuming, of course, it wasn't all a ruse and I could trust him.

Shit. What was he hiding in that damned safe? I looked away and took a step back, squeezing my eyes shut.

"What? What's going on? You've had a bug up your ass all day."

"Nothing," I lied.

"Nothing. Right." He dragged out the word, his skepticism clear.

"Can we get started?"

My suspicions had extinguished whatever had sparked between us and that knowledge hurt. I extended my hands, offering him the gun. He took his Colt and set it on a small table next to the yellow line.

"Sure. We can get started." He was all business, his voice curt. He opened the case he'd carried from the bike and handed me a pair of goggles and earmuffs. "Put 'em on. Stand to my left so you can see what I'm doing, and so the Colt won't spit brass on you."

Once I took my position, he raised his arms and fired several shots in quick succession. I jumped, even though I knew it was coming. A circle of small holes appeared on the target's chest and in the center of its head. I gaped at the target. No doubt about it, Ripper knew how to handle a gun. He could teach me what I needed to know, and that's all that mattered right now.

I squared my shoulders and narrowed my eyes. Infusing my voice with confidence, I held out my hand for his Colt. "My turn."

NINE

Ripper

My turn.

I barked out a laugh. Couldn't help it. Like a kid playing dress up, Mac had put on a mask of swaggering bravado, trying to pass herself off as a tough chick. It was cute as hell and about as convincing as a kitten spitting fire, but at least she had a backbone and was eager to learn. Could mean the difference between survival and death in the new world.

But seriously, the girl thought I was gonna teach her to shoot with *my* pistol?

"No, Mac. You're not touching my Colt." I tucked it back in my shoulder holster and pulled a Ruger SR22 from the case. "You'll be learning with a 22. Easy to shoot. Quieter. Less recoil. And it won't jam if you limp-wrist it."

She stared at me blankly. "Huh?"

"It won't malfunction if your grip isn't steady. Don't worry about that now. We got a lot to go over today."

Was it 100 percent necessary to position myself behind Mac, her ass tucked up tight against my crotch while I showed her how to stand and how to shift positions to find her shooting platform? Nope. Could I have taught her how to hold the pistol, how to line up the sights, and how to pull the trigger without wrapping my arms around hers while I pressed against her back? Sure, but I'm the kind of asshole who takes advantage of opportunity. Just like I had when I taught her how to mount my bike, when I jumped on the chance to feel her hands on me.

Mount. Christ. The way she blushed every time I dropped a sexually charged word made me think the attraction might run both ways. Except she had something on her mind, something that stood in the way of her acting on that attraction.

Part of my job was to extract information. Got good instincts when it comes to deception. Could always tell when someone was trying to hide something from me, and Mac was trying to hide something. It was obvious from the way she refused to meet my eyes, frowning and stepping back every time I asked her what was wrong.

I'd get to the bottom of it. I always did.

Wouldn't call Mac a natural when it came to shooting. Firing a weapon—shit, holding a weapon—clearly scared her, but she paid attention and followed instructions. Yeah, there were a couple of hitches. First time she fired the 22, she scrunched up her face and closed her eyes. Took the gun away from her and told her to stop screwing around. By the time we finished for the day, she didn't wince when she pulled the trigger, and she could usually hit the target. Not the body part she was aiming for, but the target. Progress.

"You need a lot more practice, but that was a decent start," I told her as we exited the shooting range and headed back to the bike. "Tomorrow, I'll teach you how to assemble and disassemble the gun, and how to clean it."

"Sounds good," she said. "I want to learn everything."

I tucked the case back into the saddlebag and turned to face her, folding my arms across my chest and staring her down. In my experience, if I pinned people in place with a wordless scowl, they started yammering, spilling their guts without my lifting a finger.

After a long moment, Mac licked her lips. Sight of her tongue wetting her lips distracted me for a couple of seconds, but I got a grip and kept my stern pose.

"I really do appreciate the lesson," she faltered.

"Yeah? You appreciate it enough to tell me what's bothering you?"

She opened her mouth, then closed it without speaking. Brow furrowed, she stared at the ground, then her gaze flicked back to my face.

"I want to tell you, but I have to figure out how."

At least she'd stopped denying that there was a problem. I could work with that.

"Got an idea," I said.

I mounted my bike and Mac climbed on behind me. Instead of returning to the compound, I rode to I-205 and followed the freeway toward the city center.

If you took your cues from disaster movies, a person might expect the freeway to be jammed full of stalled cars, but the road was more-or-less clear. Instead of a mass exodus, people who wanted to leave had trickled out of the city over the past week. Anybody who opted to stay was either too sick to drive, or they were hunkered down, obeying the governor's order to stay put. Sure, more cars than usual were pulled over on the side of the road, but I had no trouble navigating the freeway.

The Willamette River divided Portland into the more upscale west side and the working-class east. Downtown hugged the riverbank on the west side, with the appropriately named West Hills forming a backdrop to the downtown. I steered my bike toward the west side, crossing over the river on the Fremont Bridge, whose high, arching span gave us a clear view of the city and waterway. Below us, at least a hundred small boats dotted the river, probably people who hoped to avoid the flu by isolating themselves on the water.

I snorted. Like that was a good long-term plan. How much food and water, not to mention fuel, could you carry on a twenty-foot motor boat?

Didn't plan to take Mac downtown, so I blew past the exits to the commercial center of the city. Passed the exit to Forest Park, five thousand acres of wooded land on the western edge of the city. Instead, I navigated into the West Hills, following a winding road until I pulled into a parking lot and killed the engine.

Mac looked around the parking lot, recognition dawning in her eyes. "The Japanese Garden. I haven't been here since a field trip in grade school."

"I come every couple of months," I said, removing the 22 from the case and tucking it into my vest. When Mac raised her brows in alarm, I laughed. "Don't worry. No target practice in the garden, but I'm not gonna leave a weapon with the bike."

"That makes sense."

I held out a hand to her. "C'mon. I wanna show you my favorite place in the city."

We followed a paved walkway under the stone entry gate, climbed a dozen steps, then traveled a winding path toward the garden entrance.

"How will we get in?" she asked. "I can't imagine anybody is manning the ticket gate."

I cast a sideways glance and smirked. "You worry too much, Mac. This ain't Fort Knox. We'll look for a place where the ground's not too steep and find a break in the wall."

Breaking and entering was nothing new to me, but Mac was a law-abiding citizen. She chewed her lip, and her gaze darted anxiously around the garden, as if she expected a cop to jump out from behind a bush and shout, "You're under arrest."

Christ. Was I ever that uptight? Girl needed to let loose, and if I had anything to say about it, she would.

We followed along a tall wall until it gave way to a rail fence. After clambering over the fence, we squeezed through some bushes and found ourselves on a gravel path. Took no time to get my bearings. I turned right and strode down the path, Mac trailing behind me. We walked past manicured trees, shrubs, moss, and ferns, finally coming to a stop on a stone bridge that spanned a small pond. Smooth and glossy as a mirror, the water reflected the cloudless sky and the trees and bushes that overhung its banks.

"This is it." I turned to Mac. "The Moon Bridge, my favorite place."

Her forehead wrinkled, as if she was surprised that an uncivilized biker could love such a place, then her gaze swept over the scene. "It's beautiful," she breathed, the expression in her gray eyes softening as the garden worked its magic, soothing away her worries.

We stood quietly for a few minutes, admiring the view.

"Nothing that's going on in the outside world can touch this place," I said at last, trying to explain why it meant so much to me. "It's peaceful. Calm. No distractions. No shit to deal with. Let's a man stop and think, you know?"

I searched her face, hoping she understood.

Mac nodded slowly. "Yeah, I get it. It *is* peaceful. It feels like nothing bad can touch you here."

We lapsed into silence again. After a few minutes, I turned to her. "Would you like to check out the koi?" The koi pond was one of the most popular features in the garden. Bet Mac would like it.

"Yes! Seeing the fish was my favorite part of the field trip."

I pointed out which way to go, then followed Mac as she practically skipped down the path toward the koi pond. Glad to see she'd gotten over her nerves and had embraced life as a scofflaw. I'd definitely enjoy leading her astray, corrupting the good girl.

Wooden walkways suspended on stilts seemed to float above the water, allowing visitors to get close to the fish. She rushed forward and dropped to one knee on a wooden plank, leaning out far over the railing.

"Whoa." I came up behind her, grabbed her hoodie, and pulled her back. "Take it easy. I am not jumping in to haul your ass out of the water if you fall."

She rolled her eyes. "Fine. If I fall in, I'm on my own. And it's not like I'd drown in a couple of feet of water."

She bent over the pond again, her eyes scanning the surface. A pair of koi approached, their long fins undulating as they swam lazily toward us. The first fish was a bright, golden yellow. It looked like a giant mutant goldfish. The second koi really caught my eye. Iridescent white scales with distinctive orange markings covered its body.

"I remember you," Mac cried. Her eyes lit up with delight, her expression animated when she turned her head to look at me. "I saw that fish when I was a little girl. I loved it so much that I vowed I'd get a koi pond when I grew up."

"Are you sure it's the same one?"

"Yeah, I'm sure. See that mark above its left eye, the one that looks like an orange question mark? I remember it!"

I squatted next to her, watching the fish.

The koi circled and lifted their heads out of the water, mouths agape, as if anticipating a treat. When they figured out we had nothing for them, they moved on.

The joy and excitement evaporated from Mac's beautiful face. "Do you think they'll be okay? If nobody comes to feed them?"

"I don't know." Could've lied, but it's best to face the truth head on. "I think they can eat algae and bugs, but they're used to being fed. Not sure if they can fend for themselves."

She nodded, and her gray eyes filled with tears. "Dammit." She scrubbed furiously at her eyes. "What's wrong with me? Millions of people are dying around the world, and I'm crying over a couple of pampered fish?"

"Don't be too hard on yourself, Mac." I touched her shoulder. "I've seen this reaction before. Sometimes, when everything goes to shit and you're barely hanging on, the smallest thing can push you right over the edge."

Either she took my words as permission to let go, or she gave up the fight to maintain her self-control. Her jaw trembled, and her shoulders hunched, then she curled against my chest, gripping my shirt in tight fists.

"It's too much." Her tears began to flow. "It feels like the end of the world. Everything we know is slipping away. Everybody is scared. So many people are dying. When will it stop?"

"Don't know when it will stop." I sat on the wooden walkway and pulled her onto my lap. "We gotta hold on till we come out on the other side. For whatever it's worth, you're not facing it alone."

I ran one hand up and down her back and stroked her hair with the other, all the while rocking back and forth. This time, I wasn't taking advantage of the situation to put my hands on her. Not even I was that much of a bastard. Her sorrow breached my defenses, pierced right through the dispassionate reserve I usually showed the world. I held her tight while she mourned.

Mac wasn't a pretty crier. Her face turned a mottled red. She snorted, hiccuped, and her nose ran like a spigot. I felt the dampness spread onto my T-shirt and cut.

"Oh, shit." She sniffed, detaching herself from my arms. "I'm getting snot on your leather vest."

"It's seen worse." I pulled her back against my chest.

She clung to me, dragging in shallow breaths, until her despair burned itself out, her tears finally dried, and her sniffles subsided.

"Better?" I asked when she lifted her head.

She nodded and wiped her face on the back of her arm.

Time to lighten the mood. "Good." I fixed her with a stern look and tugged on my cut. "And Mac, call this a cut, not a leather vest."

"Why?"

I shrugged. "Because that's what it is."

"Okay. I guess there's no arguing with that logic."

I stood and pulled Mac to her feet. "Still want to talk to you. I thought we'd do it here, but maybe a change of scenery would be best. You up to a small detour before we head back home?"

"Sure."

We exited the Japanese garden the same way we entered, and in short order we were back on the road. Within a few minutes, I cut the engine and parked the bike again. I led the way to one of the broad stone stairways that descended into the city's famous rose garden.

"This'll do." I sat on the top step and patted the spot next to me.

Post-mounted lamps protruded from the pillars that flanked the stairs. Sunset fast approached. Soon the bulbs would flicker to life, throwing a circle of light on the spot where we sat.

Mac joined me and together we looked out over a spectacular panorama. The bushes had leafed out, but it was too early in the season for more than a few scattered flowers, so it wasn't the famous roses that caught my eye. Downtown Portland sprawled at the base of the hill.

"I'll never get tired of that sight." Mac pointed toward the heart of the city. "Just look at it. Office buildings, high-rises, and an old church tower jutting up between the park and snow-covered Mt. Hood off in the distance. There's no place else like it. It's beautiful. It's home."

The sun would be setting soon, and the streetlights would turn on as daylight waned. Shadows had begun to creep among the rose bushes, but golden light burnished the city and eastern horizon.

"Are you cold?" I asked.

"A little."

I slipped off my cut and slung it over Mac's shoulders.

She frowned and inhaled deeply, as if steeling her resolve. "You had Miles put a gun safe in his bedroom, and you told him not to tell anybody about it."

"Yeah, I did." Where was she going with this?

"And you're keeping a locked box in his safe. Miles has no idea what's inside that box."

"That's right." My eyes narrowed. "What about it?"

Mac slid her palms up and down her thighs, then clenched her hands together on her lap. “Is Miles holding something for you or the club, something you don’t want to have in your possession in case the police come knocking?”

Well, shit. The girl owned her suspicions and laid them right out in front of me. Too bad they were as insulting as fuck.

“Like drugs or weapons? That what you’re thinking, Mac?”

I jumped to my feet and stared out at the city for a long moment, before dropping into a crouch that put my eyes on a level with hers. Didn’t try to hide that I was pissed.

“Have I done anything, *anything*, that makes you believe I’m taking advantage of Miles? That I’m just pretending to be his friend?”

She shrank back. “No. You’ve been great with him. Listen, I can tell you think that I’m not being fair questioning you, but you’re not being fair either.”

She tugged my cut from her shoulders and laid it across her lap. Her fingers traced the outline of the club patch on the back, a man’s face with a handlebar mustache. He wore a white, turban-style headpiece and balanced a curved sword across his shoulders.

“You’re a Janissary,” she continued. “Janissaries were the Ottoman Empire’s super soldiers. Loyal to the sultan unto death. Kind of like the Unsullied from TV.”

“Except we still have our balls,” I interjected.

She ignored the comment.

“Janissaries were famous for being ruthless, and above all loyal. Your club is named after them. I read the news. You can’t pretend that you guys haven’t earned a reputation for some pretty shady behavior. Is it crazy for me to wonder if this mysterious box of yours—this box you’re hiding in my cousin’s safe—isn’t connected to something you’re doing for the club? Can you blame me for wondering if you put your loyalty to the Janissaries above everything else?”

I gripped her shoulders. Disappointment made my chest ache. She’d seen me with Miles, saw how I watched out for him. How could she believe that my friendship was an act?

“Miles is my friend. I would never betray him. I would never do anything to place him, or you, in jeopardy.”

“Then tell me what’s in the box,” she begged.

"Why didn't you just ask me up front instead of stewing and making such a big fucking deal out of it?" I released her shoulders and dropped down beside her again. "Fine. Remember I told you that I bought my house from a mechanic? He moved because somebody kept burglarizing the place. Four times in the last six months he lived there. When I moved in I figured I wouldn't have a problem. You know, because I'm a Janissary and everybody knows about our *shady reputation.* Last month, while I was on a run, somebody broke in and stole some tools. I decided to save up and install a good security system and a safe, but until I could afford it, thought I'd keep a box of my most valuable stuff in Miles's safe."

"What kind of stuff?" she asked.

"The deed to my house. Titles to my vehicles. Discharge papers from the army. Grandma's wedding ring. And Grandpa's medals from World War II. If you want, I'll show you first thing when we get back. Happy, now?"

Tears welled in her eyes again, like it pained *her* to mistrust *me.* "I'm sorry, but one last question. Why did you tell Miles to keep it a secret?"

I sighed. "Miles spends hours every day on his ham radio talking with his prepper buddies about how to get ready for one disaster or another. Some of them live nearby. Salem, Corvallis, The Dalles. All close enough to show up at his doorstep asking for a tour, and you can bet Miles would love to show off everything he's got. He trusts them. I don't. Can't stop him from buying weapons, but I told him the government might be listening in, and got him to promise not to tell anybody what he keeps in the safe. You know Miles. He follows rules. He promised to keep the safe a secret, so he must have decided that the box I keep in it is a secret, too. Fuck." I dragged a hand through my hair. "Is that it? Anything else got you tied up in knots?"

"That's it." She reached out to touch my arm, but pulled her hand back, as if not sure I'd welcome her touch. "I am sorry."

I inhaled a long, slow breath, trying to calm down. "Yeah. Guess I should be used to people looking at me funny because of the bike and the cut. Making assumptions. Just thought we were past that. Thought you could tell that my friendship with Miles is real, not an act."

I thought she saw *me.* Her suspicions felt like a slap in the face. I shook my head, gazing down at the city, resignation a heavy stone in my chest.

"Ripper."

I ignored her.

"Ripper, please."

She'd twisted around to face me, and something in her voice snagged my attention, pulled me outta my ruminations. I reluctantly turned to her.

She nodded and met my eyes, her expression both resolute and contrite. "I see how good you are with Miles. I *do* see it. I'm sorry I didn't look past the bike and the cut. I mean, you're right. I should have asked you about the safe first thing, let you explain, instead of obsessing over it and assuming the worst. I feel like a shit for doubting you." Her cheeks puffed when she blew out a breath. "I tend to brood over things and that's my bad. I'll try to do better."

I'd be a shit if I ignored her sincere apology.

She reached out again, laid her hand on my knee, and this time I met her halfway. I squeezed her hand, then released it to drape my arm across her shoulders and pull her to my side. She was sorry, and there was no point in holding a grudge.

The top of Mt. Hood glowed orange, then faded as the sun slipped behind the West Hills.

Despite the flu, from this distance Portland almost looked like its old self. Street lamps illuminated the roadways. Red and green traffic signals winked on and off at intersections and a few car headlights moved along the streets. Lights shone from windows in the office buildings and condominiums. Some lights were programmed to come on automatically at sunset. Others were signs of life, reminders that behind the bright windows, the city was still full of people trying to survive the flu.

I was glad that I had someone to share this moment with, this moment when—if you didn't think too hard—life could still pass for normal.

Between one blink and the next, downtown Portland went dark.

Mac gasped and her fingers dug into my thigh.

Within seconds, as the power grid collapsed, the blanket of black spread to the east side of town. The lights in the park extinguished, leaving us sitting in absolute darkness. Mac started to tremble. I tightened my grip on her shoulders.

"Shit, shit, shit," she whispered.

Sitting on a hill, with the city stretched out in front of us, we had a bird's-eye view of our world going black. Who knew if enough people would survive the pandemic to ever rebuild the grid. Might be the end of an era. Was that why Mac was shaking? Because humanity sat at a turning point? Or was it something else?

Whatever happened, whatever came next, I'd make sure that Mac was all right.

"Hey, don't be scared." I pressed a kiss to her temple. "I got you."

TEN

Kenzie

When Ripper came through the kitchen door the next morning, he found me on my hands and knees, shoulder deep in the now-empty refrigerator, scouring the interior with a mild bleach solution. Without electricity, everything in the fridge had to be tossed before it began to rot. I'd carried the limp vegetables to the compost bin, but the meats and yogurt had to be dumped into a plastic trash bag. Without garbage service, I had no idea what to do with the sack full of stinky stuff. I'd have to ask Miles.

Ripper was silent for a long moment. Aware that my ass was waving back and forth in the air as I scrubbed, I pulled my head out of the refrigerator and glanced suspiciously over my shoulder. If I found him leering—if he made some crack about enjoying the sight of a woman on her knees or my tail wagging—I'd be seriously disappointed in the man.

Instead, he angled his head toward the heavy bag full of garbage. "You want me to haul that out for you?"

I sat back on my heels, ashamed that I'd doubted him. "That'd be great. Thank you."

While Ripper took out the trash, I poured out the bucket of bleach water and washed my hands. He washed his own hands when he returned, then he straddled a kitchen chair.

"How you managing with the power out?" he asked.

"It sounds wrong, but Miles is in hog heaven. He's down in the basement counting batteries and lanterns and generally gloating over our supplies."

"Not surprised," Ripper said. "The power grid going down validates everything he's been saying for years."

I held up the coffee carafe. "You want some?"

"Yeah, thanks."

I poured Ripper a cup of coffee, then took a seat across the table from him.

"How about you?" he asked. "How are you doing without electricity?"

I shrugged. "We're in better shape than most people, thanks to Miles. His battery bank will give us enough power to run the security system and a hot plate. We have a lot of lanterns and flashlights. We should be okay."

He leaned forward, his dark brows slanting down. "Not what I asked, Mac. How about *you*?"

No way I'd confess that I spent the night with a LED lantern turned up to maximum brightness next to my bed, not when I was trying to pass myself off as a tough, capable survivor. Yesterday, he saw he break down in tears over a couple of giant goldfish, for chrissake. I scarcely knew him, but I didn't want Ripper to see me as weak, as unworthy.

"It's hard to wrap my head around the notion of no internet, no TV, no appliances, no *blow dryer*." I gasped in mock horror at the last one, trying to make light of the question.

He studied me over the rim of his cup, brows raised, clearly not happy with my jocular retort.

I squirmed like a small child caught in a transparent lie.

"I mean...of course I'm going to miss having electricity. Who wouldn't? But like I said, thanks to Miles, we're going to manage fine without power."

Ripper sipped his coffee, watching me flounder.

If she were here, Ali would hoot with laughter. In my mind's eye, I saw her pantomime digging a hole with a shovel and tossing the imaginary dirt over her shoulder.

"I'm fine," I added unnecessarily.

"If you say so." He carried his cup to the sink and rinsed it out, his movements brisk and efficient. My glib response to his concern had disappointed him, I saw with sudden clarity. I'd protected my secret—a small, embarrassing secret—but at what cost? Only yesterday he asked me to speak up if there was a problem, but this didn't count, did it? It had absolutely nothing to do with him.

If you see the real me, will you still like me?

Ripper turned around and leaned against the counter. Morning sunlight streamed through the window and brought out gilt highlights in his brown hair. He crossed his arms over his chest. "Came over to ask you to go out with me this afternoon."

"I'd like that," I said quickly, before disappointment could make him change his mind about the invitation. "Where are we going? Back to the shooting range?"

Ripper shook his head. "Can't use the shooting range in the dark. I'll set up sandbags against the back fence later so we can practice here. Today, I'm gonna check on an old friend of mine who lives in Chinatown. Harry has lung disease and needs oxygen. Wanna make sure he has enough oxygen tanks to get by and see if he needs anything."

Chinatown. The prospect of riding exposed on the back of a bike through narrow city streets made me leery, but I had to trust that Ripper could handle any trouble that might come our way.

"Is Harry a Janissary?"

"Nah. He and his wife lived next door when I was growing up. Harry's the man who got me into rebuilding and customizing Harleys. Started helping him out when I was a teenager. Learned a lot from the old guy."

"I'd like to meet the man who taught you about building bikes," I said.

"All right. Be ready around two."

Ripper left, and I finished cleaning up the kitchen. Luckily, Miles was so preoccupied double-checking his supplies that he scarcely paid attention when I told him I was going out with Ripper after lunch. He wolfed down a peanut butter sandwich and retreated back to the basement while I put on clean clothes and tied my hair back in a low ponytail.

When Ripper and Hector showed up a few minutes past two, I stuck my head in the basement door. "Bye, Miles. We'll be back in a couple of hours."

"Goodbye," he called up the stairs.

"Hector, stay," Ripper ordered.

I followed Ripper to his garage, slipped the white helmet over my head, then climbed on the bike behind him. He took the freeway toward downtown Portland, crossing the Willamette River on the old Steel Bridge. Within a few blocks, we were in the heart of Chinatown.

My arms tightened around Ripper's waist, and I pressed against his back. Despite the governor's injunction, a few cars passed us on the street, and we rode past small groups of pedestrians on the sidewalks. We weren't the only people ignoring the order to stay home.

There was little in the neighborhood that would lure people into breaking the law, a formal Chinese garden, a nightclub that boasted the world's oldest drag queen, restaurants, bars, a massage parlor, and a few Asian markets. Why were dozens of people milling around?

Ripper pulled into a parking lot bordered by a brick wall. At the back of the lot, he parked his bike between a dumpster and the brick wall, out of sight of the road. He took an LED lantern and a bottle of Jack Daniels out of a saddlebag.

At my raised eyebrows, he smiled. "Harry's favorite."

Ripper paused when we stepped onto the sidewalk, and his head swiveled back and forth while he surveyed the street.

"You mind holding the lantern and the Jack?" His gaze fixed on a pair of men watching us from across the street.

I took the lantern and tucked the booze under my left arm. Ripper moved between me and the strangers, then slung his left arm over my shoulders, drawing me to his side as we began to walk.

I glanced up at him, surprised by the intimate gesture. Maybe he wanted to make it clear that I was with him, to extend the shield of his protection over me when we were breaking the law by simply walking down the street.

Strong fingers squeezed my shoulders. "It's not far to Harry's place."

Ripper carried himself as if he owned the street. People took one look at his cut and steered clear, scuttling sideways to stay out of our path.

"Why does Harry live in Chinatown?" I asked.

"After his wife passed from cancer about ten years ago, he had to sell their house to pay her medical bills. A nonprofit agency fixes up old run-down hotels and turns them into low-income housing. Harry qualified for a unit. He's been living in Chinatown ever since." Ripper pointed at a pair of wooden doors under a striped awning. "Here we are."

We walked into a sun-drenched lobby. Tall potted plants soaked up light beneath the plate glass windows. A pair of armchairs flanked an antique fireplace, and a painting of Mt. Hood hung over the mantel. Somebody had made an effort to make the place nice, and even though I'd yet to meet him, I was glad for Harry's sake that he wasn't living in a dismal dump.

Without electricity, we would have to bypass the elevator and take the stairs to the third floor. When the door from the lobby swung shut behind us, we entered a shadowy stairwell. The steps curved up and around, disappearing into the gloom. A small skylight in the roof provided only faint illumination.

I lurched toward the bottom step. Clutching the handrail, I paused and drew in a calming breath.

"Would you mind using the flashlight?" I called to Ripper, who was jogging up the stairs ahead of me.

He glanced back over his shoulder and frowned. "Why you still at the bottom?"

"My balance sucks in the dark, and I don't want to trip." That was 100 percent true. Maintaining your equilibrium was hard when your knees were shaking.

"No problem." He clicked on the penlight and waited for me to catch up to him.

The beam of light chased away the worst of the shadows, and my racing heart slowed to normal. We emerged from the third floor landing onto a long hallway. Windows at either end provided enough light to banish the darkness. Ripper tucked the penlight back into his pocket, strode to the end of the hall, and knocked on a door.

"Harry, it's Alejandro, from the old neighborhood."

Alejandro? My lips silently shaped the name.

He cast a sideways glance at me. "Why you grinning?"

"Your name. It's beautiful."

His brows drew together, but before he could respond, the door cracked open and an elderly man peered out at us. A wide smile split the man's face, and he threw the door open.

"Alejandro, get your ass inside, boy. What are you doing out and about during a quarantine?"

"What does it look like I'm doing? Checking on you, old man. Making sure you haven't been stirring up trouble."

A tall man with a thick mane of silver hair and a potbelly hanging over his plaid pajama bottoms, Harry shuffled over and the two hugged. Harry spied me standing behind Ripper. His eyes twinkled. "And who is this young lady?"

Ripper turned to me. "Harry, meet Mac."

"Hi, Harry." I smiled and offered my hand for a shake. Ignoring it, he swept me into a bear hug. Not shy, was he? I laughed, returning the embrace.

Harry pulled back and looked me over from head to foot. "You're too pretty to be a Mac. What were your parents thinking?"

I pointed a finger at Ripper. "Blame Alejandro there." Ripper rolled his eyes at my use of his real name. "Nobody else calls me Mac. My real name is Mackenzie."

Harry pursed his lips, mulling over my comment. "No. Sorry. That's not much better. A pretty girl should have a pretty name."

"Like Belinda?" Ripper suggested.

Harry sighed. "My Belinda was a peach. And she sure loved that little scamp." He nodded toward Ripper.

"A little scamp, huh? Do tell."

"Have I got a story for you." Harry took my arm and led me into his tiny studio apartment.

An oxygen tank sat on the floor next to a well-worn recliner that was positioned so Harry could watch the street below from his window. Rubber tubing tethered the old man to the tank and fed oxygen to him from the tubes that looped over his ears and plugged into his nose.

Harry bypassed the recliner and dropped with a grunt onto a tattered love seat. He patted the cushion next to him and winked. "You come sit by me, honey. Let Alejandro take the chair."

I set the Jack Daniels and the lantern on the coffee table, and Harry flashed Ripper a thumb's up, smiling at the gift. When I sat down next to him, he took my hand. I've met some incorrigible flirts in my life, but I suspected that compared to Harry, they were all rank amateurs.

"The first time I met Alejandro—"

Ripper groaned.

"Shush now. Let me talk," Harry chided. "The first time I met Alejandro was about a week after Belinda and I moved in next door to his family. We came home from grocery shopping and found Alejandro standing on the roof of our garage with a garden hose, putting out a fire."

"So he was a hero? He leapt into action and kept your house from burning down?" I guessed.

Harry snorted. "Not hardly. It was a couple of days before the Fourth of July. He was messing around with fireworks and shot a bottle rocket onto the garage roof. He started the fire."

I glanced at Ripper, who shrugged.

"Wanted to see what would happen if I strapped three bottle rockets together. Got away from me."

"No shit." Harry laughed. "But give the boy credit. He could've run away. Pretended it wasn't him. Let the fire burn. Instead, he climbed up the rose trellis, dragging a hose behind him, and he put out the flames."

"Did you call the police?" My mom would have filed a complaint before the smoke cleared.

"No." Harry dismissed the possibility with a wave of his hand. "Neighbors don't call the cops over things like that."

That couldn't be the end of the story. "What happened next?"

"You heard of indentured servitude?" Ripper asked.

Harry cackled. "Belinda and I sat down with Alejandro's parents and worked out a restitution plan. He had to help me put new shingles on the garage roof."

"*And* clean the gutters. *And* mow the lawn every week until school started," Ripper added. "*And* help him unpack boxes of tools and bike parts, then help him set up his garage."

"You got any complaints?" Harry demanded.

"No, sir. Turned out to be one of the best things that ever happened to me. Might never have learned about Harleys if I hadn't spent the summer working for you."

"There you go. It all worked out the way it was supposed to. It usually does." Harry squeezed my hand. "Honey, will you go to the kitchenette and get us each a can of pop?"

Ordinarily, I wouldn't turn down someone's offer of hospitality, but these weren't ordinary times. Whatever food and drink Harry had in his tiny apartment might have to last him for a long time. I looked quickly over at Ripper. He shook his head, echoing my concern.

"Ripper and I just had coffee, so we're not thirsty, but I'd be happy to bring you one."

I surreptitiously checked out the contents of Harry's refrigerator when I grabbed his drink. Cans of beer and soda filled the shelves, along with ketchup and a jar of mustard. Nothing that would rot, thank goodness, but what was the man eating? I opened a cupboard door. Neat rows of chili, beef stew, fruit cocktail, and green beans filled the interior. At least he was in no immediate danger of starving.

"Are you snooping?" Harry called.

I almost lied and told him that I was looking for a glass, but thought better of it. If Harry had anything to do with molding Ripper into the man he was today—and clearly he had—he'd share Ripper's disdain for deception.

"You caught me. I'm checking to see how much food you have on hand." I walked over to the love seat and passed him the soda. "Looks like you have enough canned food to last awhile."

"Go look in that closet, Miss Nosey." He pointed to a door. When I did, I found four cases of chocolate and strawberry nutrition shakes piled on the floor. "Every time she visits, my niece brings me a case of those protein shakes for old farts. I like to chew my food, so I stick the shakes in the closet. Worse comes to worst, I could live off them for weeks."

"You're a tough old bird," Ripper said. "How are you for oxygen?"

"The agency brought me six tanks last week. And remember, the oxygen helps me breathe easier, but I won't keel over without it. I just got a ninety-day refill on all my prescriptions, too. Don't you waste a minute worrying about me, son. I'm all set."

I excused myself to use the bathroom, allowing Ripper and Harry time for a private chat. Washing my hands in the sink, I glanced over at the bathtub. Harry had no bottled water and sooner or later the taps would run dry. I jammed the rubber stopper into the drain, turned on the faucet, then sat on the toilet seat, watching the tub fill. When it was within an inch of the top, I turned off the water and rejoined the men.

"I heard the water running. You take a bath?" Harry asked.

I sat next to him again. "I filled your tub. It holds about eighty gallons of water." Miles had told me that. "That's enough to last one person for more than a month. Think of it as an emergency supply, in case we lose city water."

"I'm an old man." Harry shook his head. "I remember my mama crying after Pearl Harbor. I remember being scared shitless during the Cuban missile crisis. I remember thinking that the AIDS epidemic might end the world. What I don't remember is a time when the power stayed off for more than a couple of days, and then the city water supply dried up. I still can't believe it will come to that."

"This flu is something new," Ripper said. "Nothing's ever hit this hard or this fast. We gotta be ready for the unexpected." He leaned forward, his elbows on his knees. "Listen, say the word, and I'll get my jeep and bring you back to my place."

"I'm staying put," Harry said firmly. "Home is the only place I want to be. I got friends here, and we watch out for each other. I feel fine now, but if I get the flu, it just means it's time for me to go be with my Belinda. I've had a great life. No regrets. Anything happens to me, you remember that."

Harry smiled, clear-eyed and unafraid.

My throat ached and tears swam in my eyes. It had taken no more than half an hour to fall under the old man's spell. I couldn't bear to think of him hungry or thirsty or dying alone in his apartment. I loved the glimpse he gave me into Ripper's childhood. A scamp, he said, a troublemaker who accepted responsibility and tried to make things right when he screwed up. I could see the man in his description of the child.

"Come give an old friend a hug," he said to Ripper. "Then take this pretty girl and get back home where it's safe." The two men stood and clapped their arms around each other. Harry looked at me and tapped a finger against his cheek. "Make an old man happy. Give me a kiss."

He lowered his face, and I pressed a kiss against his withered cheek. "It was an honor to meet you, Harry. I hope we see each other again."

Harry bent over and spoke in a low voice in my ear. "Alejandro is a good man. You treat him right, and he'll treat you right."

I pulled back to meet his eyes. Harry was reading more into our relationship than existed, more than could exist after only three days. Still, the truth in his words was undeniable. Ripper was a good man, and I wanted to treat him right.

"Yes, sir. I will."

"Good enough."

Ripper and I were silent as we descended the stairs. When we reached the lobby, he halted and stared into the distance, his brows drawn together into a straight line. I barely knew Harry, and it was hard for me to walk away from him. What must Ripper be going through?

Despite his tough, laconic facade, the man felt things deeply. Facile expressions of sympathy wouldn't fly. Instead of words, I offered the consolation of touch, tentatively laying my hand on his shoulder. If he shrugged me off I'd know I'd overstepped, but he turned and allowed me to slip my arms around his waist. He wrapped his arms around me, and for a long moment we held each other.

"Suppose we should get going." He untangled himself from my arms.

I nodded.

We exited the building and stepped onto the sidewalk. I froze in place and glanced at Ripper. He sensed it, too, didn't he? The atmosphere on the street had changed, the air charged with tension. Goosebumps broke out across my skin and the hair on my arms stood up. I'd felt something like this before.

A few months ago, Ali and I had taken an Uber downtown for a day of shopping. The car turned a corner, and we found ourselves in the middle of a full-blown riot. What started as a peaceful protest had devolved into a clash between antifascists and a right-wing group. Ali and I clutched each other in the back of the car while a baying mob swarmed around us, and a line of riot police advanced up the street. The sights and sounds of that day would stay with me forever. The clamor of angry voices. The shattering glass from smashed windows. The sight of cops dodging water bottles and eggs. The blinding light and deafening blast from the flash-bangs the police deployed. The riot police eventually pushed the mob past our car and allowed us to proceed, but we had been too shaken to do anything but go back to the dorm.

Ripper was instantly on high alert. Clusters of pedestrians milled in the middle of the street. The route back to his bike was blocked by an agitated throng of people. Someone threw a brick at a plate glass window, and a spiderweb of cracks fragmented the surface. Two men pounded on the window. The glass fractured under their fists and crumbled onto the sidewalk.

A cheer erupted. Several people kicked out the remaining glass, then squeezed through the window, emerging moments later flourishing bottles of booze. The crowd surged forward, attacking every window on the block.

"Stay close." Ripper slung an arm over my shoulder and hauled me to his side. "We'll head south, where the crowd's smaller, then circle back around toward the bike."

I nodded and clung to his side while Ripper shoved his way through the crowd.

Across the street, three men pried the plywood off the storefront of a neighborhood grocery. Above the market, a second-floor window flew open, and a man climbed onto the fire escape. Brandishing a handgun, he shouted at the men below him, then fired a warning shot into the air. The men wheeled and ran. People screamed and the panicked mob scattered, rushing in every direction. Someone on the street took a shot at the man on the fire escape, who returned the fire.

Not ten feet from us, a woman dropped to the pavement, a fountain of blood spurting from her neck.

I stumbled, bile rising in my throat. She was in the wrong place at the wrong time, and now the woman was dead. It could have been Ripper or me lying in the street, the victim of a stray bullet. What was happening to my hometown?

Ripper broke into a run, dragging me along. Only his strong arm kept me on my feet as we dashed away from the melee.

At the end of the block, we veered east onto a side street, then came to a dead stop. Parked in the middle of the roadway, a van disgorged five black-clad riot police. The flu must have hit the department hard if the cops could muster only five men to quell a civic disturbance. I'd seen dozens of officers on the street when Ali and I blundered into a riot. What could five men do against a mob?

More shots rang out behind us.

"Fucking hell," Ripper muttered.

The riot police charged forward. One of them pointed a baton at Ripper.

"Right. Gotta be the Janissary." He tugged on my hand and dragged me into the group of pedestrians that filled the intersection. "Run."

We pushed our way through the crowd, then sprinted south, weaving around everyone who blocked our path. My feet slipped on a shattered windowpane, and I fell onto my knees, catching my weight with my hands. Slivers of glass pierced my palms.

"Ow! Crap!"

Ripper seized my elbows and pulled me to my feet. "Lemme see." I held up my palms for his inspection. Frowning, he plucked a few of the larger shards from my skin. "I wanna get you off the street. Got an idea. C'mon."

Jogging carefully over the broken glass, we continued down the block.

"This is it." Ripper stopped under a green awning that covered the entrance to a well-known gay bar. A man climbed out the busted front window, bottles of tequila and rum tucked under his arm.

"Better hurry, man," he said to Ripper. "Not much of the good stuff left."

"Thanks." Ripper helped me through the opening. He pulled the penlight from his pocket and directed a narrow beam of light over the gloomy interior. He strode behind the bar and plucked one of the last remaining bottles of vodka from a shelf.

"Seriously? You're looting?"

Ripper ignored me and crouched down, searching for something beneath the bar.

"Got it." He stood and held up a first aid kit. "This way." He lead me to the back of the bar, wending his way around tables, through brick archways, and down a corridor. Voices drifted toward us as other people searched the bar for booze.

Ripper hunkered down, and his fingers found an iron ring affixed to a wooden floorboard. He pulled on the ring and lifted a wooden door, revealing a narrow flight of stairs leading down into the dark.

"Couple months ago I took a tour of the Shanghai Tunnels," he said. "They run underground from Chinatown to the Willamette River. Story goes, in the old days men would get drunk at bars and end up being dragged through the tunnels and sold to sea captains as slave laborers. Supposedly, there were opium dens, gambling parlors, and brothels down there, too." He pointed down the stairs. "This is where our tour started."

I stared down into the blackness, chills racing up and down my spine. "You want us to go down there?"

"Yeah. Perfect place to wait for things to quiet down."

"Stand down." A loud crash sounded from the front of the bar. Crap. Cops were in the bar, busting looters.

"Mac, move your ass."

"Yeah."

I'm an adult, dammit, not a baby. Time to suck it up and act like it.

I curved my lips into what I hoped would pass for a confident smile. With trembling legs, I climbed down into the darkness.

ELEVEN

Ripper

How the fuck had I missed the clues?

I'd clicked on the penlight so Mac wouldn't faceplant going down the wooden stairs. Soon as she reached the bottom, I climbed down after her and swung the hatch shut. Mac wobbled—she'd warned me that the dark messed with her balance—so I grabbed her elbow and led her to a sheltered spot against the brick wall. Once we hunkered down behind an old trunk, I flicked the penlight off.

We sat shoulder to shoulder against the wall of the pitch-black room. Initially, I didn't think much of Mac's prolonged silence. Made sense to keep quiet with the cops inside the bar, barking orders and making arrests. Besides, she saw a woman shot down in the street. Dumb luck it was somebody else and not Mac who got hit. She wouldn't know how to deal with that kind of arbitrary bloodshed. Looting, civil unrest, gunfire, it'd freak out anybody unaccustomed to violence.

She sat stock-still, her arms locked around her bent knees. Hadn't shifted positions or twitched since we dropped onto the floor. She was panting, her breath coming in rapid, shallow gasps.

I recognized that sound. Trapped prey. Somebody terrified that the scary man—that I—was about to discover their hiding place and lay a world of hurt on them. Why was Mac freaking out? She had to know that even if the cops found us, I wouldn't let anybody hurt her.

I bent my head and whispered in her ear. "What's wrong?"

She shook her head.

"Talk to me."

"I...can...deal."

That didn't help. Deal with what?

I laid a hand on her hunched shoulders and touched tense, rigid muscles. Tremors racked her body. I turned to face her and smoothed her hair back from her forehead. Her skin was cold, but beads of sweat dotted her brow. I slid my hands down her face and cupped her jaw. Beneath my fingertips, her carotid artery raced.

Jesus Christ. Mac was on the brink of a full-blown panic attack, and I had no clue what caused it or how to fix it.

A crash and scuffle sounded from above ground, and Mac's entire body jerked. Fuck. If she lost it—if she started screaming or thrashing—the sound would attract the cops' attention.

Police have had a hard-on for the Janissaries for years. They find me in the tunnel, trying to restrain a hysterical woman, they'd arrest my ass for sure. Or shoot me. I wouldn't allow that to happen, wouldn't permit anyone to take me away from Mac and Miles.

I hauled her trembling body to my chest, rubbing slow circles on her back. "I'm here, Mac," I said under my breath. "You're not alone. I won't let anybody or anything hurt you. It's gonna be all right."

The tremors gradually lessened, her breathing slowed, and Mac collapsed against me, as limp as a ragdoll.

"Stupid phobia," she muttered.

Phobia? The pieces fell into place. Yesterday, when the power grid failed, she had gasped and clutched my leg. Said, "Oh, shit," or something like that. In the dark stairwell at Harry's apartment building, she stopped at the bottom step, clutching the handrail and swaying. She called out in a strained voice, asking me to turn on my flashlight. And now, barely a peep out of her since we climbed down into this black hole. Frozen in place. Panting like a cornered animal.

Mac was afraid of the dark and was trying her best to hide it. Why'd it take me so long to figure it out?

Now that I knew the problem, I could do something to help. I pulled the penlight from my pocket and clicked it on, holding my hand over the bezel so the light wouldn't travel. My fingers glowed peachy-pink where the beam passed through my skin.

"Hold out your hand," I whispered.

Mac glanced up at my face then extended her palm. I put the flashlight into her hand, careful to avoid the glass shards, then took her other hand and covered the bezel with her fingers.

"You're in charge of the light. Soon as the cops are gone, you can uncover the beam."

Mac looked down at her hands and curved her fingers over the bezel. Pinkish light suffused her skin and escaped from the cracks between her fingers. Like I hoped, having control over the penlight seemed to calm her down. She slowly inhaled, then pushed out a deep breath.

"Thanks."

"It's all right. Won't be long now."

I ran a hand through her soft hair, inhaling the scent of her shampoo. What was that? Something tropical, coconut maybe? Yeah, coconut. I liked it. I liked *this* more, holding Mac in my arms, soothing her, making her feel safe.

For so long, I've been the boogeyman, the big bad. Never questioned the role. I'm hard-wired to protect my people, whatever it takes. But *this* was new. Not *touching* a woman, for chrissakes. I've fucked plenty of women and intended to fuck Mac. Nah, what was new was seeing myself as more than simply a protector, more than a strong body standing between my people and harm. Seeing myself as the man a woman turns to for comfort, for consolation. That's a role I never imagined for myself. Until now.

Eventually, the voices and footsteps receded into the distance. Waited another couple of minutes to be sure before declaring it was clear.

Mac uncovered the beam and blinked against the sudden brightness. She shone the light around the room, sweeping over every corner. "So much better with the light on."

"Hey." I touched her cheek. "You gotta tell me if there's a problem. If I'd known you were afraid of the dark, I would've come up with a different plan."

To my surprise, she bristled and scooted over to her original place against the wall.

"Right. We're being chased by the cops. People are being shot down on the street. And I'm supposed to say, 'Hold on. Whatever you do, don't trigger my fear of the dark.'" She rolled her eyes. "Give me a break. You can't think that I'm that much of a wuss."

So, apparently I got lots to learn about offering comfort and consolation. First time up to bat, and I pissed the girl off.

"You can't wish a phobia away, Mac," I said slowly. "Try to white-knuckle your way through it, and you're asking for trouble."

"Aren't you the guy who said we all have to be strong to deal with what's coming? I'd expect you to tell me to grow a pair and get over it. Or are you cutting me slack because I'm a girl?"

Jesus. Why so prickly and defensive?

"Sounds to me like you're embarrassed, and you're trying to deflect attention from it by calling me sexist."

Mac opened her mouth to protest. Her fingertips traced over a thin white line that ran from her left eyebrow to her temple, something I'd seen her do when anxious or deep in thought. Conflicting emotions danced across her face. Denial, anger, resignation, and finally defeat. Her mouth snapped shut.

She stared into a dark corner of the room, frowning. "You're right. I'm embarrassed. It's just that I don't want to be the weak link. I want to be strong, and it's hard to believe you're strong when you have to sleep with a freaking night light on."

"Know a guy," I said. "Six one. Built like a tank. Be glad to have him at my back in any fight. He's not scared of anything, except spiders. Screams and does his spider dance every time he sees one."

"What's your point?"

"My point? Even strong people can have phobias. A therapist might tell you there are ways to get over the fear, and I bet denial isn't one of them."

"Yeah." She sighed. "No point in trying to hide what's painfully obvious."

"No. Not what I said." I had a hunch. "Who taught you that it's not safe to admit that you're scared?"

She shrugged. "Life did. Admitting that you're afraid is like giving ammunition to the enemy."

Where did *that* come from? "What the fuck, Mac?" I grabbed her hands and squeezed, determined to get to the bottom of it.

"Ow!" She yelped in pain and jerked her hands away.

"Fuck, I'm sorry. I forgot you were hurt. Lemme see." I took the flashlight and directed the beam at her hands. Her palms were red and abraded, with a few splinters of glass protruding from her skin. "Gonna clean this up," I said, reaching for the vodka.

Mac clenched her jaw but didn't cry out when I poured alcohol over her hands to sanitize the wounds. I found a pair of tweezers in the first aid kit and carefully pulled out all the slivers of glass, daubed on an antiseptic cream, then wrapped both hands with gauze bandages.

"Thanks" she said. "I definitely don't want to get an infection, not without any doctors around."

"You're welcome." I picked up the bottle of vodka. "You want some?"

"No. I don't drink."

"Never? Not even beer?"

She shook her head.

Wouldn't have pegged Mac as a teetotaler, but then Miles didn't touch alcohol either. "Is it a family thing?"

Her lips curved in a small smile. "You might say that."

I shrugged and took a swig before putting the bottle back down.

Something was going on in the girl's head that I didn't understand.

Why would a smart young woman believe that fear was a weakness she had to hide? She accused me of thinking she was a wuss. I suspected the problem was that *she* thought she was a wuss.

Interesting.

I'm a patient man. Eventually, I always get the information I'm after. Already figured out that if I persisted, Mac would spill more details. Could be my interrogation skills. Could be she naturally defaulted to honesty when pushed.

Either way, someday I'd unravel the mystery and understand what made her tick. At first glance, she might have looked like a happy-go-lucky college girl. Good-natured. Shallow. Vapid. But despite appearances, Mac wasn't easy or superficial. There were layers to peel back, and I liked a challenge.

She tilted her head and gazed upward. "What happened up there? I can't believe people would run wild simply because there aren't enough police to keep order."

"Don't know for sure. It's been—what—three days since the governor shut down the state and ordered everybody to stay put.

People are scared. They're dropping left and right from the flu. Lot of folks don't keep much food in the house, so they're getting hungry. Or maybe they're bored. Or restless. Maybe a bottle of tequila sounds like just the thing. The why doesn't matter, only what comes next."

"What comes next," she repeated. "I never thought I'd be so happy that Miles hoarded food and built a compound surrounded by razor wire. It's a safety net most people don't have. Of course, any one of us could still get the flu."

"That's right."

"But I'm not going to waste time worrying about something that's out of my hands," she said.

"No point in that. But what you *can* do is not be afraid to rely on other people. When everything goes to shit, there's strength in numbers. You gotta choose people to make a stand with."

Mac's forehead furrowed, creating a cute-as-hell little V between her eyebrows. "But you already chose. You're a Janissary. You've got your people."

"Always be a Janissary. Always have my brothers' backs."

Mac frowned. "You said that most of the men have holed up at the clubhouse. How come you're not locked in with your brothers?"

"I check in at the clubhouse. If they need me, I'm there." I unfolded my legs and stretched my back. Sitting on the cold cement floor made my muscles ache. "Some of the men chose to stay on the outside with their families. I don't know how it happened, but Miles is like a kid brother to me. Couldn't leave you two to fend for yourselves."

Mac's gray eyes widened. "You mean that you chose us, Miles and me, to be your people, too?"

"Yeah, I did." I watched her, gauging her reaction as she processed that information.

"Wait. If Miles is like your kid brother, does that mean you see me as a kid sister?"

She looked stricken. It was fucking adorable.

My lips twitched. "No, Mac. I do *not* see you as my kid sister."

If she'd seen the hard-on I was rocking when I came into the kitchen this morning and found her on her hands and knees, with her tight ass in the air, she'd know that I didn't think of her as a kid sister. Shit, I'd had to stare at the wall and go over hockey stats in my head until my condition became less incriminating.

She blushed, even the tips of her ears turned red. I almost closed the distance between us, almost hauled her into my arms. Some inner voice—maybe the hind brain that saved my ass more than once—told me to wait. Soon, but not yet. She wasn't ready.

"Sounds quiet up there," I said. "Let's go get the bike."

"Okay." Mac stood and brushed grit from the cement floor off the seat of her pants. She lifted her arms over her head, then bent over and laid her hands flat on the floor, groaning as she stretched her back. My cock perked up at the sight. "I'm stiff," she said.

I bit back a grin. "Me too."

I pointed the flashlight beam at the stairs. The hatch creaked when I shouldered it open a couple of inches, then peered through the gap into the shadowy bar. Place appeared empty, but I wasn't taking any chances. I opened the hatch and offered Mac a hand as she climbed out.

"Stay here," I ordered, passing her the flashlight. "Be back in one minute."

Treading quietly, I checked the bar for any signs of trouble. Somebody had smashed a bottle of good Scotch—now that hurt—and a few chairs and tables were overturned, but the place had been abandoned by both cops and looters.

I fetched Mac, and we climbed out the front window. Streets were as empty as the bar, except for the dead woman's body, which still lay in the middle of the road. City services had completely gone to shit. Mac didn't need to see that. I put myself between her and the body. Mac turned her face and looked the other way when we passed.

When we came to Harry's apartment building, she stopped and tugged on my shirt. "We should check on Harry."

"Yeah." I strode to the middle of the street and scanned the windows of Harry's third-floor apartment.

Like I suspected, he'd been sitting in his recliner, watching the street. He stood up when he saw me.

"Come here," I called to Mac. She joined me and together we gazed up at the old man. Harry gave us a thumbs-up, telling us he was all right. He pointed at us, then sideways up the street, toward the lot where I always parked my bike. His meaning was clear. Don't come up. Get out of here.

I nodded reluctantly. Wished to hell he'd come back home with me, but a man's got a right to choose how he lives. And how he dies.

Mac puckered up her lips and blew him an exaggerated kiss. Harry pretended to catch it, then laid his hand over his heart, before blowing a kiss back at her. Her lower lip trembled when she turned her eyes to me. "It's like walking away from your grandpa, isn't it?"

"Yeah." I swallowed my own grief and slung an arm around her shoulders. We both raised a hand in farewell before continuing up the street. I glanced back over my shoulder and saw Harry's hand pressed against the window as he watched us go.

"I just want to go home," Mac said.

"Me, too, darlin'. Let's get gone."

TWELVE

Kenzie

The kitchen door swung open then snicked shut. I cocked my head. Was that Miles coming in from the garden? Hector's nails clacked across the linoleum, followed by Ripper's heavy tread.

Yikes, not Miles.

"Mac?"

"In here." I punched at my phone's screen and turned it face down on my lap, then swung my feet onto the floor and sat up in the recliner.

"What you doing?" He leaned against the opening between the rooms.

My gaze swept over his body, from his black boots, up to his windblown brown hair. Well-worn jeans hung low on his hips and a gray T-shirt stretched over his powerful chest. My eyes lingered on his leather Janissary cut.

"Reading." I kept my voice nonchalant. Absolutely nothing of interest going on here, my tone implied. I'd sink through the floor if he snatched the phone from my hands and saw the title, *Property of Mayhem: A Dark Motorcycle Club Romance.*

Damn if Ripper didn't embody the hot, alpha male heroes of my favorite romance books. Ali always swooned over well-groomed billionaires wearing expensive suits. Not me. You could keep your penthouses, private jets, and $300 bottles of champagne. Give me a rough, fierce, working-class hero, a man loyal to the core to his chosen tribe. A man who would burn down the world to protect the woman he loved. Now *that* was a nice fantasy.

"Yeah? What you reading?" Ripper asked.

Crap. Despite my attempt at airy indifference, he must have picked up on my anxiety. "A romance novel. Please don't laugh."

Warmth crept up my cheeks. If I could choose, I wouldn't be a blusher, but I'm wired to turn tomato red at the slightest embarrassment or innuendo. Kyle delighted in making me blush. He called it adorable. I felt anything but adorable now, when I sensed my cheeks heating under the amused gaze of this dangerous and intriguing man.

"I never laugh at romance, Mac." His deep voice held not a hint of mockery.

I wriggled, and my eyes widened when they met his. It almost sounded like he was flirting with me.

"Got something for you." He held up a paper bag. "For your bedroom. C'mon."

At another time, in another context, I might get a thrill wondering what Ripper wanted to give me in my bedroom. I scrubbed that thought from my expression and followed him to the tiny room where I slept.

He pulled a lump of white fabric from the bag and twisted it in his hands. It sprang open and took the shape of a fabric-covered ball with a cord protruding from one end. He attached a small gizmo to the cord.

"What is that?" I asked.

"Gimme a minute to get it set up." Tilting his head back, he scanned the ceiling, then zeroed in on a spot kitty-corner from my bed. He dug in a pocket and retrieved a small, metal cup hook, which he screwed into the ceiling. He hung the fabric ball from the hook and pushed a button on the gizmo. The fabric ball lit up. Its gentle glow reminded me of the full moon.

I smiled, turning my eyes to Ripper. "It's beautiful."

"You can adjust the brightness. Comes with a USB base and a solar charger, to keep it powered. I know Miles has LED lanterns, but I thought you might like this better to light up your bedroom at night. You know, to chase away the dark. It's..." He hesitated over the word. "It's pretty."

Pretty. A word I never expected to hear coming from Ripper's lips. I swallowed. I'd been so afraid that Ripper would think less of me if he found out that I was afraid of the dark, but instead of judging me, he looked for a way to make dealing with my phobia easier.

"Thank you. I absolutely love it."

"Glad you like it." He turned his eyes on the fabric-covered light, but his gaze seemed to focus on something beyond the glowing orb. "Club used to ride along the Clackamas River, out toward the Mt. Hood wilderness. Sometimes we'd camp out and party. Sara, the president's old lady, loved these round lanterns. She'd hang a bunch of them from tree branches. Called them her fairy lanterns. Thought you might like them, too, so I went out this morning to track one down for you."

I laid my hand on his forearm. The muscles jumped under my fingers. "Honestly, Ripper, this is one of the nicest things anybody has ever done for me."

I'd spent the day reading, trying to lose myself in fantasy. Anything to distract me from memories of the riot. Anything to erase the horrific image of that poor woman shot down in the street. It hadn't worked. The book barely took the edge off my distress. Ripper's unexpected kindness and concern did more to restore my peace of mind than any fantasy ever could.

Impulsively, I stood on my tiptoes and pressed a thank you kiss to his cheek. Stubble scraped against my lips when he slowly turned his head, and warm coffee-scented breath grazed my cheek. My heart thumped.

If he kissed me now everything would change, and this moment—this precise point in time that separated before from after—would live forever in my memory. Breathless and eager, I wanted to leap headfirst across that divide and discover what came next.

A fraction of a second before our lips met, the kitchen door slammed against a wall. Hector barked in alarm.

"Ripper! Mackenzie!"

Our intimate moment shattered. Ripper and I raced for the kitchen. We crossed through the archway just as Miles threw open the basement door. His footsteps thundered down the stairs. Ripper and I followed him into the cellar. Miles stood over a bank of nine car batteries, wild-eyed with panic.

"I was planting tomato starts, and I noticed that the front security camera wasn't working. I checked the other three cameras and none of them were working either, so I knew something was wrong with the battery bank." His words tumbled over each other as he spelled out the crisis. The solar-charged car batteries powered the ham radio, security cameras, and the hot plate. "Look." He pointed to two of the nine power cells. "They're dead."

"Hold on, Miles." Ripper said easily. "You have extra car batteries set aside, don't you? We can fix this."

"I have three extra batteries." Hysteria colored his voice."If this happens again, we'll be totally sunk. No power for the radio. No power for the security system. Sunk."

Ripper shrugged. "So, we'll get more batteries."

"Where? All of the stores are closed. We'll have to break into some place and hope that nobody else has already taken the batteries."

"Yeah. That's exactly what we'll do," Ripper agreed. "You got a copy of the Portland Yellow Pages, don't you?"

Miles nodded. "In the kitchen drawer with all the maps."

"Good." Ripper glanced at his watch. "It's almost five. Too late to get started today. Don't wanna leave Mac home alone after dark. First thing, we switch out the bad batteries and get the security cameras back up. Then, we use the Yellow Pages to map out the location of every store and garage on the east side that might carry car batteries. First thing tomorrow morning, we go out to get them."

"All right. I'll start changing out the batteries," Miles said.

"Hey." I touched Ripper's arm and signaled him to follow me back upstairs. Once out of Miles's earshot, I turned to him. "What do you mean *leave Mac home alone?* I should be the one to go with you. Car batteries are heavy and while you're lugging them around, you might run into trouble. A pissed-off store owner, or another looter. What good would Miles do? I can at least hold a gun and look like I know what I'm doing."

"Miles can shoot. I taught him."

"What? Why in the name of all that's holy would you teach Miles how to shoot?"

"Because if I didn't teach him how to shoot safely, he planned to learn by watching YouTube videos. You tell me, which way is better?"

"Jesus." I shuddered at that thought. "It still sounds risky. I'd be more likely to stay calm if there's a problem."

"I can keep him in line. Besides, after yesterday, I don't want to take you outside the compound if there's a chance of trouble. Not right away. Take a day or two to catch your breath."

"I can do it," I insisted.

Ripper smiled and caught my chin. "I know you can, but there's another thing. Miles gets all keyed up if I don't take him out at least every couple weeks. Don't want him to develop full-blown agoraphobia. Things go south, he has to be able to leave the compound without freaking out. It'd be good for him to come with me."

"I understand," I reluctantly conceded. "Listen, you said you don't want to leave me home alone after dark. I can deal with my phobia. Especially with my beautiful new moon lantern. If you guys need to go tonight, go."

Ripper pushed a strand of hair behind my ear. "Cut yourself some slack, will you? New batteries can wait till the morning. And I'd rather stick close tonight."

After Miles traded out the batteries, we sat around the kitchen table, mapping out the men's route tomorrow morning.

I made spaghetti for dinner, adding textured vegetable protein crumbles to the sauce to increase the protein content. Any self-respecting Italian cook would probably toss it out the window, but I've eaten worse, and Ripper and Miles wolfed it down.

After dinner, Ripper placed a wall of sandbags against the back fence, and both Miles and I took turns shooting at a target. Later, we played gin rummy until close to eleven, when I began to droop in my chair.

"You promise you'll keep a close eye on the security monitor?" Miles asked for the third time, as I excused myself to head to bed.

"Cross my heart." I yawned.

"'Night, Mac." Ripper glanced up from his hand of cards. "Need me to tuck you in?"

He was definitely flirting, right?

Miles spoke up before I could reply, casting Ripper a withering look. "Grown-ups don't need to be tucked in, silly, and we're in the middle of a game."

"I'm good," I assured Miles, but my eyes strayed to Ripper's face. "'Night, guys. See you in the morning."

Early Friday morning they set out in Ripper's jeep, leaving Hector and me to keep watch over the compound.

I sat at the command post, glancing at the camera feeds every few minutes while I worked a crossword puzzle. Hector was antsy. After I'd fed the chickens that morning, I'd spent half an hour tossing him a Frisbee, apparently winning his everlasting devotion. He followed me around the house with wide, hopeful eyes, even bumping against the closed door when I took a bathroom break. If Ripper and Miles weren't back by noon, I'd treat him to another fifteen minutes of Frisbee.

I figured out a nine-letter synonym for brewing coffee—percolate—then looked up at the monitor. A blue and white car with the words Portland Police and a red rose on the door rolled to a stop on the street outside the front gate. A patrol officer climbed out of the driver's seat, approached the gate, and rang the buzzer. I froze.

We'd planned for every contingency except this one. Don't answer the buzzer. Don't open the gate to anyone. We hadn't considered what to do if a cop came knocking.

What could he want? Miles received social security disability. It's possible the city would do a welfare check on a vulnerable citizen during a state of emergency. Had the sound of bullets from our shooting lesson yesterday evening frightened a neighbor or inspired a noise complaint? Both scenarios seemed plausible. A police officer still on duty was a good thing, right? Things couldn't have completely gone to hell if cops were on the job.

The patrol officer rang the buzzer again.

I looked at Hector. "You got any ideas?"

The buzzing grew insistent.

I glanced at the 22 pistol that sat on the desk. I was supposed to defend myself if somebody tried to break in. Obviously, the cop wasn't trying to trespass; he probably just wanted to talk to Miles. I didn't need to protect myself from the police. Besides, there were no circumstances under which it was a good idea to approach a cop with a gun in your hand.

I left the 22 behind and walked to the front door. Hector followed me, whining.

"You stay inside," I ordered. Ripper had warned me that Hector was very protective of his people, and I didn't want a stranger to trigger his guard dog instincts. Besides, a police officer would defend himself if he felt threatened by an aggressive German shepherd. Best to keep the two apart.

The front door slammed shut behind me.

"Crap!" I whirled around, but the lock had already engaged, and I'd left the key hanging on a hook inside the door. I sighed. Good thing I knew which rock in the garden hid a spare.

I stood beside the heavy sliding door that separated the yard from the street.

"Yes, sir? Can I help you?"

"I need to speak to Miles Dunwitty," the officer called out in a surprisingly youthful voice.

"Miles isn't available right now." Jeez, I sounded like a voice mail recording. "He's out. I'm his cousin. Can I take a message?"

"I need to enter the premises, ma'am."

I stood in silence. What should I do?

"This is official business. You don't want to refuse to obey the orders of an officer of the law."

No, I didn't want to refuse to comply with the police. Getting arrested was the last thing I needed right now. Being locked into a jail cell during a pandemic? Worst idea ever. Even if I didn't get sick, the guards might be struck down, and I'd be stuck. Nope. Not worth the risk.

"Okay. Give me a minute." It required so much power to move the heavy gate automatically that we'd disconnected it from the backup batteries. Miles had shown me how to unlock and open it manually. It took all my strength to muscle the door along the track, and I had to catch my breath once I slid it open far enough to allow the police officer to step inside.

I bent forward, resting my hands on my knees while I recovered from the exertion. Straightening up, I offered the cop a courteous smile. "What can I do for you, sir?"

My voice faltered as I got my first close look at the man. His face was flushed and slicked with sweat. Liquid seeped from the corners of his eyes. Worse, beads of mucus dripped from his nostrils and trailed across his lips. He brushed his left hand across his mouth and wiped the goo on his pants. I would have gagged if I weren't so horrified.

Jesus Christ, the cop had the flu.

THIRTEEN

Ripper

Soon as I opened the back gate, I knew something was wrong. The domed charcoal grill lay on its side, spilling briquettes across the patio. I dropped the two car batteries I was carrying on the ground and drew my gun from my holster.

"Stay back," I order Miles. I scanned the yard, searching for other signs of trouble, but saw nothing else out of place. Hector's face appeared in the back door window. He barked frantically.

"Hector's inside going apeshit," I called over my shoulder. "I'm gonna check the front yard."

I stalked around the house, all my senses on high alert. What I saw when I rounded the corner stopped me in my tracks.

The heavy metal gate stood open by a good two feet. Any asshole passing by could waltz into the yard and help himself to whatever he found. *What the fuck?* The gate could only be opened from the inside, so Mac must have done it. Why had Mac opened the gate, and where was she now?

First things first. I slid the door back along the track, engaged the lock, then quickly scoured the yard looking for any intruders. Once satisfied that the grounds were secure, I called for Miles to follow me as I unlocked the back door. Hector paced back and forth, whimpering. I laid my hand on his head, pausing just long in my search of the house to comfort my agitated dog. He trotted at my heels when I entered the front room.

The place looked untouched. A quick search of the bathroom, bedrooms, attic, and basement confirmed that no stranger had breached the interior. Mac had left a glass of water and a crossword puzzle book on the desk in the living room. Apparently, she had been watching the monitor when whatever went down started. She left the 22 behind when she exited the house, so she hadn't been anticipating trouble.

Interesting.

The key still hung on a hook by the front door. If she went outside without the key, she'd use the hidden spare to get back in after the door automatically locked. She wouldn't open the gate and go wandering the neighborhood. Something or someone had induced her to open the gate.

Miles followed me into the front room. He hunched his shoulders and wrapped his arms around his waist, a tell I'd learned to recognize, a thing he did to comfort himself when he felt overwhelmed. His posture, slack jaw, and wide unfocused eyes told me that he was on the brink of losing it.

"Hey, buddy." I walked up to Miles, and deliberately kept my voice calm, my tone gentle.

"I knew we shouldn't have left her home alone," he said quickly. "I knew it was a mistake. We left Mackenzie alone, and now she's gone."

"Yeah. She's gone. And you're gonna help me figure out what happened to her."

His eyes darted to mine.

"The security camera has a digital recorder, right?" I asked.

"Yes."

"So we can look at the footage from this morning? Scroll back to the time we left and fast forward until we see Mac opening the gate?"

"Yes!" Miles agreed eagerly, almost stumbling over his feet as he rushed to the computer.

I stood behind his chair as Miles queued up the footage. The screen was divided into four quadrants. Each displayed the feed from one of the four cameras that covered the yard. I caught a blur of motion.

"There. Back up."

A Portland police cruiser parked on the street in front of the house, and a uniformed cop approached the gate and rang the buzzer. After a few minutes, Mac walked into view, her long hair swinging as she crossed the yard. The two exchanged words through the wall, then Mac stepped up to the gate.

"Don't do it," I said under my breath, as if I could go back in time and prevent the debacle that played out in front of our eyes.

Mac was a good girl, a solid citizen. It wouldn't have occurred to her to disobey a police officer. She struggled to open the gate. The cop stepped into the yard, half-hidden from the camera's view by Mac's body. Something he said or did frightened her. She took a step back and then another, finally allowing us to see the man as clearly as she did.

My eyes narrowed. The hair, the way the uniform fit, it was all wrong. This was no cop. And whoever he was, the man looked sick. Snot ran down his face. He pressed his hands to his head like he was in pain. A fake cop who had the flu. What kind of shit storm was this?

He pulled a gun on Mac, and I balled my fists. No question about it. The fucker was gonna die when I got my hands on him. The motion-sensitive camera pivoted, tracking them as they marched to the porch. First Mac, then the cocksucker, tried the doorknob. No success. Mac had known where Miles had hidden a key, but it looked like she hadn't been willing to let the bastard in, not even when he held a gun on her. Wouldn't have guessed she had it in her.

He waved the gun in her face now. My anger reached a white-hot crescendo.

Time for The Ripper to come out.

My rage vanished, as suddenly, as completely, as a flame extinguished by a torrent of water. I was never more dangerous than when my switch flipped. I was ice, cold to the bone, incapable of feeling fear or pity. Driven by purpose without passion.

Mac thought that my street name came from some Victorian murderer. Nah. I don't kill women. I earned the name because of my gift for putting men in the ground, for making them Rest in Peace. RIP. Once my switch flipped, I became not plain old Ripper, but The Ripper. And The Ripper was coming for this nameless dead man walking.

I watched with dispassionate eyes when he grabbed her arm with his free hand and dragged her off the porch. He circled the house, probably looking for a way in past the security bars on all the windows. He halted on the back porch and released Mac's arm before rattling the doorknob and peering into the small window.

Something scared him—probably Hector—and he jumped back, raising the gun toward the door. I tilted my head. Was he planning to shoot my dog?

Before the man could regain his footing, Mac sprang at him, knocking him to the ground. She drove the heel of her hand into his nose, and blood spurted over her fingers. Did she know how to follow through? To take advantage of his pain and disorientation by going for his eyes or his windpipe? Didn't appear so. She struck him in the chest, an ineffectual blow that did little more than piss him off.

If she survives, I'm gonna have to teach her how to fight.

The man strong-armed her onto her stomach, then wrapped an arm around her waist and hauled her to her feet. Mac didn't give up, kicking and writhing in his grip. One of her feet caught the edge of the charcoal grill and sent it toppling over onto the patio. She batted at the hand still holding the gun. He wrenched his hand away, then struck her in the temple with the butt of the gun. The same spot I'd kissed a couple of days ago.

Mac was conscious, but it looked like the fight had gone out of her. She hung limply against his arm, her eyelids fluttering as she struggled to stay alert.

He struck her again, and she lost the battle. He slung her over his shoulder. The cameras followed his progress as he carried her around the house and through the gate, before depositing her still form in the backseat of the police cruiser. He climbed into the front seat and drove away.

"Is she dead?" Miles asked in a small voice. "Did he kill her?"

"Don't think so. Most likely he just knocked her out."

"I don't understand why Jason would do this." Miles's voice cracked.

"Jason?" I turned the chair around on its swivel, then crouched down so we were face to face. "Tell me about Jason."

Miles shrank back against the chair.

Get it together. Don't scare him.

I reminded myself that he was my friend, that I didn't crowd him or try to force him to make eye contact. When The Ripper took over—when I slipped into ice cold killer mode—I sometimes forgot the ties of friendship and always regretted it later. I stood and took a step back, creating a distance between us that would allow Miles to relax and think. Allow him to give me the information I needed to track my prey.

"Jason is Chad's older brother. You know Chad, from the next block over. He sells me his Adderall."

"Yes." I remembered that Miles bought amphetamines from a teenage kid. "What do you know about Jason?"

"Chad said that Jason is the family screw-up, always getting into trouble. He spent time in juvie when he was a teenager, and he's been in jail once or twice since. Two years ago he stole a car and crashed it during a police chase. I saw his face on the news, that's how I recognized him. Anyway, he hurt his back in the accident and was in the hospital for more than a month. Chad said their mom hoped that Jason might be scared straight after the accident. Instead, he ended up addicted to oxy."

Interesting. Jason had an opioid addiction. With so many people dead or dying and the city shut down, was he having trouble scoring drugs?

"Any reason Jason might believe that you have oxy?"

Miles froze, then a horrified expression crossed his face. "It's my fault."

"Explain."

"I wanted to make sure that we had any medication we might need after the hospitals and pharmacies shut down. I bought Adderall in case we had to stay awake during an emergency. I wanted to buy a major painkiller in case somebody got hurt. I told Chad that I wanted some Oxycodone. He told me he had a source. He sold me ten pills for $75 apiece. They're in a bottle in the safe." Miles started to sway in the chair. "He must have stolen them from his brother, and somehow Jason found out and he came here to take them back. It's my fault." He struck his forehead with his palm. "My fault Mackenzie's gone."

"Miles, if you want to help Mackenzie, you need to stay calm."

He froze. "How can I help?"

"You know Chad's address?"

"Yes."

"Good. I'll start there."

"What are you going to do?" He looked like a little kid who thought he was in trouble, only to be thrown an unexpected lifeline. He met my eyes, hope lighting up his face.

"I'm going to find Mackenzie, and one way or another, I'm going to bring her home."

"You promise?"

"Yeah. I promise. And you know I always keep my promises."

FOURTEEN

Kenzie

I came to in the back of a police cruiser feeling like somebody had sucker punched me. Somebody had, and I saw the back of his head through the steel mesh that separated the front of the car from the rear.

Pain speared my temple, and it was hard to think, but I slowly pieced together what had happened. Scattered memories coalesced to paint a dire picture of my situation. Opening the gate to the impostor cop, the struggle on the back porch, the sudden blow to my head, and now, regaining consciousness in the back of a stolen police car. My situation sucked pond scum, as Ali liked to say.

I should keep quiet and give myself time to come up with a plan before dick wad figured out that I'd returned to the land of the living. If he thought I was still unconscious, he might be careless and give me an opportunity to make a move.

What's the point?

He was a walking bundle of flu symptoms, and he had put his hands on me. We were in close quarters, breathing the same air. Unless I were immune or an asymptomatic carrier, I was going to get the killer flu. What was the point in fighting back if I was doomed?

You've got thirty seconds to wallow before you get a grip.

I was no quitter, and I refused to give this creep the win.

First things first. Assess my situation.

My cheek lay on a smooth plastic seat. When the fake cop hit me, the skin on my cheekbone must have split, because blood had oozed from the wound and congealed on the hard surface. I'd leave behind a sticky smudge when I finally raised my head. My nose wrinkled. I was sprawled, face down, on the back seat of a police car. Who rode in the back seat of a police car? What wealth of bodily fluids had splashed or seeped onto this very surface?

I shifted slightly, trying unobtrusively to lift my face away from the nasty plastic.

"I know you're awake," my kidnapper called from the front seat.

If the jig was up I might as well sit up, look around, and try to figure out where he was taking me. Easier said than done. My head was swimming, and I had to close my eyes to fight a wave of nausea.

"Don't try the doors. I've been where you are. They won't open from the back seat."

Looked like I was at the mercy of an experienced criminal rather than an opportunistic amateur. Great.

"What happened to the real police officer?" I asked.

"Finally figured it out, huh?" He laughed. "The dumb shit stayed on the job. I found his patrol car parked on the side of a street a few blocks from my house. Key in the ignition. Cop dead. So I helped myself."

I can't believe I let this asshat through the gate.

"You realize that you're wearing the uniform of a man who died from the flu? It's probably crawling with the virus. Who's the dumb shit now?"

He shrugged. "Doesn't matter. My folks and brother died yesterday. I've been exposed plenty, but it's not the flu."

The skin on the back of my neck prickled. The man was clearly delusional. Was he entering the end-stage violent mania we'd heard about?

I was definitely out of my element. It was hard to concentrate, but I needed to make a plan. What did I know about dealing with a kidnapper? Only what I've seen on TV, and God knows if any of that was accurate. Conventional wisdom said I should try to establish some kind of rapport with him. Try to make him see me as a person so he would hesitate before hurting me.

How do I establish a bond with an asshole?

"I'm sorry to hear about your family. Were you and your brother close?"

He snorted, not deigning to answer. Okay, maybe that question was too transparent, too obviously manipulative.

"My name is Kenzie," I said, trying again. "What's yours?"

He was silent for so long that I thought he'd refused to answer. "Jason," he grunted.

"Where are you taking me, Jason? Do you have a plan?"

"Course I have a plan." He whipped his head around and shot me a furious look. How dare I question his competence? Bet it happened a lot, or he wouldn't be so sensitive.

Jason was a loser with a temper and low self-esteem. I could work with that.

"Of course you have a plan. Things happened fast back at the house. You couldn't have known that Miles wasn't home, or that I'd locked myself out. What did you do? You took control of the situation." The words stuck in my throat, but if I had to flatter the guy to manipulate him, I would. "I know you have a plan. It can't hurt to tell me what it is, can it?"

He wiped his nose on his sleeve, and I saw blood. At least I wasn't the only one who came away from our fight hurt.

"I'm gonna stow you someplace safe while I go back to make a deal with your cousin."

A wealth of information there. Miles had something Jason wanted, and it sounded like Jason was planning to trade me for it. That meant he'd leave me alone when he went to talk to Miles. If I were alone, I could try to escape. Unless, of course, he used the dead cop's handcuffs to immobilize me.

Worst-case scenario? I'd be chained to something in Jason's safe place, in the dark since the power was out. I'd be unable to break free of the cuffs, and if Jason keeled over from the flu before he got a chance to talk to Miles, I'd die alone in the freaking dark from hunger and thirst, unless the flu got me first. My personal nightmare. I massaged my temples, trying to think.

Get it together. Focus on what you can do to help yourself instead of spinning fantasies about everything that can go wrong.

"A deal for what?" I asked. "How do you know Miles has something you want?"

"Before he died, my brother was out of his head with the fever. He said he was sorry for stealing my oxy and selling it to Miles. I didn't know the little shit took it. I thought Mom had flushed it down the toilet."

Oxy? What would Miles want with oxy? Oh... Miles stockpiled everything he thought he might need during the apocalypse. He bought amphetamines from some kid named Chad. Maybe he thought he might need some super-duper pain killer. After hearing all the scary news stories about oxy addiction, I'd have to be desperate to touch it, but Miles liked to be prepared for everything.

I studied the back of Jason's head. He sniffed and rubbed his nose on his sleeve again. Was Jason hooked on the stuff? Oxy, or maybe heroin? Were his flu symptoms really signs of opioid withdrawal? He'd insisted that he didn't have the flu. If everybody around him got sick and died, and he didn't, maybe he was immune. Maybe it wasn't the flu. Maybe I'd been too quick to dismiss his words.

A small tendril of hope sprouted in my chest. Jason might be a low-life criminal and an addict willing to do anything to get his fix, but if he didn't have the flu, I might have a chance to survive this.

And I had an ace up my sleeve. Ripper. When Jason approached Miles to make his deal, Ripper would be there.

I saw him in my mind's eye, tall, strong, cool-headed, a man you'd want on your side when things went sideways. Jason had no clue. He thought he was dealing with the neighborhood prepper, a young man he probably thought he could bully into giving him what he wanted. Instead, he would be taking on a badass biker, a former Army Ranger. I'd feel sorry for Jason if he wasn't such a dick.

Jason had a plan. Now, I did too. I'd jolly him along. I'd try to stay on his good side and set his mind at ease, so he'd let his guard down. Then one of two things would happen. Either I'd see an opening to gain the upper hand and escape, or Ripper would come find me.

I looked out the car window, memorizing the street names along our route. If I could get away, I'd need to find my way back home.

"Are you taking me to your house?"

"No. It stinks too bad there."

He was talking about his dead family—his mom for chrissake—yet his voice held no emotion, no sadness, not a hint of loss. What was wrong with him? I'd feel compassion for anybody who got hooked on opioids after a car accident, but Jason made it easy to despise him.

We entered a part of southeast where residential neighborhoods transitioned to light industry and commerce. Jason pulled into a parking lot next to a long, low-slung, cement and brick building. I glanced at the name painted on the side of the building. It was a commercial bakery, not the kind of place that produced the high-end, artisan baked good I craved. This place cranked out the inexpensive white and wheat loaves parents used to slap together their grade schoolers' peanut butter and jelly sandwiches.

"I work here. Used to work here," Jason corrected himself.

He hopped out of the car and opened the rear door. Metal handcuffs dangled from his hand. Damn.

"Be a good little girl and hold out your wrists."

Good little girl? Grrr. I had no room to maneuver and no choice but to comply. He'd stuck the cop's gun into the waistband of his pants—the idiot—so it was easily within his reach. I doubted I could grab it before he did, although the notion of struggling over the weapon and accidentally shooting off his balls made me smile. I wiped that thought from my face and held out my wrists. At least he cuffed me with my hands in front of my body rather than behind my back. I climbed out of the back seat.

Jason pointed to a side entrance to the bakery. "You go first."

I led the way and waited for him to unlock the door. He carried a big black flashlight, doubtless purloined from the cop's stash. At least we wouldn't be fumbling in the dark while we made our way to the safe place where he intended to stow me.

Once inside, he ordered me to take the lead again. I stumbled ahead of him in the unstable circle of light cast by the flashlight. The darkness carried weight and pressed against me from every side. My heart raced and I stumbled forward on unsteady feet.

Crap. My panic pissed me off. A kick-ass woman would seize the moment and plunge headfirst into the black. Me? I trotted obediently in front of my captor. So much for my plan to snatch the first opportunity to escape. Pathetic.

Our footsteps echoed off the walls of a large room. The flashlight beam swung back and forth with each step, revealing glimpses of industrial ovens. Finally, he pushed open a door marked Employee Lounge. The flashlight barely dented the black interior, and I couldn't force myself to step into the room.

When I hesitated in the doorway, Jason shoved me. I tripped, sprawling on the floor, banging my elbow hard as I tried to catch myself.

Muttering under his breath, Jason hauled me to my feet, then pushed me onto a couch. "Stay put."

What I wouldn't give to tell him off. I clenched my jaw and squeezed my eyes shut, mentally counting down from ten. I'd blown my first chance at escape, but the rest of my plan was still intact. I *had* to control my temper and stay on his good side until I got another opportunity to get away.

Jason touched a lighter to a wick, the soft clicking drawing my eye. The flame caught, and a small pool of light added another layer of illumination to the room. He deposited the candle on the coffee table in front of the couch, then he lit three more and placed them around the room.

"Mom had a bunch of 100-hour emergency candles stuck away, in case we lost power in an ice storm."

"Good thinking." I meant her, not him, but let him think what he would.

I glanced around the break room. A refrigerator anchored one end of a long counter that held a couple of coffee makers, a toaster, and a microwave. Four sofas were scattered around the room, and two lunch tables occupied the center. A rumpled sleeping bag was balled up on one couch and somebody—probably Jason—had smashed the glass fronts of the vending machines that lined one wall. It looked like he slept here last night and had helped himself to the snacks.

Jason dropped onto the sofa next to the sleeping bag, set the gun on his lap and held his face with his hands. "My head is fucking killing me."

"Don't they have a first aid kit somewhere around here?" I asked.

"Probably. You think a band-aid or a couple of aspirin will make me all better, huh?"

His sarcasm grated on my already-frayed nerves. I gritted my teeth and swallowed back my angry retort.

"No, I don't think an aspirin will cure your headache, but if it helps even a little bit, wouldn't it be worthwhile to take some?"

"I suppose so." He sounded like a petulant child.

"And if you're dehydrated, that'll make your headache worse, too. How about I look in the cabinets for a first aid kit?" And anything I could use as a weapon. "And I'll see if there's a sports drink in one of the vending machines."

Another long pause. "All right, but no funny business." He stood and once again the gun was in his right hand, and he held the flashlight in his left. "I'm watching you."

"Got it. No funny business," I said.

Jason directed the beam of light to the counter. I crouched down and opened a cabinet door. Paper towels and paper napkins. I squinted at a box of plastic cutlery, considering, then rejecting it. Even if I could open the box without Jason noticing, I doubt I could take him on with a spork. It would probably snap in two if I got close enough to poke him, and then game over. Boxes of powdered coffee creamer and sugar packets were just as useless.

I scooted sideways and opened the cabinet under the sink. Bingo. Jammed into the back corner sat a red nylon duffel emblazoned with the words First Aid. If it had been a metal case instead of soft nylon, I might have been able to smack him in the head with it.

Next to the first aid kit, I spied a red, metal fire extinguisher. Now *that* had potential. Even with my wrists cuffed, I could wrap my hands around it and swing it at him. Or possibly, I could pull some pin or tab and blast him in the face with the fire-retardant foam.

I froze. Only a handful of days ago I'd drenched Ripper's face with pepper spray. Hadn't slowed him down one bit. He'd charged me like a bull and pinned me to the wall. If only Ripper were here now to charge Jason and take him down. But he wasn't, and it was on me to save myself.

I glanced over my shoulder, checking Jason's position. He stood ten feet behind me, his gun aimed at my back. Dammit. There was no way I could grab the fire extinguisher and run at him before he could react.

"Found it!" I smiled brightly and pulled the nylon bag out from under the sink. I stood, brandishing it triumphantly. I deliberately left the cabinet door ajar. If Jason fell asleep, I could retrieve the fire extinguisher without the snick of the cabinet unlatching waking him.

"Put it on the table." He gestured with the gun. "And get me a drink."

I dropped the bag on the coffee table and stepped gingerly through the broken glass to the vending machine. I found a grape Gatorade for Jason and a can of orange juice for me. The vending machine held an assortment of individually wrapped pastries, the kind of treats you'd pack in a kid's lunch bag. I grabbed a couple of chocolate cupcakes. They didn't sound particularly appealing, but I needed to eat and drink if I were going to keep up my energy.

I set the drinks and snacks next to the duffel. Jason dropped onto the couch, gun on his lap, and stared at me sullenly.

"First, I'm going to look for headache medicine." I unzipped the first-aid kit and found a two pack of aspirin. I placed it on the table within his reach and slid the sports drink next to the pills. "You take that, and if it's okay with you, I'll have some orange juice and eat a cupcake. I brought one for you, too, if you want it."

He nodded slowly, unscrewed the cap on the drink, and took a swig before ripping open the pills. Perching on the edge of the coffee table, I drank half the can of orange juice before taking the first bite of the sickly sweet cupcake.

"It's good." I pointed at the other cupcake. "You want to eat?"

He shook his head, his eyes never leaving my face. I shifted under his intense scrutiny. Something ominous was going on behind his eyes. I took another sip of juice to wash down the pastry.

"Feel like I'm gonna puke." He belched. "Better."

My stomach curdled, and I dropped the rest of my pastry onto the table.

"What can I do to help?" I wiped my sugar-crusted fingers on my pants.

Jason swayed slightly, watching me with a disconcerting assessment in his gaze.

"You're pretty."

"Thank you." I folded my hands on my lap and sat very still. Wherever he was going with this, I didn't like it.

"It's nice to have a woman take care of me."

What woman had ever taken care of this creep, besides his poor mother? I schooled my face into a polite mask, revealing nothing of my thoughts.

"I broke into a lot of houses yesterday, before I scored the cop car. Got run off a couple of times, but mostly I seen a lot of sick people, a lot of dead people. You know what's weird? All the women

I seen were dead. A couple of men were on the mend, but not a single woman. Makes me think."

He took a swallow of Gatorade, then nodded his head, as if he had made up his mind about something. "New plan. I was gonna trade you back to your cousin for my oxy, then hightail it out of town. Now I'm thinking, why not get my pills back and keep you? Your cousin's got a sweet setup. Security. Probably lots of food. Shit, maybe even more oxy. And even if he doesn't, it would be a good base to scope the city out for some more. Throw in a nice looking woman to take care of me, and I'd be sitting pretty."

Maybe the drugs had eaten holes in his brain, leaving it like Swiss cheese and rendering him incapable of rational thought. How could Jason imagine that I'd ever go along with that plan?

"And what about Miles?" I asked.

Jason shrugged. "I can take care of old Miles." He picked up the gun and tapped the barrel to his head. "I'm no idiot."

Seriously? Bragging about his smarts while pointing a gun at his own freaking head? And his finger was on the trigger. The brainiac just broke every one of Ripper's basic rules for handling a weapon.

"I still don't trust you, but in the end, when you figure out you got no choice, you'll come to see it my way," he said. "And you'll want a man to protect you from all the bad things out there."

Keep quiet. Don't sneer. Don't impulsively jump at a guy with a loaded gun in his hand. That didn't work out so well last time.

"Nothing to say, sweetheart? That's all right. I like a woman who knows how to keep her mouth shut."

Oh God, whatever it takes, whatever it costs, he's going down.

"I feel like shit, and I gotta sleep for a couple of hours," he continued. "Get one of those wooden chairs from the lunch table and bring it over here."

I obeyed. Jason stood up, fished in his pocket and pulled out a handful of zip ties.

"See! Your new man is ready for anything." He tossed the zip ties on the table and raised the gun at me once again. "Sit down in that chair. Tie your ankles to the chair legs, and then I'm gonna tie your wrists to one of the arms." The small hole at the front end of the barrel—the muzzle I think Ripper called it—danced back and forth as Jason swung the gun to emphasize each order.

I'm supposed to do his dirty work, to play a part in my own imprisonment. Everything about this situation galled me. I should have run into the dark when I had the chance. Even if my hands were cuffed, even if he had a gun and a flashlight and he knew the building, at least I would have had a better chance than I would when tied to a chair.

And where had my attempts to build a rapport with him gotten me? He decided that I'm so nice that he'll kill my cousin, take the compound, and keep me. My new man. My protector.

Dammit. Absolutely last time I took crisis management advice from TV.

"You deaf?" he demanded. "Sit your ass down and tie your ankles to the chair legs."

I didn't trust myself to speak, so I just nodded and sat in the chair. With my hands cuffed, it was awkward to use the zip ties, but I managed. He shoved the gun back in his waistband and roughly seized my bound wrists, then slammed them down on a wooden chair arm and fixed them in place with two zip ties.

"Sit tight while I get some shut-eye." Apparently, his accidental humor delighted him, and he giggled. "Sit tight, get it?"

When I didn't respond, he sulked. He shook out the sleeping bag and fluffed his pillow, then he slipped the gun under the pillow and stretched out on the couch. He turned his back to me, giving me the silent treatment. Within a minute, he was snoring.

I stared at the sputtering flame of the emergency candle, a small beacon of light chasing away the shadows in the unlit room. No way I'd go down without a fight. I needed a new plan.

FIFTEEN

Ripper

Parked my bike a block away from Jason's house. Not gonna let the engine sound give me away if he'd gone to ground there. I approached on foot, scanning the street for the stolen cop car. It was nowhere in sight, but that meant jack shit. He could have stashed it anywhere. I cut through the next door neighbor's property and hopped the fence into Jason's back yard.

A big-ass propane grill crowded the small deck—probably the dad's pride and joy, because sure as shit Jason and Chad were nothing to brag about. I skirted the grill and checked through the windows for signs of life. Nothing.

Somebody had left the patio slider open almost a foot, so no breaking in required. I eased my head through the open door, and it hit me, the unmistakable stink of death.

Bodies inside, but that didn't mean that Jason hadn't dragged Mac here, or that she wasn't stuck away in some back room, sucking in this foul air.

I drew my Colt and stalked through the house, inspecting every room. A man's body lay on the sofa in the small living room, a folding tray table holding an aspirin bottle, a glass of water, and an untouched bowl of tomato soup was pulled up next to the sofa.

Somebody had been taking care of him. Bet he was one of the first to pass.

The master bedroom was empty, the bed neatly made. Across from the bed, school pictures of three blond boys covered the wall, the progression of time showed them aging from smiling first graders to teenagers. No graduation photos. Chad was too young and it looked like Jason had dropped out. My gaze skimmed over the face of the youngest. His last photo placed him at around twelve, too young to be of any concern. I studied the face of the oldest boy. Jason. My prey. The passing of years hadn't been kind to him. His first picture showed a grinning, gap-toothed boy. In the last, he stared at the camera with a defiant *fuck you* expression, a young man angry at the world.

"See you soon," The Ripper promised.

Two bodies occupied the second bedroom. A teenage boy curled on his side in a twin bed that was too small for his lanky frame. A second twin bed stood against the opposite wall. It was empty, stripped down to the bare mattress. From the skid marks on the carpet, it looked like the middle-aged woman had dragged a rocking chair from the master across the hall. She died in that chair, watching over her sick son.

Impulsively, I grabbed a blanket from the foot of the kid's bed and carefully covered up her body, granting the mother a small measure of dignity.

No sign of the third kid. Maybe he died early on.

Jason's room was a pit, dirty clothes tossed every which way and half-eaten plates of food abandoned on every surface. The rest of the house was clean, shabby, but clean. Must have driven his mom crazy to live with Jason's mess and the smell of his rotting food.

Always an asshole, right Jason?

I searched every corner of the house, ending up back in the kitchen. Crossing my arms over my chest, I considered my next move. Where would Jason take Mac, if not to his home? More than half a million people lived inside the city limits. Must be thousands of houses and other buildings where Jason could hole up with his prisoner.

Maybe Jason wanted a taste of the good life. He could have broken into one of the mansions in the West Hills or Irvington, helped himself to fancy food and expensive booze.

Nah. Jason looked like shit in the security footage. If he had the flu, he'd be too weak and too sick to go far. If he was withdrawing from opioids, he was in no condition to enjoy rich food or liquor. Whether sick or in withdrawal, breaking into a mansion was out.

He had a prisoner. I'd put my money on Jason taking Mac to someplace familiar, someplace where he knew all the exits and entrances, someplace where he felt confident that he could control the environment.

If not his home, then where?

Unless he was a total leech—which I wouldn't put past him—Jason had a job. No point in using the walkie-talkie I carried to ask Miles. He'd never met Jason and his contact with Chad was minimal.

I tore apart the house looking for information about where he worked. The file cabinet in the master bedroom closet yielded the parents' tax returns, but not Jason's. I searched Jason's room, sifting through piles of crap, dumping out drawers, upending the wastebasket, looking for a pay stub or any other evidence of employment. Nothing.

Looked like Jason mooched off his parents, which left me shit outta luck.

Something nagged at the back of my mind, a half-formed notion not ready to emerge into the light of day. No point in trying to force it. Experience said that if I pushed, it would wither and die. Best to get on with things and let the idea seep up through my consciousness.

I had no clue where Jason took Mac. Where did that leave me? With no choice but to cruise the streets, looking for the stolen cop car like the proverbial needle in a haystack.

I spent the next couple of hours following a grid pattern, systematically riding up and down neighborhood streets in southeast Portland. A police cruiser parked outside an apartment complex caught my eye, but the ID number on the fender didn't match the one Jason was driving.

Rounding a block, I spied a row of cars parked lengthwise, bumper-to-bumper across a street and the adjacent yards, a barricade, blocking entrance to the neighborhood. Most likely residents were working together to prevent looting and to keep out anybody who looked sick. Not a bad plan, as long as they had healthy people to man it.

I applied the brakes and downshifted to first, stopping in front of the barricade. A burly man of around forty climbed out of the passenger seat of the center car, a shotgun nestled in the crook of his arm.

"You want something?" Lines of fatigue etched his face, but he didn't look sick.

I got no problem with men protecting their own, so instead of reacting to his hostile tone, I answered respectfully. "I'm not looking for trouble, sir, and don't want anything from you but information."

"Yeah? What kind of information?"

"I'm tracking a man driving a stolen police cruiser. He's impersonating a cop, trying to get into people's houses. This morning he got my girl to open the front door, and he took her."

"No shit?" the man said.

"You see a Portland police car pass this way earlier today?"

He rubbed his chin. "Yeah, matter of fact, I did. A couple of hours ago. Heading north. He slowed down and looked out his window at the roadblock. I thought for sure he was going to give me grief about illegally blocking a city street, but he didn't get out of the car."

The man was wearing a gray, short-sleeved work shirt, with *Taylor's Garage* embroidered over the left pocket and the name *Jamal* over the right.

"Thanks, Jamal. That could be him. Keep your eyes open because he's bad news."

"Will do. Good luck finding your girl."

I nodded, turned the bike around and started heading north. The thing struggling to emerge from my hind brain finally broke free, triggered by Jamal's work shirt. I accelerated and navigated back to Jason's house.

Acting on a hunch, I rushed to Jason's messy bedroom and dropped to my knees, pawing through the piles of dirty clothes. I dug through dingy boxers and old jeans and T-shirts, then struck gold.

My hand snagged a white, pit-stained work shirt with *Jason* embroidered over one pocket and *Sanitation Department* over the other. I flipped the shirt over and expelled a breath. Luck was with me. On the back of the shirt, large letters spelled out the name of a local commercial bakery. I'd ridden past it a hundred times. It was no more than fifteen minutes from the house.

I jogged back to my bike and sped toward the bakery. Once again, I parked a block away, so the engine noise wouldn't give him a head's up. In the employee parking lot, the police cruiser was pulled up next to a side entrance to the building.

Jason wouldn't be dumb enough to leave the door unlocked, would he? The knob turned easily in my hand. Yeah, guess he would.

I stepped inside, quietly closing the door behind me. No point in waiting for my eyes to adjust to the dark. There were no windows to allow in even a sliver of light. I had plunged into absolute blackness. I drew my Colt, then reached in a pocket for a small penlight. A decision had to be made. I could either feel my way forward in the dark, or I could risk the flashlight giving away my presence.

Fate took the decision from my hands. From somewhere deep in the building, I heard a shout, followed by the unmistakable sound of gunfire.

The fucker was shooting at Mac.

I flicked on the flashlight and sprinted toward the sound.

SIXTEEN

Kenzie

I winced and held my breath, keeping a watchful eye on Jason's motionless body. Not a twitch. He slept like the proverbial dead, one leg dangling off the side of the couch.

Emboldened, I pressed my feet onto the linoleum again and bounced the chair another few inches away from my captor. He really had to be out of it if he could sleep through the sound of the chair legs striking the floor.

After my attempt to ingratiate myself with Jason backfired so spectacularly, I'd sworn off any stratagem suggested by television. Then I remembered a scene from Ali's favorite zombie series. Our hero had been strapped to a wooden chair, much as I was now. The bad guy sicked a zombie on him, and our intrepid hero smashed the chair against the wall. The chair broke apart like kindling, freeing the good guy to stake the shuffling ghoul.

If I scooched the chair over to the wall, stood up as far as the zip ties would permit and swung the chair against the vertical surface with all my might, maybe the wooden arms and legs would come apart at the joints, allowing me to slip free.

Even if Jason slept through all the scooching and bumping, the sound of splintering wood would surely wake him. What happened next would depend on how long it took him to rally from a dead sleep. The man was sick, weak, and he had a blinding headache, all points in my favor. He also had a gun and a flashlight. Points to Jason.

For my plan to work, I'd have to bounce across the room, break the chair apart, extricate myself from the wooden pieces, and either dash out the door or make a play for the fire extinguisher under the sink. With my hands cuffed. All before Jason got to his feet and pointed the gun at me.

My plan sucked donkey balls, another Ali-ism.

So what was the alternative? Sitting like a good little girl in the chair, waiting for my *new man* to wake up and make his next move? Jason intended to kill Miles and take the compound. Ripper could kick Jason's ass with both hands tied behind his back, but what if Ripper was out looking for me when Jason approached Miles? There was no way I'd allow Jason to hurt my cousin.

My lip curled, and for the hundredth time I mentally berated myself for being too chickenshit to run away into the dark. I'd squandered my best opportunity to escape, so it was on me to take advantage of the next one.

I drew in a deep breath, steeling my resolve, then pushed off against the floor. The chair lurched another few inches toward the wall. I waited. Jason slept on, so I did it again. And again. Success made me cocky, and I launched an ambitious jump.

The chair teetered, and I imagined it falling backwards, leaving me with my feet waving helplessly in the air. After a few heart-pounding seconds, it righted itself. I scooted again.

After ten minutes or so, I landed a couple of feet from the wall. I counted to sixty, allowing my racing heart to slow down and confirming that Jason hadn't stirred. I stood, bent awkwardly forward with the chair legs firmly attached to my ankles, the seat dangling inches from my butt, and my cuffed wrists supporting the weight of the chair. Keeping my eyes on Jason, I swung the chair back and forth, gradually building momentum.

Now or never.

I slammed the chair against the wall, the force jarring my bones. Losing my balance, I tipped over sideways, but the chair arm had separated from its wooden support, allowing me to free my wrists. I kicked frantically, pounding the chair legs against the floor, trying to break them away from the seat. I almost sobbed with relief when the legs cracked, and I was able to slide the wooden pieces out of the zip ties. Free from the chair, I rolled into a crouch.

"What the fuck!" Jason roared.

A shaft of light swept the room.

Fifteen feet of open space separated me from the door, allowing him a clear shot. I dropped to my hands and knees and scrambled the opposite direction, toward the sink. The couch blocked Jason's view, giving me a few precious seconds to get my hands on the fire extinguisher.

I fumbled with the pin, cursing under my breath, until I managed to pull it out. Tucking the metal canister under my elbow, I wrapped the fingers of one hand around the nozzle and seized the handle with the other.

"Where are you, bitch?"

Jason stumbled around the corner of the couch. A beam of light skimmed over the cabinets and came to a stop when it fell on me.

"Gotcha!" he cried triumphantly.

I squinted into the glare, but unlike a deer in headlights, I didn't freeze. I pointed the nozzle and squeezed the handle, blasting Jason in the face and chest with fire-retardant foam.

He sputtered and dropped the flashlight, which bounced and spun on the floor, casting unsteady silhouettes against the back of the couch. The eerie play of shadow and light gave an aura of unreality to the scene as I raced toward him.

Please, God, let me bash him on the head with the canister before he recovers.

I slid on the spray, and my feet flew out from under me.

The canister slipped from my grasp and skated under the couch. I landed hard on my already bruised elbow and rolled onto my back. The fall knocked the wind out of me and I gasped for breath.

Jason wiped his face on his sleeve, then pointed the gun in my direction. This time he wasn't posturing; he wasn't trying to frighten me into complying with his demands. Rage contorted his features and robbed him of reason. Homicidal intent gleamed in his eyes.

My heart stuttered. I didn't want to die here; I wanted to go home. To be with Miles. To share that first kiss with Ripper. No way I'd allow this asshole to kill me.

Putting my feet together, I kicked hard against his knees, knocking him backwards off his feet just as the gun discharged.

Shaking my head to clear the ringing in my ears, I looked toward Jason, hoping that the hard fall had stunned him enough that I could wrest the gun away. No such luck. He sat up, his face a mask of malice.

He raised the gun again. I rolled onto my stomach and slithered around the corner of the sofa, propelling myself on my elbows and knees.

A bullet whistled by mere inches from my head. He was firing blind, but soon enough he'd be on me.

I reached desperately under the couch, groping for the fire extinguisher. My fingertips brushed the metal surface, but I managed only to push it further away.

Jason rounded the corner.

I was screwed. Lying on my stomach, with my arms wedged under the sofa, there was nothing I could do to protect myself.

A loud crack shattered the air. I thought for a second that Jason had fired again, that in the last moment of my life, time had crawled to a near stop. I half-expected to see a bullet flying toward me in slow motion and braced myself for the moment of impact.

Jason's head exploded, and his body toppled backward.

I blinked, and my world shifted on its axis. An invisible hand wiped my slate clean of all emotions. I stared at Jason's body with dispassionate eyes, so disconnected from reality that I might as well be watching actors in a film.

Ripper stalked forward, his eyes trained on Jason. After a moment, he tucked his Colt into his holster and swept the room with his flashlight. He found me, still sprawled on the floor in front of the couch.

"Hey, Mac." Ripper dropped into a crouch next to me.

"Hi."

"Are you hit?"

I considered his words, untangling their meaning. "He hit me in the face when we fought. Or do you mean, did a bullet hit me? In that case, no. I'm not hit."

Did Ripper think it odd that my voice sounded so flat, so listless?

He touched my bruised temple, his fingertips tracing over the cut on my cheek. "You want to sit up?"

Did I? My thoughts were muddled, and I couldn't decide what was best. "I don't know." My gaze wandered over to Jason's body. "I think he's dead."

"Yeah."

I continued to look at Jason. Curious. You'd think the blood and gore would make me want to scream, or vomit, but I felt...nothing.

"Mac." Ripper's voice was gentle. "Look at me."

My eyes turned obediently in his direction

"You're in shock. It's a normal reaction to what you've gone through. To the violence. I've seen it before. It won't last. You're gonna be fine."

"Okay."

"Let me help you." He pulled my arms out from under the sofa and lifted me into a sitting position. He extracted a small key from his wallet and held it up. "Good thing I always carry this." After unlocking the handcuffs, Ripper massaged my wrists, his gaze traveling up and down my body. "What's this white shit all over your pants? Same stuff's on Jason."

I looked down at my black yoga pants. "I found a fire extinguisher, and I blasted him with the spray."

Ripper struggled to compose his features, but lost the battle and barked out a laugh. "First pepper spray and now fire retardant. How'd that work for you, Mac?" He shook his head, biting back a grin. "You gotta learn how to fight with something more effective than foam."

That made sense. I nodded, then closed my eyes. Fatigue seized me, an exhaustion so all-consuming that I didn't know if my trembling limbs could support my weight. I wanted to crawl onto my cot, pull a blanket over my head, and sleep for a week, safe behind the walls of the compound.

Calloused fingers caressed my cheek. I opened my eyes to meet Ripper's gaze, all humor banished from his countenance. His brown eyes brimmed with confidence, reassuring me that all would be well. "You're gonna be fine."

"I know." If he said so, it must be true. "Ripper...would it be okay...would you let Hector sleep in my room tonight?"

"Sure, if it helps you feel safe." He stood and pulled me to my feet.

My legs threatened to collapse, and my teeth began to chatter. I clutched at his chest with trembling fingers. "I don't know what's wrong with me. I can't stop shaking."

"You burned through all your adrenaline. It's normal." He picked me up and cradled me against his chest. "Let's get you home."

He carried me through the bakery to the parking lot and settled me on his bike. I clung to his waist during the ride home, pondering his words.

It was normal. I was going to be fine. On one level, I knew he was correct. I'd recover from this ordeal. My strength would return. On another level, I was beginning to suspect that the world would never be normal again.

SEVENTEEN

Kenzie

I'd been so exhausted when Ripper and I returned to the compound that I'd vowed to sleep for a week. Three or four hours after making that vow, I lay awake on my narrow cot, jolted from my slumber by images of guns and blood.

"Get ahold of yourself," I whispered furiously. Jason was dead and I was safe, yet every time I closed my eyes I saw a muzzle flash or Jason's face twisted with rage.

My words woke Hector, who dozed on the floor at the foot of the bed. He trotted to my side and nuzzled my face.

"You're a good boy." I stroked the back of his head. An irresistible impulse seized me, and I patted the mattress. "Come on up." Hector hesitated. I bet Ripper had rules against jumping on the bed. "Come on," I urged. "I won't tell if you won't."

His tail thumped twice, then he leapt up onto the cot. I scooted next to the wall, creating just enough room for him to stretch out beside me. I threw an arm over his back and ran my fingers over his wiry coat.

"Such a good boy," I whispered into his neck.

Hector's presence soothed me, and eventually I drifted back into an uneasy sleep.

When I jerked awake an hour or two later—my heart pummeling my chest—the dog was gone and the bedroom door stood ajar. Hector probably nudged it open so he could go about his business.

The moon-shaped lantern glowed softly in the corner, bathing the room in muted light. My gaze fell upon Ripper's gift, and the tension gripping my throat eased.

I see the moon, and the moon sees me. God bless the moon, and God bless me. The old nursery rhyme popped into my mind.

In the Shanghai Tunnels, I hadn't been able to hide my fear from Ripper. Instead of minimizing it, he helped me to cope with the phobia. Later, he gave me a round fairy lantern to chase away the darkness.

I see the moon, and the moon sees me.

When my abortive attempt to escape my kidnapper had failed—when I was certain that Jason would kill me—Ripper had burst from the shadows and put Jason down.

To be cared for and protected. There were few thing more enticing—especially now when the old world was falling apart—and few things more likely to lead a woman down the wrong path.

My fingers traced the small scar that ran from the outer edge of my left eyebrow to my temple.

"It's hard to be a woman alone," Mom had slurred, her voice laced with self-pity.

I shook my head, dispelling the memory. I was *not* like my mother, weak and dependent, eager to latch onto any man who promised to take care of her and to smooth away life's rough edges.

Tearing my gaze from the moon-shaped lantern and its comforting glow, I glanced around the room. To my surprise, I spied Ripper dozing in a chair at the foot of my bed, his arms folded over his chest, his feet resting on a five-gallon water bottle. He couldn't be comfortable with his large body wedged into a small, hard kitchen chair, yet somehow he had managed to fall asleep.

His head drooped forward, and his dark lashes fanned against his cheeks. Even in repose, his powerful body possessed a coiled strength, a potential for violence that made me feel safe in a dangerous world. I'd no doubt that if I made a sound or stirred, he'd wake up, ready to spring into action. I held still so I wouldn't disturb him.

If Ripper were simply a muscle-bound lunkhead, a gladiator willing to stand between me and harm, I wouldn't be in so much trouble.

Alejandro is a good man. You treat him right, and he'll treat you right.

I squeezed my eyes shut. Was it so wrong—so unworthy of a strong woman—to want to be loved and protected? Did it make me a carbon-copy of my weak mother if I craved the same thing she always carried on about?

"Alejandro." I whispered his secret name, savoring the sensation of the syllables rolling off my tongue. Instantly, he stirred, and his eyes snapped open. He swung his feet down onto the floor and leaned forward.

"You say something, Mac?"

I should have known better. "Sorry I woke you."

He scooted his chair close to me. "You need anything? You hungry or thirsty?"

"No. Thanks." Actually, I *did* need something, but not food or drink. I sat up and pushed my sweaty hair back from my face. "Ripper?"

"Yeah, Mac?"

"I tried to get away from Jason. I didn't just wait for you to come rescue me. I need you to know that."

He lifted my chin so I'd meet his eyes, his expression serious. "Saw the busted up chair. The zip ties. That white shit all over everything. I know you tried. You did good."

"Thanks." Simply sitting up and talking to Ripper wiped me out. I fell back against my pillow. "I'm so tired, but I can't seem to stay asleep. I keep seeing..." I shook my head. "I mean, it's over and I'm safe, but my brain won't let go."

"Won't happen overnight, but you're gonna be fine." He tilted his head. "Got an idea. Turn over onto your stomach."

"Why?"

"Just do it."

I rolled onto my stomach, pushed my pillow off the bed, and rested my forehead against my crossed arms. The mattress dipped as Ripper sat on the edge of the cot.

"Now, take a deep breath and let it out slowly."

As I exhaled, his strong hands began to knead my shoulders.

"Oh, my God. That feels so good," I moaned.

"Shhh. Relax. Tell your brain to shut the fuck up."

The bliss of his hands massaging my tense muscles banished all the bloody images that kept intruding on my thoughts. Within minutes, I slipped into a deep sleep.

I startled awake, gasping for breath. Crap. Once again visions of bullets and gore pursued me into my dreams. I saw a thin halo of daylight surrounding the drawn window blind. Thanks to Ripper's ministrations, I'd finally slept for more than a couple hours.

I padded to the bathroom, then headed to the kitchen. In the back yard, Miles was tossing handfuls of feed to the chickens. Ripper was nowhere in sight, but that wasn't unusual. He had his own place, and he always disappeared for hours a day, probably something to do with his club.

I frowned at the old-fashioned, hand-crank coffee grinder that hung on the wall, unable to muster the energy to grind beans and boil water. Sighing, I shuffled back through the living room to my bedroom, where I crawled under the covers and stared at the ceiling.

After awhile, Miles stuck his head in the room. When he saw that I was awake, he stepped inside.

"Hi, Mackenzie." His hands were clasped in front of his stomach, a sure sign that he felt anxious.

I forced myself to sit up and offer him a welcoming smile. "Hi, Miles."

"Can I fix you some breakfast?"

I had no appetite and fought the urge to grimace at the prospect of food. "Thanks, Miles. I don't feel like eating."

"What do you feel like doing?"

Nothing. Absolutely nothing, but I couldn't tell him that. "I think I'm going to take a day," I said slowly. "You know, lie around and try to get my strength back."

"Can I do anything to help?" he persisted.

He was out of his element and trying hard to do the right thing, bless him.

"Do you remember when we had pneumonia when we were kids?" I asked. "Your mom tucked the two of us into your bed, and she read stories to us?"

"Yes, I remember."

"How about you find that old copy of *The World of Pooh*, and you read to me for a while?"

"I can do that." Miles's face brightened. He fetched the book, pulled a chair close to my bed, and began to read aloud.

When Aunt Debbie read the book to us, she gave each of the characters a distinctive voice. To my surprise, Miles followed suit. I had suggested the book in order to give Miles something to do; I hadn't expected to enjoy it so much.

Closing my eyes, I burrowed into the pillow, losing myself in the adventures of the denizens of the Hundred Acre Wood. I felt like a little girl again, safe and well-loved. Eons away from kidnappers and blood.

I must have fallen asleep again. I woke up to hear Miles and Ripper speaking in low voices outside my door.

"Has she eaten anything? Heated water for a bath? Stepped outside the house?" Ripper asked.

"She's taking a day." Miles repeated my words.

"Taking a day, huh?" Ripper said, his voice tinged with skepticism.

"Yes. I read to her and now she's sleeping."

"All right." Ripper blew out a long breath. "I'll check back in a couple of hours."

Hector pushed through the door and without invitation, hopped up next to me on the bed. I slung an arm over his side and listened to him breathe, counting his slow and steady inhalations and exhalations, until sleep claimed me once again. When I awoke from dreams of gunfire and blood, my tee soaked in sweat and my hands shaking, Hector whined and licked my face.

"I'm such a wuss," I whispered to him, choking with self-recrimination.

Ripper said this was a normal reaction to violence, that I'd be fine. I didn't feel fine. If the world really had changed forever, if there was no going back, I couldn't afford to wallow like this. I needed to conjure up some gumption. But how? How could I do that when my dreams were haunted by images of violence, when I couldn't control my trembling hands?

I really should get out of bed and do something.

Tomorrow is another day.

Good lord. If I was quoting Scarlett O'Hara, I really was losing it.

"Enough is enough," I said out loud. Gritting my teeth, I sat up and swung my legs out of bed. I shambled to the kitchen, where I found Miles stirring powdered cheese into a bowl of cooked macaroni.

"Are you hungry? I made mac and cheese."

Shaking my head, I took a seat at the kitchen table. "I don't feel like eating. Thanks anyway."

Miles frowned, but didn't say anything as he dished up his food and took a seat opposite me. "Ripper stopped by about a half hour ago. When I told him you were still asleep, he said he'd come back and check on you after he runs an errand."

Social chitchat wasn't Miles's thing, and my brain felt full of sludge, so we sat in silence while he ate. After dinner, I sat on the patio and watched Miles throw a tennis ball to Hector. Hector eventually started dropping the ball at my feet, and I threw it across the yard for him to fetch.

Sheesh. Even the dog thought I needed to buck up.

"I can read to you again," Miles offered, after the sun set and mosquitoes chased us inside.

"I'd like that." My throat tightened, his concern touching my heart. "Thanks for taking such good care of me."

He nodded, a small, pleased smile on his lips. When I got into bed, Miles surprised me by wrapping one of Aunt Debbie's crocheted afghans around my shoulders.

"Let's make you cozy." Exactly what his mother used to say when she tucked us into our sickbeds.

Miles read to me again, but this time, instead of comforting and an illusion of all-is-well, story time made me feel like a baby who couldn't face reality. I didn't have the heart to ask Miles to stop. He'd seized upon the thing he could do to make me happy, so I lay back with a fake smile on my face until fatigue got the better of me, and I fell asleep.

In the middle of the night, I rolled over onto my side, and the afghan tightened around my shoulders. I floated up out of the depths of sleep and skimmed the surface of consciousness.

Through half-closed eyes I saw Ripper once again dozing in the hard kitchen chair. I blinked, my eyelids heavy. The fairy lantern cast its gentle light across the room.

I see the moon and the moon sees me.

Nothing bad would happen tonight, not with Ripper standing guard. I yawned and sank back into slumber.

Sometime after the sun came up, Miles poked his head into the room.

"Are you awake?" he asked, rousing me from a dead sleep.

I shook my head, trying to clear the cobwebs, then glanced at Ripper's empty chair. "I am now."

"When are you getting up?"

"I'll let you know." I yawned.

"No. I need to know right now."

"Jeez! Give me a minute to wake up, will you, Miles?"

"You aren't going to take another day, are you?"

His relentless badgering was beginning to annoy me. "I'll let you know," I repeated, even though I hadn't given a thought to my plans for the day.

"Ripper won't like that," Miles muttered, before whirling around and stomping toward the kitchen.

Thirty seconds later, Ripper marched into my room. He stood at the foot of my bed, arms crossed over his leather cut while he gave me the stink eye.

"Taking another day?"

I squirmed under his disapproving gaze.

"That won't fly, Mac." He tilted his head, studying me intently, and I was suddenly aware of my grubby appearance, my greasy hair and rumpled clothes. "Tell you what, go ahead and stay in bed. Do what you gotta do, until 7 o'clock, then you and I are going out."

"What?" Memories of what happened the last time I left the safety of the compound filled my mind and my heart stuttered.

"You heard me. Be ready at seven. Dinner and a movie."

"Wait! What? You mean, like a date?" My head was spinning. A date? How could we go on a date in a dying city? Where could we dine and watch a movie without electricity?

"Call it whatever you like. Getting over bad shit is one thing. Pulling a blanket over your head and hiding in your room is another. That ain't you."

Hiding under a blanket like a frightened child? That pricked my pride. I lifted my chin and met his eyes defiantly.

"I'll be ready at seven. Is it a formal occasion? Do I need to dress up?"

His lips quirked. "Nah. Wear whatever you like." He strode to the door, then looked back over his shoulder. "But Mac, if you could manage to comb your hair and put on a clean shirt, I'd be grateful."

I threw my pillow at his retreating back.

Spending one more minute in my bed became unendurable. Still rankling from Ripper's jibe, I hopped up and stripped the sheets off the bed.

"Miles, can you help me set up that hand-crank washing machine?" I called, exiting my room.

He stuck his head out of the kitchen. "What did you say?"

"Can you help me set up the washing machine? We still have city water, don't we? So we won't have to break into the stored stuff?"

"Yes. Portland's water supply is gravity fed. The taps will keep working for a while."

Miles and I hauled the machine from the basement and set it up in the back yard. After washing my sheets and stringing them up on a clothesline, I laundered my stinky yoga pants and tee. Miles loved any new gadget, and I left him happily washing some of his own clothes when I went inside to clean up.

While I warmed a pan of water on the hot plate, I fetched my shampoo from the bathroom. Leaning over the kitchen sink, I dampened my hair before rubbing in the shampoo. One pan of water proved inadequate to rinse my hair clean, so I heated another to complete the job.

It took forever to heat a full pan on the hot plate, so I ran only a couple of inches of cool tap water into the tub for a bath. A pan of boiling water raised my bath's temperature from cold to tepid. There was no point in putting a second pan on to boil. The tub water would have cooled in the time it took to bring another pan up to temperature.

"This sucks," I grumbled, lowering myself into the tub. I soaped up, scrubbed, and splashed handfuls of water to rinse myself off while composing a mental list of things I missed from my previous life. Number one? Hot showers.

I dressed quickly in a pair of jeans and another tee—Ripper said to wear whatever I liked—then heated a can of soup to share with Miles. I kept busy all afternoon, sweeping and dusting the entire house, and pulling a few weeds in the vegetable garden. Busy meant I didn't have to think, and I welcomed the vacation from my own brooding thoughts.

Ripper came through the kitchen door promptly at seven, Hector at his heels and a bouquet of pink peonies in his hand. At my surprised expression, he shrugged. "You called it a date. Thought I better come prepared."

My cheeks flushed, and I buried my face in the flowers. Was he making fun of me for presuming we were going on a date?

I inhaled deeply. The peonies had a heavenly scent. Despite my embarrassment, it felt good to be reminded that something perfect and beautiful still existed.

"Thanks." I filled a vase with water and set the flowers on the kitchen table.

Miles hovered in the arched opening from the front room, worry stamped across his features. "You won't let anything bad happen to Mackenzie, will you?"

With three quick steps, Ripper was at Miles's side. "I promise I'll keep Mackenzie safe. You know where we're going. Nothing bad is going to happen to her there, I promise."

"And you always keep your promises," Miles said, as if repeating a mantra.

"That's right."

My cousin's expression brightened. "I'm going to eat Cheese Whiz and crackers, and see if I can reach anybody on the radio."

"Sounds like a plan." Ripper dropped a hand on Hector's head and ordered the dog to stay before turning to me. "Ready, Mac?"

I followed him out the back door into a beautiful, late spring evening. Sheets, pants, and shirts flapped on the clothesline as a light breeze stirred the air, carrying the scent of peonies from a neighbor's yard. I smiled to myself. If I followed my nose, I could probably figure out where Ripper picked the flowers.

A volley of distant gunfire ripped through the air, shattering the calm.

I collapsed onto the ground. One moment I was fine, and the next I was in the midst of a full-blown panic attack. Clapping my hands over my ears, I curled up in a fetal position. My heartbeat thrummed so loudly that I didn't hear Ripper speak when he dropped to his knees beside me.

"Mac." I saw his lips shape my name. He pulled my hands away from my ears. "No one's shooting at us. That's at least a mile away."

I heard his reassuring words and accepted them as true, but terror still gripped me by the throat. We were in no immediate danger. Intermittent gunfire had erupted around the city for days. Jason was dead. So why couldn't I suck enough air into my lungs or stop trembling? Why couldn't the rational part of my mind wrestle control away from the primitive part that insisted that we were in deadly peril?

Ripper scooped me up into his arms and jogged toward the gate separating the two yards.

"Put me down. I want to go home." I twisted in his arms, terror rising in my throat like bitter bile. Screw self-respect and dignity. All I wanted was to jump into my bed and hide.

"Sorry, Mac. That's a hard no." Ripper held me to his chest with one arm while he unlocked the gate.

I squirmed and pounded against his chest, struggling to break free. When I inadvertently thwacked his jaw, he grunted and slung me over his shoulder.

Talk about undignified.

He pinned me in place with an arm across my thighs. I kicked in protest, and he smacked my ass.

The man actually smacked my ass like some kind of misogynistic troglodyte.

He strode across the yard toward his patio door. With every step, my face bounced against the Janissary patch on the back of his cut.

He deposited me on the floor of his living room, and I wheeled on him, poking his formidable chest with my finger. "I don't care if you're a big, scary biker. You've got no right to manhandle me, or to tell me where I can or cannot go."

"Is that right?" he drawled, taking a step forward so he towered over me, crowding me. "You scared, little girl?"

"I'm *not* scared." I sputtered with rage. "I'm pissed."

Ripper smirked, his eyes alight with triumph. "From where I stand, pissed is one helluva lot better than scared shitless."

I narrowed my eyes, and my anger deflated, as if my body couldn't sustain such a powerful emotion for long. "Are you trying to tell me that you made me mad on purpose?"

He pointed to a large leather sofa. "Sit down. We need to talk."

Without waiting for my response, he installed himself at one end of the sofa, an arm slung across the back. After a moment's hesitation, I took a position at the opposite end, folding my hands on my lap while I waited for him to speak.

"The gunfire triggered a panic attack. That's normal after what you've been through. You gotta expect to be jumpy. It'll take some time to get over it, but you will."

If only I shared his optimism. Every move I made heaped failure upon failure. Who opened the gate to Jason? Who was too frightened to run away into the dark? Who let him gain the upper hand when we scuffled? And who absolutely could not shake off this crippling panic? Me. Dumb. Scared. Inept. Childish.

"I'm such a wimp," I muttered to myself.

"Oh, yeah? Would a wimp come at me with pepper spray? Would a wimp jump a man holding a gun when he threatened to shoot a dog? Would a wimp break free when she's tied to a chair by an armed psycho? Would a wimp find something she could use as a weapon and attack that psycho? Nah. You're no wimp, Mac. What you are is inexperienced and untrained."

"I could have done better," I insisted.

"You expect to go from college student to kick-ass warrior woman overnight? Do you think when some eighteen-year-old joins the army, that they hand him a weapon and ship him right off into battle? Doesn't work that way. It takes time to learn how to fight, to learn how to push past fear. And I'll help you learn. I'll train you. You'll get there."

I sat in silence for a long moment while his words sunk in. What did he see in me that I didn't? I wanted to be the person he described, somebody who was brave and capable. Somebody who could learn how to be tough.

"The world's gone to shit," he continued. "It'll never be the same, but a new normal will emerge. We're all gonna have to do things we never saw coming. Make choices we never expected. And you're gonna have to be strong to survive in that new normal."

"Is that why you wouldn't let me go back to the house when I freaked out after hearing the gunfire?"

"If you ran and hid, you'd beat yourself up. You'd convince yourself that you can't face your fears, so I took away the choice."

"And you smacked my ass to make me angry?"

Ripper's teeth flashed white, and I noticed for the first time that he had a dimple in his left cheek. "Wouldn't say that. Nothing wrong with a little friendly ass-smacking."

Why couldn't I toss my hair and laugh flirtatiously at his comment? I didn't need a mirror to know that my cheeks were stained red.

When embarrassed, deflect. "You promised me dinner and a movie. I've been racking my brain all day trying to figure out how you're going to deliver on that promise."

"Look around."

I studied his living room. A big screen television—a man-cave-sized behemoth—occupied the wall opposite the leather couch. Ripper caught me eyeing it. "I like to watch old science fiction films on a big screen," he said unapologetically.

Uncle Mel introduced me to old-school sci-fi films. We used sit up late on weekends watching 1950s films, the schlockier, the better. Any movie with irradiated mutant insects running amok, or bubble-headed aliens coming to earth in search of brides, made us happy. Aunt Debbie rolled her eyes, and Miles complained that the films were scientifically implausible, so the late night movie marathons were strictly our thing.

Ripper had better taste than Uncle Mel and me, if the framed posters on either side of the TV were any indication, *The Day the Earth Stood Still* and *War of the Worlds*, both early '50s classics.

I pointed to the posters. "It appears you're a fan of 1950s sci-fi, too."

In answer, he jumped from the couch and knelt before a low cabinet under the TV. He motioned for me to join him, then popped the door open with a flourish to reveal his blu-ray collection. I scanned the titles. It looked like he owned every sci-fi movie made between the 1930s and the 1960s, including some hard-to-find gems that Uncle Mel and I had been unable to track down.

I sat back on my heels, gobsmacked. "Ripper!" I hesitated, realizing that I didn't know his last name. "You're a man of unexpected tastes."

"Yeah? You're the first woman I've met who likes the same movies I do."

Pleasure unfolded in my chest, a happy recognition that Ripper and I shared something beyond our loyalty to Miles.

"Have you figured it out yet?" Ripper asked.

"What?"

In response, he swept the room with his finger, encouraging me to continue my search. I turned my head. Two bookcases, their shelves crowded with hardbacks and paperbacks, flanked the patio door. So Ripper was a reader, too. Magazines were scattered across the coffee table. A pair of end tables, each holding a brass lamp, stood on each side of the couch.

I frowned. The lamps were turned on, small circles of light spilling onto the table tops. I was so used to living with electricity that it hadn't struck me as odd that the lights were on. I should have noticed how easy it was to read the blu-ray titles in the cabinet.

"You have electricity," I exclaimed.

"Bingo. Powered up the generator a couple of hours ago, so we could do dinner and a movie right here."

"Nice." I was glad not to be venturing into the city again. "You made dinner?" I had a hard time wrapping my head around the notion of Ripper cooking.

"You think I want to live on pizza and takeout? I can throw together a decent meal."

It was past time for me to stop making assumptions about this complex man.

"So, what are we having?"

"Sweet-and-sour chicken over rice. I had to use canned chicken breast and pineapple, but I still had a few good carrots, and I made the sauce from scratch."

After scarcely tasting food for two days, I was suddenly ravenous.

"I am so ready."

Ripper nodded. "Pick out a movie while I dish us up."

I chose the 1953 version of *War of the Worlds*. I was still coming to grips with the idea that the world had changed forever, and it was reassuring to watch a film where humanity faced extinction, yet triumphed in the end.

We ate dinner on the coffee table, then settled back on the couch. Ripper tossed an afghan over my legs, and I recognized Aunt Debbie's handiwork. It must have been a gift from Miles. When the movie ended, I stretched and smiled happily, feeling more peaceful and content than I had in days.

"You certainly delivered on your promise, Mr…." I paused. How could I not know his last name?

"Solis."

Alejandro Solis. The name was almost as beautiful as the man.

"You delivered on your promise, Mr. Solis. That was great. Thank you."

"You're welcome."

I'd kicked off my shoes when I curled up on the sofa. Ripper pulled my foot onto his lap and peeled off my sock.

"Hope you don't mind if I strip you," he said with exaggerated innocence.

I shot him a reproachful look.

One by one, he twisted my toes back and forth, then massaged the ball of my foot. When he pushed his thumb into my arch I turned to putty. My head fell back on the cushion, and I moaned with pleasure. Ali always gave me a gift certificate for a whole-body, deep-tissue massage for my birthday. Best present ever.

Ripper was using both thumbs now.

"Harder," I gasped. "I like it so hard it almost hurts."

"I'll keep that in mind," Ripper chuckled.

Thank God I'd closed my eyes because I didn't want to see the expression on his face after my slip of the tongue. He skillfully massaged my entire foot, then started on the second, reducing me to a puddle of bliss. I was proud of myself when I refrained from telling him that he was good with his hands, but dear lord, it was true.

I needed a moment to compose myself.

"Can I use your bathroom?"

"Second door on the left."

I switched on the overhead light, expecting to see a small, shabby bathroom, the type typically found in an older bungalow. Worn linoleum, a toilet, a single sink, and a tub so small you'd have to draw your knees up to your chest to fit in.

My jaw dropped when I surveyed Ripper's bathroom. It was huge, rivaling anything I'd seen in Ali or Kyle's fancy homes in Boise. Travertine stone tiles covered the floor and counter top. He'd installed a jetted tub, a toilet that resembled a piece of sculpture, and a shower that could only be described as party-sized. A beveled mirror topped the double-sink vanity, and a framed da Vinci print hung over the toilet.

I spied a second door between the tub and what must have been a linen closet. Curiosity overcame good manners, and I carefully turned the knob and peeked into the adjoining room. As light from the overhead fixture spilled into the dark room, I saw the outline of a bed and a dresser. Ripper's bedroom.

I shut the door and slowly released the knob. After using the toilet, I washed my hands in one of the sinks. Hot water flowed from the tap, and I cast a wistful glance at the shower.

"Your bathroom is freaking amazing," I said when I returned to the living room. "Forget the king-sized garage, I'd buy the house for the bathroom alone."

"Remodeled it when I bought the place. I had no use for a third bedroom and decided to put in a shower and tub big enough to turn around in. That's why I had to postpone buying the safe and security system. Spent all my cash on the remodel."

"I love it," I said simply.

Ripper tilted his head. "You know, I turned on the hot water heater. We still have water pressure. No idea how long that's gonna last. You wanna take a shower? Might be your last chance for a while."

I scraped my teeth over my bottom lip while I debated what to do. I was dying to take him up on the offer. Miles was saving the generator for the winter months, and by then the city water would have long since petered out. This truly might be my last chance.

Would it be weird to come over to a man's place for dinner, a movie, and a shower? Once upon a time, I would have said yes. Now, when confronted with the siren call of a hot, luxurious shower, I decided that I really didn't care how weird it might be.

"If you're sure you don't mind, then yes, I'd love to take a shower."

"Wait here." Ripper hopped up, disappeared through a door, then returned carrying a gray, terry cloth robe. "There are extra towels in the bottom drawer. Take your time."

Our fingers met when he held out the robe, and we locked eyes. Nothing about his relaxed posture or facial expression suggested that he was coming on to me. I saw neither seduction nor expectation in his steady gaze, yet I felt a spark of mutual attraction flare between us.

Yesterday, we came within a hair's breadth of kissing. He'd teased me tonight and made me blush, but now, when the prospect of something real hung between us, he didn't push.

For the first time in many months, desire coiled in my sex, and I was painfully aware of my nipples grazing the lace of my bra. I licked my lower lip and Ripper's eyes hooded.

"Thanks," I whispered.

I tugged the robe from his hand, clutched it to my chest, and fled to the sumptuous bathroom. I fished in my pocket for a hair tie, then pulled my hair into a sloppy bun on the top of my head before stepping into the shower. I tried to lose myself in the experience, but as much as I had looked forward to the sensation of hot water tapping its staccato against my shoulders, back, and breasts, I found myself distracted by my jumbled thoughts.

I turned off the faucet, toweled off, then perched on the edge of the tub, Ripper's robe spread across my lap. I caressed the terry cloth fabric, brushing my fingertips over the nubby texture, then lifted it to my nose, inhaling deeply.

A hint of Ripper's scent clung to the robe, his own unique musk, separate and distinct from the smell of leather and exhaust embedded in his cut.

Separate and distinct. From the moment Ripper had strode across the yard and entered my life, I'd seen the biker first and the man second. I'd reduced him to a romance novel trope, the dangerous, sexy, bad-boy biker. The old Kenzie might have fantasized about such a man, but she knew better than to enmesh her life with one.

And the new Kenzie?

Reality was so much more complicated than fantasy. Ripper possessed the fantasy bad-boy allure. Sometimes I had to clench my fists to stop myself from reaching out to trace my finger across his chiseled face, his firm jaw, or his full bottom lip.

If I looked past the superficial layers, what did I see? A dangerous man who was loyal to his club, but who had also demonstrated loyalty toward Miles and me. A strong, smart, capable, complex man who constantly surprised me. A man who saw something in me that I had never seen in myself.

I blew out a breath. What was it Ripper had said? Our old lives were over. Everything had changed. To survive in the new world we'd have to do things we never saw coming and make choices we never expected.

What kind of life did I want to build for myself, and who did I want to share it with?

I stood, slipped my arms into the sleeves of the robe and looped the belt around my waist. The bottom hem dragged on the floor as I opened the bathroom door and marched resolutely into the living room.

Ripper dropped the magazine he was reading onto the coffee table. He slowly rose to his feet.

"You need something, Mac?"

"Yes." My heart was hammering. "You."

EIGHTEEN

Kenzie

Ripper covered the distance between us in two unhurried steps. He brushed a loose strand of hair from my face and cupped my jaw.

"You sure, Mac?"

"Yes." Then to lend weight to my words, I loosened the tie at my waist and allowed the robe to slip from my shoulders.

I'd never been this brazen with a man I barely knew, but new world, new rules.

His gaze swept over my body and he offered a slow, lazy smile. With stunning abruptness, Ripper seized my right wrist. Bending forward, he hoisted me onto his shoulder. The movement knocked the breath from my lungs. I scarcely managed to inhale again before he kicked open the door to his bedroom. He deposited me, breathless and shaken, on his bed while he stood over me, his face inscrutable.

For one heart-stopping moment I imagined that this was the face his enemies saw before he made his move, a face at once dispassionate and calculating. Did they feel as I did now, frozen in time and place, while Ripper weighed his options and decided his course of action?

This stillness, this sense of time suspended, was illusory.

Scarcely had I drawn a second breath before Ripper moved. I blinked. One moment, Ripper was standing at the side of the bed, the next, he straddled my hips, capturing both my hands in one large fist.

"Hmmm..." The impossibly drawn-out sound raised the hairs on the back of my neck.

Ripper tilted his head to one side, a speculative gleam in his eye. The smile that finally crossed his face would have assuaged my anxiety more if I was certain that it signaled goodwill and not triumph.

The smile lingered as his free hand began to explore my body, skimming over my arms, breasts, and belly before returning to my face.

"Close your eyes," he murmured, pressing with gentle insistence against my lids. His weight shifted as he leaned forward and kissed each eye, rewarding me for my compliance. "Hold still."

He released my hands so that I was no longer physically constrained, but I remained immobile, a voluntary prisoner to his will. Odd that I would cede control to Ripper in such a fashion.

Kyle once suggested that we experiment with bondage, and I had bristled with indignation. Fantasy is one thing, but in real life no right-thinking woman would give a man that kind of power over her.

Maybe I'd been overly sensitive and too hasty in my refusal. If the power truly was mine, I could chose to give it away and then to take it back again. It was mine absolutely, to do with as I pleased, and it pleased me now to comply with Ripper's orders.

I slipped obediently, but regretfully, into darkness.

Submission cost me the sight of Ripper's face as he bent over me, his beautiful eyes gleaming in the dim light. Submission always exacted a price, but maybe the benefits would outweigh the losses, as my other senses flowered in response to visual deprivation.

A glorious torment, to lie motionless and blind, awaiting Ripper's touch. My chest rose and fell, my breathing rapid and shallow. It was impossible to draw enough air into my lungs. Every molecule of my body hummed with anticipation. My skin felt charged with electricity, as if it could shock on contact.

I heard him undress. The thud as his boots hit the floor, the sound of jeans sliding down his legs, and his shirt sailing across the room. He finished stripping, and once again silence reigned.

A footstep. The bed dipped from his weight.

At last. I sighed with pleasure as his hands once again found my face, skimming over my eyes and nose, teasing apart my lips, sliding along the edge of my teeth.

Impulsively, I closed my lips around his fingertip and sucked the whole finger past my lips, trapping it between my tongue and the roof of my mouth. I bit Ripper's knuckle, holding his finger fast in its warm, wet prison.

"Unh-unh-unh," he warned, laughter in his voice. He dragged his finger out between my clenched teeth.

Why was he complaining? Had he told me not to bite?

A defiant expression must have crossed my face. Either that, or Ripper possessed an unsuspected talent for mind reading.

"Mac," he said, the word a reproach.

I smiled, a mutinous smile meant to betray not a hint of contrition.

All thoughts of defiance vanished when his mouth descended upon mine.

His lips brushed over mine once, twice, three times. His teeth gently caught my lower lip, nibbling at it and drawing it slowly into his mouth. He deepened the kiss, the tip of his tongue sliding along the inside of my upper lip before swirling over the tip of my tongue. Ripper sucked, imprisoning my tongue as I had imprisoned his finger, but unlike him, I made no attempt to escape.

Clenching his hands in my hair, he tilted my face back and forth while he rained kisses on my cheeks, eyes, and temples. His teeth sketched a chain of bites along my jaw from chin to ear. Latching onto that ticklish spot beneath my ear, he flicked his tongue against the hypersensitive skin. Forming a seal with his lips, he sucked hard. Capillaries exploded with a slight sting.

That will leave a mark. I smiled with satisfaction.

Ripper fingered the spot, then pressed my chin up, urging me to bare my throat to his attentions. From jaw to collarbone, the flats of his hands stroked up and down, and finally came to a rest spanning the column of my neck.

A disquieting pause. The moment stretched on, and my intellect waged war with my intuition. Was I crazy to lie still, pliant and trusting, while a man capable of great violence, a man I'd known for less than a week, wrapped his hands around my throat.

No sooner did the question arise than I rejected it. I knew in my heart that Ripper meant me no harm.

Not fear, but curiosity, led me to open my eyes and look at his face.

Eyes closed, forehead furrowed, with a crinkle between his brows, he looked for a moment as if he were lost in thought. His fingers began to tap against my throat, keeping time with some unheard rhythm. With a start, I realized what he was doing. His hands rested below my jaw, over my carotid artery. As my pulse reverberated through his fingertips, he drummed in time with my heartbeat.

From what I knew of Ripper's past, he fully understood how fragile humans were, how tenuous and temporary our grip on life. The flu pandemic had brought that knowledge home to everyone. Yet here, beneath his hands, my steady pulse offered proof of the life force within me.

The ominous silence signified nothing. I saw not a killer reverting to type, not a callous criminal rising true to form, but a man marveling at his connection with another human being.

It felt indecent to intrude at such an unguarded moment. I closed my eyes again before Ripper caught me spying on him.

The bed creaked when he stretched out next to me. I held my breath as his fingers played along my collarbone, slipping into that half-moon notch that marked its center, before trailing down between my breasts to my belly.

Where fingers led, mouth followed. Swirling against the hollow at the base of my throat, his tongue began its journey. A similar act marked its journey's conclusion, as the tip of his tongue delved into my naval.

Perfect symmetry. I smiled.

As Ripper kissed my mouth again, his fingertips sketched circles on my stomach. With exquisite slowness, his fingers scratched lightly over my skin, venturing near, but never quite touching the tangle of curls at the apex of my thighs.

Did Ripper intend to tease me into madness?

An unholy fire kindled in my breasts, a wildly pulsating flame that seared a path from my nipples to my sex.

I almost sobbed with gratitude when his mouth descended on my breast, his tongue flicking against my nipple. Good, but something about this man made me crave more intense sensation. I arched my back and filled my lungs with air, swelling my breasts and encouraging him to play rough.

Ripple chuckled as he responded to my silent importuning. Capturing my nipple between his teeth, he bit, lightly at first, then harder, as a moan signaled my pleasure. He rolled my other nipple between his fingers, twisting and elongating the tip.

His touch shattered my resolve and undermined my compliance. Memory and thought, all my cognitive processes, unraveled under the demands of my body to see, touch, and taste Ripper. When his hand finally slipped between my legs, the battle was lost.

Defiant at last, my eyes flew open, and I reached for Ripper, my nails digging into his shoulders. He lifted his head and met my eyes.

"There you are." His fingers glided along the slick and swollen folds. "Took you long enough."

"What?" My lust-addled voice sounded sleepy to my ears.

"Took you long enough," he repeated, a devilish gleam in his eyes.

Understanding dawned. "You were trying to make me open my eyes," I sputtered, stunned by how much I had misunderstood him. He wasn't seeking submission. He was pushing me to assert myself.

"Always do what you're told?" He continued his relentless stimulation of my sex.

I gasped as his finger brushed over my clit. Ripper raised his brows, his expression guileless.

It wasn't fair. He neatly circumvented any argument. How could I argue with a man whose hands were pushing me closer and closer to a carnal frenzy?

"You're a shit, Ripper," My head fell back against the bed.

Smiling, he lowered his head and nuzzled my throat. He nibbled and licked a line from my collarbone to my ear, then seized my earlobe between his teeth.

"Hmmm." He rumbled against my ear, the vibrations penetrating to the bone. "Never claimed to be Prince Charming."

True enough, but I was way too old to believe in fairy tales. I reached for Ripper and pulled his face to mine.

"And I'm no princess."

No longer constrained by any promise to hold still, I kissed him with eager abandon and shamelessly opened my legs to his hand. A bone-deep trembling seized me as my body opened itself to the flood of sensations his touch engendered.

With unerring precision his finger circled round and round my swollen clit, while his mouth swooped down on my hypersensitive nipple.

I held fast to his head and drew in a deep, shuddering breath as an orgasm crashed down on me with the suddenness and force of a tsunami. A guttural groan that I barely recognized as my own voice was torn from my throat. I bucked against Ripper's hand, gasping with surprise.

It couldn't be that easy. Kyle was no fumbling dud in bed—give credit where credit is due—but it always took me a while to get there, which, looking back, probably said more about me than him. With Ripper there was no frustrating advance and retreat of sensation while I inched my way to orgasm. I went off like a rocket.

Shaking my head from side to side, I laughed with amazement.

A full minute passed before I realized that Ripper was oddly silent. Lifting my head, I met his eyes.

He arched a brow. "Something funny?"

He couldn't possibly think I was laughing at him, could he? I sat up on my knees, but as I studied his wounded expression, guilt gave way to suspicion.

"Cause I'm a sensitive man," Ripper said with a straight face. "And laughter at such a time could damage my fragile ego."

That clinched it.

I pounced, propelling him backward onto the bed and pinning his hands above his head.

"You truly are a shit."

He continued as if I hadn't spoken. "If only there was something you could do to take my mind off my emotional distress."

"You are shameless." I knelt between his legs. "Absolutely shameless."

And absolutely magnificent. Smooth and flawless tanned skin covered his achingly beautiful form, skin that invited an admiring caress. I imagined my fingers exploring all the curves and hollows of his body. The dark clefts on his throat and incised pectorals. The shadowed impressions that separated his heavily muscled shoulders from his biceps, his biceps from his triceps.

I sighed. Ripper was breathtaking. Spectacular. Godlike.

A blush crept up my cheeks.

Get a grip. I'm acting like a giddy sixteen-year-old.

Through half-closed eyes he watched me ogle him. From his smirk, I suspected that he could read the nature of my thoughts. Too bad. Nothing wrong with a little honest lust. Nothing at all.

Tilting my head to one side, I contemplated what to do next. I tapped my finger to my lips, in no hurry to satisfy his curiosity about my intentions. Finally, with a half smile, I leaned over his chest.

As I lowered my mouth to his stomach, Ripper closed his eyes. "Just...don't...hurt...me."

I rocked back on my heels and glowered at him in mock rage. "You are the most aggravating man." I balled my fists and pummeled his stomach.

He allowed me to land two punches, then, in a lightning move, he captured both fists and yanked. I landed heavily on top of him, my face hovering just above his.

His fingers still wrapped around my clenched fists, he pulled one hand to his mouth and kissed my knuckles. "Play nice," he warned, his voice a shiver-inducing growl.

I didn't reply. Instead, I lowered my head and kissed his chin with a mouth so soft and yielding that his stubble scraped the delicate tissue of my inner lips. Whisker burn. I could get addicted to that.

"Mmm..." I sighed with pleasure as my lips blazed a path down his neck to his chest. I pressed open-mouthed kisses over his pecs and stomach, occasionally nipping at his sleek skin. My cheek grazed his belly as my tongue sought his naval. I bit the thin skin on the underside of the puckered dent, catching a short, black hair between my front teeth. I tugged, eliciting a grunt of surprise from Ripper.

Smiling against his skin, I nibbled down the narrow line of hairs, working my way toward the dark triangle at its base. The hairs tickled my lips as I blew warm, moist air onto the springy curls. I closed my eyes, savoring the moment as I breathed in his scent.

Ripper's fingers brushed over the back of my head and tangled in my hair. Pressing gently, but insistently, he urged my mouth lower.

I raised my eyes to his face. "Unh-unh-unh," I admonished, repeating his earlier warning.

He groaned and flashed a rueful smile, his words come back to haunt him.

I rose onto my knees and trailed my fingers over his stomach while I considered my next move.

Ripper arched his hips, flaunting a gloriously erect cock and making abundantly clear his suggestion for what I could do.

I ignored him.

Holding my body well above his straining groin, I supported my weight on my hands and rubbed my cheeks over his chest. My lips found a flat nipple and sucked it, flicking my tongue against the hard nub. As I sucked, I brushed my breasts across his belly, their diamond-hard tips signaling my own arousal.

Self-interest as much as compassion led me to relent and turn my attention to his cock.

Sitting back on my heels, I took it in my hands.

Lord have mercy, it was a thing of beauty. I stroked the paper thin skin stretched shiny and taut over the engorged organ. A tracery of veins ran just beneath the skin, pliant to the touch but springing defiantly back as soon as I lifted my fingertip. I ran my thumb across the acorn-shaped head and the sensitive ridge beneath it.

Hard to believe that an organ with such presence, such potential, could spend most of its existence curled limply against a man's groin. No wonder men found their erections to be such marvels. I would if I were a man.

Our old, familiar world might be falling apart, but life still held moments of beauty, of human connection. Not everything could be lost. My eyes welled with tears of gratitude.

"Mac." Ripper's voice pierced my thoughts. "What's wrong?"

"Nothing's wrong," I said, wiping my eyes with the back of a hand. "Hasn't the sight of your cock ever moved a woman to tears before?"

Well, that was the truth, even if it wasn't the entire truth.

I lowered my gaze demurely, then peeked to see if he bought my explanation.

Ripper's face was transparent, his expression easy to read. Frowning, he ran my words over in his mind. He pursed his lips, tilted his head to one side and shrugged, acknowledging the veracity of it.

God's in his heaven; all's right with the world.

Men! I dropped my head so he wouldn't see the laughter in my eyes. My downcast gaze focused once again on the object in question, a thing at once the source of my awe and the fount of my humor.

It twitched. I closed my eyes and bit my lip, stifling a giggle.

I inhaled, determined to regain my composure.

I bent forward and rubbed my face along the length of his shaft, luxuriating in the sensation of silky skin sliding beneath my cheek. I nuzzled the nest of dark curls, flooding my open mouth with the taste and scent of his arousal. My tongue fluttered along the underside of the shaft, from base to tip before swirling over the head.

I filled my lungs with air and slid Ripper's cock into my mouth, pausing when the tip struck the back of my throat. Willing my muscles to go slack, I pivoted my head and rippled my tongue, drawing his shade in deeper. I gagged once and panicked, but recovered. Little by little, my lips inched toward the base of his cock.

A lack of air brought my effort up short. Lungs bursting, eyes watering, I reluctantly pulled back. I leaned my cheek on Ripper's thigh, dragging in a deep breath.

"Fuuuuck," Ripper groaned.

A simple interjection, but I chose to misunderstand it.

"Soon," I promised.

Hands gripped my upper arms and hauled me over the top of Ripper's body. He grinned up at me. "I'm thinking now."

"Were you?" I dropped my head and bit his lower lip.

"Yeah." He dragged his lip out from between my teeth and kissed me, gently at first. Deepening the kiss, he pierced my mouth with his tongue and wrestled me over onto my back.

I shifted, ready for him, but instead of positioning himself between my legs, he rolled off. He pawed through his nightstand drawer and pulled out a condom.

I leaned up on my elbows.

"I have a birth control implant," I said quickly, pointing to a matchstick sized lump under the skin of my upper arm. "No babies for me for the next two years. And I had a complete physical a few months ago, after I broke up with my boyfriend. There's...um...absolutely nothing to worry about."

"Got tested a couple of months ago, myself," Ripper said. "I'm clean." He smiled, palming his rigid cock. "You telling me I can go bareback?"

"Yes." I glanced at his erection, glad to see the conversation hadn't caused his interest to...um...lag. I licked my lips, my body humming with anticipation.

"Come here," he growled.

Without waiting for a response, he slipped his hands under my hips and pulled me to the edge of the bed. Seizing my ankles, he lifted my feet to his shoulders, His hands gripped my ass and tugged, lifting my sex toward his cock.

He paused, as if relishing the final moment before consummation. A slight smile touched his lips as his fingers probed my slick wetness. With exaggerated care, he spread my moisture on the head of his cock, then raised his hand to his mouth and licked the residue from his fingers.

Good God. Amazing how such a simple act could evoke such a visceral response.

We had danced around this moment long enough, teasing and tantalizing each other as we drew closer to sexual culmination. There was no help for it. Either Ripper fucked me right now, or I would be reduced to blithering madness.

The world fell away. Nothing existed beyond this place and this moment, a universe bounded by what I could see, hear, taste, smell, and feel. At the heart of this new universe, the glowing sun, the sine qua non, stood Ripper, whose scorching touch shattered me into a million tiny pieces.

"Mac...Mac."

He leaned forward, brushed a strand of damp hair from my cheek, and captured my face between his large hands.

"Look at me."

I gathered my scattered thoughts and focused my gaze on him.

"Look at me," he repeated. "I want to look into your eyes when I fuck you."

I nodded, we locked eyes, and I drew in a deep breath and held it as he pressed the head of his cock against my aching core. His hands curled around my hips.

Time stood still again. The image of Ripper's face—contorted with passion as he drove his cock into me—imprinted onto my memory.

I gasped, rocked by the force of his rapid incursion. With my ankles resting on his shoulders, there was no retreat from the sensation, no safe ground, no shifting back from the pounding. Ripper fucked like a man too long deprived, a monk crazed with lust and longing who abandons his vows in an orgy of carnal indulgence.

After the initial shock, I relaxed, raising my hips to meet his thrusts. Good. Good. So good, I wanted even more.

I slid my legs down his arms until my knees caught in the crooks of his elbows, and my hands scrabbled across his stomach as I reached for him.

He leaned over me and nibbled at a nipple, then rasped his chin stubble over the tip.

I pulled his head to my breast, encouraging him to bite, then sobbed with pleasure when his mouth clamped down hard.

No part of me escaped unscathed from this sensual conflagration. Ripper's hands roved my body, each touch a brand. I consumed his with an equal passion, losing all sense of time as we pillaged each other's bodies.

When I felt the stirrings of impending orgasm, I turned in Ripper's arms and lifted my face to his. "I'm close. Let me see you when I come."

Color suffused Ripper's face, and a vein in his forehead stood out prominently. He'd held off his own orgasm, but now he pumped ferociously into me, as if trying to beat me to the mark.

"Oh-God-oh-God-oh-God," I groaned, the stimulation pushing me to the edge. I flushed, my eyes widening. My body arched and went rigid before convulsing in a spine-shattering orgasm. I was so lost in my own pleasure that I was only dimly aware of Ripper crying out and shuddering against me.

I collapsed onto the bed. Spots danced before my eyes and a rushing sound filled my ears, but as my pulse slowed and my lungs filled with air, the world spun back into focus. Turning my head weakly, I glanced at Ripper, who was sprawled beside me in a similar state.

I grinned. "Wow."

Ripper reached over, twined his fingers through mine, and pulled my hand to his lips for a kiss. Sighing happily, I lifted our linked hands, twisting them around as I studied the sight of my small hand engulfed by his huge one.

"You have very good hands, you know. Wonderful, talented hands."

Ripper snorted.

I let go and sat up on my knees. I needed him to hear me, to believe me. "No, I mean it. Good hands." Leaning over him, I seized both of his wrists and turned his palms up. "Beautiful hands." I stroked his long, tapering fingers. "Wise hands." I smiled, remembering what those hands could do. I kissed the tip of each finger, one after the other.

"A killer's hands. You know that, right?" Ripper asked quietly.

I straightened and met his eyes. He wasn't talking about his time as a Ranger, I suspected. He was asking me if I could live with whatever violent, clandestine acts he'd committed as a Janissary.

"I don't expect that you'll ever tell me what you've done for the club, but I believe that the people you...*dealt with*...had opted in, that they knew the risks they were taking when they crossed you," I said, choosing my words carefully. "The man I see when I look at you has a moral center, a brave and loyal heart." I wrapped my fingers around both of his large hands and held them fast. "If you're asking me if I know that these are a killer's hands, yeah, I do. But they're also a lover's hands, hands that give pleasure as skillfully as they take life. So, if you don't object, or even if you do, I'm going to stick with my original contention. These are good hands."

Ripper extracted his hands from mine and pulled my head to his chest. I sighed sleepily and snuggled against him. He was silent for a long time, and my eyes grew heavy waiting for him to reply.

At last, Ripper pressed a kiss to my forehead. "Thank you. Now go to sleep."

A furious pounding startled us into wakefulness. Ripper was already on his feet, reaching into his nightstand drawer for a gun.

"Stay here," he ordered, cracking open the bedroom door and peering into the dark hallway and beyond.

I sat up in bed, clutching a blanket to my chest, while I waited for him to return.

"It's Miles," he said a minute later. "Something's got him all worked up." He sat on the edge of the bed and pulled on his jeans and boots. He pointed to the bathroom. "Get your clothes on fast."

I scrambled from the bed and dashed into the bathroom, throwing on my jeans, tee, and sneakers. By the time I emerged, Miles and Ripper were deep in conversation.

"There's a man at the gate." Miles bounced on the balls of his feet. His voice wavered, and he had trouble getting the words out. "He keeps ringing the buzzer. He won't go away. I don't know what to do."

"It's all right, Miles," Ripper said easily. "I'll take care of it." He shrugged his cut on over his bare chest, then glanced at Miles and me. "Let's go."

We followed him through the gate and into the house. The security monitor revealed the source of Miles's distress.

A man wearing a baseball cap stood at the front gate, punching the buzzer.

"See!" Miles said. "Why won't he go away?"

The man took a few steps back from the sliding door, and the motion sensitive camera panned to follow the movement. Hands on his hips, clearly frustrated, he tilted back his head to survey the fence.

"Can you zoom in on his face?" I asked, my voice shaking.

Miles adjusted something and the man's face swam into view.

"Oh my God," I whispered, sitting down hard on the desk chair.

Ripper squeezed my shoulder. "Mac? You know him? Who is it?"

I nodded. "That's Kyle. My ex-boyfriend."

NINETEEN

Kyle

Last Sunday

Not ten miles outside of Portland, Ali began to make noises about needing a bathroom break. I loved the girl, but her bladder had to be the size of a walnut. She was never shy about demanding that Jake stop to let her pee, no matter how inconvenient it was or how late we were running.

Jake drummed on the steering wheel with his fingers, his frustration palpable. He wanted to put some distance between us and the city before taking a break, he'd said. And we both knew that Ali often insisted on stopping as a sort of preemptive strike, taking care of business before the urge got too strong. She could hold it if she wanted to, if she was properly motivated, that is.

I tapped on her shoulder to get her attention.

"Tell you what," I said. "If you can wait until the first freeway rest stop, we don't have to take turns riding shotgun."

Ali hated riding in the backseat of the pickup. Logic suggested a simple transaction—give the girl something she wanted in exchange for something that would make Jake's life easier. Least I could do for my closest friend.

"Okay. I'll try to hold it." She flopped back in the seat and started messing with her phone again.

Jake flashed me a grateful smile in the rearview mirror, and I gave him a thumbs up.

Things appeared more or less normal as we headed east on I-84, although the traffic was heavier than usual for a Sunday. Traveling back and forth between home and school, we'd made the drive dozens of times over the past couple of years.

To our left, the Columbia River flowed to the sea. To our right, the hills and rocky outcroppings of the Columbia Gorge jutted into the sky. It was supposed to be one of the most scenic drives in the country, but I was past being impressed by waterfalls and trees. In my case, familiarity bred not contempt, but indifference.

After about an hour, Ali started up again. "I really need to pee." She poked Jake in the arm. "I mean it this time."

He pointed to a road sign. "Rest stop coming up in two miles."

As he exited the freeway, we saw our first clear evidence that something unusual was going on. The parking lot was packed, even the section reserved for big rigs. People milled around, many of them wearing jury-rigged face masks, T-shirts or scarves tied around their mouths. As if a simple band of fabric could keep the killer flu virus at bay.

A few of the cars had signs in the back window: *Gas Wanted.* A couple of the signs revealed a new twist on the old gas war, the price going up instead of down. *Will pay $20 per gallon.* Scratched out. *Will pay $30 per gallon.*

Jesus, people were desperate. Looked like a whole bunch of them fled the city without a destination or a real plan. They would have been better off sticking it out at home instead of taking off on such a half-assed journey.

I threw my jacket on top of our gas cans, in case anybody got the bright idea to peek inside the window and check out what we had.

"I'm not getting out here," Ali announced, craning her neck to look at the crowd.

"Nope," Jake agreed.

He followed the ramp back onto the freeway, then after a couple of miles, eased the truck onto the shoulder.

"What are you doing?" Ali asked.

"Potty break," Jake replied, using one of Ali's preferred phrases.

"I'm not peeing on the side of the road."

"It's either that, or you hold it till we reach Boise. And we both know that's not happening." Jake hopped out of the pickup, rounded the front and opened her door. "The door will block the view from the front. I'll get your nap blanket out of the back and hold it up so nobody can see you, then you can squat down over the gravel."

"If I squat down over the gravel, people will be able to see my ass hanging out from under the door."

"All right." He sighed, rubbing his forehead. "Kyle, will you stand in front of the door so your legs will block the view from the front?"

"Sure." I climbed out and joined him on the side of the truck.

Ali jumped down, frowning. "You suck," she said to Jake.

He kissed her cheek. "I don't suck. The situation sucks. I'm your Prince Charming, remember?"

Her grumpy demeanor vanished, and she grinned. "Yeah. You are. Just make sure Kyle is facing the other way."

Seriously? Like I'd get off watching her piss on some rocks?

We got as far as The Dalles, a little shy of one hundred miles from Portland, before everything started to go south.

"Fuck, man, my head hurts too much to keep driving," Jake said. "You mind taking over?"

His skin looked pasty, and he squinted against the sunlight. Good thing Kenzie left the Ibuprofen with us. I dug the pain pills out of the backpack and handed them to Jake, along with a bottle of water.

"Shouldn't have drunk so much beer last night," he moaned.

We'd canceled the party, but the temptation of an untapped keg had proved too much to resist. Two glasses were enough for me, but Jake got shit-faced and passed out on the sofa.

We traded places. Ali tucked her nap blanket over his shoulders, and within minutes he zoned out. Ali scooted in next to him. She looked beat.

"Why don't you take a nap," I said. "I'll wake you when we get close to home."

She nodded and leaned against Jake's shoulder, balling up her hoodie to use as a pillow. Within minutes, I heard her snoring.

I smiled to myself. Ali indignantly insisted that she didn't snore and said that Jake and I were liars when we claimed she did. I thought about recording the sound to play back to her later, but decided to be a nice guy and let the opportunity to prove her wrong pass.

It was just me and my thoughts as we continued east toward home. I pulled off at one of the truck stops, thinking it might be good to fill up on gas while we had the chance, saving the cans for a later day. The lines were crazy, so I abandoned the notion. Jake and Ali slept through the stops and starts when I left the freeway and then quickly returned.

I drove in silence past the small towns that dotted I-84 and was approaching Boardman when I heard Jake retching.

I swerved onto the side of the road and stopped the truck before turning around to look at my friend. His eyes were open, but glassy, and a bright red flush stained his cheeks. His chest heaved as if he were about to puke. The retching sound should have woken Ali, but she slept on. They both looked like shit.

Fuck.

I remembered a history professor telling the class that when the plague struck Europe in the 1300s, people would go to bed feeling fine and wake up dead, so to speak. The disease could strike that fast. Jake and Ali had been fine when we started the trip, but they must have been carrying the flu virus like some sneaky stowaway.

Jake continued to retch.

I jumped out of the driver's seat and threw open the passenger door, helping him lean out of the car just before he puked. I dodged the worst of it, then handed him a bottle of water to rinse out his mouth.

"Sorry, man," he muttered.

"Don't worry about it." I tried to keep the panic out of my voice.

I glanced at Ali. The commotion had finally roused her from her sleep. Dark circles had formed under her eyes, and her face was pinched.

She rubbed her eyes and looked at Jake with alarm. "Baby, what's wrong?"

"Too much beer last night," he mumbled. He closed his eyes, and soon his head lolled against the seat back.

Ali and I exchanged glances, and I saw fear in her eyes.

"Kyle, how about we look for a motel, so Jake can sleep it off."

Was she thinking what I was thinking? That we couldn't show up at our parents' doorsteps—assuming they had escaped the contagion so far—with a flu victim in tow?

"How about you? How are you feeling, sweetheart?" I asked in a low voice.

Jake was out of it, but I didn't want to risk agitating him if he heard that Ali was sick.

"My head hurts, shit, my whole body hurts...but at least I don't have to pee."

Cracking a joke under the circumstances, when she had to know that she and Jake likely had the flu. My heart squeezed. I loved them both so fucking much, and if they had any chance of surviving this, I'd make it happen.

"I got this," I told her. "We're less than fifty miles from Pendleton. I know a place there. Close your eyes and try to rest, okay?"

"Okay." Her chin trembled and her throat worked as she swallowed back her fear. She patted Jake's face, then wrapped an arm over his chest and curled against him.

Nope. This love story wasn't going to have an unhappy ending, not if I had anything to say about it. I jumped into the driver's seat and took off, gunning the engine to ninety.

Pendleton was a big rodeo town, and for some reason my father had fallen in love with the spectacle. The man was born in Detroit. He'd never been on a horse in his life, but every September he slapped a cowboy hat on his head and family in tow, spent a happy week at the Pendleton Round-Up.

Kenzie met my parents for the first time last September when she accompanied me to the mandatory family vacation. The introduction hadn't gone well.

Mom said something to ruffle Kenzie's feathers. Mom was always saying something to ruffle somebody's feathers.

She proudly displayed both a bumper sticker and a refrigerator magnet that said *Everybody is entitled to my opinion.*

They patched things over and were painfully polite, but I could tell that they didn't really like each other.

Mom refused to stay at a "tacky" western-themed hotel, so every year my parents rented a five-bedroom house in a good neighborhood. Mrs. Malcolm, the widow who owned it, had moved into a small apartment over her garage, and she rented out the big house for corporate retreats and luxury family vacations. Dad paid top dollar to guarantee that our family had dibs on the house during every Round-Up, and he always left a pile of hundreds on the kitchen counter as a thank you tip.

I navigated the truck to Mrs. Malcolm's place, praying that the big house was vacant. Nobody would rent to people showing symptoms of the flu, so I had no chance of getting Jake and Ali into a motel.

The big house had a private entrance. With any luck I could pull the truck up to the door and sneak Jake and Ali in. It would be a crappy thing to do to the old lady, but I was sure Dad would pay to have the place sterilized afterward.

Ringing the doorbell to the garage apartment, I glanced round for any evidence of guests. No other cars occupied the driveway, which was a good sign.

After several minutes of my insistent ringing, the door cracked open and Mrs. Malcolm peered out, her face wan and haggard.

Shit, she was coming down with the flu, too.

"Hello, ma'am," I said with a polite smile. "I'm Kyle Chamberlain. My family rents the big house during every Round-Up."

She clung to the door frame. "Yes, I remember you, Kyle."

"I'm driving back home and need a place to stay for the night. All the motels in town are full, so I was hoping to rent the big house."

She frowned. "Why don't you just keep driving? It's not late."

Good question. Thinking quickly, I said, "I'm running low on gas. The lines at the stations are a mile long. I thought I'd spend the night, then get up early to get in line for gas before the stations reopen."

That explanation wouldn't stand up to much scrutiny. People would park overnight in line for gas if they were desperate, but maybe that wouldn't occur to her.

She appeared torn. I kept my expression pleasant and my tone easy. I had to approach this like another simple transaction. What did the woman value? What did she want?

"I'm sure my father will be very grateful that you came to my assistance when I was in a jam. He always remembers people who go out of their way to help the family."

When she hesitated I pressed on.

I pulled out my wallet and held up my American Express card. "I just want to get home safely to my parents. I'll pay double the going rate for the house."

There, an appeal to both her sympathy and her greed.

"Well, I don't know, Kyle. I was planning to have the carpet cleaned after the last people made such a mess, and I'm feeling a little under the weather. I'm not sure I'm up to cleaning up after you."

I bit back my frustration. "Don't worry about the carpet, ma'am. I don't care about it. All I care about is spending the night in a safe and familiar place. With all that's going on, I'd be afraid to sleep in my truck. And I promise I won't make a mess. You'll hardly be able to tell I was there. Please, Mrs. Malcolm." I offered what Kenzie called my panty-dropping smile and waved my AmEx card under her nose. "And remember, I'll pay double for your trouble."

"All right." She took a key from a hook inside the door. "You can let yourself in."

"Thank you, ma'am."

I pulled the truck up to the front door of the big house. After climbing out, I fake yawned and stretched my arms above my head, trying to look like I was shaking off the stiffness from a long drive. The movement allowed me to twist around to make sure that Mrs. Malcolm wasn't watching me through the window of her apartment. The coast was clear.

I quickly unlocked the front door and dragged Jake into the house. The master bedroom was on the ground floor, and I deposited him across the bed before rushing outside to fetch Ali. I carried her in, then stripped off their shoes and pants and tucked them into the king-sized bed. Finally, I hauled in our backpacks and secured the deadbolt.

Mrs. Malcolm kept a well-stocked guest house, including individually wrapped packets of antacid and headache pills in the master bath's medicine cabinet. After filling a pitcher with filtered ice water, I maneuvered first Jake then Ali into sitting positions, held a glass to their lips, and got them to swallow pain pills and an antacid. I lowered them gently back onto their pillows then stood at the side of the bed, staring at my hands, uncertain of what else I could do to help.

I should have listened to my mom when she urged me to major in premed instead of prelaw. I might have learned some useful skills.

What could I do? I could batten down the hatches, like Grandpa used to say. The police department was likely overwhelmed answering calls from people in crisis, leaving homeowners on their own to protect their properties. The big house was a possible target for burglars or looters, especially locals who knew that its primary occupant was an elderly woman.

I made a circuit of the ground floor, inspecting every door and window lock, then I checked the windows upstairs, in case some wise guy thought to bring a ladder. If the place looked occupied, people might be less likely to break in, so I turned on all the overhead lights.

Reluctant to stray far from my friends' sides, I heated and wolfed down a can of minestrone soup.

Mrs. Malcolm had quite a racket going. The pantry was full of shelf-stable food, all conveniently priced at hotel mini-bar rates. The can of soup I ate—worth no more than two dollars at any grocery store—bore a handwritten price tag of ten dollars. I washed it down with a five-dollar can of generic cola, then returned to the master bedroom. I dragged an upholstered chair close to the bed, so I could sit and keep an eye on my friends.

Jake lay flat on his back, his mouth hanging open, his body drenched with sweat. To keep him from overheating, I pulled off all the covers except for the sheet and turned on the ceiling fan over the bed. I hoisted his dead weight up far enough that he wouldn't choke on the can of ginger ale I tipped into his mouth. Most of the liquid dribbled out over his chin, but he swallowed twice before groaning and pushing the can away.

At first I thought that Ali had a less severe case of the flu. She woke up and agreed to my suggestion that she drink some lemon-lime soda—Ali hated ginger—and then, with my assistance, she shuffled to the bathroom to pee. Afterwards, she fell asleep once again.

In the middle of the night, Ali began to thrash wildly in the sheets, as if she were fighting off some unseen assailant. I leapt to my feet and glanced at Jake, but he was sleeping so hard he looked like he was in a coma. While I stood on the side of the bed and debated whether I should try to wake Ali, her eyes flew open and she looked up at me.

"I'm sorry," she said, and her face crumpled.

I sat carefully on the edge of the bed and took her outstretched hand. Her fingers were hot and damp, and I resisted the instinctive urge to pull my hand back.

"Hey, you've got nothing to be sorry about, Ali."

She shook her head back and forth, vehemently rejecting my reassuring words, then she squeezed my hand with startling strength. "No. It was stupid of me to pitch a fit over those dumb tickets."

Tickets? What was she talking about?

Tears seeped out of the corners of her eyes. "I'm sorry, Jake. Please don't be mad."

Fucking hell. Ali thought I was Jake. My breath froze in my lungs. I'd never felt more helpless, more heartsick than I did at that moment.

"I'm sorry," she repeated. Hectic color marked her cheeks and her pillow was sodden from sweat. I touched her forehead. Damn. Ali was burning up with fever.

If ever a situation required manning up, this was it.

"It's okay, ladybug." I used Jake's nickname for her. "That thing with the tickets was no big deal. Even if I got pissed off at the time, you know I could never stay mad at my best girl."

"You promise?" She looked at me with wide hazel eyes, eyes that stared through me to see another man.

I had no clue what happened between Jake and Ali, or why this event was preying on her mind, and it didn't matter.

"I promise." I brushed damp hair away from her brow. "How about you drink some water. Will you try for me?"

She nodded and pushed herself up on trembling elbows. I wrapped my arm around her shoulders to hold her steady while I lifted a glass of water to her lips.

She managed a few swallows, her glazed eyes never leaving my face.

"I'm so tired, Jake."

"I'll get you a fresh pillow," I said, remembering that Mrs. Malcolm kept extra ones in the bedroom armoires.

I slipped a dry, clean pillow under her head and tossed the damp one into a corner.

"Better. Thanks, baby. You always take such good care of me."

I couldn't speak past the lump in my throat, so I nodded.

"Will you hold my hand while I fall asleep?"

I swallowed. "Of course I will."

I pulled the upholstered chair to her side of the bed and took Ali's hand in mine. Her eyelids drifted shut and then snapped back open, as if she remembered something important.

"I love you, Jake. I love you more than anything."

A knife twisted in my heart, and I glanced at the man who was like a brother to me. He was unconscious, his chest barely moving as he drew breath. My gaze returned to Ali and I spoke for Jake, said what I knew was in his heart, the only words that could bring her comfort.

"I love you, too, ladybug. I love you with all my heart."

Ali lapsed into a deep sleep, our fingers entwined. I held on tight, as if I could keep her with me as long as our hands touched. Eventually, exhaustion and stress got the better of me, and I sank into a heavy slumber.

When I awoke with a start in the morning, Ali's hand was cold in mine. A quick look confirmed that Jake, too, had died during the night.

Thank God they were spared the violent mania that sometimes struck near the end.

I found a shovel in the shed and dug a double grave in Mrs. Malcolm's rose garden. I couldn't think of a better place to lay my friends to rest.

Afterwards, I took a shower and put on clean clothes. I raided the pantry, loading my backpack with food and water bottles for the road. Her prices might have been exorbitant, but I tallied the cost of everything I took and left Mrs. Malcolm an IOU on the kitchen table, instructing her to call Dad's business manager to get paid for the food and lodging.

Emotionally drained, I felt disconnected from reality, as if I were watching everything from a distance.

Jake dead. Ali dead. The full impact would hit me sooner or later, but right now I carried out my tasks with calm detachment.

Hanging over my head was the likelihood that I'd get sick, too. You'd think I would have developed symptoms by now. Maybe I was immune. Maybe I was just a carrier. Maybe the virus took a different course in different people, and symptoms would develop days later.

I knew what to watch for. Headache, sensitivity to light, lethargy, fever. If I came down with the flu, I'd stay the hell away from everybody and find a quiet spot to curl up in. Until then, I'd move forward as if I still had a future.

Time to make a decision. I could continue to Boise and reunite with my family. They had generators, fuel, food, and water, everything they needed to ride out the pandemic. They lived in relative isolation, safe behind the walls of a gated community. With a little luck, they would be fine.

Thoughts of Jake and Ali rose to the fore once again. They had loved each other, and the flu stole their chance for a life together. I'd lost Kenzie, and I still didn't understand what went wrong, why she left me. Angry, hurt, and proud, I'd never demanded an explanation. I'd respected her decision. Maybe that was a mistake. Maybe I'd blown my chance at a happily ever after. Life and love were precious and fragile. Jake and Ali's fate had taught me that.

Kenzie was alone in Portland with her prepper cousin while a flu pandemic raged.

The decision wasn't so hard after all. I was going back to Portland to try to work things out with Kenzie. I slung the backpack over my shoulder and pulled the keys to Jake's truck from my pocket. Now that I had decided on a course of action, I couldn't wait to get started. I locked the front door behind me and took two steps toward the driveway before I stopped in my tracks.

The truck was gone.

TWENTY

Kyle

I couldn't blame the people who drove right past me as I trudged west along the freeway, my thumb stuck out to ask for a ride. Who could expect a stranger to risk exposing himself to the flu or to a man who might be desperate and dangerous? It's illegal to hitchhike on a freeway, so clearly I was willing to break the law. Still, with more than two hundred miles separating Pendleton from Portland, it was worthwhile to try to get a ride.

Even in late spring, a couple of months before the high desert heat kicked in, carrying a backpack filled with food and water was hot work, especially since the freeway had a steep uphill grade heading out of town.

Yeah, dripping with sweat and illegally hitchhiking, I couldn't wonder why people sailed on by.

How long would it take to walk two hundred miles? No idea. I was in good shape. I worked out at the gym three times a week. It might take four or five days to walk to Portland, assuming I didn't run into trouble along the way.

I'd look for water at the next town, but if I couldn't find any, I'd have to ration my supply. If I stumbled across a motel that by some miracle was still open, would I be able to rent aroom? Looking the way I did, probably not, which meant I'd have to sleep somewhere on the side of the road.

I cast a wary eye at the arid, hilly landscape. Are their rattlesnakes in eastern Oregon? I had no clue. I was a city boy. Dad suggested once that we take a family vacation to a dude ranch in Montana. Mom fixed him with a death stare. We spent two weeks at a spa resort in Thailand, instead. Roughing it was not part of my skill set, and I definitely didn't want to cozy up with a rattlesnake.

I heard another car approaching, and I turned to face oncoming traffic, flashing an *I'm a nice guy* smile as I waggled my thumb at the red sedan that whizzed past. I tried the friendly smile on the next two cars and again, they blew by me with barely a sideways glance. I didn't bother to turn around for the next approaching vehicle.

A black pickup towing a horse trailer pulled onto the shoulder a hundred yards ahead of me. Somebody actually stopped. Staring at it in disbelief, it took a good ten seconds before my brain relayed the message to my feet. I jogged to the truck, my heavy backpack swaying with each step. A horse whinnied as I ran past the trailer.

Silver letters on the driver's door spelled out the name *Valhalla Ranch.*

The driver examined me through the side window, probably trying to decide if I was sick or dangerous. I smiled slightly and nodded at him through the glass, trying to appear healthy and harmless. Finally, he rolled down the window.

"You looking for a ride?"

"I sure would appreciate one," I said, studying him in return. My potential Good samaritan looked to be a few years older than me, somewhere in his midtwenties. His sun-bleached blond hair and deep tan told me that he spent a lot of time outdoors. The callouses on the hand gripping the steering wheel and the ropes of muscle in his forearm spoke of hard physical labor.

"You an ax murderer?" he asked.

"No. You?"

"Nope." He offered a slow smile. "Well, now that we've cleared that up, I suppose you might as well get in." He leaned over to open the front passenger door.

"Hold on." My conscience got the better of me. It'd be a dick move to meet this guy's generosity with self-serving deception. "I've got to be honest with you, man. I was traveling with some friends. They got sick and died. I've been exposed to the virus."

"I appreciate the warning, but unless you've been holed up in some cabin in the woods, you've been exposed to the flu. Climb on in."

I slung my backpack onto the rear bench seat and settled into the front, sighing with pleasure when a cool air-conditioned breeze blew across my overheated face.

"Cold drinks in the cooler in the back," the stranger said. "Help yourself."

He didn't have to offer twice. I twisted around and raised the lid on the old red and white cooler. At least a dozen cans of soda and beer were nestled in a bed of half-melted ice.

My hand paused over a can of pale ale. I'd give anything for a cold beer, but since it's against the law to have an open alcoholic beverage in a moving vehicle, I reached for a cola.

"If you want a beer, take a beer. Haven't seen a police car all day."

With one sentence, he graduated from Good samaritan to guardian angel. I snatched up the pale ale and collapsed back in my seat, watching the beads of moisture drip down the side of the can. I'd never looked forward to a beer more in my life.

"Thanks, man." I popped the top and took a long pull. "My name's Kyle."

"Bjorn," he said, steering the pickup back onto the freeway. "But most people call me Bear."

"Thanks for taking a chance on a stranger, Bear."

He inclined his head, silently acknowledging my thanks. "Where you heading, Kyle?"

"My friends and I were going home to Boise when they got sick." I paused, the painful memories threatening to intrude. I pushed them back. Not here. Not now. "They died during the night. Somebody stole our truck, so I decided to walk."

Bear cast me a sideways glance. "You got turned around, son. Boise's the other way."

"Yeah." I looked out the window at the dusty hills. "I changed my mind and decided to go back to Portland."

Bear was silent. I sensed he wanted to ask me why I changed my mind—curiosity was only natural and I was being cryptic—but he held his tongue on the subject.

"I turn south on Highway 97," he said. "I'll need to drop you off at Biggs Junction. That'll put you about a hundred miles from Portland."

"You cut the trip in half. I'm in your debt."

He nodded again. "Mind handing me a bottle of water?"

I dug in the cooler and handed Bear his drink.

"Where were you when the flu broke out?" I asked after he downed half the bottle.

"I had to see a man about a horse."

"What?" Considering he was towing a horse trailer, I suspected he meant it literally, but it was the first time I'd heard that phrase used to mean anything other than needing to take a piss.

He grinned, then his face grew serious. "I was in Wyoming, picking up a horse from a breeder, when the news about the flu started to get bad."

"You work for the ranch?"

"My family's owned Valhalla for more than a hundred years."

"Valhalla, that's the Viking heaven, isn't it?"

"Something like that," he said.

I let that knowledge percolate for a moment. "Your real name is Bjorn. That's a Scandinavian name."

"Yup. Full name is Bjorn Knut Rasmussen. Doesn't get much more Scandinavian than that."

Bear looked like a Viking, tall, blond, and muscular. I could imagine those powerful arms wielding a battle ax, although he didn't seem like the kind of guy who would terrorize the countryside. In fact, he seemed downright chill.

I sat up straighter as something occurred to me. "You're Bear Rasmussen? The rodeo star? The guy who came within spitting distance of winning the all-around champion award at the last Round-Up?"

I remembered Bear Rasmussen from the Round-Up last September.

Kenzie had been leafing through a program when she'd stopped to ogle a photo of Bear leaning halfway off a horse while he roped a calf. Her eyebrows had lifted in that tell-tale sign that she thought a man was hot, before she glanced at me and flipped the page. Later that day, at the tie-down finals, she casually asked to borrow the binoculars and kept them glued to her eyes during Bear's performance. Later, we spotted him sauntering through the crowd, a gaggle of giggling teenage girls trailing close behind.

Kenz and I had a deal. As long as we were in an exclusive relationship, it would be rude and disrespectful to leer at another person. She never flirted at parties. I didn't check out other women.

Celebrity crushes were another matter. You could love one person and have lascivious fantasies about another. That was human nature. I didn't give a damn that Kenzie drooled over a popular British singer, and she never gave me grief for crushing on the hot actress from that hospital series on TV. Maybe she tried to play it cool over Bear because he fell into some sort of gray zone, a celebrity who was practically within arms reach.

Yeah, I remembered Bear Rasmussen, and I didn't hold Kenzie's interest in him against him.

"That's me," he said.

"You qualified to go to the National Finals Rodeo in December."

"Didn't make it. I dropped out of the rodeo circuit in October after my dad had a heart attack."

"I'm sorry," I said.

He shrugged. "Dad recovered, but I couldn't let my mom worry that he'd push himself too hard running things. Anyway, I always intended to work the ranch full time someday. It's all good."

It's all good? He gave up a promising and potentially lucrative rodeo career to return home to work the ranch full-time. Helluva guy. My respect for him ratcheted up a notch.

"How about you? You compete in any sports?" he asked, changing the subject.

"Yeah." I hesitated for a moment. My sports had none of the swagger or panache of being a rodeo cowboy. "Archery in high school and fencing in college."

While Bear was busting broncos and roping steer, I was practicing to be one of Robin Hood's merry men. Or a musketeer. No way I was going to tell him that I was also junior trap shooting champion at the country club.

His brow furrowed. "They have college teams for competitive fence building?"

It took a moment for his meaning to register. I barked out a laugh before I could stop myself. "Sorry, man, I didn't mean to be rude." Of course a guy who grew up on a ranch would think fencing had something to do with...well...fences.

Bear groaned and shook his head. "You mean sword fighting with those skinny swords. Duh." He thumped a palm on his forehead.

"Don't feel bad," I said. "I know squat about cattle or horses or ranching."

We shared stories of our childhoods for a while, laughing and bonding in a way that surprised me, considering our disparate backgrounds. When a road sign showed that Biggs Junction lay three miles ahead, Bear grew quiet.

"Listen," he said finally, turning his head to give me a concerned look. "You sure you want to go on to Portland? A big city might not be the safest place during a flu pandemic. You could come back to Valhalla with me. The ranch is at the ass end of nowhere. We've got everything we need to survive. Dad could put you to work earning your keep."

"You think a tenderfoot like me could do anything useful on a ranch?" I asked.

"Tenderfoot?" He snorted. "You've seen too many John Wayne movies. Seriously, though, what do you think?"

Bear had made an amazingly generous offer.

"I can't, man," I said with genuine regret.

"Why not?"

"Last night, two of my closest friends died. Jake and Ali." I shoved a hand through my hair, finally permitting the sadness to filter through. "They were in love. It was end game. I had no doubt that someday I'd be toasting them and telling embarrassing stories at their wedding reception. The flu killed them, ended their love story like that." I snapped my fingers.

"I'm sorry. That's tough," Bear said.

"My girlfriend and I broke up a couple of months ago," I continued. "I still love her. I want another chance to make things right. She's practically alone in Portland. I've got to find her, so much as I appreciate the offer, I can't go with you to Valhalla."

"I understand."

He pulled onto the shoulder just before Highway 97 split off from I-84.

"Hold on." He turned and reached into the back of the truck.

He pulled a brown lunch sack out of an insulated bag. "Roast beef and smoked provolone on sourdough. I found a deli open this morning and grabbed a couple of sandwiches for the road." He took a cold cola from the cooler, then leaned farther over and picked up a black baseball cap with the words Valhalla Ranch embroidered on the front.

"Sometimes we get paying guests, people who want to see ranch life up close. Mom ordered these as a souvenir of their stay. You'll need to keep the sun out of your eyes while you're walking." He handed the lunch sack, soda, and the baseball cap to me.

I'd known Bear just a couple of hours, and I already felt like I was saying good-bye to a friend.

"You've been a lifesaver." I extended my hand.

We shook hands.

"If you get to Portland and you can't find your girl, or if things get too crazy in the city and the two of you decide to get out, you'll always be welcome at the ranch." He took a business card from his wallet.

I glanced at it. Underneath Valhalla Ranch were the address and phone number, with a small map printed on the reverse side.

"In case you ever need to find the ass end of nowhere," he said.

I tucked it into my wallet and grabbed my backpack from the rear seat.

"Thanks again."

I jumped out of the truck. As he pulled away and followed the ramp to Highway 97, I raised a hand in farewell. After tucking the sandwich into a zipper compartment on the front of the backpack, I slapped the baseball cap onto my head. I glanced back at the truck just in time to see it disappear over a rise in the road.

A hundred miles separated me from Kenzie. I shouldered the bag and continued my march west, sipping what might be my last ice-cold soda.

Once again, I-84 hugged the banks of the Columbia River, the freeway's curving route matching that of the water. On the Washington side of the river, giant windmills dominated the horizon. To my left, low rocky hills lined the roadway.

I walked about five miles, planning to stop and eat my sandwich in a campground just before the Deschutes River emptied into the Columbia. Like the rest stop we drove through while fleeing Portland—just one day before—this place was jam-packed with refugees from the city. I found a tree at the far edge of the campground and sat down in its shade to rest and eat.

Bless Bear. I groaned with pleasure when my teeth sank into the sandwich. To compensate for the weight of the bottled water and soda, I'd filled the backpack with light-weight, high-calorie foods. After tonight I'd be living on granola bars, peanut butter crackers, and packages of roasted almonds. Bear mentioned that the governor had declared a state of emergency this morning and had ordered all businesses to shutter, so what I carried was all I'd have till I made it back to Portland.

It was late afternoon, and I had no time to waste. I decided to push on to The Dalles, a small city about fifteen miles away. With any luck, I could find a hose to refill my empty water bottles and a porch or awning to sleep under.

I arrived on the outskirts of The Dalles after dark and passed a used car lot. Acting on a hunch, I found the neatly coiled hose employees used to wash the cars and filled the five empty water bottles in my pack.

Exiting the lot, I eyed the cars lined up in rows on either side of me. Impulsively, I put my hand on the rear door handle of an SUV. It had started to rain and the idea of sleeping dry and snug on the back seat of an empty vehicle held an almost irresistible appeal. I tested the handle. Locked, of course.

I shook my head, annoyed with myself for trying it. It was a stupid move. I knew better.

"Stop right there," a voice cried out.

I whirled around to face a young man wearing a security guard's uniform. He had to be at least twenty-one to carry a firearm on the job, but he looked like little more than a pimple-faced kid. To my utter amazement, he pulled his weapon from the holster on his hip and pointed it at me.

"Put your hands up," he ordered in a breathless voice.

I complied.

"Is there a problem, sir?" I asked with deliberate calm. He was a bundle of nerves, and I didn't want to do anything to set him off.

"I'm making a citizen's arrest." The barrel of the gun wavered in his unsteady hand.

From my prelaw classes at the university, I knew that a security guard could make a citizen's arrest only if he witnessed a person committing an actual crime. Suspicious behavior wasn't enough.

"On what charges?" I kept my tone even and nonthreatening.

"Theft. You stole water from the hose. And I saw you try to break into that SUV to steal it."

I stole water from a hose? I touched a door handle? Good luck getting any DA to file charges on that, but potential charges weren't my problem. My problem was the twitchy-as-fuck rent-a-cop holding a gun on me.

"What's your name?" I asked.

He shifted his weight from one foot to the other, frowning. "Marty."

"Marty," I repeated. "Let's think about what's going on here. People need water to live. Every store in town is closed. There's no place for me to buy water. I don't want to scare any of the good people of this town—your neighbors—by knocking on their doors and asking for water, or by helping myself to some from their outdoor faucets. The car lot is closed. There's nobody here to alarm."

Marty scoffed.

"I just want to go home, Marty. You get that, don't you? And I don't believe that under the circumstances, the car lot owner would object."

I smiled, the nice guy smile I'd been practicing all day. It worked no better on Marty than it had on the cars zooming past me on the freeway.

"You took the water without permission. That's stealing."

Shit. A black or white, right or wrong thinker, probably with an IQ somewhere south of one hundred. No point in attempting any nuanced arguments with Marty. Another tack was required.

"Have you called the city police for backup, Marty?"

He frowned. "I tried, but all the lines were busy."

"That's right. All the lines were busy because a lot of bad things are happening. The police have their hands full. Let's say you get through to them. What do you think will happen if they send an officer out here, and they find out that you arrested me for stealing water from a hose?"

"And for breaking and entering. And for trying to steal a car," he insisted.

"Come on, Marty. Think about it. What did I break? What did I enter? Nothing. You'll look like a damned fool if you call the police in on this."

That was a mistake. I realized it as soon as the words left my mouth.

His face flushed, and he reached with his left hand for a pair of metal handcuffs. "Turn around and put your hands together behind your back."

No fucking way I was letting this flustered hack cuff me. I took a step back, scanning the lot for the best escape route.

"I mean it." His voice quaked.

I spun and darted to my left, between two rows of cars.

A bullet whizzed past my head and I stumbled. He actually fired his weapon? Un-fucking-believable. I recovered and plowed straight ahead toward a break in the line of cars.

The way his hands were shaking, it would be a miracle if he could hit me, so rather than take cover, I ran.

Adrenaline gave my feet wings. I leaped over the short wall separating the lot from the sidewalk and started sprinting across the street. Something punched my shoulder.

I glanced behind to see if Marty had caught up with me, if he'd landed a blow, but he stood frozen in place where I'd left him, holding the gun in his outstretched hands.

I ran for two blocks, then dodged right into a residential neighborhood. Gasping for air, I staggered onto the driveway of a small ranch house. A row of garbage cans were lined up against the exterior garage wall, and I dropped behind them, pulling my knees to my chest to make myself small.

I cocked my head and held my breath, straining to hear sounds of pursuit. Nothing.

Relief robbed my limbs of all strength, and I leaned my head against my knees, willing my galloping pulse to slow.

That's when I saw it, a dark stain spreading from my shoulder. I touched the spot and my fingers came away wet with blood. I stared at my fingertips while my brain put two and two together.

Intense pain suddenly lanced my shoulder, as if a red-hot poker had been laid across my skin. I gasped.

Holy hell. I'd been shot.

TWENTY-ONE

Kenzie

"Kyle is supposed to be in Boise with Ali and Jake. I have no idea what he's doing here."

Ripper dropped down into a crouch and spun the chair so we were face to face. He cupped my chin and fixed me in place with the intensity of his gaze. "What do you want to do, Mac?"

"We have to let him in. We can't leave somebody I know standing on the street outside the gate. The city isn't safe."

"He's your ex for a reason, right?"

I nodded mutely.

"If he hurt you, you owe him nothing, and I can make him go away."

A shiver ran down my spine.

"No," I said hastily. "No. Kyle isn't a bad guy. We just..." I shrugged, at a loss for words. "We just weren't good together. I wish he'd stayed in Boise, but now that he's here, I can't in good conscience leave him on the street. And I need to hear what he wants. Maybe he has a message from my best friend."

"All right. Your call." He leaned forward and pressed a brief kiss on my lips. Over his shoulder, Miles's eyes widened. Ripper stood, caught my hand, and pulled me to my feet.

"Miles, you wanna wait inside, or do you wanna come to the gate with us?" Ripper asked.

My cousin's eyes moved from Ripper's face to mine and back again. "I'll wait inside with Hector."

I followed Ripper as he strode to the gate. He released the locking mechanism and pushed the heavy, rolling door along its tracks, creating an opening a few feet wide. He stood back to allow Kyle to step inside the compound.

Kyle hurried through the entrance, his gaze sweeping the yard until he found me.

"Kenz." A huge smile broke across his face, and he rushed toward me, his arms outstretched.

Ripper stepped between us and held up a hand to block Kyle's advance.

"Hold on." He looked Kyle up and down. "You sick?"

Kyle's head jerked back, and his posture grew stiff, rooting him in place. He glanced back at me, confusion written across his features.

"I said, are you sick?" Ripper repeated. He crossed his arms over his chest and planted his feet apart, making it abundantly clear that Kyle wasn't getting past him until he answered.

No wonder Ripper was cautious. Kyle's clothes were filthy, as if he had been sleeping in a ditch. He used to spend as much time fussing over his hair as I did mine—the man loved his styling products—but today his hair was a lank and greasy mess. But it wasn't his clothes and grooming that gave me pause. His face was pale and pinched, and he held himself as if he were in pain.

Did Kyle have the flu? Dear lord, please no. No matter what had passed between us, I'd never want to see him suffer.

"No, I don't have the flu. At least, not as far as I can tell," Kyle said stiffly. "I've been on the road for almost a week, walking most of the way. A bullet grazed my shoulder in The Dalles, and I laid low for a couple of days."

"What?" I exclaimed. "Somebody shot you?" I took a step toward him, but Ripper held out a hand to keep me back.

"Not yet, Mac." He kept his eyes laser focused on Kyle, as if Kyle posed a danger he wasn't ready to dismiss. "You have a headache, nausea, fever, any of the symptoms?"

Kyle stared at Ripper's palm pressed against my rib cage.

"Kenzie, who is this guy?" He ignored Ripper's question.

I glanced at Ripper and saw what Kyle saw when he looked at him. A tall, shaggy-haired man wearing the leather cut of an outlaw motorcycle club over his bare, heavily muscled chest. A dangerous man. A man who laid his hand on my body as if he had the right to.

He did. I gave him that right. I ran my palm down Ripper's muscular forearm, then settled my hand on top of his. "Ripper is a friend. I trust him. You can trust him, too."

"More than a friend, wouldn't you say?" Ripper snaked his arm around my waist and pulled me to his side, staking a claim in front of a potential rival.

"Yes, more than a friend," I agreed.

An awkward silence hung between us. Kyle's mouth went slack before he turned his head and looked to the side, staring fixedly at the ground.

I don't know if he was taking this badly because he'd come here hoping for some kind of reconciliation, or because he hated to see me at the side of a man he'd likely dismiss as a thug. I'd absolutely no desire to hurt Kyle or to make him uncomfortable, but he had to understand that I'd moved on. The world had changed, and I had chosen a man with whom I wanted to face it.

"If I could refill my water bottles before I go, I'd be grateful," Kyle said at last.

"You didn't answer my question. You have any symptoms of the flu?" Ripper was as tenacious as the proverbial dog with a bone.

"No. None."

"All right. Come inside the house. We'll get you cleaned up, give you something to eat. I'll take a look at your wound."

"What?" Confusion creased Kyle's face.

"Nobody is asking you to leave," Ripper said. "Don't have to tell you that it's dangerous out there. Mac is worried about your safety. She says you're a good man. We're not gonna throw you out onto the street."

Despite the macho posturing, despite his menacing demeanor, Ripper listened to me and cared about what I said. A warm sense of gratitude flooded my chest.

"Thank you," I whispered into his ear.

He squeezed my waist and flashed a smile before stepping away to roll the heavy door back into place and secure the gate.

Kyle wobbled on his feet, looking exhausted, defeated, and uncertain.

"Please come inside, Kyle." I gently touched his arm.

"You sure, Kenz?" His eyes were clouded with pain.

I'd been with Kyle long enough to know that there were layers of meaning behind his simple question. Was I sure I wanted him to stay? Sure that there was still room for him in my life? Sure that I wanted Ripper? Sure that choosing him was a good idea?

Yes, an emphatic yes, to all the questions.

"I'm sure. Come on." I smiled and tugged on his arm. "I want you to meet Hector and my cousin Miles."

"Who's Hector?"

"My dog," Ripper answered, catching up with us on the porch steps.

"Only the sweetest, bravest, cuddliest dog in all the world," I offered.

"Still goofy for dogs," Kyle muttered. "Some things don't change."

Ripper's eyes narrowed, and he shot me a suspicious look. "You the reason Hector started jumping onto the bed at night?"

I smiled innocently and batted my eyelashes. "I'm sure I have no idea what you're talking about."

"Hmm...We'll continue this conversation later," he promised, a promise that made my insides flutter.

I laughed and led the way into the kitchen.

Miles was seated at his command station, where he'd probably watched our encounter on the security monitor. When we entered the room, he stood. Introductions—any of the social niceties—made him awkward, and he preferred that they be formal and by the book.

"Kyle, this is my cousin Miles. Miles, I'd like you to meet my friend Kyle."

"Hello." Miles bobbed his head to acknowledge the introduction.

"Pleased to meet you," Kyle said. He didn't extend his arm for a handshake. Good.

Ripper patted his thigh, and Hector trotted over and sat by his feet. He laid a hand on the dog's head. "And this is Hector. Kyle, step closer and let him sniff you." As Kyle approached, Ripper squatted down. "Hector, Kyle is a friend." Hector nosed Kyle's legs.

"Hey, Hector."

"Mac, how about you get Kyle something to eat while I check out his shoulder."

"Sure. Eggs okay for you, Kyle?"

"Sounds great. If I never see another granola bar it will be too soon."

The words were appropriate but his tone was stilted, as if he were struggling to make polite conversation, which had never been a problem for Kyle. He was born to schmooze. He must have been feeling worse than he let on.

I heated a skillet over our hot plate and diced a small potato, setting it to cook in a little oil while I went into the back yard to gather eggs, a few stalks of late asparagus and some chives. Back in the kitchen, I glanced up from whisking eggs to see Miles carrying the first aid kit.

I poked my head into the living room. Kyle sat in the rolling chair, bare chested, while Ripper examined the angry red gash across his right shoulder.

"How'd you treat it?" Ripper asked.

"Pieces of fabric from my shirt were stuck in the wound. I pulled out as many as I could find, then I tried to sterilize it with a miniature bottle of vodka I had in my pack."

"Bet that hurt," Ripper said.

"You mean dumping alcohol over an open wound or wasting a perfectly good bottle of vodka?"

"Both." Ripper smiled.

"It stung dumping it over the laceration, but not as much as using up all the booze. I raided the minibar at the place in Pendleton where I spent the night. I only took the one bottle, trying to keep the weight down in the backpack."

Kyle spied me standing in the doorway. "You know the place, Kenz. The big house where we stayed with my folks during Round-Up. You and I had the room overlooking the rose garden."

Was Kyle trying to get a rise out of Ripper? I glanced at Ripper to see how he'd react to the mention of Kyle and me on vacation together, but his face showed not a hint of jealousy.

I didn't know what to make of that. Maybe he wasn't the jealous type. Maybe he didn't get bent out of shape by things that happened in the past. Maybe he didn't really care enough to be jealous.

Kyle picked up the story. "I cleaned the wound with the vodka, then wrapped it in a clean T-shirt."

"Could have been worse," Ripper said. "The bullet didn't carve into the deeper layers of skin and tissue. No sign of infection."

"I broke into an...um...empty house," Kyle said. "Dug around in the medicine cabinet and found some antibiotics. I took it easy for a couple of days, to make sure there were no complications, then I started to walk again."

"Breakfast can be ready any time," I interrupted.

"We can wrap this up in a minute," Ripper answered.

The edges of the potatoes had turned golden brown and crispy. I tossed the asparagus pieces into the pan and sauteed them for a minute before adding the eggs, salt, and the chives. Two minutes later, I set the plate on the kitchen table and called Kyle in for breakfast. I put a pot of water on to boil and cranked the coffee grinder, so I could prepare a carafe of French press coffee for everybody.

Kyle sat at the table. After one bite, he groaned with pleasure, then started wolfing down the rest.

I was pouring boiling water into the insulated carafe when something occurred to me. "I bet Ali was glad to make it home to Boise. Was everybody okay back there?"

I glanced at Kyle. He'd dropped his fork on the table and wore a stricken expression.

"Kyle?" My hands were shaking when I carefully set the pan of boiling water down, then turned to face him.

"Fuck," he whispered. "I should have told you right away. We never made it to Boise. Ali and Jake got sick on the road. We stopped in Pendleton. I tried to take care of them, but they died. Ali and Jake are dead."

In movies, when you saw people keeling over from shock, I always assumed that such an overwrought reaction was a plot device, an unlikely but effective visual cue to let the audience know that something very bad had happened. Nope. There was nothing bogus or contrived about it. My knees buckled, and I fell hard to the floor, catching myself on my hands.

In an instant Ripper was there. He sat on the floor beside me and pulled me onto his lap, rocking me back and forth, offering the same comfort he had when I broke down by the koi pond. This time, instead of clinging to him, I curved into myself, wrapping my body around a grief so sudden and intense that I was incapable of seeking solace.

My best friend was dead. Jake, too. Shuddering, I gulped for air.

"I'm so sorry, Mac," Ripper murmured. He held me fast, cradling me in his arms, while my heart thudded in my chest like a frozen lump. If Miles or Kyle spoke, it didn't register, didn't pierce the veil of my grief. My eyes burned, but I didn't cry. After a while, I shifted in Ripper's arms, laying my cheek and palm against his bare chest.

Without conscious intent, over time I matched my breaths to the tempo of his inhalations and exhalations, our chests rising and falling in harmony. I leaned heavily against him, heartbeat echoing heartbeat, breath echoing breath, linked to Ripper in a way that allowed me to draw upon his strength, his calm.

I lifted my head and looked into his eyes.

"I'm here." He cupped my face. "We're all here for you, Mac. You aren't alone."

I nodded and pressed my cheek against his palm, absorbing the warmth and reassurance of his touch.

I glanced over his shoulder at Miles, who leaned against the wall, wringing his hands. He'd stayed, despite what must have been an overwhelming urge to flee such an emotion-laden scene. He stayed for me.

Turning my head to look at Kyle, I recoiled when I saw his expression. His eyes were fixed on Ripper. Jaw clenched, cheeks flushed, he stared at Ripper with such open hostility that I gasped. I blinked and the bitter antagonism had disappeared from Kyle's face, as if an unseen hand had erased it..

Kyle met my eyes and offered a slight smile. "Ripper's right. We're all here for you." The words were reassuring, but they were at odds with the anger I'd seen flashing in his eyes. What was going on in Kyle's head?

Had I made a mistake insisting that we bring Kyle into the compound?

TWENTY-TWO

Kenzie

After dinner, we gathered in the living room. Miles brought a package of sandwich cookies up from the basement stockpile, his way of welcoming Kyle to the compound. No fan of chocolate, I shook my head when Ripper offered me one.

"You *know* Kenzie doesn't like chocolate, right?" Kyle asked.

Ripper swung his eyes toward my ex, then shrugged. "Guess Mac and I have been too busy with other things to talk about cookies."

Kyle flushed, Ripper stared him down, and a knot twisted in my stomach.

"We need to figure out where Kyle will sleep." I changed the subject.

"We could clear a space against the far wall for an inflatable camp pad and sleeping bag," Miles suggested.

"And if Kyle wants some privacy, we could tack a sheet to the ceiling to create a visual barrier." I added.

"Got a better idea." Ripper leaned against the arched opening between the rooms. He turned his gaze on me. "I want you in my bed. Kyle can take your room."

An awkward silence followed his suggestion. Miles frowned in confusion. Kyle's expression hardened into stony lines.

I want you in my bed.

My heart fluttered. Ripper was asking me—no, he was telling me—that he wanted to sleep with me every night.

A kaleidoscope of enticing images flashed through my mind. Falling asleep in his arms. Watching his chest rise and fall when I stirred awake in the middle of the night. Waking up, warm and safe, next to the hottest man I've ever laid hands on. Dashing to the bathroom to gargle and pee before I jumped him.

I suspected that Ripper could read my thoughts, because a slow, self-assured smile crossed his face.

He took a long pull from his beer, apparently unconcerned that this was a discussion most people would have in private.

I want you in my bed, a brazen declaration made by a man unencumbered by the rules of polite society. Certainly not words most men would utter in front of my cousin and ex-boyfriend.

Miles spoke up before I could unscramble my brain cells enough to respond. "But, Mackenzie lives with me. I like having her here. I don't want her to live someplace else."

"Nothing to worry about, Miles. She'll still be around every day," Ripper said. "The only change will be at night, when she comes to my place to sleep."

Miles turned pleading eyes toward me. "Mackenzie, do you want to sleep with Ripper?"

Ripper's lips twitched. "Yeah, Mac, do you want to sleep with me?"

I did, more than anything, but Miles's distress tugged at my conscience. "I'd like to stay with Ripper at night, but maybe we could work out a compromise. Maybe Kyle and I could take turns using the second bedroom. One or two nights a week I could stay here, the rest of the time I'll sleep over at Ripper's."

"I don't mind sharing a bed with Kenzie." Kyle offered Ripper a smug smile. "Won't be the first time."

They locked eyes, and Ripper's expression chilled. "Past is past, boy. I won't have you *sharing* Mac's bed."

Tension choked the air.

I walked over to Ripper, and laid my hand on his chest. "I've got another idea. How about we haul the washer and dryer out of the back porch? Then there'd be plenty of room for Kyle to spread out a sleeping bag. He'd have his own space, with a door he could close."

The back porch was scarcely bigger than a closet, certainly nothing Kyle would once have deigned to call his own, but times had changed.

My breath caught as my mind dredged up an unwanted memory—the closet door closing, the snick of a lock, my mother's voice calling out *Party time!* Shit. Not now.

I pushed the image away with both hands, locked it away next to my grief over Ali and Jake's deaths, and focused on the here and now.

Ripper's expression softened when he looked down at me. "That could work. Good thinking."

Kyle was still recovering from the bullet wound, so Ripper and Miles wrestled the washer and dryer out of the enclosed porch and rolled the appliances to the side of the house. After sweeping up dust bunnies, I brought a camp pad, sleeping bag, and pillow up from the basement and spread them out on the floor.

Kyle watched me from the doorway. "Your new boyfriend is quite the gentleman, isn't he? 'I want you in my bed.'" He mimicked Ripper's deep rumble. "Jesus, Kenz, what are you thinking? You slumming?"

Slumming? That was rich, coming from Kyle. The apple didn't fall far from the tree, did it?

I stood up and brushed my hands off on my jeans, before turning to glare at my ex. "You're out of line. You don't know him."

"And you do? After a whole week?"

"Yeah. I do. In case you haven't noticed, the world is falling apart. Things are changing quickly. Ripper and I have shared a lot since we met."

"No, I haven't noticed things falling apart." Kyle's voice was heavy with sarcasm. "I've been too busy watching Jake and Ali die and getting shot by a trigger-happy security guard."

The reminder of Ali's death was like a body blow. I reached out to steady myself on a wall. Regret flashed in Kyle's eyes, and he drew in a deep breath, then exhaled.

"Listen, I get it. I'm not blaming you. You were alone. There was nobody here to take care of things."

My brows raised and I heard Aunt Debbie's voice in my head. *What am I, chopped liver?* And what about Miles? He'd created this well-stocked sanctuary. Really? Nobody here to take care of things?

Kyle either ignored or didn't see how his words gave offense.

"You shouldn't be too hard on yourself," he continued. "You've always had a thing for bad boys. I've seen the covers of those romance books you like to read, all those ripped, bare-chested guys. Ripper shows up with his muscles and tats and motorcycle vest, and he must have seemed like your dream come true. But it's obvious that the man is a lowlife. Nobody you can rely on. Nobody you can trust. It's time to start thinking with your brain and not your—"

"You patronizing asshole." I jabbed my finger in his face. "Just shut up." I sucked in a calming breath before continuing. "Know what I've noticed, Kyle? You have a gift for making me feel less than. You tell me I'm stupid, I'm deluded, I'm doing the wrong thing. Do you want to know how Ripper makes me feel? Like I'm good enough, like I'm capable." I squeezed my eyes shut and scrubbed at my face, suddenly very tired. "I'm not sorry you're here. I don't want you to leave. But you have to be civil to Ripper, because he's not going anywhere."

"Everything all right in here?" Ripper asked, coming through the kitchen door.

I'd spoken my peace, so I could call the situation all right with a clear conscience. "Just helping Kyle settle in."

Miles followed Ripper into the house. "There are extra clothes in the basement. Toiletries, too. I can get you a toothbrush and toothpaste."

Kyle nodded. "Thanks, Miles. I appreciate that."

"You want to grab your stuff?" Ripper asked me. "Then we'll head over to my place."

"Yeah. I'll be just a minute." I went to my room and collected my toiletry bag and a change of clothes. Back in the kitchen, I paused to speak to Miles. "I was thinking blueberry pancakes for breakfast tomorrow. Would you like that?"

He nodded, biting his lips.

"It'll be fine," I assured him. "I'll be back by eight-thirty in the morning, and we'll spend the whole day together." I wished Miles tolerated hugs. I had to fight the impulse to wrap my arms around him. Instead, I briefly touched his shoulder. "Good night, Miles."

"See you in the morning, buddy," Ripper said.

"Good night," Miles said, frowning.

"Night, Kyle," I called over my shoulder as I followed Ripper out the door.

Ripper took my hand, and we crossed through the yards to his house.

Once inside, I waited by the door while Ripper walked through the dark living room, touching a lighter to the wicks of several tall pillar candles. As he made his way from the coffee table to the cabinet under the television, to an end table, and back to me, his passage stirred the air. The flames wobbled, and his shadow danced against the walls.

He stopped a foot away from where I stood. With the candles to his back, his face lay in shadow, so I couldn't read his expression. "Can't run the generator every day, but if you'd like, tomorrow night we can power it up and watch another movie."

"I'd like that," I said.

"It's a plan."

An uneasy silence filled the space between us. Ripper loomed in front of me, a dark figure, tall and imposing. I wasn't afraid of him, but I felt uneasy, my thoughts perturbed.

What do you say to a man who baldly asserted *I want you in my bed*? What do you say to a man who just allowed your ex-boyfriend to intrude into his life? I couldn't imagine a less-welcome complication, yet Ripper hadn't hesitated.

I reached out and traced the line of his jaw, brushing over the thick stubble. He angled his head, so my fingers stroked his cheek and across his full lower lip.

"Would you have asked me to share your bed if Kyle hadn't shown up?"

"Yeah. Eventually. I saw how he looked at you and thought it was important to set boundaries. Let the kid know I've staked my claim."

Staked his claim? The sentiment was inherently primitive and chauvinistic. No modern, right-thinking woman wanted to be claimed. If Kyle had said it, I would have hooted with derision. Claimed. I should protest. Instead, I clung to the words and wrapped them around myself like a security blanket.

With Ripper at my side, I could do anything, be anything.

I smiled up at him. "You mean, so he doesn't get any ideas about winning me back?"

"So he doesn't make a fool of himself trying."

"How magnanimous of you. You sound very self-confident, Mr. Solis."

Ripper shrugged. "I got anything to worry about?"

"Absolutely not." My hand drifted from his face to his chest. Through his T-shirt, I played with the metal bar piercing his right nipple. "You told me that there's strength in numbers. We're going to need allies going forward. Kyle could be a good addition to our group. But like I said, you have nothing to worry about. Who wants a *kid* when you can have a *man*?"

Ripper caught my fingers and pressed them against his piercing, encouraging me to handle it more roughly. I obliged, twisting the bar until he hissed, then I scraped my fingernail over the hard tip of his nipple. He shuddered, drawing in a deep breath. I gloried in the power I had to make this tough man tremble. Emboldened, I reached out with my other hand and cupped his cock, rubbing my palm up and down the already rigid shaft.

His hands settled at my waist before sliding down over my hips. He tugged, yanking me against his jean-covered erection.

"Enough about Kyle." Hot breath tickled my ear and his fingers dug into my ass. "Gonna fuck you now, Mac." He sucked my earlobe into his mouth and tongued the fleshy nub. I gasped, and goosebumps erupted across my shoulders and arms.

God damn. Despite everything—despite the horrors that tomorrow might rain down upon us—at this moment, with this man, life was sweet.

TWENTY-THREE

Kenzie

I could never last as long as Ripper.

Whether it was a question of stamina or temperament, I couldn't say. He was tough, both physically and mentally, and I did my best to keep up with him, but it was a lost cause. I learned the limits of my endurance at Ripper's hands.

Forty-five minutes into our latest session, I was light-headed and short of breath, with a steady trickle of sweat stinging my eyes.

"If you don't ease up, you're going to break her," Kyle called from the sidelines.

"Yeah?" Ripper raked his hands through his sweaty, disheveled hair. "If you think you can do better, be my guest."

"Nah, I like watching."

While the men squabbled, I bent forward and rested my weight on my knees. When I straightened, the world spun around me, and only Ripper's quick reflexes kept me from smacking into the ground.

"Told ya," Kyle called.

"You've had enough for today," Ripper said in a low voice, an arm wrapped around my waist to hold me up. He turned to Kyle, smirking. "You're right. Mac needs a break. Think I'll take her back to my place for a bath and a nap."

Kyle jumped down from his cross-legged perch on top of he picnic table and stomped into the house, muttering under his breath.

"Do you have to push his buttons?" I demanded.

"He's been a pissy little bitch since he got here, and he's getting on my last nerve," Ripper said.

I turned in his arms and splayed my hands across his bare chest, which glistened with sweat from my lesson. "He needs more time to adjust to things," I said, with an optimism I didn't feel.

True to his word, in addition to our daily shooting instruction—where I'd graduated from a 22 to a Sig P938—Ripper had been teaching me how to fight. I might never have a future as a kickass assassin, but I'd become adept at escaping when someone snuck up and grabbed me from behind. And if forced to fight, I knew all the vulnerable spots on the human body.

The first time I managed to plant my knee in Ripper's groin, he'd bent over double, grunted, then told me my offensive skills were improving. All while Kyle howled with laughter.

It had been five days since Kyle arrived at the compound, five days in which the situation had gone from awkward to downright unpleasant. Give the man credit, Ripper had been patient and tolerant at first, willing to cut Kyle some slack, not rising to the bait when Kyle frequently reminisced about the good old days when we were a couple.

"I know you got history with Kyle that makes it hard to turn your back on him, but I'm done taking his shit," he said, his hands curving around my hips. "We've all lost people. No telling how many of the folks we knew before the flu are gonna survive. If any. The chance to stay connected with somebody you know from your past, it should mean something. Should be something you fight to hold on to. But it's as if Kyle is hellbent on pissing away any chance to fit in."

"He just needs a little more time," I said. "I think Kyle expected to show up at the door like a white knight coming to rescue me from all my problems. He had good intentions. It'll just take him a while longer to wrap his head around the situation."

Ripper sighed and tugged on my hips, drawing me so close that his jean-clad groin pressed against my belly. He tangled his fingers in my messy hair and dragged my mouth to his for a kiss, angling my head back, the way he liked it.

I resisted at first, embarrassed by my sticky, sweat-slicked skin, but he would have none of it. When his tongue slid between my lips, my awkward hesitation fled. I felt his cock jump, and I moaned, imagining it piercing my core the way his tongue penetrated my mouth.

My mouth securely in his possession, Ripper released my hair and grabbed my thighs, hoisting me up until my legs wrapped around his waist.

He broke the kiss and straightened up. Swiveling my head to follow his line of sight, I saw Kyle's face in the kitchen window.

"You knew he was there?" I gasped.

"Yeah." Ripper carried me toward the gate separating the two yards. "Just helping him wrap his head around the situation."

"Sure you weren't rubbing it in?"

"I got something I want to rub in," he said with a slow smile as he unlocked the gate.

My brain stuttered and I totally forgot what I planned to say next.

Two hours later, we returned to the compound. Ripper strode across the yard with an easy, unselfconscious lope, while I swear I floated, trying and failing to keep a silly grin from my face.

I'd been brought up to practice discretion, while Ripper's attitude was a brash "We'll be back after we fuck." He wasn't doing it for Kyle's benefit, despite what the little charade in the yard might suggest. Uninhibited, shameless, and unconstrained by convention, he shrugged off any suggestion that our behavior be more guarded.

Miles spied us through the window and stepped through the back door to meet us on the patio. "Something bad has happened," he said, clenching his hands.

My happy glow burst like a bubble.

Ripper came to a stop in front of my agitated cousin. "Tell me what happened, and we'll see what we can do to fix it."

Kyle appeared in the doorway behind Miles, his gaze shifting uneasily from Ripper to me, then back to Ripper.

My heart sank. Dammit. Kyle was responsible for whatever bad thing had happened. I almost groaned. Just what we needed, another bone of contention between the two men.

"Let me explain," Kyle began.

"Kyle lost Hector," Miles blurted out.

Ripper's head jerked back. "What?"

"Kyle lost Hector," Miles repeated.

Ripper's head pivoted, and he fixed Kyle with an icy stare that would send most men scurrying for cover. "What did you do? Where the fuck is my dog?"

Kyle dropped his head and dragged his hands through his hair. "I don't know where he is. I've been running up and down the streets looking for him for the past hour. I got back here five minutes ago. I was about to come knocking on your door."

"What happened? How did he get out?" I asked, stepping between Kyle and Ripper.

Kyle raised his head and met my eyes. "After you and Ripper went to his place, I needed to blow off some steam. I decided to go for a run. I thought it would be nice for Hector to get out of the yard, you know, to get a chance to stretch his legs, so I took him with me. Everything was fine until this orange cat jumped out from behind a bush and hissed at him. Hector took off after the cat, ran through a back yard and under a hedge, and I lost him."

"Had to be Murphy, old Mrs. Mowbray's cat," Ripper said. "Murphy and Hector have history."

"I'm sorry, man," Kyle said. "I should have put Hector on a leash, but he's so well-behaved that it didn't occur to me that he'd take off. I feel like an idiot. What can I do to make it right?"

I laid a hand on Ripper's arm and squeezed. "What can we do?" I asked quietly.

We had to find Hector. The thought of losing him was unendurable. We all loved him. His presence brightened every day. I couldn't bear the thought of anything or anybody hurting him.

"Hector's smart," Ripper said. "Chances are, he'll make it home on his own. I'll leave the dog door open. Miles, would you mind hanging out at my place and letting me know if Hector shows up?"

"I can do that." Miles nodded.

"Odds are nobody would try to hurt Hector, but there's no point in taking a chance that he runs into a trigger-happy fool. I want him home, the sooner the better," Ripper said. "He knows the sound of my Harley pipes, so I'm gonna take my bike. Mac, you're with me. Kyle, you can take my jeep."

"If you come across him, how would you get him home on your bike?" Kyle asked.

"We'll keep in touch by walkie-talkie. Miles has a set in the basement. If I find Hector, I'll signal you to come pick him up in the jeep."

Ripper fished the keys out of his pocket and tossed them to Kyle. Miles brought the walkie-talkies up from the basement, then we all traipsed over to Ripper's house. Miles took a seat at the kitchen table across from the dog door. I had no doubt he'd sit staring at the dog door until we returned.

While Kyle backed the jeep out of the garage, I turned to Ripper. "You okay?"

He shook his head. "Anything happens to Hector, I'm gonna kick Kyle's ass."

My stomach muscles clenched. Lately, it felt like I was dancing on a tightrope, trying to keep the peace between Ripper and Kyle. Kyle had made a mistake, but he had no malicious intent. He'd never endanger Hector on purpose.

"He didn't mean to do it," I said hesitantly. "It was an accident. He said he's sorry."

"World's not a forgiving place anymore, if it ever was. We can't afford careless accidents. Kid's gotta step up his game." He swung his leg over the bike and handed me a helmet. "Sorry don't cut it."

He kicked the engine into life, and I climbed on behind him.

For the better part of an hour, we rode up and down neighborhood streets, pausing every few blocks to call for our runaway dog. We crossed paths with Kyle a few times. The first time, he raised a hand to acknowledge our presence, but after Ripper ignored the gesture, the following times he drove past without a nod or wave.

The walkie-talkie came to life and Ripper pulled over and cut the engine. He pressed a button on the device. "Yeah?" After he released the button, we heard Miles's voice come through the speaker.

"Hector's home."

I sagged against Ripper, relief robbing my limbs of all their strength.

"On our way," Ripper replied.

Kyle pulled into the driveway ten seconds before we arrived, but stood beside the jeep waiting for us before entering the house. Ripper killed the engine on his bike and led the way into his kitchen.

Hector sat on the floor, scratching his ear with a hind leg as four pairs of human eyes fixed on him. I dropped to my knees beside him and threw my arms around his neck. "You little shit," I whispered into his fur. "You scared me to death." I pulled back, wrinkling my nose. "He got into something."

Ripper knelt beside me and sniffed his dog's fur. "He needs a bath." Hector tilted his head, unashamed and unrepentant after his little adventure. Ripper glanced over at Kyle. "Proud of yourself? Scared Mac and let Hector out to roll around in something dead?"

"Let it go, will you?" Kyle eyes flashed with annoyance. "I said I'm sorry. What else do you want me to do?"

"Really? That's what your life has taught you? You say you're sorry, and it's all good?"

"Please stop." Both men ignored me. I raised my voice in an attempt to get their attention. "Ripper. Kyle." Their bickering ceased and they looked at me. "Give it a rest, please."

Kyle nodded and Ripper clamped his jaws shut, grudging acquiescence writ large across his features.

They listened. They gave it a rest, but the tension in the pit of my stomach told me that this respite was merely a break in the hostilities and not the end of the war.

TWENTY-FOUR

Ripper

Before the flu, life threw softballs, the kind of crap a man could deal with. Over the past few weeks—when the flu grabbed the world by the balls—life had lobbed bombs. It fucked over our plans, kicked the shit out of our hopes, and stole away people we cared about.

After living through all that, you'd think a man would reach the point where he could shrug off a mere annoyance, but sometimes it's the petty stuff that pushed you right over the edge.

Locking the gate between the yards, I dreaded what lay ahead. Another shit task in a day that had already gone down the crapper. I was gonna break Mac's heart, but it had to be done. I turned around and stopped dead in my tracks, face to face with a perfect storm of aggravation.

A shirtless Kyle had parked himself in a lawn chair. Looked like he had appropriated a pair of sweatpants from the basement stockpile and had cut them into shorts. Feet up, legs and chest bare, a pair of sunglasses protecting his delicate eyes from the glare, the kid was sunbathing.

My lip curled in disgust. I stalked across the yard, my blood pressure rising with every step.

I stopped next to him and planted my hands on my hips. Ear buds blocked the sound of my approach, and his head bobbed to music only he could hear. Unearned sweat covered his body. Not the sweat born of honest work, but the useless moisture that seeped from a man's pores when he was lying like a beached whale in the sun.

I shifted position, so my shadow fell across his face and chest. That got his attention. Something blocked the sun; somebody stood between him and his golden tan.

Frowning, he pulled out the earbuds and slid the sunglasses to the top of his head, then he squinted up at me.

"You want something?" he asked.

"You can't find anything better to do with your time than work on your tan?"

He shrugged, slipped the sunglasses down and settled back in the chair. "Still recovering from being shot."

I glanced at the thin, red line etched across his upper arm, just below his shoulder. A bullet grazed his skin two weeks ago. Big fucking deal. My Janissary brothers would laugh their asses off at a man who bitched and moaned over a scratch.

"Your owie still giving you grief?" My voice was steeped with false sympathy.

"No, man. The only thing giving me grief is you."

I almost laughed. This was me dishing out grief, huh? Kid had no fucking clue.

Couldn't let it go.

"When I left this morning, Miles was hauling water from the rain barrel to the vegetable plants. Mac was hanging laundry up to dry. Did it occur to you to offer to help?"

That got his attention. He turned his head. Through the dark glasses, I felt rather than saw his eyes on me. "If Kenzie wants *anything* from me, all she has to do is ask, and I'll happily give it to her."

My fingers itched to bitch-slap the boy, but I saw Mac watching us through the kitchen window, so I tamped down my irritation.

"Mac's not gonna ask for help if she thinks you're hurt. You gonna let her baby you? Or you gonna man up and make yourself useful?"

"I washed and dried the breakfast dishes," Kyle said, yawning.

Color me impressed. While Miles carried bucket after bucket of water to the thirsty plants and Mac wrestled with wet sheets, Kyle spent a whole ten minutes doing the dishes.

He rolled onto his side and reached for something on the cement patio, then lifted a brown bottle to his lips and took a long pull.

My blood pressure spiked again. How the hell had Kyle gotten his grubby hands on a bottle of *my* beer?

"Enjoying the beer?" I asked.

"S'all right. I prefer a pale ale, but this'll do."

Little shit stole my beer, then dissed it?

Before I could respond, the back door swung open, and Mac stepped outside. A frown clouded her face as she looked from Kyle to me. "Everything okay?"

"Never better," Kyle answered. "Your boyfriend got back from his joyride, and we were shooting the breeze, right Ripper?"

Joyride? Fuck. That reminded me why I came over here.

Mac grabbed my hand and tugged, urging me inside. When the door closed behind us, I let out a slow breath.

"The fucking flu is killing good people right and left." I pointed toward the patio. "But that waste of space is just fine. Lying around getting a God-damned tan. Sucking down my beer."

"Kyle isn't a waste of space," Mac said. "That's not fair."

"No?" I whirled on her, not in the mood to hear any defense of his lazy ass.

In the face of my anger, Mac shrank back. Now that really pissed me off. Had I ever done *anything* to make her think that I'd lose my shit on her? That I'd hit her? If she was afraid of me, *that* was the real injustice here, not my criticism of Kyle.

I glowered at her. Yeah, maybe giving the girl the stink eye only added fuel to the fire, but watching her flinch stung.

To my surprise, instead of retreating further away from me, Mac drew herself up. Her jaw tightened. "Kyle *isn't* a waste of space. He's smart. He's loyal to his friends. He'll be an asset someday."

"An asset? All I see is a guy lying on his ass and helping himself to my beer."

"Kyle didn't help himself to the beer," Mac said. "I gave it to him."

I stared at her, thunderstruck. Miles had laid in a supply of my favorite beer and once that was gone, I'd be outta luck. Grocery store shelves were picked clean of beer. I knew. I'd checked. Hadn't occurred to me that Mac would share it with her ex.

"You gave Kyle *my* beer?"

Mac spun around, marched over to the junk drawer and took out a black Sharpie.

"I didn't realize that any of us had exclusive rights to the supplies." She slapped the pen into my hand. "Here. You like to claim things, don't you? If you want to call dibs on something, go put your name on it. Use big, capital letters. Let everybody know what belongs to Ripper, and that it's off limits to everybody else."

I held the pen up, then swung my gaze to her face. Girl had no idea what it meant to be claimed.

Narrowing my eyes, I considered her words. I imagined wrapping a hand around her neck, dragging her to my chest, then writing RIPPER across her forehead in permanent ink. Calling dibs on Mac so everybody—especially Kyle—would know she's mine and back the fuck off.

I quashed the impulse before it took root, restrained the mother-of-all dick moves, but it was too late. Mac must have read the thought in my expression.

She held up a hand. "I swear to God, if you try to write your name on my forehead, you'll be sorry."

"Yeah?" Threatening me? Never a good idea.

I fought the urge to step closer, to crowd her. Physical intimidation was part and parcel of my trade, often the best way to prevent a situation from devolving into violence. Fear kept people in line, kept them from doing something stupid.

Ain't nobody bigger and badder than me, and don't you forget it.

But that was club business and this was Mac, and no way I'd blur that line. Besides, I liked an angry Mac a helluva lot more than a cowed and intimidated one. Meant she had grit. Meant she knew better than to be afraid of me.

Still, I liked the idea of putting my mark on her, locking things down so there was no question that I'd claimed her. Hmmm...had to think on that. New world, new rules.

I held my hands up in the classic *I surrender* pose, then laid the Sharpie on the counter. "Sorry, Mac."

Her brows drew together, as if my apology took her by surprise. "Thank you."

I shoved a hand through my hair, hating like hell what came next. "Listen. There's something I gotta tell you—"

The back door flew open, and Kyle stomped into the room. "What's going on in here? Why is Kenzie yelling?"

Stepping between Mac and me, he shoved at my chest. The little fuckwad actually summoned the wherewithal to climb out of the lawn chair and launch some kind of kamikaze attack on me. I didn't so much as rock back on my heels when he shoved me. Instead, I put my hands on my hips and scowled, daring him to try it again.

"What did you do to her?" he demanded.

Jesus. The white knight charged into battle to rescue the damsel in distress, except I was no fire-breathing dragon, and Mac didn't need rescuing. Not from me. Not ever.

Mac laid a hand on his arm. "Ripper didn't do anything to me." Her patient, soothing tone rubbed me the wrong way. Why was Mac trying to placate him? We didn't need to justify anything to this interloper.

"I'm done with your shit," I said to him. "Done with your snark and your snide comments. Done with you trying to butt in between me and Mac. And I've had it with you lying around while everybody else works."

Mac's head pivoted between Kyle and me. "Ripper, he's taking it easy because he's recovering from being shot." She used the same cajoling voice on me that she used on Kyle, like a teacher trying to make peace between two rowdy schoolboys.

I snorted. "That scratch? He's milking it for all it's worth."

"Maybe to somebody like you, getting grazed by a bullet is no big deal, but to the rest of us, it's huge," Kyle said.

"'Somebody like you,'" I repeated slowly. "What does that mean, huh? A Janissary? A criminal?"

Kyle shrugged. "You said it, not me."

"You were an Army Ranger," Mac interrupted. "You've been shot at during the war. That's what you really meant, isn't it Kyle?" She turned pleading eyes toward her ex.

"Not what he said, darlin'." I used the endearment on purpose. Knew it would get a rise outta Kyle.

"Fuck you," he spat, glaring at me.

Here we go. I smiled with grim satisfaction. Past time for this to come to a head.

"You got a problem with me, Kyle?"

"Are you fucking kidding me?" The boy prince lost it, his eyes full of contempt. "Instead of going home to my family, I came back to Portland to be with Kenzie. And what do I find? She's shacking up with a biker."

"Kyle, stop it," Mac begged.

I raised a hand to silence her protests. "Let him talk. Where were you in your story, Kyle? Oh, yeah. You came back to Portland—uninvited—and discovered that life went on without you." I made a circular gesture with my hand, encouraging him to keep going.

"Asshole," he muttered before continuing his story. "I tried to be understanding. Kenz was alone and scared, and you showed up, with your muscles and your badass attitude. She needed somebody to protect her, and you must have seemed like the perfect solution to all her problems."

"Doesn't think much of you, does he, Mac?" I said in an aside. "No wonder you dumped his ass."

"Please, stop. This is so unnecessary," Mac whispered.

No. This was *exactly* what was required. Kyle and I needed to clear the air once and for all.

"Do you honestly think that Kenz would have anything to do with someone like you if it weren't for the flu?"

I shrugged. "Doesn't matter. The flu happened. Mac and I found each other. Now you gotta deal with what is and stop whining about what you lost. Or this isn't gonna work out, and you'll have to go."

"No." Mac touched her temple, as if our argument hurt her head.

"Kenzie would be a fool to trust you. Everybody knows that the Janissaries are low-life scum. They—"

I cut him off. Hand around his throat, I shoved Kyle against a wall. "Don't ever disrespect my club."

The kitchen door opened and closed.

"Maybe I've been too easy on you, let you talk shit to me for Mac's sake. But listen up, Kyle. This is a line you will not cross. Not one word against my brothers, or you're done. You feel me?"

He nodded, red-faced and sputtering. I dropped him, and he collapsed to his knees on the floor.

After a few minutes, he struggled to his feet and grabbed a bottle of water from the counter. He scowled at me through bleary eyes, but had the sense to keep quiet while he sipped the water.

The kitchen door opened again, and Miles walked into the room, pulling off his gardening gloves. Wide-eyed, he took in the scene.

"Where's Mackenzie?" he asked.

"She went outside a few minutes ago," I said. "Did you see her?"

He shook his head.

I glanced at the hook by the door and my blood chilled. The keys to the gate were missing.

TWENTY-FIVE

Kenzie

I had no particular destination in mind when I locked the gate behind me and started to walk up the street. The only place I wanted to be was somewhere else. Anywhere else. Anywhere I wouldn't have to listen to the relentless bickering that was sucking the joy out of our already fragile existence.

Civilization and humanity were circling the drain. The flu might still kill us all. Every day spent in health and safety, in the company of familiar faces, was a precious gift. Instead of cherishing that gift, Ripper and Kyle were pissing it away.

I carried a knot of tension in my stomach that never eased up, and I popped antacids like candy. Constant vigilance, the urge to keep the peace at any cost, the compulsion to mediate between the two men, was wearing me down.

Would Ripper and Kyle be at each other's throats forever?

I walked aimlessly up one neighborhood street and down another. Once tidy lawns sprouted knee-high grass turning crispy brown in the summer heat, and weeds choked the flowerbeds. While the flu raged, people had retreated into their sanctuaries to die. Curtains drawn, blinds down, the houses now displayed a blank, closed-off face to the world. Behind those shuttered exteriors, death reigned.

Corpses surrounded me, a thought that gave me the heebie-jeebies.

Eventually, I found myself nearing 82nd Avenue, once a major commercial thoroughfare. I cut through a Japanese car lot, then on a whim, headed south on 82nd.

Eerie silence reigned on this formerly bustling street. Neither a car nor a person disturbed the quiet. Within a block, the unaccustomed stillness began to give me the creeps. The skin between my shoulder blades itched, and I tried to shake off the suspicion that someone was watching me. Vulnerable and exposed, I found a spot between two bushes near the front door of a pancake restaurant. I sat cross-legged on the ground, resting my chin on my fists.

My gaze roamed around the parking lot, coming to a stop on the cinder block wall of the bar next door. Somebody had tagged it, scrawling *Back 2 Eden* across the surface in green spray paint. It caught my eye, both because I rarely saw green graffiti and because it was new, or at least I'd never noticed it before.

Back 2 Eden. It could be a religious or maybe an environmental message. I'm sure somebody believed that the flu pandemic was God's judgment on sinners, or that depleting the human population would allow the earth to revert to a pristine, preindustrial state.

The familiar sound of Ripper's bike interrupted my deliberations, and reality crashed down around my ears. Of course, he was out looking for me. I'd abandoned the safety of the compound and had wandered off, exposing myself to the dangers of the outside world.

Ripper and Kyle would worry. Miles would be frantic. Crap. No matter how much Ripper and Kyle's bickering upset me, running away had been an impulsive, lame-brained move, one that embarrassed me now that I'd gained some distance from the situation. I wouldn't compound it by hiding behind a bush like a naughty child. When the bike drew near, I stood up and walked to the edge of the street, ready to face the music.

Ripper pulled over, killed the engine, then swung off his bike. I braced myself for an angry outburst. Lately he spent a lot of time with his jaw clenched and a vein throbbing in his forehead. I didn't possess Kyle's gift for passive-aggressive needling, but apparently I'd mastered the grand, stupid gesture.

My heart sank as he stalked toward me. Nothing good ever came from confronting an angry person.

Suck it up. I'm not a scared kid anymore.

I drew in a deep breath and forced myself to stand up straight.

Ripper stopped a few feet away from me, his face unreadable, his posture tense. "You all right?"

I nodded, trying to decipher his expression.

He turned his head, scanning the surroundings. "Why were you sitting on the ground? You hiding from somebody?"

"I didn't see anybody, but I started to feel conspicuous walking around, like I had a target on my back."

"Least you showed *some* sense. C'mon." He gripped my arm and pulled me toward his bike.

Yeah, he was mad. He had a right to be mad after chasing me down like a wayward child. What he didn't have was the right to manhandle me.

I dug in my heels and jerked my arm back. I couldn't shake him off. His strong fingers braceleted my wrist, but I got his attention.

"You don't get to grab me," I said in a quiet voice.

Slowly and deliberately, he released my arm and withdrew his hand. He narrowed his eyes, frowning at my recalcitrance. "Get on the bike, Mac."

"And you don't get to tell me what to do." If I caved whenever he barked out an order I'd be setting a dangerous precedent, reshaping our relationship in a way that would completely undermine my self-respect.

Ripper folded his arms over his chest and regarded me coolly.

"Miles is at home freaking out. We aren't safe. Somebody's watching us—you can feel it, can't you? And you pick *this* moment to assert your autonomy? Because no matter what else is going on, you gotta stand up for your rights?"

Heat colored my cheeks. I might not be willing to concede the overall argument, but I saw his point. This wasn't the time or place for a debate. Still, I felt compelled to defend myself.

"Maybe I shouldn't have left the compound by myself—"

"Maybe?" He gave an exasperated huff. "You and Kyle both need to wrap your heads around the idea that the world's gone to shit. There's no room for stupid mistakes. You don't get to stamp your foot and say, 'It's not fair.' Life isn't fair. Get over it." He leaned forward. "So, I'll repeat myself. Get on the fucking bike."

I bristled. He expected me to obey, and clearly he'd brook no disagreement. His strength and self-confidence always made me feel safe, but this was the dark underbelly of my desire to be protected by a strong alpha male. The mantle of authority sat too easily on his shoulders. Instead of seizing my wrist, as he did before, he held out his hand, inviting me to take it, a small sop to my pride.

I saw movement over his shoulder. Two men emerged from the open bay of the car wash across the street. One lifted a walkie-talkie to his mouth.

"Oh, shit." My eyes widened with alarm, and Ripper whirled around.

A third man stepped around the corner of the bar next door to the pancake house.

Three strangers converged on us. If they were friendly or harmless, they'd keep their distance. They'd raise a hand and call a greeting, allowing us to establish that we're all good people just going about our business. They wouldn't silently stalk toward us.

Why hadn't it occurred to me to bring my Sig on my walkabout? Talk about stupid, impulsive mistakes. I half-expected Ripper to draw his Colt, but he didn't. Maybe he didn't want to start a shoot-out if the men were armed. Instead, he pulled me toward his bike. I jumped on behind him as the engine roared to life.

I held on tight as Ripper raced south on 82nd, heading away from the compound. I watched over my shoulder for signs of pursuit. After several blocks, it became clear that no one was tailing us. Ripper swerved onto a side street, then veered north toward home. He down-shifted and paused on the street in front of Miles's gate.

The security camera panned in our direction, confirming that Miles saw me on the back of the bike and knew I was safe. Ripper rounded the block, pulled into his driveway, hauled up the garage door, then parked his Harley inside, out of sight. He strode into his living room and watched the street from the slit between his curtains for a few minutes, before stepping back and dragging his hands through his hair.

He pivoted to me, his usual cool, self-possessed facade shattered. His eyes flashed, and his face twisted with strain.

"Do you realize what would've happened if I hadn't got there in time? Those fuckers could have taken you. Done anything they want to you, and I wouldn't have a clue where to find you." He gripped my shoulders, holding me at arm's length. His fingers dug painfully into my skin. "You scared the shit outta all of us, running off like that."

I'd anticipated his anger, but not *this*, not his anguish.

"I'm sorry," I whispered. I'd been unfair, expecting him to handle everything with calm assurance, but Ripper wasn't a stock character, a stoic, square-jawed hero who could shrug off inconvenient emotions. I'd seen anger and arrogance in his reaction. I should have seen the fear. I'd scared him. Scared them all.

What the hell had I been thinking? Suddenly, Ripper and Kyle's bickering shriveled in importance. I'd felt sorry for myself because I had to mediate between two men who cared for me? Pathetic. What would my life have been like if those strangers took me away? If I never saw Ripper, or Miles, or Kyle again?

You'd think my misadventure with Jason would have knocked some sense into me. Apparently not. The fear on Ripper's face brought home how vulnerable I was—we all were—in a world without laws and authority.

He sucked in a breath, visibly composing himself, then he cupped my face. I swear his hands shook.

"Lemme make this clear. You can't run off like that. It's not safe. I get why you did it. The constant arguing. Hasn't been fair to you. To Miles." Ripper shook his head ruefully. "You see that he's chewed his fingernails down to the quick? We gotta do better. I'm gonna talk to Kyle. Can't promise we'll ever be friends, but we can cut back on the open hostility."

"Lately it feels like I'm living in a powder keg, waiting for something to blow," I said. "But that's no excuse for doing something so risky, for making you all worry. I'm really sorry, Ripper."

He dropped his head and pressed his forehead against mine. "That was too fucking close."

"Yes." I shuddered, a bone-deep quivering that started in my stomach and slithered out through my limbs.

I wrapped my arms around Ripper's waist, clutching at him as if he were my anchor, the only thing holding me steady in an insecure world. I wanted to burrow into him and become so inextricably connected that nothing could tear us apart. I wanted *him*.

"S'all right, darlin'," Ripper whispered, tightening his own grip on me.

Sudden lust obliterated my inhibitions. "I need you." My fingers fumbled with the button on his jeans. "Now. Please, Ripper." I scarcely recognized my own voice, breathy and filled with desperate longing.

He coiled my hair around his fist and yanked my head back so he could look into my eyes. "You're mine. You got that, right?"

His gaze bore into me, piercing through my tangled thoughts and conflicting impulses.

I'd never be a doormat, someone who would smile and acquiesce whenever he laid down the law. But...I wanted to be his. I was a disgrace. If anybody survived from the Women's Studies department, they would seize and burn my feminist credentials. Yet my truth was undeniable. I wanted to be his.

I tried to incline my head, to signal my submission to his demand, but he gripped my hair so tightly that I managed only a slight nod.

"Good." Ripper eased his grasp. His hand slid to the waistband of my yoga pants. "Because I protect what's mine, even if that means protecting you from yourself."

"Mm-hmm," I agreed, squirming with anticipation when his hand slipped into my panties, and his finger circled my clit.

"Mean it, Mac. I expect you to be smarter moving forward."

"Will you shut up and fuck me?" I toed off my sneakers while my hands worked his fly. Enough talking. I didn't want sweet words. Didn't need foreplay. The only thing I needed was Ripper's cock inside me *right now*.

I shoved his jeans down his thighs and past his knees, then paused. In my rush, I'd forgotten his boots. Dropping to my knees, I quickly worked the inside zippers and wrestled the boots off his feet. He kicked off his pants and pulled off his T-shirt.

I rocked back on my heels, distracted by his naked glory. His cock jutted out—proudly erect—from his powerfully built body. Smiling to myself, I rose up on my knees. I slid my hands along his muscular thighs, stopping only when my thumbs caught under his balls and my hands framed his massive hard-on.

I licked my lips, eyeing the bead of pre-cum on the tip of his cock. I definitely still wanted him to fuck me, but maybe first I could—

Strong hands seized my wrists and hauled me to my feet. "You suck me off now—looking up at me like that—and I'll blow in thirty seconds." Ripper dragged my shirt over my head and tossed it aside.

He didn't bother unhooking my bra. Instead, he shoved it up so my breasts spilled into his hands. He palmed them for only a few seconds—twisting my nipples until I gasped—before he shoved my pants down my legs.

Stepping out of the pants, I braced myself for whatever came next.

Eyes hooded, breathing hard, Ripper had fallen sway to the same undeniable urge to fuck that held me in its grip. Maybe horniness was simply contagious. Maybe this carnal craving was the consequence of our brush with danger, this intense arousal the inevitable, life-affirming byproduct of almost losing it all. Either way, my need to be filled and consumed by this man was like an itch that had to be scratched, and Ripper had caught my sense of urgency.

"Mine," he snarled, kicking my legs out from under me and bearing me down onto the floor. Rough hands pried my thighs wide apart and he settled between my outstretched legs, his weight crushing me onto the carpet.

I expected to feel his fingers probing my slick folds, confirming that I was ready for him. Instead, within the space of one heartbeat, the blunt head of his cock slammed home, breaching my core.

Ripper raised up on his elbows and seized my chin. "Look at me."

I stared into his brown eyes and trembled at the stark hunger, the dark purpose I saw in his gaze. He rocked backward and his hard shaft slid out of my pussy, leaving me empty and bereft.

I whimpered a protest.

He arched forward and the tip of his cock brushed my dripping slit. "Tell me you're mine."

It took my lust-addled brain a moment to process the command. What would I be giving up if I said the words, if I confessed my own shameful longings? What would I gain? Honestly, at that moment, I didn't care. The only thing I cared about was easing the desperate, aching emptiness inside me.

"I'm yours," I said in a shaky voice.

Smiling exultantly, Ripper drove his cock back into me.

I locked my ankles behind his back, opening myself to his merciless pounding. He rode me fast and hard, with none of his typical finesse, not one whit of our usual playful banter. I might have imagined it—projected my need for certainty and assurance on the encounter—but it felt like a claiming, like some fundamental shift in our relationship.

My vision blurred. I screamed and clawed at Ripper's shoulders as I came, leaving crimson tracks on his smooth skin. With an animalistic growl, he pulled his cock out and rose up on his knees between my thighs.

For one heart-stopping moment, I was afraid that the bloody gashes I'd scratched onto his skin had angered him. I froze and held my breath.

With a feral grin, Ripper leaned over me, supporting his weight on one hand while the other pumped his cock.

One, two, three rough strokes. Thick, warm ropes of cum spurted over my belly and breasts.

As the musky scent floated in the air, my nostrils flared and my tongue darted out to trace my lips. Ripper's eyes glittered as he rubbed the sticky fluid over my skin, smearing cum across my nipples, into the hollow of my navel, and over my ribs.

He held his hand up to my mouth. "Lick it clean."

I gazed up at him, wide-eyed, startled by the demand. Lick it clean?

If any other man said those words I'd be repulsed. For some reason, there was a difference between swallowing—which I'm totally down with—and licking semen off a surface. But when Ripper ordered me to lap up his cum, my sex clenched and my nipples tightened.

He was a dangerous man, not only because of his propensity for violence, but because he invoked in me a deep longing to please him, to succumb to his wishes.

With a broad, flat tongue, I laved his palm. Then, one after the other, I sucked his fingers into my mouth, my tongue swirling over each digit as it sought every last drop of his seed.

"Good girl," he breathed.

I sighed happily and collapsed against the carpet, physically and emotionally spent.

Ripper sprawled on his stomach beside me, resting his head on his crossed arms. He must have been as exhausted as I was, because he fell asleep easily.

I dozed for a while, but found it impossible to get truly comfortable while naked on the hard floor. I rolled onto my side, facing him.

You're mine. I've staked my claim. His exact words, but what did he mean by them?

Uncle Mel used to say that a wise man knows what he doesn't know, a concept that elicited a confused "Huh?" from me the first time I heard it. I was beginning to develop an inkling of what he meant.

Ripper was a Janissary, maybe the last surviving member of his club. As much as I loved reading motorcycle club romances, I knew next to nothing about genuine biker culture. When I read the novels, I thrilled to the notion of being formally claimed as some hot biker's property. As tantalizing as the stories were, I always assumed that their depiction of life in a motorcycle club was essentially bullshit, a combination of fantasy wish-fulfillment and alpha male romance tropes. I had no clue about the expectations and assumptions that a real biker—a Janissary—would bring to a relationship.

You're mine. I've staked my claim. Were the words hyperbole, something a man said in the heat of passion? Or did they mean something else to Ripper?

I could ask him. Poke him in the shoulder and introduce the subject by saying, "In *Property of Mayhem*, when he claimed Raven in front of his club and gave her a vest with a Property of Mayhem patch..." Um, no. If Ripper wasn't already lying on the floor, he'd probably fall down laughing at the question.

I sighed. Someday I'd find the right way to ask him what the words meant, but not today, not when my brain was still in a sex-induced fog.

I leaned up on my elbow to study the club tattoo that covered his back, the turban-wearing Janissary with a handlebar mustache and a curved sword. I longed to trace the lines of the image, run my fingers over Ripper's sweat-slicked skin.

"Go ahead and touch it," Ripper mumbled groggily, his eyes still closed.

Smiling to myself, I cupped the firm mound of his ass and squeezed.

His shoulders shook with laughter. "Mac," he drawled, his voice a shiver-inducing rumble. "You know I was talking about the ink."

I sat up and swung a leg over his waist, straddling him. "It *is* beautiful." I touched the tattoo, my fingers gliding over the colorful design, an emblem he shared with men he considered brothers, men who were now likely dead.

My hand stilled and my heart constricted. Ripper's club had been his family, yet he never moaned about their loss, never indulged in self-pity. He swallowed his grief and kept going, creating new bonds with Miles and me, and even—after a fashion—with Kyle.

"Can hear you thinking," Ripper said.

I bit back what I suspected would be unwelcome words of sympathy over his loss. Instead, I leaned forward, kissed the center of his back and mentally shifted gears.

"If you and I had met before the flu, do you think I would have fit into your world?"

Ripper groaned and rolled over. He wrapped his hands around my waist and pulled me snug against his body. "You sound like Kyle."

"Seriously. I don't drink. I'd *never* do anything sexual in public. I'm not a wild party girl."

It was Ripper's turn to sigh. "First, we didn't meet before the flu, so the question's pointless. Second, I decide who and what I want. Why you gotta complicate things? It's a new world. Here and now, we fit."

He was right, of course. Ali would have said that Ripper and I were fated to meet, that flu or not, we would have found our way to each other. I've never subscribed to that kind of woo-woo thinking. I wasn't quite a hard-nosed realist, but life had stripped me of any confidence that things would work out for the best. Before the pandemic, no matter how attracted I was to Ripper, we wouldn't have stood a chance. The world tipped on its axis, and now we did.

"You're right." I splayed my fingers across his chest, admiring the hard lines of his pecs. Something occurred to me. "This afternoon, before everything went south, you said that there's something you needed to tell me. What is it?"

In an instant, Ripper's expression changed.

"Fuck!" He sat up so our faces were level. The pain I saw reflected in his dark eyes made me tremble, even before he said a word. "Rode downtown this morning to check on Harry." Ripper hesitated, as if struggling to find the words. "He's dead. Fucking flu.

Died sitting in his recliner, holding the empty bottle of Jack in his hands."

Another body blow. Not Harry, too. Not that funny, wise-cracking old man who was like a grandfather to Ripper.

"I'm so sorry." How do you comfort a man hardened by years of battle and loss, a man who had turned stoicism into an art?

I reached out and tentatively touched Ripper's face, half-expecting him to pull away. Instead, he angled his cheek into my palm and closed his eyes.

All day long, while squabbling with Kyle and then searching for me, he'd carried this secret knowledge, this secret pain. I'd put him through hell while he was suffering this gut-wrenching loss. Ripper didn't cry—wouldn't cry—but he allowed me to wrap my arms around his shoulders and drawn him close.

I thought the flu had wrung me dry, but I was wrong. Tears streamed down my face. There was always more to lose.

TWENTY-SIX

Kenzie

Neither man shared details of their private conversation—I'd no idea if Ripper and Kyle had a meeting of the minds, or if Ripper simply laid down the law—but the men achieved a workable truce.

Well, maybe it was more of a cold war than peace in our time, but at least the overt hostilities had ceased. Kyle stopped his sniping and innuendos. Ripper abandoned his homicidal glowering. And I hadn't chugged Maalox once in the past five days. Win, win, win.

Ripper and I flopped across his leather sofa, our legs entangled as we watched the final moments of a sci-fi movie on his giant TV. Every few days, Ripper fired up his generator, and we had a movie date. This afternoon, we watched a silent 1929 film, *Woman in the Moon* by the German director Fritz Lang. Uncle Mel and I had never ventured into silent, German films—way too artsy for the likes of us—but Ripper loved the classics and enjoyed sharing his enthusiasm with an willing audience.

"My first silent film, and I loved it." I smiled up at Ripper. "Great story. Gorgeous cinematography."

"Thought you'd like to watch a movie the Nazis banned in Germany." He shifted, pulling me onto his lap. "Seeing how you hate Nazis."

"Why did they ban it?" I asked.

"The rocket in the movie looked too much like the one in their V-2 rocket program."

"Amazing."

"Yeah."

"So." My fingers toyed with his metal piercing. "Miles and Kyle are making noise about a group movie night. Would you be willing to invite them over to watch a movie with us?"

"Course. How about we set something up in the next couple of days?"

"Great. Thank you." I sighed happily, perfectly content.

"And Mac?"

"Hmmm?"

"How about you keep doing what you're doing with your fingers, and I'll do this." His hand slid into my pants.

An hour later, we headed back to the compound. We passed Miles in the backyard. For the past few days, Miles had been obsessed with the solar oven. Taking advantage of a stretch of sunny weather, he'd tinkered with recipes from one of Aunt Debbie's old cookbooks and finally produced a passable loaf of bread from an outdoor oven powered by the sun.

You don't realize how much you miss fresh bread until you live without it for a few weeks. Tonight, he'd proudly announced, we were having grilled cheese sandwiches and a salad made with baby lettuce from the garden. The cheese was one of those garishly hued, shelf-stable products, something I'd normally turn my nose up at, but I was genuinely looking forward to it. Fresh bread, something green from the garden. Heaven.

"Ripper, Mackenzie, come check this out," he called excitedly, leaning over his latest obsession. He pointed at the glass panel on top of the oven. Obediently, we peered inside. "See! I figured out how to make the bread crust brown better."

"Good job, buddy," Ripper said. "You want to high five?" Miles nodded and the two men slapped their palms together. "What was the trick?"

"I sprayed water on the loaves before they went into the oven."

"They look fantastic, Miles," I said. "Congratulations. Now that you've mastered bread, what do you want to try next?"

He rocked in place and stared off to one side, his lips parted. I recognized that look. It meant the wheels were turning in his brain while Miles considered some delightful new idea.

"I haven't thought of what to do next. Is there something you'd like me to make, Mackenzie?"

"Yes," I answered without hesitation. "Cookies. You know my favorites."

"Do you want mom's sugar cookies? Or her molasses crinkles?"

"Surprise me. Either one would make me do a happy dance."

Miles's face was lit from within, an excited smile curving his lips. He was rarely demonstrative, but it always gave him great satisfaction to know exactly what to do to make somebody happy. "I'm going to go look at mom's recipe box." He ran to the house.

"Happy dance, huh?" Ripper said. "I wanna see that someday."

"Maybe you will." I smiled at a sudden memory. "Ali strong-armed me into taking a strip dance class with her last year. Maybe—if you're very good—I'll show you some of my moves."

I'd grumbled at first when Ali proposed taking the class, telling her we were betraying the sisterhood and reinforcing sexist stereotypes, but the truth was, I loved every minute of it.

"No maybe about it." Ripper's eyes narrowed with interest. "I'm getting a private show later."

"We'll see." Can't let a man think he calls all the shots.

He swatted my ass, and I jumped, huffing indignantly.

"Mr. Solis, that was uncalled for."

"You think?" He grinned.

Miles emerged from the back door, waving a small knife and carrying a bucket of water, Hector at his heels. "I'm going to water the tomato plants and pick lettuce for dinner."

They disappeared around the side of the house, heading for the vegetable bed in the front yard.

"Sugar cookies or molasses crinkles." Ripper took my hand and lead the way toward the house. "Why couldn't you say chocolate chip."

I wrinkled my nose. "Not all women go gaga over chocolate. If you give me a chocolate chip cookie, I pick the pesky things out and flick them across the room."

That statement stopped him in his tracks. "That's heresy, woman. You don't like chocolate. You took a strip dance class. Ms. Dunwitty, you're full of surprises."

I shrugged. "What can I tell you? I'm a woman of surprising depth."

He chuckled. "So I see."

We found Kyle sitting at the command station, keeping one eye on the security monitor while he read one of Uncle Mel's old paperback spy thrillers.

"Hi, Kyle," I said.

He grunted a response, not taking his eyes off the page.

A sour expression crossed Ripper's face. I squeezed his hand, silently begging him not to start another argument. He rolled his eyes, but nodded, acceding to my request.

I glanced at the security monitor on the desk. On one quadrant of the security feed, the motion-sensitive camera had focused on Miles working in the front vegetable garden. He pulled a few weeds, then bent over to examine a tomato plant.

Something bright sailed over the chain-link fence.

I gasped as a fireball exploded mere feet away from Miles, wicked flames dancing as high as his head. He stumbled backward, then picked up the bucket of water and flung it onto the flames. Instead of sputtering out, the flames spread, lashing at Miles's legs.

Ripper was out the door in a flash, hurtling down the steps toward Miles, Kyle and I close on his heels. He yanked Miles back from the inferno, slapping at the scorch marks on Miles's jeans and shirt.

"Let the fire burn itself out," he barked.

Kyle grabbed Hector around the neck and hauled him back from the flames.

I almost tripped over my feet rushing to Miles's side. He stood petrified, clutching his elbows, his eyes wide with shock. I couldn't stop myself. I grabbed my cousin's arms, frantically scanning his body for signs of injury. His face and arms were red, as if he had a bad sunburn. Flames had licked at his cheeks and singed his eyebrows, but he appeared otherwise unharmed.

"Miles," I sobbed with relief.

He shuddered and pulled himself out of his shocked stupor.

"I want mom." His lips trembled.

It took all of my willpower not to pull him into my arms, but instead of giving comfort, such a gesture would overwhelm his already-frayed senses.

"I know, Miles," I said. "Your mom's not here, but I am. Ripper is. Kyle is. We're all here for you. It's going to be all right."

The flames had died down, and I saw a shattered glass bottle on the gravel path.

"What the fuck was that?" Kyle stood with his hands on his hips as he surveyed the scene.

Ripper stared grimly at the dying flames. "Somebody threw a Molotov cocktail into the yard."

TWENTY-SEVEN

Ripper

"What are we going to do?" Kyle leaned forward in the chair, his elbows on his knees, his voice low.

Last I checked, Miles was lying in bed with his face turned to the wall while Mac read him some children's book about a stuffed bear.

We? I had neither the time nor the inclination to keep making nice with Kyle. "Best I can tell, the only thing you bring to the table is sarcasm and a shitty attitude. I'll handle this. You do you. Stay put and pout. Or maybe go work on your tan."

Kyle clenched his teeth. Looked like the little piss ant wanted to argue. Bring it, boy. I was so angry I'd welcome the chance to pound something. Or someone.

An hour ago, Miles was the happiest and most relaxed I'd ever seen him. He had a job—baking bread and tending the garden—and he was doing good, making a contribution to the group. He was proud of himself, and it showed in the expression on his normally guarded face and the bounce in his step.

And now? Curled on his side and nearly catatonic.

The burns weren't too bad, thank fuck, but he was in pain. When he found out he'd made the fire worse by throwing water on it, Miles called himself stupid and kept bashing his head against the wall.

Mac cried, unable to calm him down or to make him stop. I couldn't take it. Human touch upset Miles, but I locked him in a bear hug anyway, whatever it took to make him stop banging his head. He tensed, then leaned into me, his eyes leaking tears.

I'm only seven years older than Miles, but watching him suffer was like watching my kid in pain. Helpless rage and a deep protective instinct roiled in my blood.

"I've been an asshole, but you're a dumbshit if you don't think two people going after this guy is better than one," Kyle said.

I'd been pacing the room, letting off nervous energy. I spun on him, my fists balled for a fight.

Kyle met my eyes defiantly, his jaw set. "Kenzie. Miles." He emphasized the names, calling my attention to what was really important. "How are we going to protect them?"

I blew out a long breath, trying to expel the useless, self-indulgent rage. Where was The Ripper when I needed him? Asshole was right. In a city this size, with an unknown arsonist, two men going after the target was better than one. Extra eyes. Extra ears. Extra weapon?

"You know how to shoot?" I asked.

He hesitated before answering. "I can handle a shotgun."

Nothing wrong with that answer, so why was my bullshit meter pinging?

"You any good?"

Kyle threw his hands in the air. "Yeah, I'm good. I was junior trap champion at my county club. The only thing I've shot at is clay pigeons. Go ahead and laugh."

Fuck me. I'm going into battle with a spoiled rich kid, a college boy who'd probably never done a lick of real work in his life. I bit back my snide retort and focused on the good news.

"All right. Means you got good aim."

Country Club appeared braced for an insult. When one didn't come, he continued.

"The question is, who is our target? We don't know if we were attacked at random—some fire bug running around the city tossing Molotov cocktails at whatever strikes his fancy—somebody who just likes to make things go boom, or if was a targeted attack." He lifted his brows and glanced pointedly at my cut. "You got any enemies?"

"Of course, make this is about me and the club. You want to catch the man, or do you want to persuade Mac that it's all my fault? Get your head screwed on straight."

"No, man. My point is we don't know what this is about."

He was right. We were fumbling in the dark right now.

"If there's a firebug in the city, wouldn't we have seen evidence of it before now? Without a fire department, any blaze he set could burn out of control. We haven't seen or smelled smoke."

"Maybe he's been setting fires someplace else—the suburbs or a small town—and he just started on the east side. Maybe he started with something small, like a dumpster or something else that would burn out without spreading, and now he's escalating."

"And we just happened to be his first target?" I asked doubtfully.

Kyle shrugged. "Somebody has to be."

"That seems like a stretch. Or, like you said, it could be personal." I shoved my hair out of my face. "I can't think of anybody who'd have that kind of a grudge against me. No personal enemies. If somebody had a grudge against the Janissaries, it'd make more sense to attack the clubhouse. Besides, this is Miles's property, not mine. Can't imagine anybody would have it in for Miles."

Kyle blew out an exasperated breath. "There's too much we can't know. Let's focus on what we do. An unknown person threw a Molotov cocktail into Miles's yard. We want to track him down in a big city, full of empty buildings and houses. We don't know how he's getting around."

"Didn't hear a vehicle, and the motion-sensitive camera had focused on Miles, not the street," I noted. "Could be he came up the sidewalk, hugging the fence, out of range of the camera. Which means he was on foot, or he had stashed a bicycle or car a block away, out of earshot."

"A bicycle," Kyle repeated. "That reminds me of something. I took a psych class where we profiled arsonists. They're usually white males with low IQs. If they're under eighteen, they're most likely pyromaniacs. Kids with poor impulse control who like to watch things burn. If our arsonist is walking or riding a bike, it could be a teenage pyromaniac. If his parents died, there's nobody to supervise him, and the city's wide open."

Still didn't feel right. Why here? Why now? "We won't know for sure till we find him. The big question is, how do we stop him?"

"If he's just getting started on an arson spree, we'll see evidence. He'll start other fires. If it's personal, he'll want to hit us again," Kyle said.

We both fell silent, deep in thought.

"It's gonna be dark in a couple of hours," I said. "How about you and I take positions at opposite ends of the block, in case the arsonist comes back after dark. My hunch is that we were targeted. No fucking clue why, but that seems more likely than we just happened to be the first place in the city he hit."

"It beats driving around the city hoping we spot him. Talk about searching for a needle in a haystack."

"You want to try to get a couple of hours shut eye before we go out?" I asked.

"No, I couldn't sleep if I tried. How about you?"

"Not my first all-nighter," I replied. "If you need help staying awake, Miles has Adderall."

Kyle shook his head. "I tried that once during finals week, and I don't want to do it again. It left me so jittery that my hands wouldn't stop shaking. A couple of cups of coffee will do me fine."

"All right. We got a plan. I'm gonna check on Mac and Miles."

Mac sat quietly in a chair, her hands clenched on her lap, the discarded book face down on the nightstand. She put a finger to her lips when I stuck my head in the door. After tip-toeing out of the room, she shut the door and followed me to the hall.

"He finally fell asleep." Mac's face was pale, and she looked wrung out.

I folded her in my arms, wishing I could shield her from all the bad things in the world.

"Hey." I put a finger under her chin and tipped her face up to mine. "I want you to lie down and try to sleep. We have a big night ahead of us, and I need you sharp."

She drew back. "What's going on?"

"Got a hunch the arsonist might come back tonight. Kyle and I are going to lie in wait at opposite ends of the block, try to catch him red-handed."

"You're going to leave Miles and me alone?"

"Anything goes wrong, we're thirty seconds away. I won't let anything happen to you."

"We won't let anything happen to you," Kyle interrupted.

Irritation spiked through me, but I tamped it down. Two men standing guard was better than one, and if he demanded credit for watching out for her, it made no real difference. Mac chose me, not him. And the college boy had finally decided to step up. Couldn't hurt to toss him a bone.

"We won't let anything happen to you," I agreed.

Mac stared at the floor, clearly troubled.

"What's wrong?"

"I'm what's wrong," she said. "You tell me I'm going to be alone here with Miles and my first thought is, 'Who's going to take care of things if something bad happens?' Dammit. I can't afford to be such a dependent wuss. Give me a job. Give me something I can do to help."

Unfortunately, my knee-jerk reaction mirrored hers. Mac was mine to protect, and I'd gut anyone who threatened her, but I'd be doing her no favor if I let her rely on me to keep safe.

I'm not invincible. The virus might still get me. I might come up against a bigger and badder opponent who could get the better of me in a fight—although my ego scoffed at that suggestion. If I died, I couldn't leave Mac helpless to face a dangerous world.

"You're right," I said. "If I'm not around someday, you'll need to know that you can take care of yourself. I believe in you. You're no wuss, remember?"

She stiffened, then extracted herself from my arms, probably troubled by talk of my death or the reminder of her ordeal with Jason.

Mac swallowed and was silent for a long moment. "Tell me what I can do."

"Keep an eye on Miles. I'm worried about how withdrawn he is. And I'd like you to monitor the security feed tonight. Nobody is going to sneak past Kyle and me on the street, but there's a remote chance the arsonist could hop fences and attack from a side yard."

"Okay, I can do that. We should eat dinner, so our energy doesn't lag overnight. I'm going to go check the solar oven and see if the bread's still good."

While Kyle and I finalized plans for our ambush, Mac set three places at the kitchen table and warmed a couple of cans of chili over the hot plate. Nobody had the heart to eat grilled cheese sandwiches and a salad without Miles. We didn't have butter, but we tore off chunks of the fresh bread and dipped it in the chili, sopping up the savory juices.

"Damn, that was good." Kyle leaned back in his chair after polishing off his meal. "I don't care if the crust was too brown, that bread was fantastic. Thanks for making dinner, Kenzie."

Mac managed a halfhearted smile. "It's Miles you should thank for the bread."

"I will, as soon as he's up. In fact, I'm nominating him for official baker."

Her smile grew wider, and this time it reached her eyes, but it faded quickly. "He'll like that."

Mac retreated to Miles's room after dinner. Kyle warmed water to wash the dishes and I ground beans for coffee.

"Is Kenzie all right?" Kyle glanced over his shoulder as he rinsed a bowl. "She seems down, even more than I'd expect under the circumstances."

"She had some trouble coping after the kidnapping," I said. "She had been getting better, but could be the Molotov cocktail set her back, made her feel vulnerable again."

Kyle wheeled around to face me, wiping his hands on his jeans. "Kidnapping! What the hell are you talking about?"

"She didn't tell you?" I was incredulous.

"Not a word."

"A few weeks ago, a drug addict posing as a cop talked Mac into letting him in the yard. He kidnapped her. He had some hare-brained scheme to force Miles to turn over his stash of prescription drugs. She tried to escape. Attacked him. He shot at her. Missed twice. I got there when he was about to finish her off. Took care of him and brought her home."

"Jesus." Kyle sat down hard on a kitchen chair. "You saved her life."

I shrugged. "I protect my own."

"Well...damn. Good thing you were there, man."

I brought Mac a cup of coffee, dropping a kiss on her upturned face while she sat at her cousin's bedside, then I went back to my place to fetch a pair of night-vision goggles. I carried my Colt, and Kyle took one of the shotguns.

We took up positions at opposite ends of the block, concealed vantage points where we could keep our eyes on both the street and the house. Standing watch was nothing new to me, but I hoped the inexperienced college kid could stay alert and not doze off.

Two houses down from the compound, a light moved behind a window shade, proof that we weren't the only survivors on the street. A car's headlights caught my attention as it drove through an intersection a quarter mile away, then sped off in the opposite direction. If it was the arsonist, we weren't his target at the moment.

Old Mrs. Mowbray's orange cat Murphy sauntered up the middle of the street, king of the road now that cars had all but disappeared. Fat and happy, apparently living large on a diet of mice and birds. The damned thing meowed when he spied me and twined around my legs, purring. Hector would just love smelling cat on me when I came home.

"Scat," I whispered, shaking my leg to discourage him. Murphy slunk off, curling up under a bush a few feet away. Guess I had company during my watch.

The streetlights had stopped working weeks ago. A crescent moon hung in the sky, doing little to illuminate the dark landscape. I slipped on my night-vision goggles and settled back to wait. Hours passed. Murphy eventually wandered off, chasing a bug.

Sound carried at night. Must have been after midnight when I heard the familiar whoosh of bicycle tires rolling over pavement from about a block away. I braced, ready to spring into action if he passed my position.

A bicycle careened around the corner, its rider little more than a black shape huddled over the handlebars.

I jumped into the street and the bike slowed. The rider twisted in the seat, glancing over his shoulder. He took off, pumping hard on the pedals, only to find his path blocked by Kyle, who held the shotgun at the ready.

Whaddaya know. Country Club didn't let me down.

The bike skidded to a stop, and the rider's head swung back and forth as he looked from Kyle to me.

"Get off the bike," I ordered.

"Fuck you!" The defiant shout would have been more impressive if his voice hadn't cracked. Definitely a kid, with a baseball cap pulled low over his eyes.

"Get. Off. The. Bike." I imbued my voice with a menace that had stopped grown men in their tracks.

Kyle pumped the shotgun, and the kid's gaze flitted nervously from Kyle to me.

"Have it your way, asshole." He slid off the banana seat and engaged the kickstand, leaving the bike upright. It was a little girl's bike, with streamers dangling from the handlebars and a basket decorated with plastic flowers. Inside the basket, I saw half a dozen bottles nestled together, rags sticking out of the open ends.

Kid had a busy night planned.

"Put your hands up and step away from the bike."

He jutted his chin out. "Make me."

Really? Did the twerp have a death wish?

Five seconds later, he was face down on the pavement, his arms pinned behind his back. He bucked and let loose with a string of expletives that would do any foul-mouthed biker proud.

"Shut up," I said, jerking on his arms. I pulled a zip tie from my pocket and secured his wrists, then hauled him to his feet. His baseball cap had fallen off during the tussle. I pulled a penlight from a pocket and shined it at a freckle-faced kid with tousled blond hair who was spitting abuse at me.

Shit. I recognized that face.

TWENTY-EIGHT

Kenzie

If I'm not around someday, you'll need to know that you can take care of yourself.

What was that old proverb? Knowledge is power. Now that I knew how things stood between Ripper and me, I could look into the future with clear eyes, rather than through rose-colored glasses.

Ripper didn't intend to be around for the long haul.

I shouldn't be surprised. If life had taught me anything, it was that people leave.

I saw a counselor a couple of years ago who told me I have abandonment issues. Duh. The thing is, I thought I'd wrestled those issues into submission. When Aunt Debbie and Uncle Mel were killed, I knew that a stupid accident took them away. It wasn't fate depriving me of the people I loved. And when the writing was on the wall, I'd dumped Kyle before he got around to dumping me. The flu killed Ali and Jake; their deaths had nothing to do with me.

The demon had been vanquished, until Ripper told me that someday he'd be moving on. Suddenly, I was five years old again, my nose pressed to the window, wondering what I'd done to make the man I loved best not want to come home anymore.

Pathetic.

It is what it is, another truism. Time to put on my big-girl panties. God, I was full of cliches today.

Ripper had never told me that he was going to stay. He'd claimed me, told me I was his, but maybe I'd read too much into that. Maybe all he'd meant was that I was his for as long as he chose to stick around. I'd foolishly assumed that we all were banding together, creating a new sort of family to face a radically changed world.

I vaguely recalled some old adage about making an ass out of yourself when you make assumptions, but my brain was finally tired of regurgitating trite phrases.

I slumped in the desk chair, staring glumly at the security monitor. I'd better make peace with this new knowledge, or Ripper would be taking off sooner rather than later. Nobody wanted to hang around a moper.

I drew in a deep breath and sat up straight.

What were my priorities? Helping Miles recover from the Molotov cocktail attack was number one. It broke my heart to see his spirit wilt after the fireball exploded at his feet. I'd do anything to help him regain his confidence. Number two, stopping the arsonist. With no functioning fire or police departments, ordinary people would have to step up to keep the city safe. Number three? Enjoying every moment of my remaining time with Ripper and summoning the strength to say goodbye with grace when the time came.

Big-girl panties tugged up nice and snug, it was time to take care of business.

I quickly checked on Miles and found him still asleep. Hector lifted his head from the floor, and I paused to give him a pat before returning to the command post. Crossing my arms on the desk, I leaned forward and kept my eyes firmly focused on the monitor screen.

Minutes ticked by slowly, then hours. Every time my attention wandered, I snapped it back to the screen.

Finally, I saw the heavy front gate roll open. Ripper stepped in and gave a thumbs up to the camera. They got the arsonist.

He marched toward the front porch, a young boy in tow. Kyle followed him through the gate, pushing a child's bike. He paused to lock the gate before following Ripper and the boy up the steps.

I rushed to unlock the front door, then stood back while Ripper escorted the boy into the house. The boy had the face of a cherub, with cupid's bow lips and messy blond curls.

The kid looked me up and down, his churlish expression morphing into a leer. "She's hot. Which one of you is fucking her? Or is it both?"

"Shut up," Ripper and Kyle said in unison.

The face of a cherub with the mouth of a sailor.

Kyle fetched a chair from the kitchen table and placed it in the middle of the room. Ripper pushed the kid onto the chair, then pulled two zip ties from his pocket and fastened the boy's ankles to the chair legs.

That brought back memories, and I had to look away. Ripper touched my arm, concern on his face.

"I'll be a minute," I said. "I want to make sure Hector has food and water."

I called for Hector who followed me into the kitchen. He had plenty of water, but I added a scoop of dry food to his food dish. The patient dog allowed me to hug him for a long moment before he began nosing the bowl.

"I can take a hint." I gave him a slight smile. Returning to the front room, I leaned against the wall, well back from the interrogation to come.

Ripper retrieved another kitchen chair and took a seat facing the boy. "There's no point denying it, kid. We caught you red-handed."

"So? What are you going to do, call the cops? Good luck with that," he scoffed.

"No cops. No jail. No court. Just us." Ripper pointed to Kyle and himself. "Judge. Jury. And executioner."

Startled, I glanced at Kyle. Ripper wasn't implying that he'd hurt the boy, was he? That couldn't be part of any plan.

"Am I supposed to be scared?" The boy sneered. "Because you're a Janissary? What a bunch of pussies."

I expected Ripper to explode, the way he had when Kyle insulted his club, but he laughed instead. "Did you actually call us pussies? Got to work on your insults, kid."

"Got to work on your insults, kid," the boy mimicked in a falsetto voice.

"I know who you are." Ripper folded his arms over his chest.

Uh-oh. That was his I-mean-business, and I'm-getting-pissed pose.

"Do not," the boy said in a songsong voice.

"Jason and Chad's baby brother."

I stifled a gasp, staring at the boy. Now that I looked for it, I could see the resemblance between him and the man who had kidnapped me.

His surly expression returned, but he held his tongue.

"The baby of the family." Ripper drew out the word baby.

"I'm no baby," the boy mumbled.

"No? What are you? Nine? Ten?"

"Twelve," the boy said indignantly.

"Twelve," Ripper repeated. "Still a kid, but you weren't living at home when the flu hit. Your bed was stripped, and your half of the room looked empty. What happened? Your parents kick you out?"

"They didn't kick me out. I got sent away, locked up because I'm more of a badass than you'll ever be."

"That right?" Ripper leaned forward on his elbows, cocking his head to one side. "What'd you do, badass? Wet the bed?"

The boy flushed. I bet he *was* a bed wetter. Ripper was needling him, goading the boy into revealing essential information. It was hard to watch a child being picked on.

I opened my mouth to protest the cruelty. Kyle shot me a warning look and shook his head. I pressed my lips together, reluctantly keeping my silence.

"What'd I do?" The boy bristled. "I burned down the neighbor's garage. Torched the Jackson's travel trailer. Burned old lady Wang's chicken coop. You should have seen the birds! Squawk! Squawk! Squawk!" He laughed, reliving the memory.

His shoulders rose and fell. If his hands weren't tied behind his back, I bet he'd be flapping imaginary wings.

"Cops caught me when I started a fire in the school library. I saw a movie where some Nazis piled up books on the street and set them on fire. It was so cool! I tried to do the same thing. I dumped lighter fluid on a big pile of books. The janitor saw me and called the cops. I got sent away to residential."

He smiled proudly at Ripper. "That badass enough for you?"

Good lord. A twelve year old firebug roaming the streets unsupervised.

"What's your name?" I asked impulsively.

"Caleb."

I crossed the room and knelt in front on his chair, trying to create some kind of a bond with this wretched child. "Caleb. Were you locked up when everybody started getting sick? That must have been so scary. How were you able to get away?"

He hesitated, torn, I suspected, between suspicion and the innate human need for connection. "A lot of the kids and teachers got sick and died. I didn't, because I'm strong and tough, like my big brother."

I felt genuine sympathy for a twelve-year-old, locked into a facility, surrounded by dying people. "How did you get out?"

"One of the nurses decided to go home. She unlocked the door and said anybody who felt good enough to leave could go. So I did."

"And you went home?" I gently prodded.

"Yeah. Everybody was dead but Jason." His lip trembled, and suddenly he looked more like a little boy than the angry preteen we'd confronted.

"I'm sorry, Caleb."

Unable to use his hands, he wiped his cheek on the shoulder of his shirt.

Ripper picked up the questioning. "Did Jason take care of you?"

"He wanted to take care of me, but he couldn't because he was sick. He said it wasn't the flu. He said the neighborhood weirdo stole his medicine, and he was gonna come over here and get it back. Then he'd feel all better, and we could go someplace nice."

Jason left to retrieve his oxy, and he never came back, leaving this kid alone in a house with his dead family. How horrible.

"I saw you." Caleb glared at Ripper. "I saw you come in the back yard, so I hid behind some boxes in the garage. Why did you break into our house?"

"I was looking for Jason." Ripper surprised me by admitting the truth.

"Why?"

"Because he kidnapped Mac." He pointed to me. "He thought Miles would give him the medicine if he took her."

"What happened to Jason? Where is he now?" Caleb demanded.

Brutal honesty was not what this child needed. It would serve no purpose to fill his head with bloody images of his adored big brother's actual death.

I spoke quickly, before Ripper could reveal the truth. "Jason got really sick. He died from the flu. That's why he never came back for you. After he died, I got away and went home. I'm sorry you lost your brother, Caleb."

Caleb squeezed his eyes shut, absorbing the news. "I knew there was a reason he didn't come back home."

"Did you throw the Molotov cocktail into the yard because you're mad at Miles?" Ripper asked, letting my lie pass.

Caleb's eyes glittered with spite. "It's all his fault, and I want him to burn."

Ripper stood and gestured to Kyle and me. "We need to talk." He whistled and Hector trotted to his side. "Hector, sit." The dog obediently sat back on his haunches. "This is a trained guard dog," he told Caleb. "Hold still and there won't be any problem. If you move..." Ripper shrugged, the gesture implying a world of hurt.

Kyle and I followed Ripper into my small bedroom, a room where we could close a door to muffle our conversation.

"We can't leave that little monster running around the city," Kyle said. "He'll burn the place to the ground."

"Agreed," Ripper grunted.

"The police, social services, they're all gone," I said. "We'll have to take him in. There's nobody else."

Both men looked at me as if I'd lost my mind.

"We are not taking him in, Mac. That's a hard no."

Kyle nodded in agreement. "Did you hear him, Kenzie? Caleb loves to set fires. He laughed when he described chickens burning to death. The kid is vicious and absolutely lacking in empathy. He said he wants Miles to burn, remember. You think Miles should live with that? You expect him to recover if he has to share a home with the kid who tried to set him on fire and who wants to do it again?"

Miles, my number one priority. Oh, God. Kyle was right.

I collapsed onto the cot and dropped my face into my hands, my mind desperately seeking a solution to this mess.

Kyle sat beside me and laid a hand on my shoulder. "How would it work if we took Caleb in? We'd have to keep him locked in a room or chained to a wall. We could never let down our guard. We'd be living with a surly, foul-mouthed prisoner who would make our lives hell. And it would be no picnic for him, either."

"Maybe we could help him get better," I suggested in a small voice, lowering my hands and meeting Kyle's eyes. "Teach him right from wrong."

"No, sweetheart," he said gently. "He's a rage-filled pyromaniac. He has a mental disorder we're not qualified to treat."

Ripper squatted in front of me, his expression implacable. "We're not debating this, Mac. The kid's not staying. I won't allow anything or anybody to jeopardize your safety."

"Then what are we going to do with him?" My eyes filled with tears, and I furiously brushed them away. "Because I'm not going to let you kill a twelve-year-old child, if that's what you're thinking. That's where I draw the line."

Eyes grim and jaw set in a hard line, Ripper seized my hands. "I've never killed a kid, and I don't want to start now—"

"Good," I interrupted. "I mean it. Find another way."

"Hey, Kenzie." Kyle spoke up. "Why don't you go see if Caleb wants something to eat and let Ripper and me come up with a plan we can all live with."

I should have protested on principle. The little woman is sent to rustle up some grub while the men make plans? Except...it would do my heart good to show some kindness to this lost soul, and I truly didn't want to participate in the discussion.

"That's a good idea. Thanks, Kyle."

Ripper squeezed my hands, then released me. I slipped from the room, shutting the door behind me.

"You have fun back there with your boyfriends? Two on one, woo-hoo!"

I ignored the taunt. "When's the last time you ate?"

Caleb shrugged. "I ate three candy bars and some corn chips tonight. Got them from a quickie mart. There's a lot of good shit lying around. Not going hungry anytime soon."

"When's the last time you ate a hot meal?" I persisted.

"Don't remember."

"Would you like some spaghetti?" That would be quick and easy to throw together on the hot plate.

He eyed me suspiciously. "How come you're being nice? Is this one of those condemned man last meal things? Are your boyfriends gonna kill me?"

Despite his bravado, I saw fear on his young face.

"Nope. We're not going to kill you, but I am going to feed you. How about the spaghetti?"

"Do you have some of that cheese in a green can?"

"I do."

"Okay," he said grudgingly. "I'll eat your spaghetti."

Ripper and Kyle emerged from the back room as I was dishing up the food.

"Can you untie his hands so he can feed himself?" I asked Ripper.

"Sure."

He pulled a knife from his pocket and cut the zip tie binding Caleb's wrists. I handed Caleb a bowl of pasta—along with a plastic fork—and he dug in. When he polished off the food and handed me the empty bowl, Ripper once again took a seat facing the boy.

"Smart thing to do would be to kill you," Ripper said without preamble.

The stark words chilled me. After everything I said, had the men decided to kill the boy anyway? I glanced at Kyle. He shook his head, assuring me that the implied threat wasn't real.

"We can't risk you setting a fire that will burn out of control." Kyle stepped up to stand beside Ripper.

Caleb glared at me, his expression rife with reproach. "How about if I promise not to set any fires?"

Ripper snorted. "Your promise ain't worth shit, kid."

"No promise will make you behave," Kyle said. "But you know what might?"

The question hung unanswered in the air.

Caleb squirmed in the chair. "What?" he finally asked.

"Fear." Ripper leaned forward in the chair. "We got a simple proposition for you. You stay on the west side of the river. Lots of houses and stores where you can find food and a place to sleep. You will *never* cross a bridge and come back to the east side. If I see you over here, the deal is off. And you will never set another fire, because if you do, if I see any sign of flames or smoke, I will hunt you down. It's what I do. There's no place you can hide where I won't find you. And when I do, well, I won't be so forgiving a second time. You feel me, kid?"

Caleb glared at Ripper. "Yeah, I got it."

"All right. I'm gonna pull my jeep up to the front gate." Ripper tossed Kyle another zip tie. "Fasten his hands together again, then free his legs and bring him to the gate."

"Will do."

"You're going tonight?" I followed Ripper toward the back door.

"I want him out of the house before Miles wakes up."

"Wait a moment, please."

Ripper turned to me and raised his brows. "What is it, Mac?"

"Are you really going to drop him off on the other side of the river? This isn't like that story that parents sometimes tell kids about an old, sick pet who needs to be put to sleep? That they took him to live out his days on a nice farm in the country?"

Yeah, it was an insulting question, but I had to know that this wasn't a lie he and Kyle had concocted to shield me from an unendurable truth.

He put his hands on his hips and stared at the floor for a minute, then lifted his head, his expression weary. "Have I ever lied to you, Mac?"

"No, but I thought you might to spare me this."

"I won't lie to protect you from a hard truth." His eyes drilled into mine as he spoke slowly, emphasizing every word. "I won't lie to make your life easier, or mine. I won't lie to make you think I'm a better man than I am. I want a relationship grounded in honesty. Nothing less."

"That's what I want, too." My eyes swam with tears and an ache in the back of my throat made it hard to speak. "I'm sorry. You're right. I shouldn't have questioned your honesty. I won't do it again."

"Come here." His expression softened as he pulled me into his arms.

I held on tight, committing to memory the sound of his heart beating beneath my cheek, the scent of leather, soap, and musk that was uniquely his own, the sensation of hard muscles flexing beneath my fingertips as he held me.

One day, these memories would be all that remained of our time together. One day, I'd find the courage to ask him when he intended to go, secure in the knowledge that he'd tell me the truth.

One day, but not today. I wasn't ready to face a future without him.

TWENTY-NINE

Kenzie

Nobody would ever accuse them of launching a bromance, but the tension between Ripper and Kyle had eased considerably since they worked together to catch the little pyromaniac.

I watched out the kitchen window as Ripper and Kyle—both shirtless—sparred in the yard.

Just weeks ago, the sight would have thrown me into a panic. I probably would have rushed outside with a pail of water, threatening to drench them like a pair of hissing tomcats if they didn't break it up. Now, instead of intervening, I watched the men hone their fighting skills.

Sweat glistened on their bare chests as they circled each other, muscles rippling. They were beautiful, each in his own way. Ripper had at least three inches and forty pounds of powerfully sculpted muscle on Kyle's six-foot, lean, athletic frame.

Ripper shoved his shaggy hair back from his eyes, then caught sight of me in the window. Grinning, he lunged forward and in a blur of movement flipped Kyle onto his stomach. Was he showing off? Kyle slapped the ground, yielding, before he hopped to his feet. Kyle said something to Ripper, who tossed back his head and laughed. They circled each other again.

I tore my eyes away from the sight when Miles shuffled into the kitchen. He poured himself a cup of coffee from the thermal carafe and without a word, wandered back to his position at the command center.

Physically, he'd healed from the Molotov cocktail attack nine days ago. Like a bad sunburn, the red skin on his face and arms had blistered and peeled. His singed eyebrows and eyelashes were growing back. Mentally, his recovery wasn't going nearly as well.

After taking to his bed for two days—following my I'm-taking-a-day example after the kidnapping—Miles reemerged, a listless shadow of his former self. Dispirited and lethargic, he wandered restlessly from one task to the next. Nothing held his interest or sparked his enthusiasm. He even shoved the solar oven on top of the defunct refrigerator.

When I asked for help cranking the manual washing machine, he sighed and lent a hand, but it was a joyless exercise. I jollied him into helping me plant beans and carrots, but again, he was merely going through the motions. His exuberance, his sense of purpose, had died on the day of the attack.

I poured myself a cup of coffee and followed Miles into the front room. Perching on the edge of the desk, I watched my cousin turning knobs and flipping switches as he scanned radio frequencies.

"You owe me cookies," I said.

He pulled off his headset. "What?"

"I said, you owe me cookies. Sugar or molasses, I don't care which one you make, but I'm tired of waiting."

Miles frowned. "The solar oven is in the kitchen. You know where all the ingredients are. You can make them yourself."

I blew on the hot coffee to cool it. "I can, but you promised to make them for me, and I'm holding you to that promise."

I had him there. For Miles, promises were sacred, a nonnegotiable commitment to do something, and I'd called due his debt.

"Can I make them some other time? Maybe next week?" he hedged.

"Nope. I have a hankering, and I want cookies today."

He rocked back and forth, reluctance battling with his sense of obligation. I waited patiently, sipping coffee, while his conscience forced him into action.

"Okay." He was clearly annoyed that I'd forced his hand. "I'll make your darned cookies."

Darned! Miles must be angry. Aunt Debbie never tolerated foul language, and darned was as close as he got to swearing a blue streak. He stomped into the kitchen, every step a protest.

Ripper and Kyle burst through the kitchen door, laughing and dripping with perspiration. Ripper poured water from a bucket into a basin in the sink. He splashed water on his face and chest and rubbed a bar of soap over his sweaty skin.

"You can't do that," Miles cried, snatching the bar of soap from Ripper's hand and throwing it through the open back door. "You're making a mess. It's sloppy. The kitchen sink is not for washing up."

"Somebody's cranky," Kyle said under his breath.

Ripper leaned over the basin and rinsed the lather off his face and arms. He pulled a kitchen towel out of a drawer, patting his skin dry before tossing the damp towel onto the counter. He turned to face Miles, who stood trembling with anger in the middle of the room.

Miles clenched and unclenched his fists and for one terrible moment, I thought my cousin might launch a sort of suicide attack against his friend.

"What's going on, Miles?" Ripper asked mildly.

"You broke the rules!" Miles shouted.

Ripper leaned back against the sink, his expression imperturbable, a counterpoint to Miles's irrational, out-of-left-field fury.

I hadn't seen Miles fly into such an absurd rage since his adolescence, after relentless bullying forced him to drop out of school. The slightest provocation would set him off then. We'd all tiptoed around him for months.

"Miles!" I said, aghast. Had I started this by twisting his arm to make cookies? I'd been attempting to snap him out of his funk, to reanimate his love of baking, not to drive him over the edge.

Ripper raised a hand to still my protest. "What rules did I break, Miles?"

"You...You don't clean yourself up in the kitchen sink. It's not safe. You'll splash soapy water on the floor and make it slippery. Somebody might fall down and hit their head or break their arm. And there are no doctors. I've worked so hard to make everything safe and I can't...I can't..."

Miles wrapped his arms around his waist and bent forward, his mouth opening and closing on a wordless cry.

With slow, easy steps, Ripper approached him. "Hey, Miles."

My cousin ignored him.

"You *have* worked hard to keep everybody safe," Ripper said. "Food, water, weapons, medicine, security cameras. Bars on the windows. Doors and gates reinforced. Shit, you even stretched razor wire on top of the fence."

Miles straightened and glanced briefly at Ripper's eyes. "And you helped me put rebar along the fence line so nobody can drive into the yard."

"That's right. You tried to think of everything. Nobody could have done a better job making the place secure than you have, Miles."

Miles bobbed his head, acknowledging Ripper's praise.

"But a kid threw a Molotov cocktail over the fence and burned you. Didn't see that coming, did you?"

Miles jerked his head back, surprise and betrayal etched across his face.

"The thing is, nobody can predict the future. Nobody can think of everything that can go wrong, least of all prepare for it. No matter what we do, it's a crap shoot. Any one of us could still get the flu and die. An arsonist tried to burn the place down. Who saw that coming? Somebody could get their hands on military ordnance, breach the fence, and take the place. One-hundred-percent guaranteed safety is a pipe dream."

"That's unacceptable," Miles said.

"That's reality." Ripper shrugged. "You gotta live your life, Miles, despite the uncertainty. Do things that give it meaning. Spend time with the people you care about."

Miles was silent for a long moment. "Mackenzie wants cookies," he said at last, looking at me.

"Yeah? So make your cousin happy by baking her some cookies." Ripper leaned forward and stage whispered, "And if you want to make me happy sometime, bake chocolate chip cookies. My favorite."

"Let me clean up, then if you like, I'll lend you a hand with the cookies," Kyle said, bending over the sink. "I've been meaning to learn how the solar oven works."

Miles's eyes lit up with some of his old enthusiasm. "It's an amazing device." He launched into a long-winded explanation of how the oven functioned. Kyle nodded, then winked when he saw me watching them.

"Come here." Ripper tugged me into the living room.

"Thanks for talking him down," I whispered. "He used to wig out like that all the time, but I haven't seen it for years."

"Miles has a hard time handling stress, and the fire pushed him over the edge." Ripper wrapped his arms around my waist and hauled me close. "He needed to vent."

"He looks better now," I said. "Almost like his old self."

Up close, I caught a whiff of sweat, not a rancid funk, but the fresh scent of masculine exertion. I dragged the tip of my tongue across his chest, tasting the salt on his skin. My lips curved into a smile as I remembered the ease with which Ripper took command of the bout, wrestling Kyle into submission.

"What's that smile about?" he asked, chuckling.

"I like watching you spar." My fingertips skated over his powerful shoulders, tracing the groove where his shoulder muscles swept down to meet his rock hard biceps.

"Got an idea," he said in a low voice.

"Mmmm?" My eyelids had drifted shut, and I pressed an open-mouthed kiss to his nipple piercing, my tongue flicking against the metal.

"Ms. Dunwitty, unless you intend to put on a show for your cousin and Kyle, I suggest we go back to my place. Afterward, I wanna take you for a ride."

Lifting my head, I gazed at him with wide-eyed confusion. "I thought you were going to ride me first?"

His hands slid down to cup my ass and squeezed so hard that I jumped, barely repressing a shriek. "That's the plan."

He took my hand and led me back to the kitchen.

Kyle was sifting flour into a bowl while Miles was lining the rest of the ingredients up on the counter. Miles had donned Aunt Debbie's favorite apron, an old-fashioned blue and yellow floral apron that tied at the waist with a big bow.

"It's been a while since Mac's been out of the compound," Ripper said. "I thought I'd take her on a ride. Will you two be all right for a couple of hours while we're gone?"

"Sure," Miles said, once again happily preoccupied with baking. "And when you get back, the cookies will be ready."

"No problem," Kyle said.

His smile had faded when we walked into the room. I suspected that it was obvious from my demeanor that we wouldn't be hitting the road first thing.

Watching Ripper and me together had to hurt. Kyle's grand gesture—showing up on my doorstep—had fallen flat, and his impassioned attempts to paint Ripper as a dangerous thug had only driven a wedge between us. Still, I wasn't sorry he had decided to stay.

I was starting to imagine what the post-flu world would be like, how it would reconfigure itself after the loss of billions of souls. Every friend who survived, every familiar face, would be a blessing. If Kyle would respect my choice, we could find a way to restore our friendship. I suspected that those who thrived in the post-pandemic world would be those who bonded together to create new families, new communities, however unlikely the members.

"See you later, guys." I followed Ripper out the back door. As we crossed the patio, I whistled to get his attention. "Hunker down, will you?"

He glanced backward over his shoulder. "What's up, Mac?"

"Can't you just do as you're told without arguing, Mr. Solis?"

"All right. I'm game." Ripper bent his knees, and I leapt onto his back, wrapping my legs around his waist.

"I decided that I want the first ride. Giddyup, cowboy."

"Cowboy?" He straightened and jogged obediently toward the gate. "You got a thing for cowboys, now? Not just bikers?"

"What did you say?" I demanded, my voice an octave too high.

"Didn't I tell you? Kyle let me in on your little secret." Ripper unlocked the gate and locked it again once we were through. The process took no more than thirty seconds, but it felt like an eternity while I waited to hear what he said next. "Told me that whatever you're feeling for me isn't real. Turns out it's a byproduct of your obsession with bad-boy bikers. Even showed me your Kindle library. Some very interesting titles you got there, Mac. I read a couple of chapters from one. Meant to ask you if you'd like to act out a scene or two."

You could fry an egg on my face. Use the radiant heat from my cheeks to light the Olympic torch. I tried to shimmy down his hips.

"Whoa," Ripper said, then laughed, apparently delighted by his own wit. He hoisted me back into place. "Where do you think you're going, little lady?"

"Put me down. I've got a man to kill."

"Nah. Kyle didn't tell me anything I didn't already know. I saw it in your face the first time we met."

Could a person actually die from mortification?

Our relationship had been reduced to a fetish. Bad-boy biker and—what—sexy coed? Good girl taking a walk on the wild side? No wonder Ripper was planning to bail. You could only sustain a relationship based on fantasy wish fulfillment for so long before the novelty wore off.

Ripper carried me into his house and deposited me on a kitchen counter. Nudging my legs apart, he stepped close and leaned in to kiss me. Something in my expression must have given him pause, because he reared back, a frown creasing his brow.

"Mac?"

I fixed my eyes on his Adam's apple, too humiliated to look him in the eyes.

"Mac." His fingers caught my chin and tilted my face up. I squeezed my eyes shut in a lame and craven attempt to evade his scrutiny. "You embarrassed?"

I nodded, miserable.

"Hmmm. How about you open your eyes?"

Nope. I shook my head. I'd embraced the most juvenile dodge imaginable, ranking right up there with sticking my fingers in my ears and humming to avoid a painful conversation. And I was going to see it through to the bitter end.

"All right." He stroked my hair back from my face, then his hands settled on my shoulders. "No need to be embarrassed. Lot of relationships start with a superficial attraction. Nothing wrong with that. Something's gotta spark interest. You think bikers are hot. I got a thing for long-legged smart girls who blush when they get flustered."

I winced. Ripper was confirming my worst suspicions. We were archetypes, nothing more.

"Pay attention." He tapped my nose. "Once you get past the initial attraction, it's what happens next that matters. If you were mean, or shallow, or stupid, I would have moved on without a second thought. You're not, and I didn't. And I'm hoping that you stuck around because you've come to see me as something more than a hot man in leather who rocks your world in bed."

My eyes flew open. "Hot man in leather who rocks my world in bed? You've got some ego, Mr. Solis."

"There you are." He smiled down at me. He'd manipulated me into opening my eyes. Can't believe I fell for it so easily. "You telling me I don't rock your world?"

No. No, I absolutely was *not* telling him that.

"You know you do." I'd promised Ripper honesty. Why was this so hard to confess when the proverbial cat was already so completely out of the bag? "Kyle was partially right. I have a thing for bad-boy bikers in novels, and when we met, the first thing I saw was a gorgeous, sexy man wearing a Janissary cut."

Ripper flashed a self-satisfied grin. No doubt about it. I wasn't the first woman to melt when he swaggered into a room. He's probably parlayed his panty-dropping good looks and bad-boy demeanor into dozens of hook-ups.

Now that I'd started talking, I couldn't seem to stop. "You think I'm a smart girl? I am. I'm way too smart to get involved with a man merely because he's a walking embodiment of my fantasies. By the end of that first night, after we said goodbye, you know what I was thinking about? How impressed I was by your kindness toward Miles. And how being with you made me feel safe. Those things have nothing to do with any obsession."

"That wasn't so hard, was it?"

"Yes, actually, it was. I've never discussed my sexual fantasies with a man The only reason Kyle knows anything about them was because he snooped and then teased me about them."

"What a chump move." Ripper shook his head, brows raised as he contemplated Kyle's bone-headed action. "Never a good idea to mock a woman's sexual fantasies. Helluva lot more fun to make them come true, but he's young. He'll learn."

"You sound mighty magnanimous, considering how much you two disliked each other not too long ago."

"Country Club's not so bad, once he got his head out of his ass. He admitted he was being a dick. And he stepped up when it counted. That says a lot. There's hope for the kid."

"He's twenty-two. That's hardly a kid. I mean, I don't turn twenty-two for a week and a half. You don't think I'm too young, do you?"

He gave me a reproachful look, then kissed the tip of my nose. "What I mean is he's had an easy life up till now, with his family's money to grease his way. None of that's worth a damn anymore. The flu leveled the playing field. He's gonna succeed or fail on his own. But like I said, there's hope."

I was tired of thinking about my ex, especially since the hottest man I'd ever met was wedged between my legs. I leaned back on the counter, supporting my weight on my elbows. Narrowing my eyes, I allowed everything to go slightly out of focus while I admired Ripper's six-pack.

I sketched the grid pattern in the air with my finger. "If I had a Sharpie, I could play tic-tac-toe on your abs."

He snorted. "Try that, and I'll play connect-the-dots with your freckles."

I grinned. Jake had given Ali a jar of chocolate body paint for Valentine's Day. Bet I could find some someday, maybe at one of those sex toy, lingerie shops that dotted the city. Panicked people might have stripped grocery stores clean, but I doubted that anybody had made looting a sex toy store a priority. A field trip might be in order.

"What are you thinking about?" Ripper asked.

I smiled broadly. "How about, some time in the next couple of days, you and I go on an expedition? There are a couple of things I'd like to pick up. You said it's a hell of a lot of fun to make a woman's sexual fantasies come true. Here's your chance."

Ripper shook his head, regret etched across his features. "Sounds fun, but there's no time for an expedition. I gotta hit the road in three days."

THIRTY

Ripper

I'm not getting laid tonight.

Not one minute ago, sex seemed a sure thing. Mac had been lolling back on her elbows, a wanton smile on her lips, her eyes gleaming with lascivious anticipation. I knew that expression. I fucking *loved* that expression. An uninhibited, turned-on Mac was a wonder to behold. She'd come right out and said she wanted me to make her sexual fantasies come true. Yeah. Barring divine intervention, I was getting pussy. And then I went and opened my big mouth.

I gotta hit the road in three days.

Soon as I said the words, Mac stiffened and slowly sat up, the color draining from her face.

Could have told her later—you know, after we did the deed—but it didn't occur to me that she'd take the news so hard. It wasn't God, but my own big mouth and shit sense of timing that shut things down.

"Mac?"

"It's okay." She fixed her gaze on the floor. "You warned me. You've been nothing less than honest about your intentions."

No fucking clue what that meant. "What are you going on about?"

"You told me that the day would come when you're not around anymore." Her brows lifted, and she raised suspicious eyes to mine. "Is that why you tried to whip Kyle into shape, so you could leave with a clear conscience?"

I threw my hands in the air, both confused and indignant. "What the fuck are you talking about? When did I say that I was planning on ditching you?"

"After Caleb threw the Molotov cocktail into the yard. You agreed that I had to stop acting like a dependent wuss, because someday you wouldn't be around to take care of things. You were warning me not to get too attached because you were planning to take off."

Frowning, I replayed that conversation in my mind. Nothing I said should have triggered Mac's suspicions. This miscommunication was on her, not me. Girl had a positive gift for twisting innocent words into the worst possible meaning.

"Anybody ever tell you that you hear what you want to hear and then jump to conclusions? This isn't the first time you've rushed to judgment. When Miles told you that I keep a box in his safe, you decided that I had to be hiding club contraband from the cops. You accused me of being the kind of dickwad who'd take advantage of a friend."

"I was wrong then, and I said I was sorry," Mac shrank back.

"Didn't stop you from doing it again, did it?"

"But...you told me—"

"Try to remember the conversation. *You* called yourself a dependent wuss, and I told you that you were wrong. I said *if* I'm not around someday, you have to be able to take care of yourself. How you twisted that to mean that I intend to abandon you, I don't have a fucking clue. At the time I was thinking shit happens. The Molotov cocktail might have burned me to a crisp. I might die from the flu. *If* I'm gone, you have to be able to take care of yourself, even though there's nothing I want more than to stick around and keep you and Miles safe."

I slapped my hands on the counter, 100 percent fed up with her lack of faith.

"You heard what I said and concluded that I'm some asshole who intends to run off and leave you to fend for yourself. So tell me, are you just bound and determined not to trust me? You think I'm a good lay but nobody you can count on?"

Mac opened her mouth to reply, then clamped it shut. I could practically see the wheels turning in her head as she considered my words. Nothing to say, huh? I'd tried so hard to do right by Mac. Her lack of faith cut deep. The prolonged silence tweaked my last nerve, and I needed a break.

I whirled around and strode from the room, feeling a vein throb in my forehead. I sat on the edge of the sofa and buried my face in my hands.

"Ripper?"

"Go home, Mac." I was so tired of this shit.

Instead of obeying, she crossed the room and dropped to her knees in front of me. An almost palpable emotional miasma clogged the air, making it hard to breathe. She was silent for a long time before she finally spoke.

"Did Miles ever tell you why I spent so much time with his family when I was growing up?"

I didn't answer.

"I came home from kindergarten one day to find out that my daddy was gone. He ran off with a waitress from a diner up the street. I loved him more than anybody, but he left, and he never looked back. Mom and Dad weren't happy. My mom was a difficult person. Bitter, angry, impossible to please, always feeling sorry for herself."

She paused, maybe hoping I'd respond. When I didn't, she continued.

"She got depressed after dad left, and she self-medicated with alcohol. She'd invite men home from the bar and lock me in my room and turn off the light, so they wouldn't know that anybody was there. That she had a kid. She was so desperate and needy that she hooked up with some real losers..."

Her voice trailed off. She laid a tentative hand on my knee, as if unsure that I'd welcome her touch.

I lowered my hands and stared into her eyes, then shifted my gaze to the thin, white scar that ran from her eyebrow to her temple. I traced a finger over the line.

"Did one of those men hit you?" Helpless fury roiled in my gut, as I imagined a little girl abandoned by the father she loved, left alone to deal with the losers her alcoholic mother brought home.

She shook her head. "No."

No?

"Then how'd you get this?"

She hesitated. "It was an accident. Mom threw an empty bottle of vodka, and it hit me in the face."

"An accident?" I snorted. "She threw a vodka bottle at her kid by accident?"

Mac sighed. I wrapped my fingers around the small hand resting on my knee, rubbing her palm with my thumb.

"She...she didn't mean to do it," Mac faltered. "Mom couldn't pay the electric bill, so our power was shut off. I woke up and heard her stumbling and cursing in the dark. I got out of bed and fumbled my way to the living room. Maybe the sound of my footsteps startled her. Maybe she was frustrated and didn't realize I was there. She threw the bottle. It clipped the side of my head. Just missed my eye."

Mac fell silent, lost in the memory.

"What happened next?"

"Mom was sorry. She knelt on the rug next to me sobbing. Said she would never, ever, ever hurt her baby on purpose, but I had to understand we couldn't go to the emergency room for stitches. There was no money for it. Besides, this was family business, and we couldn't risk them taking me away from her over an accident."

Jesus. Even after almost putting out Mac's eye, her piece of shit mother made it all about her. Didn't want them to *take Mac away from her*.

Yeah, I could be an unforgiving bastard. Got no sympathy for anybody who failed to protect their kid. I felt a stab of gratitude for my loud, loving, grizzly bear mom. What must Mac's childhood have been like with a runaway father and a drunk mother?

"Come here."

I pulled her onto my lap and wrapped my arms around her. She settled against my chest, her ear over my heart.

I wasn't surprised when her tongue darted out, and she licked me. It wasn't a sexual thing. I'd come to realize that over time. Whenever I held her—especially if we'd been apart for more than a few hours—she tasted my skin, nosed my throat, inhaled my scent, and listened to my heartbeat.

For some reason, she needed sensory validation. Never asked her why, just figured it was one of the quirks that made Mac Mac.

After a long second, she turned in my arms, and her eyes found mine. "I don't want to make things sound worse than they were.

Mostly things were okay. Lots of people had a harder time. Mom was able to keep a job, and she usually paid the bills. She made sure I got to school. She yelled, but she never hit me. And the one time one of her boyfriends came on to me, she kicked him to the curb and said she'd call the cops if he came back."

"Yeah. Mother of the year material." My voice dripped with sarcasm.

"Obviously, she didn't have the wherewithal to be much of a mother. One evening Uncle Mel stopped by to fix a leaky toilet, and he found me eating dry cereal for dinner while mom was passed out on the sofa. I started spending a lot of time with Uncle Mel and Aunt Debbie and Miles after that."

She twined her fingers through mine, then clutched at my hand.

"When I graduated from high school, Mom must have figured that her job was done. She went on the road with a long-haul trucker. Sometimes she calls me on my birthday and Christmas, but that's the extent of our contact. A month after mom left, a drunk driver killed Aunt Debbie and Uncle Mel."

"I'm sorry, Mac," I murmured, my hand stroking up and down her back.

"I didn't tell you about all this because I want sympathy."

She sounded defensive.

"I want you to understand why I sometimes mess up. It's not because I don't trust you. Deep inside, I think something in me is out of whack. I look for trouble. I expect good things to fall apart. I expect people to leave and never come back."

"Kyle came back," I said. "He came back for you."

"Are you saying that you think I should be with Kyle?"

"Fuck no." I couldn't keep the exasperation out of my voice. "I'm not trying to hand you off to Kyle. I'm pointing out the flaw in your belief system."

"See!" Her gray eyes were full of self-recrimination. "I jump to conclusions, and I have abandonment issues. Not to mention, I'm afraid of the dark. I'm a real prize. I wouldn't blame you if you just gave up on me."

"Not giving up on you." I tightened my grip on her to make the point. "It takes a special kind of asshole to walk away from a kid. I understand why it haunts you, but Mac, you got to work on keeping this shit in check. Don't let the past ruin what you got now. You recognize the problem. That's half the battle. You wonder about something between us, you ask me. Don't stew. Don't decide you know what's what before you get all the facts. If you can do that, we'll be all right."

"I want that. More than anything. I promise, I'll do my best."

"Good enough." I tightened my grip on her hand.

"And in that spirit," she said. "I have a question for you."

I groaned. "Hope I haven't created a monster. Go ahead."

"You said you're hitting the road Friday morning. You said you're not ditching us, and I believe you, but I have no idea where you're going or why."

Reasonable question.

"Got a promise to keep. I saw the president of my club before he died. He asked me to go to Grants Pass to check on his ex. I gave my word that I'd go as soon as I could. I couldn't leave until I was sure that you had gotten over the kidnapping and Miles had recovered from the Molotov cocktail. I do feel better about going with Kyle here, especially since his attitude's improved."

"How long do you think you'll be gone?"

My cheeks puffed out as I blew out a breath. "Hard to tell. It's only about a 250-mile trip to Grants Pass, but I have no idea what I'll encounter on the road. I'd guess no more than two, three days if I don't run into trouble. Chances are I won't find Sara alive, but I gotta try."

"Why are you so sure that Sara is dead? She could be holed up somewhere safe—relatively safe—like we are."

I paused before answering. "I didn't tell you. When I go out, I've been checking on my brothers and their families. They're either dead or scattered. One of the men—Wheezer—got the flu and recovered. His old lady and two sons died. He buried them in their back yard, and he refuses to leave their house. I've been bringing him supplies. Lot of people have died." I shook my head, haunted by memories of the carnage. "Wheezer is the only survivor I've found from the club. Can't say I have much hope that Sara's still alive, but I made a promise."

"That reminds me." Mac sat up straight. "I meant to say something earlier. When he was holding me prisoner, Jason told me that he'd been breaking into houses. He saw a lot of dead and dying people and only a few who had got the flu and recovered. All of the people who recovered were men. Is it possible that only men can survive the flu? Can a virus work that way?"

I shrugged.

"Damned if I know. Wouldn't have thought so, but this virus is an unpredictable monster. Some people die within a few hours. Others linger for days. The incubation period varies. It's got a mortality rate to rival Ebola. And why do some people get violent episodes near the end, but not others? I don't know how to make sense of it. Just hope somebody's alive at the CDC working on it."

"Amen to that."

She wriggled in my lap and my cock twitched, happy for the unintentional stimulation. Maybe it wasn't too late to salvage the date.

"Hey," I said, shifting gears. "I promised you a ride." I waggled my brows suggestively.

"Ripper, if I'm going to be totally honest—."

I threw my head back against the cushion and sighed a martyr's sigh. "Now I know I created a monster. Go ahead."

She smacked my leg with the back of her hand. "Listen. Before you go on your trip, I want to go at it like a pair of rabid mink. I really do. Just not tonight."

"What happened?" I frowned. "You were gung-ho not too long ago."

"I've never been one of those people who gets turned on by conflict. The emotional roller coaster knocked the horny right out of me."

"Bet I could knock it back into you," I suggested.

"I'm sure you could, but..."

"But?"

"Could we just sprawl on the sofa and hang out?" Her teeth worked her lower lip while she waited for my reply. Time to step up and show her that her feelings mattered. I'd remind her of that rabid mink promise later.

"Yeah." I smiled. "We can do that."

I scooted back against the corner of the sofa and spread my legs, motioning for her to crawl between them and settle against my chest. She nestled into the crook of my arm, then trailed her fingers along my collarbone.

"Ripper?"

"Yeah?"

"You'll be careful on the road, won't you?"

I didn't respond, surprised by the question. I'm not used to having anybody worry about me.

She glanced at my face, frowning. "I'm not questioning your ability to take care of yourself. You're the strongest, most capable man I know. It's just...there's no telling who or what you'll run into out there. And I need you to come back home to me."

I need you to come back home to me.

For a long time, home had been the place where I parked my stuff, a base of operations, not a place where I belonged, a place where I mattered to somebody. That had changed; I saw that with a sudden clarity. Mac and Miles were my home. I hated like hell to leave them, but I had no choice. Couldn't live with myself if I ignored my duty to my dead president.

I was a realist. Mac was right to be worried. I would be heading out into a lawless landscape where I'd face unknown dangers. Sure, years of service as a Ranger, then a Janissary, had made me a match for any man, but the flu or a lucky bullet could still take me out.

I looked at her anxious, upturned face. Couldn't lie to Mac, couldn't offer her a false assurance that I absolutely would return. I brushed her hair back from her brow and dropped a kiss on the top of her head.

"I promise to be careful and to do everything in my power to come back home to you."

"I can't ask for more than that, can I?" She offered a weak smile. "Thank you, Mr. Solis."

"And you know what Miles says," I added.

"Yes. You always keep your promises."

THIRTY-ONE

Kenzie

I started looking for Ripper at the end of the second day after his departure for Grants Pass.

It was only a 500-mile round trip. If he didn't run into trouble, he could easily return within forty-eight hours.

On the morning of the third day, I reminded myself that Ripper was a conscientious man. If Sara wasn't at home, of course, he'd spend a day scouring Grants Pass trying to locate her. If he found her alive, he'd either have to convince himself that she was safe, or he'd have to persuade her to return to Portland with him.

On the fourth day, it occurred to me that he might have had trouble locating gasoline to refill the tank on his Harley. He'd packed a short length of hose so he could siphon gas from abandoned vehicles. Maybe other people had the same idea, and it was taking longer to locate fuel than he'd expected.

On the fifth day, my imagination ran amok.

Ripper had crashed his Harley and was lying in a ditch with a broken leg. He'd run afoul of a survivor from a rival motorcycle gang. He'd been shot by a panicked citizen who believed every man wearing a cut was bad news. The flu had struck him down, and he was dying a miserable death all alone.

I kept my fears to myself. Miles puttered contentedly around the compound. He tended the garden and chickens, baked bread and cookies in the solar oven, and played Frisbee with Hector.

I'd overheard Ripper speaking to Miles before he left, assuring him that he'd do everything he could to make it back home to us. Apparently Miles had so much faith in Ripper's promises and in his ability to take care of himself, that he didn't worry that Ripper's prolonged absence could spell trouble.

I was careful not to plant any seeds of doubt in my cousin's mind.

If Kyle was worried, he kept it to himself, although I occasionally found him surreptitiously watching me. We kept up our daily target practice, and by unspoken agreement, made sure our weapons were always within reach. We were vigilant about monitoring the security feed at night, alternating six-hour shifts.

Our caution may have been excessive. Portland's population was dwindling. Fewer and fewer cars passed by the house. Gunfire—once a nightly event—erupted sporadically. Only occasional pinpricks of light pierced the blanket of darkness that lay over the city at night. Every evening, we covered the windows with blackout shades so our lights wouldn't betray us.

At night, when the gloom pressed in from all sides, I carried an LED lantern with me from room to room. And when I curled up on my lonely cot, Ripper's moon lantern kept watch over me, banishing the shadows and reminding me of my absent man. I'd fetched Ripper's pillow from his king-size bed and fell asleep every night hugging it.

Hector, bless him, sensed who needed him the most and padded from room to room during the night.

Six days after Ripper left, Miles banished Kyle and me from the back yard. His eyes dancing with excitement, Miles escorted us into the house. He pulled down the kitchen shades and fixed us with a stern gaze.

"I'm making something wonderful. It's a surprise, so no peeking." After filling a pitcher with water and carrying it out to the picnic table, he filled a box with mystery ingredients from the basement food storage.

"You up for a small wager?" Kyle asked me, watching Miles haul mixing bowls and other kitchen tools outside.

"Probably. What do you have in mind?"

"Guess what Miles is making. If either one of us gets it right, he—"

"Or she," I interrupted.

"Let me finish. He *or* she will be handed a hot, fresh cup of coffee by the loser first thing every morning for a week."

Lazing in bed while Kyle delivered my coffee? I was so down with that idea.

"You're on." I pursed my lips, considering what Miles might be up to. "I got it." I snapped my fingers. "My birthday is the day after tomorrow."

From his stricken expression, I could tell that Kyle had forgotten. It didn't matter in the slightest. The only thing I wanted for my birthday was Ripper safely back home. "I bet Miles is baking my favorite birthday cake, vanilla layers with seedless raspberry jam filling."

"Not German chocolate?"

"Why would Miles make your favorite cake for my birthday? You can drop hints in September when your birthday rolls around."

He made a face, no fan of white cake.

"What's your guess?" I asked.

"He's been making noises about missing pizza. So my guess is pizza."

We shook hands, sealing our bet.

A few hours later, Miles summoned us to the backyard. He'd set the picnic table with Aunt Debbie's wedding china, crystal candlesticks, and a vase full of yellow roses from a bush that straddled the back fence. It was an incongruous sight, dainty Limoges china on redwood-stained planks, but entirely charming, especially since Miles had taken such care to make things nice.

I flashed Kyle a triumphant smile. This certainly looked like a birthday dinner.

My triumph was short-lived. With a flourish, Miles produced a platter of pizza slices.

"I take mine with sugar, in case you're forgotten." Kyle flashed a smug grin.

"This looks wonderful, Miles," I said.

It was impossible to summon even a twinge of disappointment—and really, who would complain about pizza—in the face of his pride and pleasure. He must have baked the pizza on a rectangular cookie sheet because the slices were cut into squares, but other than that, it looked like a real pizza. Gooey melted cheese and a glistening tomato sauce covered a homemade crust. Black olives and pepperoni rounds had been scattered with a heavy hand across the top.

"Oh, man," Kyle groaned. "You've outdone yourself."

"Where did you get the ingredients?" I asked, stunned. Without refrigeration, we hadn't seen real cheese for more than a month.

"Freeze-dried mozzarella. I rehydrated it with water. The pepperoni was in a vacuum-sealed bag. Don't worry. Dried meat is supposed to be good for months at room temperature."

Sometimes it was the insignificant, ordinary moments that took root in your memory and lived there forever, a cherished snapshot of a perfect point in time.

When I thought of the happiest times from my childhood, I remembered standing on a stool at the kitchen counter while Aunt Debbie showed me how to roll out a pie crust. Sitting safely in the crook of Uncle Mel's arm, Aunt Debbie's Siamese cat Taz purring on my lap, while we watched a monster destroy Tokyo. Building a Lego fairy-tale castle with Miles, only to have him add a working drawbridge to it. I'd always remember the earnest expression on his face as he explained the necessity of fortifying the battlements.

I smiled. I guessed I should be grateful that it hadn't occurred to Miles to build a moat around the compound.

You rarely recognized such moments when they occurred, but this was a moment I knew with absolute certainty would live in my heart forever. Kyle licking his fingers and telling Miles that he'd made the best pizza ever. Miles bobbing his head and smiling. The golden light of the setting sun casting a brilliant hue over the tableau. A rare moment of contentment in the midst of devastating change.

Only Ripper's absence cast a pall over my perfect happiness.

After dinner Miles pulled out the family's old badminton set, and we batted the birdie around the back yard, dodging the barbecue, the chicken coop, and the vegetable beds. The goal was to keep the birdie in the air, rather than to score points. Kyle made a heroic dive over the picnic bench to keep the birdie in flight. Hector watched, enraptured.

The game ended when he leaped into the air and seized the birdie in his mouth, denting it enough that we decided its wonky flight path was a good reason to call it quits.

Sated and worn out, we cleared off the picnic table and retired indoors to play cards—Old Maid and Go Fish—around the kitchen table.

After an hour, a loud gurgling sound disrupted our play. Kyle and I glanced at Miles. His shoulders jumped, and he burped, a warbling belch so protracted that it took on a life of its own.

"I apologize," he mumbled.

"You okay, guy?" Kyle asked.

"I thought the pepperoni would be safe to eat. I hope I wasn't wrong."

Me, too, although I'd peeled half the pepperoni from my pizza and had furtively passed the slices to Kyle, who could never get enough of the stuff.

Miles burped again.

"Why don't you take an antacid and lie down?" Kyle suggested.

Miles nodded and headed toward the bathroom's medicine cabinet.

"Do you think it was the pepperoni?" I asked Kyle. "I feel fine, but how about you? You ate more than anybody."

"Salami and pepperoni constitute my favorite food group, remember? I've got a cast-iron stomach. I feel fine. Maybe Miles isn't used to the salt and fat."

Kyle washed the dishes while I pulled the blinds and took Hector out for his evening potty break. I volunteered to take the first shift watching the security monitor. Kyle retreated to the back porch with a paperback.

Peering into his bedroom, I found Miles sound asleep, flat on his back and snoring lightly. I took my position at the command center and kept an eye on the monitor while I worked on a scarf I was knitting for Ripper.

Six hours later, Kyle tapped me on the shoulder and took my place. I collapsed into bed and instantly fell asleep.

Sometime later, I awoke to the sound of retching.

I rushed out of bed and rapped on the bathroom door. "You need anything, Miles?"

I heard him dump a bucket of water in the toilet tank, followed by the sound of the toilet flushing. Thank God the sewer system still functioned, although we had to fill the tank for every flush.

Miles opened the door and squinted at me through bleary eyes. "My stomach hurts, so I took another antacid. Sorry about the pepperoni. I'll throw the rest of it away tomorrow."

He stumbled back to his bed. Standing in the door, I watched him for a few minutes, until he fell back asleep.

"How do you feel?"

I whirled around, pressing a hand to my heart.

"Fine," I whispered. "You?"

He shrugged. "Nothing wrong." Kyle peered over my shoulder at Miles's sleeping form. "I've read that people with his condition sometimes have gastrointestinal issues."

"That's true. He's always had a sensitive stomach. Since we feel fine, it's probably that and not the pepperoni."

Kyle squeezed my shoulder. "Go back to bed. If Miles wakes up and needs anything, I'll take care of it."

"Okay. Thanks."

I awoke hours later to Hector nuzzling my face, probably a sign that he was ready for his morning visit to the back yard. I tiptoed past Kyle, who had fallen asleep at the command station with his head resting on his crossed arms. Not wanting to disturb Kyle, I carried the hand-crank coffee grinder out onto the patio.

I shivered. The sky was overcast and the air weighed down with the promise of rain, not unusual weather for Portland in late June. While Hector went about his business, I ground the beans. Kyle won the bet fair and square, and I'd deliver his coffee with a smile.

After making coffee, I filled three mugs with the steaming brew and carried them to the living room on a small tray.

"Here's your coffee." I tapped Kyle on the shoulder.

He jerked awake, then nodded his thanks, clutching the mug against his chest.

"Ambrosia." He yawned.

"Nectar of the gods." I replied without thinking.

We used to say that every morning during our first cups of coffee, one of those silly habits couples fall into. He glanced at me and I flushed. I hadn't intended to reanimate that old custom.

I picked up a mug from the tray. "I'm going to see if Miles is up to drinking coffee."

I knocked lightly on his door. "Miles?"

When he didn't respond, I cracked the door open and stuck my head inside.

Immediately, I drew back, wrinkling my nose against the wretched smell that assaulted my nostrils.

Had his poor tummy been roiling all night long, compelling a sleeping Miles to cut loose with some truly noxious fumes? I wouldn't say a word to Miles in case I embarrassed him, but I'd be sure to air his room out as soon as he was up.

"Hey, Miles?"

My foot slipped in something as I approached the bed, and I struggled to stay on my feet, sloshing hot coffee over my hand.

"Crap!" I placed the mug on his nightstand and blew on my hand to cool it.

Miles hadn't stirred.

"Miles?"

I crossed to his window and rolled up the blind, bathing the room with soft morning light.

Miles groaned and covered his eyes with his arm.

"Turn off the light, Mom. It hurts my eyes."

I pulled the blind halfway down, then took a faltering step toward the bed. Miles had vomited on the floor then gone back to sleep, an unthinkable act for a young man as obsessively tidy as he was. Holding my breath, I edged closer to my cousin.

Hectic red color suffused his cheeks, and his sweat-slicked hair clung limply to his head. He'd thrown aside his blanket, and his bottom sheet was discolored, soaked through with perspiration.

"Miles?" I whispered. My heart hammered so loudly that I couldn't hear the word.

I stepped over the mess on the floor and laid a hand on my cousin's forehead. He grimaced and twisted his face away, but not before my fingers registered the blistering heat. His dry, cracked lips were pressed together, and his pulse beat a frantic staccato in his throat.

My legs couldn't support me. I sank to the edge of his sodden mattress.

Sweet Jesus. Please God, no.

THIRTY-TWO

Kyle

I needed caffeine to function at 100 percent—at least one full cup of morning joe—before the gears in my brain engaged, before I could interact with the world with more than a vacant "Huh?"

I'd downed half a cup when the silence penetrated my brain fog. Instead of the soft murmur of voices, I'd heard nothing since Kenzie carried a cup of coffee to Miles. If he was awake, they'd be chatting by now. If he was still asleep, she would have quietly left the room.

Frowning, I set the cup down and walked to the bedroom.

The stink hit me first and I reeled.

The ominous silence and the smell triggered a flood of memories from the worst night of my life. I held onto the door frame while the world swam around me.

Miles. Not Miles.

Visceral panic seized me at the sight of Kenzie perched on the edge of Miles's bed, her hand pressed to his sweaty, red cheek.

"Kenz, you need to step away from Miles."

"If you think I'm going to keep my distance from Miles when he's sick, you can go fuck yourself." Her expression was blank and her voice flat, at odds with the vehemence of her words.

Dammit, she was right. What was the point? We had to be exposed. Nothing could protect us from the viral intruder that had wormed its way into the compound.

My fingers tightened on the door frame. We faced a life-and-death struggle against an implacable enemy. Maybe another death watch. I had to suck it up and do everything in my power to make this easier for Kenzie.

"Some people recover," I reminded her. "Isn't that what Jason told you? We got a fight on our hands, but we're going to do everything we can to save Miles."

Maybe there was hope for Miles. Maybe all I could do was give Kenz time to accept the inevitable. Damned if I knew.

She looked at me expectantly, as if I had some answers. I *had* been through this before, although without a lick of success. I let go of the door frame and crossed to the bed.

Miles lay hunched on his side, his lips parted, his face glistening with perspiration.

"He has a fever. I've never seen anybody sweat so much, and he's been throwing up. He must be dehydrated," Kenzie said.

"Yeah." I nodded. "First job is to get fluids in him. I'll clean up the puke and open the window to let some fresh air in. You get a glass of water, and we'll try to make him drink. Then we'll figure out what to do next."

I slid open the window, then I followed her to the kitchen and grabbed one of those small, plastic bags we used to clean up after Hector. I scooped the mess into a bag, tied it off, then deposited it in a wheeled trash can in the corner of the yard. After cleaning up, I joined Kenzie in Miles's room.

I hoisted Miles into a sitting position, and Kenzie held the water to his lips.

"Swallow, Miles," she ordered.

"Leave me alone." He turned his head, pressing his lips together. Kenzie squeezed his nose, forcing him to open his mouth to breathe, then she tipped in the liquid. Despite his initial resistance, once the water hit his tongue, Miles drank greedily. After he took a few swallows, I touched Kenzie's shoulder.

"We should get something in him to lower his temperature."

"You're right, especially since he's able to swallow. Keep him upright. I'll be back."

She dashed to the bathroom and returned with a bottle of Ibuprofen. We managed to get Miles to swallow two pills.

"His bed is gross," Kenzie said. "Can you pick him up so I can throw on some clean sheets and pillowcases?"

"Sure."

Miles was tall and lanky, but regular workouts had packed enough muscle on my frame to allow me to swing him up into my arms and stand.

Kenzie whipped the wet sheets and pillowcases off the bed and replaced them with clean ones.

"Hold on." She retrieved a large, flat sheet from the linen closet in the hall, folded it in half, then tucked it across the bottom sheet. "I think they do something like this in hospitals, so that if this one gets damp, we can pull it off and still have a fresh sheet underneath."

"Good thinking."

I settled Miles back onto his dry bed.

"I don't think the pills are going to do enough to bring down his fever," Kenzie said.

I didn't think so, either. They hadn't done a damn bit of good for Jake or Ali, but I wouldn't tell Kenzie that.

"Let's give the pills a little time to take the edge off his pain, then we can fill the tub with water and try to bring his temperature down with a cold bath," she suggested.

A knife twisted in my gut. I was a fucking idiot. Why hadn't it occurred to me to try that with Jake and Ali? Could I have saved them if I'd been able to cool them off? I'd never know. Now I'd have to live with that uncertainty.

"Good idea," I said through numb lips.

"Dammit, I wish we had electricity." She blew out an exasperated breath. "Then we could set up a fan next to his bed and make ice."

That was something I could tackle. "Miles has a generator, doesn't he? The refrigerator is probably a big power suck, but it'll be worth it if we can make ice to cool him down."

"That's right! Do you know how to set it up?"

"I'm on it." I sprinted to the back yard and threw open the door to the cinder block shed where Miles kept propane and gasoline. Neatly stacked rows of fuel on shelves reached to the ceiling. Wow. He 'd stockpiled enough gas to run the generator for weeks, or to fuel up Ripper's jeep many times over.

I'd helped Dad run the generator back home when winter storms knocked out power in Boise, so getting it up and running was a cinch. I plugged in the refrigerator, and its familiar hum told me that it was working. It would take a while for the freezer to chill enough to make ice, but I filled all the ice trays with water and added some gallon-sized plastic bags full of water to the freezer.

Kenzie had climbed the rickety wooden ladder that gave access to the attic, where she'd retrieved a table fan that now blew cool air across Miles's bed.

"Can you help me fill the tub?" she asked.

Even though Miles had accumulated hundreds of five-gallon water bottles, we always tried to preserve the precious resource. All rules went out the window now. We dragged four water bottles from Kenzie's room and dumped them into the tub.

"Miles is going to hate this." Kenzie dipped her hand into the room temperature water.

Miles lay in a fever stupor, hovering between sleep and wakefulness. If we spoke to him, he'd rouse and mumble a somewhat coherent response. Otherwise he'd float in a fitful slumber.

"On your feet, dude." I grabbed him under the armpits and lifted him from the bed.

Fortunately, he was able to bear some of his own weight as we stumbled to the bathroom. I balanced against the sink while Kenzie stripped off his socks and T-shirt. She left his boxers in place, probably to spare him the embarrassment of his cousin seeing him naked, but I doubted he was with it enough to care.

When I lowered him into the water, he began to flail.

"Please don't fight us, Miles." Tears filled Kenzie's eyes. "We're just trying to help."

Either her words pierced his stupor, or he lacked the energy to continue to struggle. Miles lay back quietly in the water. When he began to shiver, I lifted him from the tub and carried him back to his bed.

Miles opened his eyes. "I'm thirsty." He downed half a glass of water before he collapsed back against his pillow. His eyelids fluttered, then he fell asleep. Some of the angry red color had retreated from his cheeks, and he seemed to be breathing easier.

"I want to sit with him," Kenzie whispered.

I dragged the recliner next to his bed and Kenzie sat vigil. I took care of all the chores, watering the garden, washing Miles's sheets and clothes, and hanging them on the line to dry. In the middle of the afternoon I heard Kenz speaking to him. I poked my head into the room.

"Look who's awake." Kenzie smiled.

"Hey, man. How you doing?"

Miles's head bobbled on his neck when he turned to look at me. Haggard and hollow-eyed, he looked like shit, but awareness of his surroundings had returned to his eyes.

"I feel better." His voice was raspy and weak. "My head hurts, but at least I don't feel like I'm floating above the floor anymore."

"It's a start, man."

Kenzie helped him swallow a couple more pain pills. "Can you try to eat something, Miles? Maybe some soup? You have to keep your strength up so you can fight this thing."

"I'll try."

"Let me get it," I said.

I warmed a can of chicken and rice soup and brought the bowl to his bedside. Kenzie sat on the edge of the bed and raised a spoon of soup to his mouth.

Miles ate, obediently opening and closing his mouth, his eyes never leaving Kenzie's face. "Thanks for taking care of me, Mackenzie." He finished half the soup.

Her hand stilled halfway between the bowl and his mouth. "I love you, Miles. I'd do anything to make you better."

"You aren't mad at me?"

She dropped the spoon into the bowl and set it on the nightstand. "Why on earth would I be mad at you?"

"It's my fault Jason kidnapped you. If I hadn't bought his oxy, he never would have come here."

"Miles." Kenzie took his hand and instead of pulling away—which I would expect given his distaste for human touch—Miles held on tight. "If we're going to play the blame game, I expected you to be mad at me for letting Jason into the yard. It's the stupidest thing I've ever done."

"That wasn't your fault," Miles rasped.

"I appreciate your saying that, and I want you to know that I never blamed you for Jason. Things happened that we couldn't anticipate. Let's call it even, okay?"

"Okay." Miles yawned. "I'm sleepy, but there's something I have to remember." He frowned.

"Whatever it is can wait until tomorrow."

"Tomorrow! That's it. Tomorrow is your birthday."

"That's not important. What's important is that you rest and get better."

"*No.* I made a promise to Ripper, and I have to keep my promise, just like he always does. Go look in the top drawer of my dresser."

Kenzie stood, walked over to the dresser and opened the drawer. She pulled out a pale blue gift bag and held it out to Miles.

"That's it. He asked me to give it to you on your birthday if he hadn't made it back yet, but I want to give it to you now, in case...you know."

Kenzie clutched the bag to her chest and her eyes filled with tears, maybe at the reminder that Miles could take a turn for the worse, maybe because Ripper had cared enough to leave her a birthday present.

She cleared her throat. "I'm going to go put this in my room. I'll be right back."

Thirty seconds later, Kenzie returned to Miles's side.

Kenzie held his hand until he fell back asleep, then she stood and stretched.

"You need a break," I said. "Go outside. Get some fresh air. I'll keep an eye on Miles."

Kenzie played with Hector, then fixed herself something to eat before returning to Miles's bedside.

He slept off and on for the rest of the day. Every time he awoke, one of us helped him drink water or Gatorade. We gave him more pain pills late in the evening. He fell into a hard sleep. Kenzie refused to lie down on the cot, insisting on staying by his side.

Around four in the morning, I found Kenzie in the kitchen, smashing a baggie full of ice with a meat mallet. Bleary-eyed with fatigue, she came within an inch of bringing the mallet down on her finger. I took it from her and finished the task.

"Miles is awake, and he asked for ice chips," she said.

"Let me watch him for a while, You won't be any good to him if you're dead on your feet. Go lie down."

Reluctance warred with exhaustion on her face. Her shoulders sagged when she conceded defeat. "Just for a little while."

"Go." I swatted her ass, trying to scoot her from the room. Startled, she glanced back over her shoulder and frowned. Damn. I forgot. It was too easy to slip back into old habits.

"Sorry."

She yawned and shoved her hands through her hair. "Just wake me if anything happens, promise?"

"Will do."

I fed Miles the ice chips and more pain meds. I could feel a headache coming on—no wonder considering the stress we were all under—so I popped two of the pills myself. Despite my best intentions, I fell asleep a couple of hours later.

I bolted upright, torn from sleep by a familiar nightmare, the terrifying dream that had haunted my childhood. The monster who lived under my bed had backed me into a corner with no escape. Wide awake, I slapped my face and shook my head, trying to dispel the image, but I swore I could still hear his claws scrabbling across the floor and his heavy breathing.

Wait. I *could* hear claws and heavy breathing.

I blinked. Bright sunlight flooded the lower half of the room from the partially raised blind. I spied Hector pacing the room, his toenails clacking against the floor. I scrubbed my face with my hands, trying to come completely awake.

"What's up, boy? You need to take a leak?"

Swinging my legs onto the floor, I glanced toward Miles's bed and froze.

He lay on his side, and his chest hitched as he sucked in a rattling breath, then exhaled with an almost explosive force. Scarlet blotches stained his cheeks, and his eyes appeared sunk into his head. Once again, his sheets were sodden with sweat. The monster had returned with a vengeance, but it wasn't the boogeyman who lived under my bed.

Fuck. I staggered toward Miles and lay my hand on his forehead. He was burning up.

"Kenzie!"

Within seconds, she stumbled into the room, clearly rousted from a deep sleep.

"Put ice in the tub. We have to bring down his fever."

She turned and ran toward the kitchen.

A minute later, ice plunked into the tub. I grabbed Miles and dragged him to the bathroom. He was too weak to protest when I lowered him into the water. He lay inert, despite the shock to his system when the icy water touched his superheated skin.

Kenzie dropped to her knees beside the tub. "Shit. I thought he was getting better."

"Me, too." I supported Miles's head with my hands so it wouldn't slip under the water. If Kenzie felt as helpless as I did, she needed something to do to make her feel useful. "Can you switch out his pillowcase and bottom sheet? They're soaked."

She jumped to her feet without a word and dashed to her cousin's bedroom.

I had no fucking clue what I was doing, no idea how long Miles should stay in the ice bath. I'd always taken it for granted that emergency medical help would be within reach. At the very least, that I could look for advice on the internet. What do you do when it's all gone, and you have nothing to rely on but your own piss-poor skills?

"His bed is ready," Kenzie said from the doorway. I tested Miles's cheek, chest, and arm. His skin felt cool to my touch. That had to be a good sign. I carried him back to his bed and carefully laid him down.

Now what?

"The last time we cooled him off, he got better for a while," Kenzie said.

I nodded. "Did you notice what time it is?" She would have walked past the battery operated wall clock when she fetched ice from the kitchen.

"Yeah. It's a little past one in the afternoon."

My headache had returned, making it hard to concentrate. "Maybe we should let him sleep for an hour, then see if his temperature has spiked back up."

"Okay." Kenz sounded as uncertain as I felt, both of us out of our element. "I need coffee. You want some, Kyle?"

"Yeah, please." It had been thirty hours since my last cup. I'm such an addict that caffeine withdrawal could easily be the cause of my headache. I dropped onto the recliner and slumped forward, exhausted and demoralized. When I heard Kenzie's light footsteps approach the room, I sat up and manufactured a confident expression.

"Thanks, Kenz." I smiled, accepting the mug of coffee.

"I put more bags of water in the freezer. In case we need ice later."

"Good idea."

She pulled a wooden chair away from Miles's desk and sat facing me while we sipped our drinks.

Today was her twenty-second birthday. There was absolutely nothing happy about her birthday, nothing worth celebrating. *Happy birthday* would sound glib and insulting. Her cousin was hanging between life and death. Her boyfriend—lover—I had no clue how they defined their relationship—was missing and possibly dead. I wouldn't ask her if she opened his gift.

I thought I'd made some sort of peace with the idea that she chose Ripper over me. Turned out he was a better man than I first thought, smart and competent, and good to her and Miles. It hurt like hell to see them together, but I could either leave in a huff or accept reality and stay.

I still loved Kenzie. If Ripper truly was gone…

"Earth to Kyle."

"Huh?"

"I was saying, I'm a mess. I'm going to heat some water and use the sink to rinse off. Give me the kitchen for fifteen minutes, okay?"

"Sure."

While Kenzie cleaned up and changed her clothes, I leaned back in the recliner and rested my eyes. She returned with a towel wrapped around her shoulders to protect her fresh tee from her damp hair.

"You want a turn?"

"Nah. Think I'll doze until it's time to check Miles's temp."

I awoke with a start when Kenzie touched my arm. "His temperature is 103. The ice hasn't set yet, but I put a couple of bags of half-frozen water into the tub to bring the water temperature down."

I nodded. We repeated the process of carrying Miles to the tub and immersing him in cold water. Hefting his dead weight was starting to wear on me, although I didn't say a word of complaint to Kenzie.

Afterward, we crushed Ibuprofen tablets into water, and I held his jaw while she poured the solution down his throat. We checked his temperature again an hour later, and it was still 103.

"Do you think the cold baths are keeping his temperature from rising even higher?" Kenzie asked. "I hate to put him through this if it isn't doing any good."

"I have no idea." I supported his weight while Kenzie tipped a sports drink into his mouth. He dribbled out as much as he swallowed, which I supposed was better than nothing.

Kenzie pinched the skin on the back of his hand. It remained in a narrow peak for several seconds before slowly flattening to its normal shape. "Did you see that? It means he's dehydrated."

"How do you know?"

"When I was little, Aunt Debbie had a Siamese cat. Taz developed kidney disease. The vet showed us how to pinch his skin to tell if he was dehydrated. If his skin was slow to return to normal after a pinch test, it meant the cat needed fluids. The vet said she either had to put Taz to sleep, or we had to give him subcutaneous fluid every day to keep him hydrated. Taz was Aunt Debbie's baby, so she opted for the sub q fluids."

"Are you thinking we could give sub q fluids to Miles?" I asked.

"Maybe. I mean, the best thing would be for a doctor to give him intravenous fluids, but that's not possible." She dragged her hands through her hair. "I don't know what to do. I don't know if it's safe to give sub q fluids to humans, but I think it's worth the risk. All you do is stick a needle under the skin and let gravity pull the fluid into the body. At first, there's a big lump of liquid where the needle goes in, but over time, it disperses throughout the body."

"We'd have to go to a vet clinic to find sub q fluids," I said slowly. "I bet most hospitals and pharmacies have been picked clean, but most people probably wouldn't go to a vet to get emergency medical supplies."

"That's what I'm thinking," Kenzie said. "Miles has a phone book in the kitchen. We could check the Yellow Pages and make a list of local vet clinics."

"You should stay with Miles, and let me go get the fluids. I'll take Ripper's jeep. You can't drive a manual transmission, so it's gotta be me."

"Okay. You make a list of nearby vets, and I'll fix you something to eat before you go. We can't have you breaking and entering on an empty stomach."

My stomach flip-flopped at the prospect of eating, but I suppose Kenz was right. If I ran into trouble, I needed to be at full strength. "All right. Something simple, like soup and crackers."

Sitting at the small kitchen table, I copied down the addresses of the five closest vet clinics. Kenzie set a bowl of soup in front of me. My pounding head and the cloyingly sweet scent from the vase of roses combined to rob me of any appetite. I forced down the soup while Kenzie told me what to look for, bags of subcutaneous fluid, needles, and tubing.

When she wasn't watching, I swallowed a few more pain killers. I didn't want to let her know that my headache was getting worse.

Kenzie emptied out one of Miles's backpacks and handed me the keys to Ripper's jeep.

The soup didn't agree with me. I kept swallowing the saliva that flooded my mouth.

"Are you all right?"

The question barely registered, as if Kenzie's voice was coming from a distance.

"I'm fine." I rose unsteadily to my feet. I balanced one hand on the kitchen table, then took a step. The world tipped sideways, and the floor rushed up to meet me.

THIRTY-THREE

Kenzie

Kyle's eyes rolled back in his head, and he crashed to the floor, taking the vase of yellow roses with him. He lay surrounded by shards of crystal and rose petals.

I stared blankly at his sprawled form, my mind initially refusing to acknowledge what was happening.

Within seconds, I shook off the inertia and dropped to my knees beside him.

"Kyle?" I touched his face, which looked pale and drawn. When he began to retch, I rolled him on his side so he wouldn't choke if he vomited.

"Oh, Kyle."

Had I been so consumed with Miles that I hadn't noticed that Kyle was falling sick? Had he pushed himself too hard, trying to take care of Miles and me while ignoring his own symptoms?

Crap. Crap. Crap. I was the last man standing—so to speak—and it was on me to take care of everybody.

Hector poked his head into the room. "Stay back, boy."

I didn't have time to tweeze tiny crystal shards out of his paws if he stepped on glass. He obediently sat and watched me with curious eyes that seemed to ask what I intended to do. Damned if I knew.

Kyle and I had worked together to try to save Miles, and I wasn't sure if our combined efforts would succeed. How could I take care of two sick men by myself? I wasn't unwilling to take action; I had no clue what to do.

When you bite off more than you can chew, take things one step at a time.

Uncle Mel used to say that. When I was a snarky teenager, I had laughed at the visual image—chewing and stepping mixed together as if the adage made sense—but now his words snapped me out of my frozen funk and propelled me into action.

"One step at a time," I said out loud. Kyle was lying in a puddle of water on the hard floor. "Kyle. Kyle!" I stroked his face, trying to wake him up. His eyelids fluttered, and he focused on me with an effort.

"There you are." I winced. Ripper had said those exact words to me less than two weeks ago, but thinking about Ripper right now wouldn't help one bit, so I pushed the memory away. "I want you close to Miles, so I can keep an eye on both of you. We need to get you to my bedroom. If I help get you on your feet, can you walk?"

"Yeah, I can walk...but I'm supposed to go find a vet's office."

"Don't worry about that now." I hooked my arms around his waist and pulled. He wobbled to his feet. Leaning against me, he stumbled toward my bedroom and sat heavily on my cot, swaying as I knelt to remove his shoes and socks. "Lie back so I can pull off your jeans."

"Never thought I'd hear you say that again," he mumbled, falling back against the mattress.

Never thought I'd do it again, but instead of a straight path toward a predictable future, my life—everybody's lives—was a road full of unimaginable twists and curves. Kyle raised his hips. I unfastened his belt and tugged his jeans down his legs.

"Kenz, if this is the flu, I need to talk to you."

"You need to save your strength." I neatly folded his jeans and placed them on top of the dresser.

"Come on. You saw how it went with Miles. Before long I could be totally out of it, and then it will be too late."

Kyle had a strategic mind. He always looked ahead, weighing options and possible outcomes while he charted his next course of action. He could argue circles around anybody. That was probably why his dad encouraged him to go to law school.

I bet he wanted to have an agonizing *what-if* conversation. *What if Ripper never came back? What if Kyle and Miles both died? What would I do?* Kyle would want to help me plan for a future when everybody was gone, and I was totally alone.

Nope. Call me a wimp, but that was a conversation I couldn't face.

"You have time," I said. I turned, heading to the kitchen to get him a glass of ice water.

Kyle caught my wrist. "You owe me, Kenzie."

"What do you mean, I owe you?" I pivoted to face him. That didn't sound like the preamble to the conversation I'd imagined.

"We dated for nine months and then, out of the blue, you dumped me. No explanation. You refused to talk about it, to give me a chance to fix whatever went wrong. You were done and that was that."

My cheeks heated with humiliation as I remembered that fateful Easter visit to his family home in Boise. Breaking up with Kyle had been a face-saving preemptive strike, the only way I could protect my shredded dignity and heart. Why was Kyle acting like the injured party? He had been there. He said what he said.

I swallowed my pride and tried to stay grounded in the present. "We don't have time for this. I need to focus on taking care of you and Miles, not rehashing the past."

"This might be the only time I've got, and this discussion is way overdue. Please. The best thing you can do for me now is to finally answer my questions."

The one saving grace from the Easter debacle was that Kyle didn't know that I'd heard what he said. I sighed. If I had to embarrass myself in order to give Kyle peace of mind, it was a small price to pay. He was right. He might not have a lot of time left with a clear mind.

"Okay." I pulled up a chair and sat facing him. "What do you want to know?"

"What happened in Boise to make you change your mind about us? Did my mom say something?"

"Your mom said plenty." I paused, remembering all the subtle and not-so-subtle jibes that made it clear that she thought I wasn't refined enough to fit into their genteel world.

"Who are her people?"

I had paused at the bottom of the curved staircase, my hand still on the banister. It was the day before Easter. I was coming down to the kitchen for a glass of orange juice when I'd heard Kyle's mother's voice and had known she was speaking about me.

"What am I supposed to tell my friends? Kenzie's mother spends her days riding shotgun in a semi-truck? Her father and some floozy high-tailed it to parts unknown years ago?"

Kyle's sister had replied, but her voice was so low that I couldn't make out the words, although her tone was unmistakable.

"She's an embarrassment and the sooner Kyle realizes it, the better," his mother continued.

"Mom."

My heart had stopped when I heard Kyle's voice.

"When you're right, you're right."

I'd fled back upstairs on stockinged feet, packed my bag, and called an Uber to take me to the bus station. If Kyle was so weak-willed that he allowed his mommy to talk him into dumping me, screw him. I was better off without him. Abandoning him before he abandoned me was a small sort of victory.

"What did my mom say?" Kyle asked, bringing me back to the present.

"Nothing I hadn't heard before. It was what you said that changed everything."

"What I said?" Kyle frowned in confusion. "What are you talking about?"

"Puh-leeze, there's no point in playing coy. I heard everything. I was right outside the kitchen. Your mom said that the sooner you realized what a low-class embarrassment I am, the better. And you said, 'Mom, when you're right, you're right.'"

Kyle's face went slack. Dammit. What was I thinking, arguing with him when he needed to conserve his strength?

To my amazement, Kyle heaved himself into a sitting position and turned, dangling his legs off the bed so he could face me. He braced his weight on his hands. His body might be weak, but his voice was strong with outrage.

"What. The. Fuck? *That's* why you broke up with me?"

"You mad I beat you to the punch?" The intensity of his reaction took me aback.

Kyle threw his hands in the air, then put them back on the mattress when he swayed.

"Let me tell you what happened that morning. Mom asked me to go get the box of stuff she uses to decorate the table for Easter dinner—ceramic bunnies and chicks and painted ostrich eggshells. I remembered that she stored the Easter decorations in the attic. She told me they were in the basement. I bet her a buck I was right. Guess what? The box wasn't in the attic. I carried it up from the basement. You heard me telling mom that she had won the bet."

If I hadn't been sitting, my legs would have given out. Too stunned to speak, I stared at Kyle with wide, horrified eyes.

"You made a life-changing decision based on a snippet of conversation you overheard while eavesdropping," he continued. "If you had just asked me what was going on, we could have settled this in thirty seconds. Instead, you blew up our relationship. For nothing."

Another voice echoed through my memory, a voice whose absence left a gaping hole in my heart.

Anybody ever tell you you hear what you want to hear and then jump to conclusions?

Kyle and Ripper. My track record for fucking up in relationships was 100 percent. I rushed to judgment, putting the worst possible spin on innocuous comments. Was I really so afraid of being abandoned that I leaped at excuses to leave first?

Ripper had called me on my shit, and I'd promised to talk to him instead of jumping to conclusions. Here and now, I made another promise, this one to myself. I'd get this monkey off my back if I had to throttle it with my bare hands. The next time my fear of being left behind raised its head, I'd stop and think before I reacted. I'd ask questions. I'd behave like a normal, well-adjusted adult instead of a scared little girl.

Too bad it took me twenty-one years—no, twenty-two—to figure this out.

"I'm sorry. You're right. I blew it." My voice was heavy with regret.

His brow furrowed, as if he had expected me to argue with him.

"You're sorry," he repeated. The false energy born of anger evaporated, and he fell back against the pillow. "I don't know why I thought I'd feel better if I understood what went wrong. If anything, I feel worse. We broke up for the dumbest possible reason."

I opened my mouth to point out that his mother had been bad-mouthing me just seconds before he made his ill-timed comment, then closed it without speaking. Defending myself was pointless. If I had handled things better, Kyle and I never would have broken up. We'd been happy enough together. Chances are, we'd still be together and facing the flu pandemic as a couple.

And now? I wouldn't have allowed myself to fall in love with Ripper if I was still with Kyle.

I was in love with Ripper.

It was the first time I admitted it to myself. I had no idea if he loved me. Probably not. Knowing his forthright nature, he would have said so if he did, but he liked me and had promised to try to come back to me.

If—when—he came back, we could build on that. I'd fallen for a complex man who surprised me every day with his unlikely interests and passions. I wanted a future with this smart, strong, sexy, man who pushed me to be my best self, who saw me, and judged me good enough.

There was no place in the world that I felt safer than in his arms.

What about Kyle? Our break-up was a mistake, but I couldn't pretend that I hadn't fallen for Ripper. The situation truly sucked, and I'd carry the guilt from it forever. Kyle deserved better, but I couldn't undo the past months.

My gaze fell on Kyle's pale face. His eyelids drifted shut, then snapped open as he struggled to stay awake.

I took his hand. "I'm glad you're here, Kyle. No matter what happens, I'll always care about you and want the best for you. I want you to fight to live. Don't give up. Promise me."

He nodded and squeezed my hand.

"Good. Rest now. I'll be back in a little while."

I turned on Ripper's moon lantern, then left a bottle of water and some pain meds on the kitchen chair, within reach of the bed.

I tiptoed into Miles's room and found him curled on his side, his breath coming in ragged gasps. A digital thermometer revealed a temperature of 104.

After filling a basin with cold water, I swabbed his body with cool liquid, then moved the fan closer to his bed. When I lifted his head and tried to give him water, he coughed and sputtered. Afraid that he might aspirate the water into his lungs, I stopped.

I kissed his damp forehead then leaned over his ear. "Hang in there, Miles. I love you, cousin."

I carried my unopened gift from Ripper to the living room and sat down in the office chair, the bag on my lap. Reaching into the bag, I pulled out a long, narrow box with the name of an exclusive downtown jewelry store embossed on the lid.

A smile pulled at my lips when I saw the necklace tucked inside. With much of the city's population dead and the luxury shops abandoned and unguarded, Ripper could have selected the most expensive necklace in the store, some over-wrought, diamond-encrusted monstrosity that would look at home on the neck of a drug lord's mistress. Instead, Ripper's choice reflected how well he knew me and what I'd like.

A simple platinum circle pendant hung from a thin cable chain. What made my heart constrict were the five small charms dangling from the circle. Ripper hadn't simply swooped into the store and grabbed the first likely necklace. No, he'd spent time customizing the necklace for me, welding five jump rings closed to permanently attach the charms to the pendant.

He created something unique and special, the way he did with the Harleys he built. Every charm carried meaning. A letter R and a letter M, our initials. A sun, to chase away the darkness. A moon, to remind me of my fairy lantern watching over me at night. And a padlock and key. I couldn't quite figure out what to make of that last one. It might refer to the safety we found behind the locked gates.

The chain was long enough to slip over my head. Once in place, the charms nestled in the valley between my breasts. I pressed my fingers against them and closed my eyes, connected to Ripper by the cool metal he had worked with his hands.

"Come back to me," I whispered.

My chin wobbled. I missed him so much that it was like a physical pain, an ache deep in my bones. I forced my eyes open and willed myself to stand up and walk to the kitchen.

Hector watched from the arched opening to the living room while I carefully cleaned all the crystal shards and rose petals from the kitchen floor. The empty backpack and map to the closest veterinary clinics lay on the counter next to the keys to Ripper's jeep.

I dumped a can of food into Hector's dish and while he ate, I stepped out onto the patio and inhaled the damp night air. Clouds obscured the moon and an oppressive shroud of darkness blanketed the city. Only a scattering of lights and a car's engine that revved some distance away revealed the presence of other survivors.

Returning to the kitchen, I pulled a black hoodie over my tee and stuffed the map and a penlight into the pocket. A couple of water bottles, a granola bar, and an extra flashlight went into the backpack, along with a crowbar and a hand towel. I fastened a holster around my waist and tucked the gun Ripper had given me—a Sig P938—into it, along with a second magazine.

A leash and a lanyard holding keys to the houses and both gates hung by the back door. I slipped the lanyard around my neck.

"You ready?" I asked Hector, who was finishing up his food. He ambled to my side and I clicked the leash onto his collar.

Hector followed me outside, and I secured the door. I strode across the dark yard toward Ripper's gate and tried to ignore my racing heart and the sensation that something was watching me from the shadows. Reaching out to put the key in the lock, I heard a noise behind me.

Dropping to my knees, I wrapped an arm around Hector's neck and strained to listen for a repetition of the sound. Nothing. My eyes slowly adjusted to the dark. I scanned the yard for any sign of movement.

I couldn't make out a thing. Maybe a leaf had rustled in a breeze. A raccoon or possum might have stepped on a branch. My imagination might insist that a monster lurked in the gloom, biding its time until I let down my guard, but my rational mind knew better.

It was past time to set aside my childish fears. Miles and Kyle were depending on me. I stood and unbolted the gate, stepped into Ripper's yard, then locked the gate once again, leaving behind the safety of the compound.

"Time to save the day," I said to Hector.

We set off into the dark night.

THIRTY-FOUR

Kenzie

When I used to fantasize about morphing into a kick-ass heroine—projecting myself into some movie or novel—it never occurred to me to worry about the small, pragmatic details. I imagined using my mad martial-arts skills to kick butt or my steady hand and deadly aim to blast away the bad guys. All the while sporting perfect hair and tossing out snarky quips.

Reality was nothing like fantasy.

Scared and alone, there wasn't an ounce of snark in me, only a grim determination to bring back the supplies I needed to save Miles and Kyle. I paused, frozen with indecision on the street in front of Ripper's house.

When you're setting off on a hero's journey in the middle of the night, do you use a flashlight or not?

The moon was hidden behind clouds, and the streetlights had given up the ghost weeks ago. At first thought, relying on a flashlight to navigate through dark streets seemed like a no-brainer. If I tripped over something and sprained my ankle or broke my wrist, I'd be in trouble. It was better to see what lay ahead than to blunder through the darkness. But if I could see what lay ahead, the reverse was also true.

In a pitch-black city a flashlight beam that bobbled with every step might attract unwanted attention.

Alrighty then, I'd proceed in the dark, trusting my keen-eyed canine companion to steer me around any obstacles on the road.

I crouched down and pulled the map from my pocket. Using the hoodie as a shield, I flipped on the penlight and quickly scanned the map, memorizing the directions to the closest vet clinic. One block north, east until I hit 82nd Avenue, then north again.

I gave my eyes a moment to readjust to the dark.

"Okay, Hector. Let's go."

We kept to the middle of the street, keeping a buffer between us and the overgrown bushes and parked cars that lined the roadway. It was unlikely that anybody lay in wait, ready to spring out as we passed by, but maintaining a distance between us and potential danger gave me comfort. At least I'd have time to react if somebody jumped us.

Hector walked confidently forward, apparently sharing none of my trepidation. I hadn't stepped outside of the compound for weeks—not since my foolhardy solo outing—and the urge to scamper back behind its walls was strong. But the safety it promised was an illusion, wasn't it?

All of Miles's planning and precautions hadn't kept a determined criminal out, or stopped an arsonist, or held a deadly virus at bay. I might still fall sick myself, a fact I couldn't afford to dwell upon.

Why was I so afraid of imaginary monsters lurking in the shadows, when genuine dangers had already threatened everything and everybody I loved?

I stopped dead in my tracks and turned slowly around, gazing at the black silhouettes that loomed against the inky landscape.

"Here I am," I called out, confronting my phobia, challenging the bug-a-boo that had haunted my life since childhood. "I dare you. Come and get me."

I held my breath, waiting for the hushed night to fracture, for a blur of movement, for a crackle of energy, for a shriek.... Nothing happened, of course. No monster leaped out of the darkness. No one called to me from the gloomy shadows, whispering my name in a paper-thin rasp.

My panic shriveled to a tiny kernel. When faced with the prospect of losing Miles, Ripper and Kyle, maybe there was simply no room in my heart or mind to play host to other terrors.

Hector patiently paced ahead of me as we trekked through the neighborhood. Here and there, lights glowed behind drawn shades. The clouds thinned and the moon appeared for a brief moment, a pale circle haloed by insipid light. A cat sprawled on the roof of a car, the moonlight reflecting in its eyes as it followed our progress.

As we drew close to 82nd, we passed an old cemetery. Graveyards didn't spook me. In fact, I used to enjoy wandering through historic cemeteries, reading the inscriptions and admiring the intricately carved tombstones. The flu changed everything.

Funeral homes and coroners couldn't keep up with the deluge of bodies. With nobody left to transport corpses, desperate people dumped their dead on the cemetery grounds. Tonight, I kept to the far side of the street as I scuttled past heaps of mouldering corpses, holding my breath.

When my street intersected 82nd, I paused, and huddled against the wall of a drugstore, reconnoitering.

Eighty-second Avenue was a major thoroughfare, four lanes wide, lined on both sides by large and small commercial establishments, stores, restaurants, medical offices. The street would be a magnet for any people searching for food, tools, anything they might need to survive. I bet the gun shop a few blocks away had been picked clean within a week of the outbreak.

The windows of the drugstore had been smashed, the pavement littered with shattered glass. I couldn't let Hector walk over broken glass. Instead of hugging the storefronts, as I had planned, we'd have to abandon the shelter of the buildings and expose our position to anybody who might be lurking nearby. I didn't expect to run into anyone in the middle of the night, but I couldn't afford to be careless, not when my task was so critical.

We headed north. The moon peeked out from behind the clouds, and everywhere I saw evidence of looting. Busted-down doors, broken windows, boxes of discarded goods scattered across parking lots.

A car's headlights approached us from a few blocks away. I pulled Hector behind a parked car and waited until its taillights had disappeared before resuming our trek.

We walked right past the veterinary clinic and had to double back when the pawn shop on the next block told me that we'd gone too far. The vet clinic was separated from the road by a small parking lot.

Nothing indicated that the place had been ransacked. No broken glass crunched beneath my shoes. I didn't trip over any boxes abandoned in the parking lot. My spirits rose.

Above the door handle, a rectangular window filled the top of the entry door. Better and better. I'd come prepared to pry a door open, instead I bashed in the glass with the crowbar, then covered the jagged glass with the small towel, so I could reach inside and unlock the door without cutting myself.

If we still had power, I probably would have activated an alarm, but there was no danger of that now.

Once inside, I clicked on my penlight. Hector and I skirted the reception desk and headed into the back of the clinic. The first three doors led to exam rooms, the fourth opened into a room lined floor to ceiling with crowded shelves.

I worked my way around the room, systematically examining the contents of every shelf. When I reached the back wall, I hit pay dirt. I opened a box containing bags of electrolyte injection solution. The next held cartons of disposable needles and IV tubes.

I hadn't expected it to be this easy. Knowing my luck, I'd figured we'd have to check out three or four clinics before we found one that hadn't been plundered. All I had to do now was retrace my steps back to the compound and administer the fluids to Miles.

Aunt Debbie and I had taken turns injecting Taz with the life-extending fluid. The first time I felt the needle pop when it punctured Taz's skin, I'd cried, certain I was hurting him. That experience would make it easier to stick a needle into my cousin, and maybe into Kyle, if it came to that.

I packed eight bags of sub q fluid, a box of needles, and a package of tubing into the backpack. On impulse, I squeezed a bag of bison dog treats on top of the medical supplies, a reward for my faithful companion.

I dropped to my knees and scritched Hector's neck. "We did it. Now we get to go home."

I settled the pack on my back and switched off the flashlight as we exited the clinic. I walked quickly, my steps buoyant, as Hector and I headed home.

The sooner I got fluids into Miles, the better. Maybe I could nail an old wire coat hanger to the wall above his bed and suspend a bag of fluid from that, allowing gravity to force the liquid down the tubing.

Preoccupied with my plans, at first I paid no attention to the sounds coming from the side parking lot of a small tavern. As soon as the grunts and thuds penetrated my awareness, I shrank against the front wall of the tavern, pulling Hector close.

"Whadaya got there?" a man's voice demanded. "You trying to hold out on us?"

The unmistakable whomp of a heavy blow landing on a human body sounded, followed by a low moan.

"Bobby, see what he's trying to hide," the same voice ordered.

A scuffling sound, then a second man—Bobby presumably—spoke. "It's one of those things a doctor uses to listen to your heart."

"A stethoscope?" The first man snorted. "Why you hiding a stethoscope? You like to play doctor?"

"I am a doctor," a third man said. He wheezed, obviously in pain. "Please. You can't have any use for a stethoscope."

"Don't think you'll be needing it either, dickwad. Not where you're going."

A doctor. My heart thumped so loudly that I was afraid the assailants would hear it from around the corner. If I could bring a doctor home to treat Miles and Kyle it might mean the difference between life and death. After finding the subcutaneous fluid at the very first vet clinic and now stumbling upon a doctor, maybe my luck was turning.

I'd told Ripper that I look for trouble and expect good things to fall apart. Maybe this was more evidence that I should let go of my default pessimism. But first, I had to intervene to help the doctor.

With my left hand, I took the penlight from my pocket and switched it on, directing the beam at my chest until I was ready to move. I unclipped the leash from Hector's collar, then drew my Sig from the holster and used my thumb to sweep the safety off.

Leaning forward, I whispered in Hector's ear. "With me." The dog tensed. After one deep breath to settle my nerves, I stepped around the corner.

If this were a movie, I probably would have made a grand entrance, shooting into the air to get their attention and snarling a command. In reality? Nope. Firing my weapon was a last resort. I didn't want to announce my presence to any other bad guy within earshot.

I rounded the corner, took a position squarely facing my target—the stable platform Ripper had taught me—and shone the flashlight beam in the men's eyes.

"Let him go and walk away," I called.

Hector punctuated the command with a low growl, leaning forward as if eager to lunge.

The men froze, blinking into the light.

Please God, don't let the men be armed. I might just have initiated a wild-west type shootout. I'd been practicing every day for almost six weeks. Ripper called me a decent shot. If it came to it, was decent good enough, especially if I was aiming at a live, moving target? I sure hoped so, because after stirring up this hornet's nest, I had no choice but to brazen it out.

"You heard me." I put as much conviction as I could muster into my voice. "Let him go and walk away."

A burly man of about fifty raised his hands in the air and smiled. "Why don't you put the gun down, honey, before you hurt yourself."

His partner in crime, a scrawny man in his thirties, stared at my Sig with wide-eyed alarm. I bet he'd never touched a weapon. Good. Now, what about his pudgy, sexist friend?

"Worry about yourself, not me. I've got a gun that I know how to use. I've got a trained police dog." I tilted my head toward Hector. It was a total lie, but a credible one. "If you're smart, you'll walk away."

I spared a glance for the man sprawled on the ground between them. His right eye was beginning to swell shut and blood trickled from his mouth. He sat up, pressing a hand against his side. That sound I heard had probably been the two men kicking him in the ribs. He edged away from his assailants, scooting a couple of feet toward me.

"Hank?" The scrawny man—Bobby—deferred to his older companion.

"Now, honey, there's no need to get testy." The smile lingered on Hank's face, but his hard eyes gave the lie to the friendly gesture.

When he took two quick steps toward me, I put my finger on the trigger and fired, cracking the windshield of a car parked behind him. So much for avoiding unwanted attention.

Bobby took off, running south on 82nd.

"Stupid bitch." Hank rushed me. I had a split second to decide if I wanted to shoot again.

"Attack," I shouted.

Hector launched at the man, knocking him to the ground. When Hank tried to punch Hector, the dog sank his teeth into the man's forearm.

"Get your fucking dog off me." Hank attempted to wrench his arm from the dog's jaw.

"Sure. I'll call my dog off. Then I'll give you five seconds to get out of here. If you don't..." I pointed the Sig at Hank, my threat clear.

"All right," he spat. "I'll clear out."

"Hector, release." The dog obeyed and retreated to my side, his eyes still fixed on the man, ready to spring into action again.

Hank sat up, cradling his injured arm against his chest, his expression baleful. Blood dripped from the torn flesh.

"Five." I began the countdown.

Hank struggled to his feet, obviously in pain.

"Four."

He glowered at me, his teeth clenched.

"Three."

Hank whirled around and shambled off into the darkness, following the direction his friend had fled.

"Two. One." I finished the countdown. I blew out a long breath, staring after him for a minute before turning my eyes to the injured doctor. He'd managed to get to his feet and now leaned against the wall for support.

I holstered the Sig, then approached the stranger.

"How badly are you hurt?" I asked, shining the flashlight on him.

"I'll have a black eye and a split lip. Superficial injuries." He lifted his shirt to examine his side, gingerly pressing against his rib cage. "I think my ribs are bruised, but not broken. All in all, it's not too bad." He raised his gaze to my face. "Thank you for coming to my aid."

I couldn't answer for a moment, struck dumb by the lustrous beauty of his deep brown eyes. Not even the puffy and discolored skin surrounding his right eye could diminish its impact. The last thing I expected tonight was to stumble across a doctor with the soulful eyes of a Renaissance angel.

"You're welcome. Are you really a doctor?"

"Yes. I am—or rather I was—on staff at the community health clinic a mile south of here."

I was impressed. Only altruism—or an abysmal medical school grade point average—could motivate a doctor to accept a modest salary at a sliding scale clinic that served the homeless and people without health insurance. Perhaps my mystery doctor had more in common with an angel than heavenly eyes.

Or not. I'd carelessly trusted the wrong man once, allowing a dangerous stranger into the compound. Not a mistake I'd make again, but still, my breath quickened at the possibility of finding a real doctor to treat Miles and Kyle.

"I'm sure you were overwhelmed at the clinic once the flu hit," I said.

He frowned. "It was a mad house. At the best of times, we're understaffed and patients must wait a long time to be seen. Once the flu struck, it became impossible to keep up. Desperately sick people filled the waiting room and lined up outside the building. One by one, the staff fell ill, leaving fewer of us to tend our patients. And the truth is, there was little we could do to help. Anti-virals did nothing to stem this strain of virus. Eventually, every member of the staff died except me, and people gave up seeking medical help."

A block of ice settled in my chest as I listened to his bleak account. "Are you telling me that there's nothing a doctor can do help a flu patient recover? That it's hopeless?"

"Are you falling ill?" he asked gently. "Do you have a headache or a fever?"

I shook my head, then slipped the backpack from my shoulders. I held up a bag of sub q fluid. "I'm fine, but my cousin and a friend have the flu. I thought that if I could keep them hydrated, that they'd stand a better chance of surviving." My voice broke.

I hadn't allowed myself to think of anything beyond my mission, or to consider what would happen if the fluids did no good.

"Are your friends men or women?"

"Men."

"I don't want to offer you false hope, but I have seen a handful of men recover from the flu. I suspect that giving your friends subcutaneous fluids might slightly increase their odds of survival. It's a good plan. You did well to think of it."

The panic squeezing my chest eased. I nodded my thanks for his reassurance.

"What have you been doing since the clinic closed?" I asked.

"What little I can to be of assistance." He offered a small, rueful smile. "I wear my white lab coat to identify myself as a physician and go door to door, asking if anyone needs help. Few people open their door to me. Perhaps they think I'm a fraud, seeking to take advantage, but some let me in. At first, when I still had medication to bring down fever and intravenous fluids, I did some good. Later, when I exhausted my supplies, I could do little more than sit at their bedside and offer comfort as they passed."

Good lord. My initial reaction was correct. His compelling eyes revealed a deep well of compassion and a commitment to his profession. It took a lot of courage to brave the streets when civil order was breaking down and to knock on frightened strangers' doors offering to help. I'd been a gullible fool when Jason demanded admittance to the compound, but I sensed I could trust this man.

"That sounds dangerous. Nowadays, a lot of people are likely to shoot first and ask questions later."

"I did carry a gun for a while. My brother-in-law is a police detective. We used to go to his gun club together. He taught me how to shoot and helped me get a permit for a concealed weapon. It seemed like a good idea since I often worked late in rough neighborhoods." He shrugged. "I hope to *never* shoot anyone. I've treated too many gun-shot victims and know how much damage a bullet can do, but I wanted to be ready to defend myself or an innocent bystander."

"How come you didn't have the gun with you tonight?" I asked.

"I gave it to a woman I treated a few weeks ago. A man had broken into her house and ransacked it. He dislocated her jaw and ruptured her eardrum when she resisted. She was afraid he'd come back. I decided she needed the gun more than I did."

"You're a real bad ass." I held out my hand for a formal introduction. "My name is Kenzie Dunwitty."

He grinned. "My little sister might disagree with that assessment, but I'll take it. Dr. Sahdev Chowdhury, but please call me Sahdev."

We shook hands.

"Sahdev, would you be willing to come home with me and take a look at my friends? Help me administer the sub q fluids?"

"Of course." He inclined his head. "I'd be pleased to help."

From his bruised face and his awkward posture, it was clear that Sahdev was in pain.

"It took me almost an hour to walk here from home. Are you in any condition to walk that far?"

"I'm fine," he said through gritted teeth. "I spent the past two days with a flu patient. There was no food or water in the house, so I haven't had anything to eat or drink for more than forty-eight hours. I'm lightheaded, but that won't stop me from doing what needs to be done."

I dropped to my knees and dug through the pack. "You're living proof that doctors make the worst patients. Here." I handed him a bottle of water and a granola bar.

"Can you spare this? I don't want you to do without for my sake."

"Please, take it. I'm not hungry or thirsty, and we have plenty of food back home."

"Thank you." He twisted the cap, downed half the bottle of water, then wiped his mouth with the back of his hand. "We took so much for granted before. Clean water is a blessing."

I nodded. After Sahdev tended to Miles and Kyle, I'd fix this man a hearty meal. It would give me pleasure to repay his kindness with a plate of hot food.

"We probably should get moving," I said. "We don't want Hank and Bobby to come back with a gun and find us here."

"Hank struck me with his right fist, so I believe that is his dominant hand. Your dog bit his right forearm. I doubt Hank will be able to use a gun until his arm heals, but you're right. It isn't safe to linger on the streets."

I shouldered the pack and clipped the leash to Hector's collar while Sahdev peeled the wrapper from the granola bar. After we walked south for a few blocks, I turned to him.

"I'm curious. When Bobby tried to take the stethoscope from you, why did you refuse to give it to him? It's not the kind of thing looters would take. You could find another one someplace else. Why risk being hit again to hold on to it?"

"Ah, this is a special stethoscope." Sahdev pulled it from his pocket and held it up. "My parents immigrated to the United States from Ahmedabad, a city in northwest India. My grandfather is a physician there. When I graduated from medical school, he flew here for the ceremony. He gave me his stethoscope as a graduation present. It's a sentimental connection to my family, to my grandfather, that's impossible to replace."

"I understand." I liked him even more for his explanation.

With Hector in the lead, we navigated the route back to the compound. Optimism put a spring in my step. I had a doctor in tow and everything we needed to cure Miles's dehydration, to give him his best shot at surviving the flu.

Dear God, I silently prayed. *Please let this work. Please don't let it be too late.*

Out of the blue, goosebumps erupted on my arms and a prickle of fear crawled up my spine.

Hurry, an inner voice urged. *Hurry home.*

THIRTY-FIVE

Kyle

I awoke with a start, shuddering from the conviction that something was very wrong. A shit ton of things were wrong. My head hurt so much that I felt like puking. My parched tongue stuck to the roof of my mouth like a fat, desiccated slug, and it required real effort to peel it away from my palate. Gross.

With a grunt, I rolled on my side. Squinting against the pain ricocheting through my skull, I reached for the bottle of water Kenzie had left on the kitchen chair next to the bed.

Halfway to the plastic bottle, my hand stilled.

What was I hearing? It sounded like the panting of a winded animal. Hector was the only mouth-breather in residence, and Kenzie had taken him along on her expedition. If not Hector, who or what was quietly gasping for air?

The monster under my bed, my imagination suggested. I snorted. My imagination could shut the fuck up. What was I, five?

I glanced around the room. A shadow danced against the wall. My bleary eyes homed in on its source, then widened in surprise.

Miles stood at the foot of the cot, his mouth hanging open, his glassy eyes fixed on me. He rocked gently back and forth, as if keeping time to music only he could hear.

I raised up onto my elbows. "Hey, buddy. What are you doing out of bed?"

He ignored my question, shifting his weight from side to side, an image that brought to mind a scene from an old 1930s-era movie that Kenz and I had watched. A snake charmer in India played a flute, luring a captive cobra from a basket. The beguiled cobra swayed, his pitiless eyes fixated on the charmer, while the crowd waited with bated breath for the snake to strike.

Miles stared at me with as much comprehension, as much humanity, as that mesmerized snake. If Miles was the cobra in the scenario my mind constructed, what was I, the crowd of observers, or the intended victim?

"Miles, snap out of it." I summoned the strength to sit up and swing my legs off the cot. The world went cockeyed. Everything in my field of vision upended. I groaned and dropped my head, squeezing my eyes shut against the nauseating visual kaleidoscope.

After a minute, I lifted my head and opened my eyes. Miles had moved to the side of my bed. In his right hand, he clutched a large chef's knife.

I sat up straight, my disorientation forgotten.

End-stage homicidal mania, the stuff of nightmares, the characteristic that distinguished this particular virus from all others. From the earliest days of the flu outbreak, rumors had circulated that some patients devolved into a murderous frenzy. I'd rejected the rumors as bullshit until I saw the murdered girl in Kenzie's dorm. When Jake and Ali got sick, I'd held my breath, waiting for one of them to show signs of violence. Thank God, it hadn't happened.

Thought I'd dodged a bullet. Until now.

Why Miles? The poor guy couldn't catch a break. All his life, he'd struggled with social anxiety and obsessive interests that left him lonely and isolated. He lost his parents when he was barely twenty.

When Kenzie and I were dating, I'd been a shit, dismissing him as a weirdo survivalist I refused to meet. If only I could go back and change that. Yeah, he had some whackadoodle notions, but he was a good guy doing his best. He'd come into his own in the past month, surrounded by people—Ripper, Kenzie, me—who cared about him and who valued what he brought to the table.

This sucked. It wasn't fair.

Miles sidled closer, and I got my ass in gear. Snagging my jeans from the dresser, I stumbled from the room, swinging the door closed behind me. I pulled my belt from the loops and wrapped it around the bedroom doorknob, yanking it tight. Turning around, I frantically searched for some way to hold the bedroom door shut.

I managed to reach into the coat closet and grab an old wire hanger. I twisted apart the hanger, straightened the wire, then threaded it through the last hole in the belt strap. I quickly twisted the wire again, firmly attaching it to the belt, then I wrapped the wire around the knob on the coat closet door. The wire held the bedroom door firmly shut.

Try as he might, Miles would be unable to get out. I hoped.

I collapsed to the floor, dripping with sweat, my heart pounding, my limbs trembling, totally exhausted by my efforts.

Now what? I'd succeeded in locking Miles in the bedroom. According to the rumors, violent flu victims possessed an unnatural strength. He couldn't batter down the door, could he? What would happen if he did?

I wasn't sure I'd have the strength to fight him. If I lost consciousness—or worse, if I fell victim to the same mania—I couldn't allow Kenzie to arrive home and walk into a life-threatening situation.

I had to find the energy to warn her. I crawled over to the command station and clambered onto the desk chair. A quick search of a drawer revealed a spiral notebook, a pen, and a roll of tape.

Spots swam in front of my eyes, making it hard to see what I wrote in large, block letters. "KENZIE. MILES IS VIOLENT. BE CAREFUL ENTERING HOUSE."

Too weak to stand, I pushed off with my feet and rolled the chair to the back door, where I taped the note to the window. A shotgun hung next to the door. I lifted it onto my lap and rolled back to the hall, where I took a position outside the bedroom door.

Weak, racked with pain, and lightheaded, I felt like shit, but it didn't matter. As long as I was conscious, as long as I had any strength in my arms, I'd protect Kenzie. I wouldn't let anybody hurt her, not even the cousin she loved, a man I'd come to consider a friend.

Leaning my head against the wall, I fought the compulsion to close my eyes.

Damn, I was cold. I glanced longingly at one of Aunt Debbie's crocheted afghans, one that usually covered the back of the old recliner, but now was folded on the long table. I didn't dare use up my limited store of energy propelling myself across the floor to fetch something so self-indulgent. Instead, I tucked my fingers under my arms.

So cold. I swore I could see my breath hanging in the frosty air. How was that possible? Is was summer, wasn't it? June or July? Maybe August? Why couldn't I remember?

I shook my head to dispel the haze and was rewarded with a pain so sharp it felt like someone had driven a pick ax into my skull.

"Fuuuck," I groaned.

The bedroom door knob rattled. I peered through narrowed eyes at the belt and wire contraption I'd jury-rigged. It better hold. Not sure I could take on a determined kindergartner right now.

A thump. Shit. Miles had given up on the doorknob and was now throwing his body against the flimsy, hollow-core door. Again and again, the door shuddered in its frame, but didn't buckle.

Another moment of silence.

"That's right, Miles," I whispered. "You can't get out. Give up, buddy. Just give up."

My neck couldn't support the weight of my head, which teetered like one of those bobblehead toys.

What was that? A scraping sound, like a cat scratching at a door to be let out. Miles didn't have claws, but he had a knife, didn't he?

I jerked backward in the chair when he pounded on the door again. The wood cracked and the thin tip of the knife poked through the flat surface of the door.

He struck again and the wood splintered.

Miles punched through the disintegrating veneer, his knuckles streaked with blood. He twisted his hand, as if trying to enlarge the breach, then withdrew his fist.

A few seconds later, the knife appeared again. Miles hacked frantically at the ever-widening hole, the borders crumbling under the blade's onslaught.

How the fuck did he find the strength to do this?

"Please stop," I said, a plea to Miles or maybe the universe. I glanced down at my hands cradling the shotgun. Tears swam in my eyes. I didn't want to hurt Miles.

His hands tore the edges of the uneven opening, breaking off huge pieces of it, then they suddenly retracted.

Silence.

Had Miles given up? Had he passed out, his flu-ravaged body finally exhausting all of its manic energy? I held my breath as the seconds ticked by.

Miles thrust his face through the gaping maw, twisting it from side to side as he rammed his head through the saw-edged hole. The jagged wood tore at his skin, leaving a bloody slash from his temple to his chin.

When his eyes fixed on me, he stilled.

There was nothing left of the man I knew behind those glittering eyes. The young man who eagerly explained the workings of the solar oven, the guy who smiled shyly and ducked his head when we complimented his baking, was gone. He'd become a soulless automaton, driven to violence by a virus that sparked some irresistible impulse in a corner of his dying brain.

He opened his mouth and howled.

Chills ran up and down my body, and for a moment I couldn't see past the spots dancing before my eyes. In my weakened state, these adrenaline surges wiped me out. My fight-or-flight instinct had been triggered one too many times, and now I lacked the energy to either do battle or flee.

I'd black out soon. Already, oblivion nibbled at the edges of my consciousness.

I wasn't afraid of dying. Shit, I figured I was going to die since the first flu symptoms appeared. Why would I be spared the fate that had claimed so many people?

What terrified the crap out of me was leaving Kenzie alone to face the future. To face Miles. If she came home and Miles attacked her, would she be able to bring herself to shoot him? If she did, would she ever forgive herself?

I wouldn't let her move forward in life with that kind of guilt eating away at her soul. Maybe the last thing I could do for the woman I loved was to take that burden from her shoulders. She'd never know why I did it. She'd probably hate me, blame me for not finding another way. Didn't matter, as long as she was safe and her conscience clear.

I conjured Kenzie's face in my mind.

Miles pounded and kicked like a berserker, tearing off huge chunks of wood.

I remembered how Kenzie laughed, her nose crinkling adorably as we shared a private joke.

Miles roared with rage or triumph—I couldn't tell which—and squeezed his body through the opening. Bloodied, he stood up straight, the knife gripped in his fist.

In my mind's eye, Kenzie touched my face, a soft smile curving her lips. *I love you, Kyle.*

"I love you, too, Kenz," I murmured.

Everything in my field of vision dimmed as my consciousness ebbed.

It took a Herculean effort to pump the slide on the shotgun's stock, advancing a shell into the chamber. I didn't have the strength to raise the gun to my shoulder, so I braced it against the seat of the chair.

Miles rushed me in a blur of movement.

"I'm sorry," I mumbled, squeezing the trigger.

Something damp splattered against my skin, and Miles's body tumbled to the floor at my feet. I coughed, choking on the blood-clogged air.

Heartsick, yet somehow at peace, I lapsed into unconsciousness.

THIRTY-SIX

Kenzie

By the time I unlocked the gate to the compound, my feet were dragging and I was fantasizing about coffee. I needed sleep more than caffeine, but that wasn't going to happen, so I'd have to content myself with a jolt of java.

I had a plan. While Sahdev checked on Miles and Kyle, preparing to administer the subcutaneous fluids, I'd brew a carafe of coffee. Fortified against the mind-numbing fatigue that made my feet stumble and my brain glitch, I'd get on with the day.

A hand-written note taped to the window caught my eye as we approached the back door.

"KENZIE. MILES IS VIOLENT. BE CAREFUL ENTERING HOUSE."

I would have rushed in, heedless of the warning, if Sahdev hadn't placed his hand over mine on the doorknob.

"Perhaps I should go first," he suggested.

"If Miles is throwing things or taking a swing at Kyle, I need to get in there to help."

Sahdev kept his hand on mine, preventing me from turning the knob. "I must insist."

I bristled. What kind of sexist bullshit was this? Had he forgotten who just saved his ass?

"Please, Kenzie, allow me to explain. If your cousin has developed the flu mania, he will do far more than throw objects and punches. I've seen flu patients fly into a homicidal rage, attacking their closest family members. Your friend warned you to be careful entering the house. I suggest we take that warning seriously."

I couldn't imagine Miles in a homicidal rage—the mere idea should have been laughable—but Sahdev's words stilled my hand. The flu mania made killers out of the most unlikely people, didn't it? I'd seen it for myself in the dorm when Jenna suffocated Lauren.

"Okay," I said reluctantly. "We'll be careful, but I'm not staying outside. You're a stranger to Miles and Kyle. If you walk in without me, they'll think you broke into the place. And Kyle has a gun."

"As you wish."

We stepped into the kitchen and a strange smell washed over me, a pungent combination of wet rust and something sickly sweet. Hector strained at the leash, whining and agitated. I swirched on the LED lantern we kept on the counter by the door and another from the table.

Sahdev twisted to face me and gripped my elbows hard. "Please trust me when I tell you that there are some things in life you can't unsee. Whatever happened in the next room is not an image you want to plant in your memory, especially not when it involves people you care for."

My chest constricted with panic, and I tried to wrench my arms out of his hold. "Miles! Kyle!"

Hector growled a warning, and Sahdev released my arms. We stared at each other for a long moment. Pity and regret mingled on his features. I shook my head, helpless against my need to know, to understand what transpired while I was out seeking help.

"I'm sorry," I whispered. Perhaps I shouldn't see what lay in the next room, but I had to.

I took one step into the front room. Across the room, Kyle slumped sideways in the rolling desk chair, a shotgun loosely cradled in his limp arms. When he fired the gun, the recoil must have spun the chair on its axis, because he was facing me and not the hallway.

I thought he was dead, until I saw the slight rise and fall of his chest. From head to foot, his body and clothes were stained red, as if he'd walked through a cloud of atomized blood. Looking past him to the floor, I saw those things that Sahdev had warned me about, images that would haunt my dreams for the rest of my life.

Miles. Oh, my God. Miles.

I collapsed. My knees buckled, and I caught myself on my hands, swaying while I retched. Sahdev knelt beside me and helped me to my feet, gently guiding me back to the kitchen. He eased me onto a wooden chair, took a cold bottle of water from the refrigerator, twisted off the lid, and put it in my hands.

Crouching in front of my chair, he waited until I met his eyes to speak. "You told me that your friend Ripper lives in the house on the other side of the gate. Do you have a key to his place?"

I nodded numbly and held up the key ring dangling from the lanyard around my neck.

"I want you to take the dog and go to your friend's house. Barricade the doors and wait. I'll come and find you as soon as I've taken care of everything here."

"Kyle's alive," I said, looking past him into the front room.

"Good. The care of the living takes precedence over everything else," Sahdev said. "Once I've stabilized him to the best of my ability, I'll take care of the other matters."

The other matters. He meant Miles's body. My cousin was dead. I'd been too late to save him. My hands shook, and I spilled water on my lap.

"You hardly know me." My teeth began to chatter. Why were my teeth chattering? "It's not fair to ask you to deal with this mess."

He grasped my hands. "Kenzie, look at me." When I lifted my gaze to his, I saw compassion and strength in his eyes. "I'm a doctor because the desire to alleviate suffering, to be of service, is bred in my bones. I've served in war zones with Doctors Without Borders. I'm not squeamish. There is nothing here I haven't seen before. Allow me to do this for you, please."

My eyes filled with tears, and I was beyond grateful that I wouldn't have to face the horrors in the next room. Within a few seconds I pulled myself together, wiped the tears from my face, and straightened in the chair. What would Sahdev need to "take care of the other matters"?

"There are two bedrooms in the back of the house and clean sheets in the linen closet in the hall. We have lots of five-gallon water bottles. The generator is running, so you can heat water on the hot plate, if you need it. We keep cleaning supplies—rubber gloves, buckets, and bleach—on the shelf at the bottom of the basement stairs." I pointed to the basement door.

He nodded. "Very good."

"There's a shovel in the garden shed and a small wheelbarrow." My breath caught in my throat, and I had to swallow before I could continue. "And there's an empty spot of land in the corner of the yard, past the chicken coop."

"Leave it all to me," Sahdev said. "Now, you go to Ripper's house, and I'll attend to your friends."

I stood and set the backpack on the kitchen table, then paused at the back door.

"We never leave the yard without locking the gate behind us. You'll need a key. There's an identical lanyard hanging by the front door. Use this key to unlock the gate." I held up a bronze key. "And this one to get into Ripper's house." I held up a silver key.

"Go rest, and let me take care of Kyle."

I tapped my leg to summon Hector and took an extra lantern from a cupboard. Weary and demoralized, I shambled through the yards to Ripper's house. Once inside, I crawled onto his king size bed. When I burrowed my nose against the sheets, I caught a faint whiff of Ripper's scent.

Ripper would be gutted by Miles's death.

"Where are you?" I whispered. "Please be all right. Please come home."

As soon as we had crossed the threshold, Hector had abandoned me to explore his old home. After a few minutes, the bedroom door creaked, and Hector stuck his head inside. I patted the bed and the dog jumped up beside me.

"You won't leave me, will you?" I stroked his furry back. He licked my face, and I closed my eyes.

Miles was dead. My sweet cousin.

Oh, God. I couldn't wrap my head around the knowledge of what he and Kyle must have gone through. Sleep seemed impossible, despite my exhaustion.

Miles. Ripper. Kyle. What would I do if I lost them all? I clung to Hector's side, taking comfort from his familiar presence and the sound of his steady breathing.

The universe must have taken pity on me, because I tumbled into a deep and dreamless sleep.

"Hello? Kenzie?"

"Five more minutes, Mom," I mumbled, barely awake and pulling the covers over my head.

Someone rapped on the bedroom door. I lifted my head and looked around me at Ripper's bedroom. Memories flooded back, and I sat up.

"Sahdev? Is Kyle okay?"

"He's still alive," he replied from the hallway.

"I slept in my clothes. I'm decent. Come on in." I scrubbed at my face, trying to banish the last vestiges of sleep.

He hesitated inside the door, glancing around at the masculine bedroom. "I brought you a cup of coffee." He crossed the room and handed me a still-steaming mug.

"Thank you." I took a sip and sighed. "Tell me about Kyle."

"He's resting in the smaller bedroom. He regained consciousness after receiving the subcutaneous fluid. He took a cool bath and managed to keep down a bottle of sports drink."

"Did he talk about what happened?"

"Yes. As you can imagine, he's quite distressed."

"I want to see him," I said, slipping on my shoes.

"I buried your cousin and cleaned up the aftermath. Before you see Kyle, I'd like to show you a few things that will help you understand the events of last night."

Saying thank you felt totally insufficient for all Sadhev had done. Impulsively, I touched his arm. "I don't know what I would have done if you hadn't been here."

Sahdev patted my hand. "I suspect that the same woman who frightened away my assailants would have risen to the occasion and done what needed to be done."

We locked up Ripper's house and headed back to the compound. I glanced at the corner of the yard where Miles was buried, but didn't stop there. The living take precedence over the dead, Sahdev had said, and he was right. If I stopped at Miles's grave, the grief would overwhelm me. I'd be useless in helping Kyle.

I wasn't surprised by the strong scent of bleach that greeted me as we crossed the threshold. Before my courage failed me, I walked into the front room and looked at the scene of last night's horrors.

Every drop of blood had been scrubbed clean, even the rolling desk chair was returned to its position at the command center. Hesitantly, I approached the hall leading to the bedrooms and bath.

"This is what I want you to see," Sahdev said at my shoulder. He pointed to a belt-and-wire-contraption linking two door knobs that held the door to my bedroom securely shut.

"When Miles threatened him, Kyle managed to lock your cousin into the bedroom. Miles had a knife. The flu mania gave him unnatural strength. As you can see, he broke through the door."

A jagged hole—just large enough for a man to squeeze through—had been ripped through the center of the door.

"Kyle was weak and losing consciousness, but was determined that you not come home and be confronted with a violent man."

I wrapped my arms around my waist. Yes. It was obvious how the nightmarish scene had played out and how hard Kyle had tried to contain Miles before killing him.

"When Kyle regained consciousness, he was beside himself with regret for killing Miles," Sahdev continued.

"He didn't have a choice, did he?"

"No, he didn't." Sahdev laid a hand on my arm, his touch tentative. I turned to face him, meeting his compassion-filled eyes. "I've never seen a patient recover after the flu mania. The violence would have continued until Miles collapsed and died. If he were in his right mind, I believe your cousin would be thankful that Kyle stopped him from hurting the people he cared about."

"I'm sure you're right. Miles would never want to hurt anybody. It's all so...horrible." I needed to stay focused on Kyle, so I pushed all thoughts of Miles from my mind. "I want to see Kyle now."

"Of course."

Kyle occupied Miles's bed. Although clearly sick, he looked better than I dared hope. Instead of ragged gasps, his breathing was slow and even. His face appeared flushed, but without the dark red stain that had marked my cousin's cheeks as he deteriorated.

"Does he have a fever?" I asked in a low voice.

"One hundred and two. Higher than I'd like, but I've seen much worse. He isn't out of danger, but I have hope that he may recover."

I sat on the edge of the bed and took Kyle's hand. "It's not your fault," I whispered.

His fingers tightened around mine, and his eyelids fluttered as he wrenched himself from sleep. With an obvious effort, he turned his head and his sunken, bloodshot eyes sought mine. "I'm sorry, Kenz."

"It's not your fault," I repeated. "I don't blame you. The flu killed Miles. You just put him out of his misery."

He shook his head, as if rejecting my words, then winced and sucked in a breath. Kyle always liked to play the tough guy, shrugging off any injury. Based on the grimace, he must have been in a lot of pain.

Kyle's gaze traveled from me to Sahdev. "I don't know who you are or where you came from, but I wouldn't have made it through the night without you. I wouldn't have had this chance to talk to Kenzie. I'm grateful, man."

He closed his eyes, as if the effort of speaking depleted his strength.

I stood. "Talking is wearing you out. You need to rest."

"No. Wait." Kyle clutched my hand, refusing to let me go.

I sat down again and gently brushed the lank hair back from his forehead. "What do you need?"

"There's a card in my wallet." His raspy voice was barely audible and I had to lean over to hear his words. "For Valhalla Ranch in central Oregon. Map on back. The owner said...to go there if things get bad in Portland. If I die, pack up the jeep and go to Valhalla...You'll be safe."

"Don't talk about dying," I said. "You're getting better."

Frowning, he lifted his head from the pillow, agitated by my reply. "I need to know you'll be all right."

"I will be all right. You're going to recover. Ripper will come back. We have a new friend in Sahdev."

Kyle tried to lift himself up on an elbow, but fell back, as if the effort drained every bit of strength from his limbs.

"If everything goes wrong, I'll remember what you said about the ranch." I tried to placate him with a noncommittal response.

In his fevered state, he'd forgotten that I couldn't drive a stick shift. And he couldn't seriously believe that I'd pack up and leave the city without Ripper. My somewhat cagey assurance seemed to satisfy him. He nodded, and his eyelids grew heavy again.

"Rest." I stood and kissed his forehead. "I'll check back soon."

I found Sahdev in the kitchen dumping a can of dog food in Hector's bowl.

"He'll love you forever if you feed him," I said, entering the room.

"That's good. I have no desire to be on Hector's bad side." He washed his hands in the basin in the sink, then pointed to the carafe. "More coffee?"

He poured two cups and we sat at the small kitchen table. Despite the caffeine and his unfailing civility, fatigue was beginning to weigh heavily upon him. He slumped against the back of the chair and watched me through red-rimmed eyes.

"Where have you been staying?" I asked.

"My home is in Lake Oswego. I live in a guest house on my parent's property. When the flu epidemic struck, it made sense to sleep at the clinic, so I could be close to my patients."

"Have you gone back home to check on your parents?" Lake Oswego was only ten miles from southeast Portland, close enough for a quick visit.

"A few days before the governor closed down the airports, my parents, my sister and her husband and daughter, all flew to Ahmedabad for a cousin's wedding."

"Your entire family is in India?"

"Yes." Sahdev lowered his head and took a long sip of his coffee, hiding his expression from my scrutiny.

Did he regret staying behind in Portland while the rest of his family was half-way across the world? How could he not? Who knew when—or if—commercial air travel would resume. Even if some of his relatives survived the flu, he was unlikely to see them again. My heart ached for a good man bereft of kith and kin.

"Have you heard from them since they flew to India?" I asked hesitantly.

"One call, shortly before the phones went down. They're staying at my grandparents' house. There's a comfort in knowing that they're all together to face whatever comes."

"But you're alone."

He shrugged, clearly reluctant to indulge in self-pity. "I had my work. I did some good."

I didn't doubt that for a moment. Lonely, but resolute, Sahdev had tried to hold the line against a relentless foe, against an unstoppable plague.

"Sahdev, would you consider staying here with us? The compound is as secure as any place in the city. We have food, water, and fuel." I leaned forward, eager to make my case. "I can't imagine what the future will be like after the flu burns itself out. So many things will be gone or will be different. We've all lost family and friends. After the flu, people will have to come together to form new family bonds. I'd like you to stay and be part of our new family."

Sahdev closed his eyes and dropped his face into his hands.

Had I overstepped? Made unwarranted assumptions?

I could almost hear Ripper snort. When do I *not* make unwarranted assumptions? Crap. Maybe Sahdev liked the autonomy of living on his own. Maybe he shared the back room of the clinic with a kindhearted nurse who was equally devoted to patient care. Why did I presume he'd want to join our tribe?

After a few awkward minutes Sahdev lifted his head and met my eyes. "It's hard to be alone in a dying city. I've missed talking to someone over a cup of coffee. Sharing a meal. Making plans. All the simple things that shaped my life before the flu."

"Does that mean you'll stay?" I scarcely dared hope it was true.

"For now." Sahdev inclined his head. "As you say, we can't know what the future will hold. Perhaps you'll come to see my presence as a burden. Perhaps I'll feel constrained by life in a compound. If you ever wish to rescind the offer, I will go on my way with nothing but gratitude for your generosity."

My mind shifted to the practical challenges of adding another person to the household. "There are sleeping bags, pillows, and a memory foam pad in the basement. You can take Kyle's spot in the back porch if you like."

"I'd rather sleep near Kyle so I can monitor his condition."

"You can sleep in the recliner next to the bed until he's better. You look exhausted. Let me fix you something to eat. Is there anything you don't eat?"

"My parents and grandparents are vegetarians, but I eat everything except beef."

I figured that he hadn't had fresh vegetables for a while, so I sauteed some sugar snap peas from the garden, made a simple lettuce salad, and scrambled three eggs with chives. After eating, Sahdev checked on Kyle, then fell asleep in the recliner.

I decided to wash the sheets on my bed and hang them to dry inside the house, since it looked like it would rain soon. I approached my bedroom with trepidation, the shattered door a stark reminder of Miles's fatal mania.

Sahdev had cleaned off any blood splatters, but the jagged hole would always remind me of my cousin's death. When he woke up, I'd ask Sahdev to help me remove it from its hinges and store it in the basement. I could tack up an old sheet to cover the opening when I wanted privacy.

I unwound the belt and wires securing the doors and entered my room. I peeled the sheets from the bed, warmed some water, then hauled the hand-crank washing machine to the patio, taking advantage of the lull before the rain. My arms were cramping when I finished washing the last sheet.

I walked around the house to the front yard, stretching my arms above my head to shake out the stiffness.

Halting by the front gate, I tilted my head back to sniff the air. I did it again to be sure, then whirled around, frantically scanning the sky.

No. No. No.

THIRTY-SEVEN

Kenzie

The clouds dumped rain over the city on Sunday night, but bright sunlight greeted me Monday morning when I went outside to feed the chickens and gather eggs. Tendrils of mist spiraled into the air above puddles and wet foliage as the sun burned off the residue of last night's rain.

No hint of smoke lingered in the atmosphere.

Maybe I'd imagined it, maybe I'd smelled somebody's charcoal grill and jumped to the conclusion that Caleb—or another firebug—had started setting fires again. Ripper and Kyle had put the fear of God into Caleb. Since the kid couldn't know that Kyle was sick and that Ripper had been away for eleven days, he wouldn't dare risk bringing their wrath down on his head, would he?

I fed Hector and made coffee, then stuck my head into the smaller bedroom and found Sahdev bending over a sleeping Kyle. Sahdev glanced over his shoulder and joined me in the hall.

"Kyle's temperature has dropped." He showed me a digital thermometer.

99.4, close to normal.

"What does it mean?"

"It's too soon to declare victory. His fever might spike again, but it's a very good sign."

I sagged against the wall, weak-kneed with relief. "When will we know if he's going to make it?"

"If his temperature remains stable for twenty-four hours, I believe there's an excellent chance that he will recover."

I opened my mouth to thank Sahdev for everything he had done, but found myself unable to utter a word.

For so long, I'd been hardwired to expect everyone I cared about to go away. My rational mind rejected the idea—insisted that Ripper would come back and Kyle would get better—but a small part of me still believed that inevitably I'd end up alone.

Aunt Debbie sometimes read the Bible to us at bedtime, and I vaguely remembered a verse about putting away childish things. Maybe it was time to get over my childish fears once and for all. The dark held no terrors I couldn't face down. The universe had no scheme to take away everyone I loved. How grandiose was that notion, anyway?

Sahdev said there was an excellent chance Kyle would recover.

Impulsively, I stepped forward and wrapped my arms around his waist, holding him tight. He patted my shoulder, and I realized that hurling myself into a near stranger's arms was inappropriate.

"Sorry." I pulled away. "I really needed a hug."

He smiled, the expression in his eyes warm and reassuring. "Doctors are used to people swooning in their arms. It's an understandable reaction to stress."

I made breakfast while Sahdev added gas to the generator's tank. The day promised to be a scorcher, and I wanted to make sure we could run the fan by Kyle's bedside and have ice and cold drinks ready for him.

Kyle slept for most of Monday, waking occasionally to down water or a sports drink. In the middle of the afternoon, he roused enough to drink half a mug of chicken broth. By evening, his temperature had dropped to normal.

Before bedtime, I picked a bouquet of Aunt Debbie's yellow roses and placed them on Miles's grave, then sat beside the freshly turned earth, Hector's head resting on my knee.

"Hey, cousin." My voice broke. "I can't believe I'm never going to see you again." I closed my eyes, remembering the serious little boy who'd grown into an intense and complicated young man, a man whose doomsday obsessions had saved us all. "You did good. You made a difference. You were loved. And I'm going to miss you everyday for the rest of my life. Tell Aunt Debbie and Uncle Mel hi, and that I'll see you all again someday."

I woke at dawn on Tuesday and spent an hour hauling buckets of water to the vegetable garden. Another blistering hot day was in the offing, and I couldn't afford to risk our vegetable crop wilting and drying up.

Kyle felt well enough to sit up in bed. He was restless and eager to stretch his legs, but Sahdev insisted that he spend one more day recuperating before abandoning his sick bed. His head and eyes still hurt too much to focus on a printed page, so Sahdev and I took turns reading aloud to him from one of Uncle Mel's spy thrillers.

In the afternoon, Sahdev took an LED lantern and descended to the basement to examine our food stores. He emerged with an armful of canned foods and containers of spice. He prepared dinner, his grandmother's recipe for cholle, a north-Indian chickpea stew with tomatoes served with rice. The stew was far too spicy for Kyle—who downed a bowl of chicken broth—but I loved every bite. We finished the meal with fresh strawberries from the garden.

Before bedtime, I opened all the windows to allow the cool night air to circulate through the house. It felt odd to leave the house open while I slept, but worth the risk. Nobody had tried to scale the fence or bash through the gate since I'd moved in. The windows were all barred. Even if an intruder snuck into the compound, he was unlikely to break into the house.

It wasn't a person who infiltrated the house overnight.

I woke up Wednesday morning to the sound of Hector barking. My throat tickled, and my eyes stung from the tiny particles of soot, tar, and ash wafting through the house.

Coughing, I leapt to my feet and slammed my bedroom window shut. I ran into the second bedroom and flung that window shut, too. Sahdev jumped to his feet and helped me close up the house.

We ran into the back yard. A pinkish-gray mist filled the sky. I could look directly at the sun, which appeared a glowing yellow disc behind the haze. We couldn't see any flames. Kyle staggered out the kitchen door and collapsed on a picnic bench, wheezing.

"Can you see where the fire's coming from?" he asked.

"No, but it's got to be somewhere in town," I said.

"I'm going to take Ripper's jeep and see if I can spot the fire. We need to know how close it is." He struggled to his feet.

"You're in no condition to drive." Sahdev placed a hand on Kyle's shoulder. "Give me the keys. I'll go."

Instead of protesting, Kyle sunk back onto the bench.

I grabbed the lanyard from the hook inside the kitchen door and led Sahdev to Ripper's garage.

"Be careful." I clutched at his arm.

"I'll return as quickly as I can." He climbed into the driver's seat and backed the jeep out of the garage. I watched until it disappeared into the murk, then raced home.

Kyle refused to get back in bed, so I pulled the recliner into the living room. He sat at my side while I watched the back yard on the security monitor, waiting for Sahdev to unlock the gate.

"If the fire is close, we need to start thinking about evacuating the city."

I ignored him, all of my attention focused on the monitor. One step at a time, as Uncle Mel used to say. The last thing I wanted to think about was leaving Portland.

"Kenz," he persisted. "I know you want to be here in case Ripper comes back, but it's time to get real."

I shot him a dirty look over my shoulder. "It's way too early to talk about abandoning the compound. Let's wait and see what Sahdev says."

Arms folded across his chest, Kyle lapsed into a grudging silence. When the gate finally swung open, I rushed to the back door to let Sahdev in. He followed me to the living room and sank onto the desk chair.

"I drove to the top of the Fremont Bridge so I could get a good view of the city. It looks like Forest Park and the West Hills are on fire. Downtown doesn't seem to be burning, although it's hard to be certain through the smoke. Office buildings and skyscrapers are built to resist flames. It makes sense that trees and houses would burn first."

"Jesus." Kyle shoved his hands through his hair. "Five thousand acres of forest land are burning less than ten miles away. Hundreds of houses in the West Hills. Is there any sign that the fire has jumped the river?"

"No. It looks like only the west side of town is burning."

"There you go," I said to Kyle. "We're in no immediate danger. There's no reason to talk about leaving."

Unless the flames were on top of me and I faced imminent death, I'd fight anyone who tried to drag me from the compound. Miles had devoted the last years of his life to creating a secure, well-stocked haven. And he was buried in the yard. I couldn't leave my cousin behind, alone. Every corner of the familiar house reminded me of Aunt Debbie and Uncle Mel.

And Ripper—leaving the compound would guarantee that I'd never see him again. We could hunt for each other for the rest of our lives and never reconnect. He'd promised to do everything in his power to come back to me, and I wasn't about to give up on him.

Kyle and Sahdev exchanged a worried glance, as if they were dealing with a crazy person, which pushed all my buttons.

"Ripper wouldn't have wanted you to—"

"Don't you dare talk about him in the past tense, as if he's not coming back," I erupted. "If you want to pack up and hightail it out of town, go right ahead. I'm not going anywhere."

"Seriously, Kenz? You think I'd take our only vehicle and leave you behind in the middle of a freaking fire? Don't be stupid!"

Sahdev stiffened."There's no reason to resort to name-calling."

Kyle sucked in a breath and held it, then slowly exhaled. He nodded at Sahdev before turning to me. "I get that you don't want to do anything hasty, so let's compromise. As long as the fire is restricted to the west side of the river, we'll stay put. But if it jumps the river and starts to burn houses on the east side, or if the smoke gets too thick, we have to be packed up and ready to evacuate."

I opened my mouth to protest. He silenced me with a glare. "What if a burning ember blows across the river and lands on a roof? What if Caleb's been setting fires and decides to start up on this side of town? It makes sense to be ready for anything."

Kyle and his deals. I couldn't argue with his logic. I'm not suicidal, but every part of me rebelled against the prospect of abandoning Portland, of giving up on Ripper.

"Okay," I conceded. "As long as you understand that I won't leave unless it becomes a matter of life or death. Packing the jeep is just an exercise in caution."

"Who's Caleb?" Sahdev asked.

While Kyle explained our dealings with the little pyromaniac, I retreated to my bedroom. Sitting on the cot, I leaned against the wall and hugged my legs to my chest. Hector stuck his head into the room and I patted the bed, encouraging him to join me.

"Hey, you." I slung an arm over his shoulders and buried my face in his neck. "I wish your daddy were here."

Ripper was counting on me to take care of Hector. If we had to pack up the jeep and get ready to flee, I'd make sure we brought everything Hector needed. Dog food, his water bowl, a leash, his Frisbee. My mind began to race, thinking of everything we'd need to pack if worse comes to worst.

Miles had anticipated this possibility. An entire shelf in the basement was devoted to bug-out gear. "You thought of everything, Miles," I whispered, tears welling in my eyes as I thought of my lost cousin. Kyle and Sahdev wouldn't know about the emergency evacuation supplies Miles had set aside. I wiped my eyes and went back to the living room to talk to the men.

Despite his protests to the contrary, Kyle was too weak to do more than shuffle from room to room and sit up in a chair. Uncle Mel had been a Luddite who preferred old school maps—the folded kind you used to buy at gas stations—to modern GPS technology. He left behind a drawer full of maps from all the states he and Aunt Debbie visited on summer road trips. Kyle sat at the kitchen table with a state map spread out in front of him, using a yellow highlighter pen to trace a route to Valhalla Ranch in central Oregon.

Sahdev backed Ripper's jeep up to the gate that separated the two yards.

Since space was finite, we debated what to pack.

We should be able to scavenge for food and clothing, so we'd take only about a week's worth of food and a couple of changes of clothing each. Gasoline was a priority. We might be able to siphon some from abandoned cars, but we wouldn't want to count on that. After filling the gas tank, Sahdev and I heaved five five-gallon gas cans into the back of the jeep, more than enough to get us to central Oregon.

We loaded a few cases of bottled water and a large bag of dog food. I filled a several boxes with assorted canned foods and a case of Hector's food. It should take less than a day to get to Valhalla, but we needed to be prepared in case we ran into trouble and it took longer.

Sahdev sorted through Miles's medical supplies and filled a duffel bag with everything we might need for any medical emergency. I packed several LED lanterns, batteries, and a solar charger. I even took a small box of Miles's trade goods, cartons of cigarettes and a bottle each of scotch and vodka. We packed up the walkie-talkies and Miles's ham radio set.

I insisted that we prepare four bug-out bags, including one for Ripper. Each bag held everything we'd need to survive for three days if we had to take off on foot—water, light-weight foods, a sweatshirt, and socks, a sleeping bag, a ground tarp, and other essential supplies. I put a gallon-sized Ziploc bag full of dried dog food in each bag. I packed extra magazines for our weapons, including Ripper's Colt. Last of all, I tucked Ripper's moon lantern and its solar charger into a bag.

Sahdev and Kyle took extra clothing Miles had stockpiled for himself.

I kept telling myself that I was packing up the jeep on the off chance things went completely to hell. It was nothing more than an exercise in caution, as I told Kyle. The flames weren't likely to jump the wide Willamette River. Caleb wouldn't dare cross a bridge and set fires on the east side, not if it meant Ripper would hunt him down. And we lived in Oregon, after all. The rain was bound to return in the next couple of days and extinguish the flames.

As long as I kept busy I could hold my fears at bay, but as soon as the jeep was packed, my thoughts were free to wander. What if we really had to leave? What if I never saw Ripper again? I didn't even have a photograph of him.

I grabbed the keys and a flashlight and raced to Ripper's house. Taped to the front of his refrigerator was a photo of Ripper sitting astride his bike, his hands on the ape hangers, one foot on the pavement. It looked like he had been caught unawares by the photographer, as if he had glanced over when somebody called his name. Unsmiling, he gazed into the camera with serious, intelligent eyes. I peeled the photo from the refrigerator and touched the image of his face.

"Please, Ripper. Please come back to me before it's too late."

I walked to his bedroom and tugged open the top drawer of his dresser. Coiled in a small box was a chain holding his dog tags. I hesitated for a moment before slipping them over my neck and tucking them into my shirt next to my necklace.

It seemed disrespectful, somehow, to take them for my own, to wear unearned the symbol of military service, but I wanted to hold against my heart something that Ripper had worn next to his skin. Something important to him.

If the fire passed us by, I'd put the dog tags back. If it didn't, it would serve no purpose to let them burn.

I pulled a black tee sporting a Harley logo from another drawer, stripped off my shirt, and replaced it with Ripper's tee. The well-worn shirt swam on my smaller frame, hanging down halfway to my knees, but I didn't care. After one last, lingering look around Ripper's bedroom, I braved the smoky haze and returned home.

I packed my most precious items into a small, leather zipper pouch, the photo of Ripper, a small framed picture of Aunt Debbie, Uncle Mel, and Miles, my phone with its photographs and books. True to his word, Ripper had shown me the contents of the box he kept in Miles's safe. He hadn't locked it afterward. I fetched his grandmother's wedding ring and his grandfather's medals from the box and stuffed them into my leather pouch.

If the worst happened, I'd be ready to dash to the jeep.

Nobody had much appetite for dinner. I picked strawberries and peas from the garden and carefully rinsed off the soot, so we'd have something fresh to nibble on. Kyle had a craving for tuna fish and crackers—blech—but at least he was eating protein. Sahdev opened a can of lentil soup for himself. I ate an entire can of cherry pie filling.

Still weak and exhausted, Kyle went back to bed right after dinner. Sahdev and I boiled water and poured it into the tub. After I bathed, I offered to help Sahdev boil more water for his bath.

"No need," he said. "I took a whore's bath while you were bathing."

My eyebrows shot up. "You took a *what*?"

He grinned. "A sponge bath. When water use is restricted—back in Ahmedabad or when I was working with Doctors Without Borders—you learn how to clean up with a small amount of water."

We retired early, me to my cot, him to a bedroll in the back porch. After reading for an hour, I finally fell asleep, my fingers clenched around Ripper's dog tags.

When I rolled out of bed Thursday morning, I dressed quickly in Ripper's Harley tee and a pair of yoga pants.

The smoke hadn't dissipated overnight. If anything, it seemed thicker and more pungent, but the red glow the flames cast against the sky was visible only to the west. That had to be a good sign. The fire might have engulfed more of the city, but at least it was limited to the other side of the river.

Looking through the kitchen window, I saw Sahdev pacing the yard, a towel held over his mouth and nose. He head swung back and forth as he scanned the sky, probably checking for any sign of encroaching flames. After a while, I offered to take a turn watching for flames, but he insisted on remaining outdoors.

Kyle slept for seventeen hours, until a little after one in the afternoon. I was glad, both because he needed the rest and because he couldn't nag me to leave while he was sleeping.

I was sitting at the kitchen table, distracting myself with a game of solitaire, when Kyle finally emerged from his bedroom.

"How about some coffee?" I smiled brightly, as if nothing in the world were wrong.

Shaking his head at my sunny greeting, he crossed the kitchen and exited into the back yard, where I saw him speaking to Sahdev.

He stepped back into the kitchen.

"No sign of fire on the east side, right?" I said before he could speak, trying to forestall any argument about leaving.

Kyle crouched in front of my chair and took my hands, his expression solemn.

I dropped my gaze to my lap, unable to meet his eyes. It was easy to fall into old habits, to argue with Kyle, almost on principle. We'd always enjoyed verbal sparring. If he yelled at me or gave me grief, it was game on. What I couldn't handle was the sympathy in his eyes when he hunkered down in front of me.

He squeezed my hands. "Sweetheart, look at me."

I shook my head.

"I'm afraid that you're going to die because you refuse to face reality. We're in danger. The smoke is getting thicker. The temperature is rising. Portland is going up in flames. Ripper has been gone for fourteen days. If he could have come back to you, don't you think he would have done it by now?"

His fingers caught my chin and tilted it up so I had no choice but to meet his eyes. "And what about Hector? Hector loves you and trusts you. Are you willing to betray that trust? To let him burn? Would Ripper want that? Do you want Hector and Sahdev to die, do you want me to die, because you can't let go of the hope that Ripper will return? If we wait too long, none of us will make it out of the city."

Shit. My heart twisted with guilt, and I laid my hand on Kyle's cheek.

Once upon a time, he'd been the center of my universe. He was a good man, and he'd always have a place in my heart, even though my heart now belonged to Ripper. And brave, kind Sahdev? I couldn't let Kyle and Sahdev risk their lives because I was unable to face losing Ripper. And Hector? I'd do anything to keep that dog safe.

Sahdev burst through the kitchen door. "I see flames shooting into the sky north of here."

There was nothing left to debate, no decision to be made. Our only course of action was to abandon the compound and flee the city. A bleak and joyless future stretched before me. My heart was breaking, but I had to do the right thing for everybody else.

We had to go.

THIRTY-EIGHT

Ripper

Two weeks ago

When I hit the road late Friday morning, Mac and Miles had both sent me on my way with a smile on my face. Miles had got up early to bake a batch of my favorite chocolate chip cookies. I was loading the tail bag on my bike when he proudly handed me a plastic container of them. Had to take out a T-shirt to make room, but hey, priorities.

And Mac? True to her word, we spent most of Thursday night fucking like crazed animals. When she rolled off my bed the next morning, she hobbled like a bow-legged cowboy, wincing and cursing my name. I smacked her ass—which always got a rise outta her—and said I wanted to leave her with something to remember me by.

If looks could kill, that woman would be on death row.

I'd made the trip from Portland to Grants Pass dozens of times. Straight shot south on I-5, two hundred and fifty miles from the top of the state to the bottom. On a good day, the trip took around four hours. Trip didn't get off to a good start. Heading out of Portland the freeway curved like a snake. Couple of semis had jack-knifed, blocking the freeway. I diverted to the old highway, a narrower roadway lined with businesses.

Despite the massive death toll from the flu, in a city the size of Portland, there had to be thousands of survivors. Even law-abiding citizens grew desperate when food and water ran out, when there's nobody to call for help.

I felt people's eyes on me whenever I rode through town, peeking out from behind closed blinds or watching me from their hidey-holes. Most of them probably saw the cut and kept their distance, figuring I was bad news. Smart decision. Nobody who confronted me was likely to walk away, but I knew that some wannabe hero might hide somewhere and take a shot, thinking he was ridding the world of a dangerous criminal.

Given a choice, I'd stick to the open road, where I didn't feel a target on my back as I rode past so many potential hiding places.

Had to slowly wend my bike through a highway clogged with vehicles. Didn't make sense at first. Cars trying to bypass the semi-trucks blocking the interstate should have been able to hop back on the freeway once they were past the accident.

When I drew close to the next freeway entrance, the reason for the backup became clear. A roadblock spanned the old highway—piles of tires, probably from the nearby tire store—and had prevented any vehicles from turning back onto the freeway. Best I could figure, somebody had been shaking down the drivers attempting to flee the city.

Cracked windshields and bullet holes in the sides of cars gave clear evidence of trouble. Bodies littered the ground and slumped behind steering wheels. Whatever had gone down had happened weeks ago, but I proceeded cautiously past the mayhem.

Once back on the freeway, I sped away from Portland. Everywhere I saw evidence of a world undergoing a metamorphosis.

When you lived in a big city, you learned to tune out the commotion of urban life, the barrage of voices and traffic sounds inevitable when people lived and worked together in close quarters. The total absence of that commotion left behind an eerie quiet. My bike was the only vehicle moving on the road, its motor the only sound breaking the silence.

Some people had waited too long to flee the city, setting out either ill-prepared or too sick to drive. They ran out of gas or died behind the wheel, leaving hundreds of cars parked on the side of the freeway. I rode past half a dozen serious accidents.

Hour after hour, as I rode without seeing another living soul, the scope of everything we'd lost hit home.

Instead of pulling into a gas station and chatting with the attendant who filled my tank, I siphoned gas from an abandoned car. I ate alone on the side of the freeway, leaning against the tire of an abandoned pickup while I polished off three of Miles's cookies.

I'd never considered myself a particularly gregarious man, but within a few hours of leaving Portland, I began to miss human contact. I missed home and wondered what Mac and Miles were up to. I missed the brotherhood I'd found with the Janissaries. I missed bantering with a waitress over lunch, people watching while I sat at Starbuck's drinking coffee, and nodding to fellow patrons at a quickie mart.

Shit. Maybe I wasn't as much of a loner as I'd thought.

In the middle of the afternoon, I took exit 58 toward Grants Pass. Sara lived in a trailer park close to the Rogue River. I pulled up to a shabby, green and white, 1980s era single-wide. I cut my engine and swung off the bike.

Giant pots of pink flowers flanked the step leading to the front door. The flowers and leaves had wilted and drooped over the sides of the pots. A garden gnome sat in the middle of the dying foliage. Not an encouraging sign. Sara was crazy about flowers and if she were alive and well, I wouldn't put it past her to haul water from the river to keep them alive.

I rapped on the door, not expecting an answer. When none came, I tried the knob and found it unlocked. Covering my nose so I wouldn't be bowled over by the putrid stink of decay, I stepped into her tiny living room.

The air smelled musty, as if the windows hadn't been opened for a while, but the unmistakable reek of decomposition was absent. No body, then. She hadn't died in her small house.

Cabinet doors hung open and a can of beer had spilled across the coffee table. Somebody had dumped the contents of the hall closet onto the floor. Sara was as neat as Jethro was sloppy, so I could tell at a glance that the place had been ransacked.

Where was Sara, and who had tossed the place?

"Hello?" a voice called from the open door.

I drew my Colt and turned around to confront a wide-eyed boy who couldn't have been more than thirteen or fourteen. He raised his hands in the air and staggered back, tripping over one of the flower pots and sprawling on the dirt.

Fuck. Terrifying kids was getting to be a habit with me. Still, you never knew. My experiences with the Rangers had taught me that kids could pose as great a danger as any adult.

"What do you want?" I didn't holster my Colt, but I didn't point it at the kid either.

"If you're looking for Sara, she's not here." His voice wavered, either because he was scared or because he was at that age when a boy's voice cracked uncontrollably.

"You know where she is?"

He shook his head.

"How do you know Sara?" I asked.

"I live next door. Sara and my mom were friends. She's nice. She used to bake brownies and bring them over sometimes."

I held up my Colt and when the kid's eyes latched on it, I returned it to the shoulder holster.

"What's your name?"

I offered the kid a hand and pulled him to his feet, then gestured for him to come inside the trailer.

He slapped the dirt from his pants before stepping into Sara's house, a simple, spontaneous act that made me warm up to the kid. His parents had raised him right.

"Gustavo Dominguez. But everybody calls me Gus."

"Tell me what's been going on, Gus."

He frowned, his forehead wrinkling. "Everybody died," he said in a small voice. "I'm the only one left. Well...Mr. Paterson got the flu, but he got over it. His wife and kids died. For a while he helped me go out and look for food and water, but then one day he hanged himself. I think he missed his family too much."

"How about your family, Gus?"

"My mom and sisters died about a month ago. My dad was away on a job in California. I kept waiting to get the flu, but it didn't happen. I must be immune or something."

"What can you tell me about Sara."

"I think she went to stay with her boyfriend. He rents a house over by Gilbert Creek Park."

"You know his name or the address?"

"No. Sorry."

"That's more information than I had before. Thanks, Gus. Hey, you got any idea who's been in here since Sara left?'

He flushed and looked guilty. "I came in and took all the peanut butter and crackers and canned food. Mr. Paterson started going into people's houses looking for booze and weed. I guess he made the mess."

When I was his age, I'd be the one looking for booze and weed, but I believed the kid when he blamed the late Mr. Paterson. *I* blamed Mr. Paterson. Depressed or not, what kind of a man offed himself and left a kid alone to deal with the post-flu world?

I thought of something. "Wait here."

I retrieved the container of cookies from my tail bag, popped the lid, and held it out to Gus. "Baked fresh this morning. Take two."

"Thanks." He bit into a cookie and sighed with pleasure. "Chocolate chip. My favorite."

"Mine, too."

I studied the skinny, dark-haired boy. His tee was swimming on him. He'd either lost weight or was wearing one of his dad's shirts. He appeared more or less healthy, but could a kid his age take care of himself for the long run?

What was I going to do about Gus?

My first obligation was to Sara and to the promise I'd made to my president. She might have dumped him and moved on, but Jethro had still cared about his former old lady, and that was good enough for me.

If I found her alive, I'd offer to bring her back to Portland. Maybe I should consider bringing Gus back, too. I could hot wire a pickup truck and put the bike in the back if I had to.

"How are you for food?" I asked.

He brightened. "I got lots. Mr. Paterson and I brought home tons from the grocery store. And we went to the sporting goods store and got a bunch of freeze-dried food and things to filter water. If you want to eat dinner with me, I can heat up freeze-dried lasagna on my dad's propane grill."

"Sounds good. I'm going to go start scoping out the neighborhoods around Gilbert Creek Park. I'll be back before dark."

The next couple of hours I cruised up and down the residential streets near the park. I didn't seriously expect Sara to come running out a front door, waving to get my attention, but if she were alive, she'd recognized the sound of a bike's engine. If she peeked out a window and saw my Janissary cut, she'd know I was a friend.

Lotta ifs and none of them likely to pan out, but it was as good a place to start as any.

I returned to the trailer park before sunset and ate dinner with Gus, who chattered away like we were old friends. After crashing at Sara's place, I got an early start the next morning. Gus surprised me by getting up early and handing me a cup of instant coffee and a cellophane-wrapped blueberry muffin.

Caution was essential as I hunted for Sara. Couldn't blame anybody who looked out their peephole, saw an unknown biker pounding on their front door, then hid, praying I'd go away. I couldn't go away, not without searching every house for Sara's body.

Every time I crashed through a door, I was aware that I might be met by the barrel of a gun. After ten hours of knocking on doors and then breaking them down, I came up empty. So many people had shut themselves in and died in their beds. House after house after house, nothing but corpses.

Discouragement weighed me down when I returned to the trailer park at sunset. Gus offered me a warm beer—his dad's favorite brand—and a dinner of freeze-dried chicken and dumplings. For dessert, he proudly produced two astronaut ice cream sandwiches made from freeze-dried ice cream. They tasted better than I expected.

During his foray to the sporting goods store he had picked up a few of the same LED lanterns Miles had bought for the compound. We sat at his family's kitchen table and played chess until bedtime.

Sunday was a repeat of Saturday as I systematically looked for Sara. Late in the afternoon, I approached a tidy, gray bungalow. Two giant planters full of wilted pink blossoms, identical to the flowers by Sara's trailer, stood by the front door. A gnome riding a Harley perched in one of the planters. My heart hammered as I beat my fist against the door.

"Sara, it's Ripper. Open up."

Nothing.

"Sara, I'm coming in."

Two hard kicks and I was inside. The familiar smell of decomposition washed over me.

Swiveling my head, I looked into the living room. I opened the curtains so I could examine the body huddled under a blanket on the sofa. The sunlight caught Sara's strawberry-blond hair tumbling across a pillow.

I sank down onto my heels next to her body. "I'm sorry, sweetheart."

Truth be told, I hadn't expected to find her alive, but it was a kick to the gut to find this vibrant and funny woman dead.

Fucking flu had laid waste to the world, indiscriminately striking down old and young, sinners and saints, leaving only a handful of survivors to pick up the pieces. I wanted to jump on my bike and speed back to Portland, to Mac, to Miles, shit, even to country club Kyle. I needed see a familiar face, to hear a familiar voice. To know that life goes on, and that I have a place in it and people to share it with.

Couldn't do it, of course. Got business to take care of.

A man's body lay on the kitchen floor, a bottle of water next to his hand. Must be the boyfriend Gus mentioned. I'd like to think he was bringing the water to Sara when he was struck down, to know that somebody was taking care of her at the end.

A door in the kitchen led to the garage. I clicked on my penlight and searched until I found a shovel. I dug a grave for two in the back yard—figured the guy had earned a place next to her—then buried Sara and her man.

On impulse, I fetched the gnome from the planter and stuck in on top of the grave. Sara always liked flowers and other girly shit, and the butt-ugly figurine meant something to her.

Gus must have read my face when I got back to the trailer park. "You found Sara?"

"Yeah." Didn't need to share the grisly details with the kid. "Could you put some water on to boil? I wanna wash up."

"Sure."

Before he turned chickenshit and offed himself, at least Paterson had helped Gus stockpile dozens of jugs of water and extra tanks of propane. Gus filled a pan and fired up the grill.

The kid was smart and competent and he was sitting pretty. For now. Sooner or later he'd run out of food and water, or scavengers might steal his supplies.

I filled a bucket halfway up with cold water, then Gus carefully dumped the boiling water into the pail. Back in Sara's trailer, I grabbed a bar of soap, stripped, and cleaned up as best I could.

Didn't have much of an appetite, but I didn't want to disappoint Gus, so I joined him for dinner.

We ate the last of Miles's chocolate chip cookies for dessert, then lounged on a pair of rickety lawn chairs that Gus had snagged from a neighbor's patio. He brought me one of his dad's beers and we sat in silence, watching the sun go down.

"Gonna take off tomorrow morning," I said, after the sun had dipped below the horizon.

"Okay." He shoulders drooped, and he pressed his lips together, clearly upset by the news. After a minute, he nodded to himself and sat up straight, as if determined to man up. "I'll fill a couple of water bottles for you, and you can help yourself to my food."

I set my empty beer bottle on the ground and leaned forward. "I got a place in Portland with friends. We have food and water, everything we need for at least the next year. Don't want to leave you alone here, Gus. I want you to come back to Portland with me."

His eyes filled with tears, and he shook his head. "I can't."

"Why not?"

"I'm waiting for my dad to come back. If I'm immune to the flu, maybe he is, too. Maybe I inherited it from him. Maybe he's on his way home right now. I can't go anywhere. I have to wait for him."

What was the chance that Gus's dad was still alive? Next to zero. Only a total shit would crush a child's hope that he wasn't alone in the world, but I had to be real with him.

"How many people lived in the trailer park before the flu?"

"A little more than two hundred."

"And how many of you survived?"

He squirmed, obviously knowing where I was going with this. "Two."

"Two people out of two hundred. Gus, you gotta know that the odds are that your father is dead. He wouldn't want you to be alone. He'd want you to go someplace safe."

Gus jumped to his feet. "I don't care about the odds. I'm not leaving. Don't you get it? If I go to Portland with you, and he comes back, I'd never know. I...I couldn't live with that, with wondering if my dad made it home, and I missed my chance to be with him."

What was I supposed to do? Tie the kid on the back of my bike and drag him kicking and screaming back to Portland? No. Staying put might be a foolish decision, but it was his to make.

"Think about it overnight. You change your mind, you let me know."

He nodded, wrapping his arms around his waist. All I wanted was to sleep, but if this was my last evening with Gus, I wanted to spend it with him. We played gin rummy until he started to yawn and his eyes grew heavy.

Monday morning, as I was packing my tail bag, Gus brought me a cup of coffee and a banana muffin.

"Change your mind?" I peeled the cello wrap from the muffin.

"No." To my surprise, the kid launched himself at me, wrapping his arms around my waist. His tears dripped onto my cut. "I'm going to miss you."

"Gonna miss you, too, kid." I tousled his hair. "Wish I could be around to watch you grow up. Wherever they are, I bet your parents are proud of you."

He pulled away and rubbed his eyes, then handed me an astronaut ice cream sandwich and two water bottles. "For the road."

"Thanks." I swung onto my bike and started the engine. When I glanced over my shoulder, Gus raised a hand in farewell. I swallowed the unexpected lump in my throat, nodded to him, then rode out of the trailer park.

At first, I intended to head north out of Grants Pass, toward the freeway back to Portland. With any luck, I could be in the city by the middle of the afternoon. Home called to me with a powerful allure.

As I approached the freeway, I saw a sign for Medford. We'd lost contact with the Janissary chapter there when the phones went down. The city was just shy of thirty miles away. Wheezer was the only Janissary I'd found alive from the Portland chapter, and the man was a shell of his former self, broken by the deaths of his entire family.

I'd no idea if any of the Medford brothers had survived. Like as not, searching for them would prove as disappointing as my hunt for Sara.

Gus's words came back to haunt me. He couldn't live with uncertainty, without knowing if his dad ever came home. Turns out,

I couldn't live with uncertainty either. I had to try to find out if any of my Medford brothers had survived.

Since I didn't know where any of them lived, all I could do was to check the clubhouse for signs of life. I could be back on the road to Portland in less than two hours. Home by late afternoon. Eating dinner with Miles and everybody by evening. Balls deep in Mac by midnight. I could spare the time.

Sighing, I turned onto I-5 and headed southeast toward Medford.

The clubhouse was built on a couple of acres of land just outside the city limits. The sliding gate that secured access to the property stood open, an ominous sign. I recognized Bulldog's bike parked out in front of the main building. Ought to know it; I customized it for the Medford president. Almost a dozen other bikes and a handful of cars filled the lot.

Walking through the unlocked main door, I immediately knew that I was on a fool's errand.

No one challenged me as I crossed the threshold. Deadly silence reigned.

I walked from room to room and found bodies strewn throughout the building. Some of the men had brought their families in, probably hoping to isolate them from the virus. Hadn't worked. The fucking flu had wormed its way into their stronghold.

After the past few days, you'd think I'd be hardened against the sight of dead women and children. Turns out I wasn't. My hide wasn't as thick as I liked to pretend.

The desire to get back home morphed from an urge to a compulsion. Holding my breath, I raced from the building and dropped into a squat in the parking lot, covering my eyes with my hands, as if I could block out the images. I sucked in lungfuls of the fresh air.

A few feet behind my head, I heard the unmistakable clickety-clack of a shotgun being racked.

THIRTY-NINE

Ripper

"And here I thought the vermin were all dead. I guess not. Go ahead. Reach for your gun, Janissary. I dare you."

Fucking hell. I lost focus for one freaking moment, and someone got the jump on me.

"Hands behind your head," the same voice ordered. "Get on your belly."

I fell forward onto the gravel, shaking my head with disgust over my sloppy carelessness. I probably could wrestle a handgun away from a less-experienced shooter, but a shotgun at close range was nothing to mess with.

Rough hands seized one of my wrists and slapped a metal handcuff around it. The stranger pulled my other hand behind my back and cuffed my wrists together.

"Sit up," he growled, circling in front of me.

Rising up on my knees, I studied the man, who looked to be in his late forties, with a receding hairline and a beer gut. He wore a khaki shirt, navy pants, and a navy tie. Above his left shirt pocket, he sported a six-pointed gold star.

A Jackson County sheriff's deputy. Fuck. The sheriff's department had long had it in for the Janissaries.

"Is there a problem, officer?" I asked politely, as if the usual laws and regulations still held sway. He had no reason to suspect my involvement in any crime, not even a bogus offense like littering or not using my blinker. Nothing I'd done justified him pulling a weapon on me or cuffing me.

The criminal justice system was dead, and the deputy was operating outside the law, with absolutely nothing to check his behavior except his personal commitment to doing the right thing.

He called us vermin. I was screwed.

Ignoring my question, he reached inside my cut and pulled my Colt from the holster. "Well, lookie here." He held up my pistol. "You got a concealed-handgun license to carry this?"

I gritted my teeth. "Yes, sir. Card's in my wallet."

He strutted behind me, and he reached into my back pocket. Out of my peripheral vision, I saw my wallet fly through the air and land behind a car.

"What wallet?"

Smirking, he hunkered down in front of me so we were eye to eye. "In the state of Oregon, your failure to produce a valid concealed handgun license can be considered prima facie evidence that you don't have one. I'm placing you under arrest for unlawful carrying of a weapon."

If only one deputy survived the flu, why couldn't it have been a decent man instead of this piss-poor excuse for a law enforcement officer?

No point in continuing this charade after the fucker tossed my wallet. "That's bullshit, and you know it."

"You resisting arrest, son?" He stepped back and raised the shotgun. "Get up. I'm taking you downtown."

I could rush him. I imagined ramming my skull into his soft belly, knocking him to the ground, and wresting my Colt and the handcuff keys away from him.

Mac's face appeared in my mind. I'd promised to do everything in my power to make it back to her. Launching myself at the deputy would be suicide. I couldn't die doing something stupid and leave Mac to wonder what happened to me.

I rocked back on my heels and stood. The deputy jerked the shotgun barrel, gesturing for me to lead the way through the gate. I deliberately didn't glance back at my bike. Wouldn't put it past the asshole to trash the Shovelhead if he knew it was mine.

His green and white patrol car was parked outside the gate. He shoved me into the back seat, put my Colt into the glove compartment, then drove to the county jail in Medford, a large cement building surrounded by chain-link fence.

After the power grid collapsed, generators probably provided electricity to the jail complex for a while, but the building was dark now. The deputy switched on a flashlight and led me to a narrow jail cell holding only a bunk, a toilet, and a sink.

"You can cool your jets in here." He locked the cell door.

Without another word, he walked away, leaving me alone in the pitch-black cell.

Mac would hate this. I groped my way toward the bunk. Dark never bothered me and no boogeyman haunted my dreams. Imaginary phantoms stood no chance against the real-life horrors I'd witnessed. And participated in.

Leaning back against the wall, I considered my situation. Worst-case scenario? The deputy abandoned me here, and I'd die from starvation or thirst. I'd tucked the astronaut ice cream sandwich from Gus into an inside pocket in my cut. Couple of hundred calories at best, which wouldn't hold me for long. And with my hands cuffed behind my back, it'd be a trick to get it out of the pocket and tear it open.

I'd have to check to see if any water trickled out of the tap. In a place this large, maybe some water remained in the pipes, enough to keep me alive for a while.

I'd need to conserve my energy and hope to hell the deputy came back. If not, I was gonna die in here like a trapped animal.

I got up and paced the cell, memorizing how many steps to the toilet and the door. To my relief, water dribbled from the faucet, and I drank a couple of mouthfuls before returning to the bunk.

Much later in the day, I awoke to the sound of approaching footsteps. A flashlight beam cut through the darkness then pierced the cell.

"Brought your dinner," the deputy said cheerfully.

Unless he was fucking with me—which I wouldn't put past him—that meant it was Monday evening. He squeezed a bag of potato chips and a warm can of cola through the bars. Not exactly fine dining, but I'd welcome the calories and caffeine.

Best not to piss him off. Let him play the big shot. Think he'd cowed and intimidated me. Think he held all the power. Then when I made my move, he wouldn't see it coming.

I squeezed my hands into tight fists, imagining I was throttling the bastard. "Thank you, sir."

"Good boy. You're learning."

Whistling a cheerful tune, he spun around and left me alone again.

I had to drop to my knees and feel around behind my back for the can of cola. I picked it up and carried it to the toilet tank, the only elevated, flat surface in the room.

Took a minute to pop the tab. When I heard the familiar hiss of escaping carbonation, all the spit in my mouth evaporated, and I felt parched. Hunkering down, I pushed the can against the wall with my chin and managed to tilt it into my mouth. I groaned in frustration when some of the precious fluid spilled down my chin. After a few swallows, I forced myself to stop drinking and save some for later.

I tore open the bag of potato chips and set it on the bunk. I had to bury my face in the bag and retrieve chips with my tongue. The deputy would've laughed his ass off watching how I had to contort myself in order to drink and eat while cuffed, like a pig in a trough.

I'd make him pay.

He returned Tuesday morning and called out "Breakfast" before shoving a candy bar and a can of root beer through the bars. Was he raiding vending machines in order to feed me? Didn't matter. Whatever crap he brought provided energy and hydration.

"Hey, any chance you could take off the cuffs? Not like I'm going anywhere."

He pursed his lips, making a show out of his deliberation. "Nah. Not today. Maybe tomorrow."

Dinner was corn nuts and orange soda. I managed to open the can behind my back and drink without spilling any of it, a first.

I fell asleep fantasizing about the garden back home. Miles had told me that the strawberries and sugar snap peas would be ready to eat soon. When I got home, I planned to stand in the middle of the garden and eat my fill. No more of this processed shit.

By Wednesday morning my shoulders were on fire, my muscles protesting the strained position. Bruises braceleted my wrists, despite the care I took not to pull on the cuffs. My fingers tingled. Was that a sign of nerve damage?

The deputy appeared outside my cell, and I knew from his gleeful expression that something was up.

He set a cardboard carton of orange juice and can of beef stew on the floor by his feet. Compared to corn nuts, a can of beef stew was haute cuisine. And real fruit juice? My mouth watered.

"You want those cuffs off, don't you?"

I kept my expression neutral, refusing to give him the satisfaction of seeing how very much I wanted the cuffs removed. "Yes, sir."

"Tell you what. You got a choice to make. I'll take the cuffs off right now, but then you won't get any food or water today or tomorrow. Is it worth it? Can you go two days without eating or drinking?"

I pretended to think about it. Drop by drop, I'd managed to fill the three empty pop cans with water from the tap. Half of the candy bar and a handful of corn nuts were hidden underneath the pillow. Gus's astronaut ice cream was still in my pocket. Besides, I'd gone longer than two days without eating while serving as a Ranger.

"Okay," I said reluctantly, as if the decision pained me. "Take the cuffs off. I guess I can go two days without food or water."

"Alrighty. Back up to the cell door and hold your wrists out."

I climbed off the bunk and shuffled toward the door, deliberately making myself appear weak. Slowly, as if unsure of my balance, I turned around and extended my wrists so he could unshackle me.

A lightning bolt struck between my shoulder blades. I lurched forward, then dropped to the floor, my body rigid, my muscles spasming. Gasping for breath, I finally managed to roll on my side.

When the deputy offered to remove my cuffs, I half-expected it to be some mean-spirited mind fuck: He'd brandish the key, mess with the lock, then announce that he'd changed his mind. I hadn't expected the bastard to taze me.

Bet he pressed the taser directly against my back, using something cops liked to call pain compliance. It hurt like a son of a bitch, but I was done complying.

"Fuck you," I said through clenched teeth.

He snorted, then dropped into a crouch, shining the flashlight beam onto my face.

"No, fuck you, Janissary."

He stood and without another word, turned and walked away.

He was done toying with me, I suspected, finished exacting whatever retribution he had against my club. He was gonna leave me here to die. Sure as shit this wasn't the first time I'd faced death, but it was the first time I faced it filled with regret for what I was leaving behind.

What would they think when I disappeared from their lives? Would Mac believe that I'd abandoned her? Would Miles decide that I lied when I promised to do everything in my power to come home? Would they come to hate me?

I rolled to my feet and hurled my body against the bars, howling with frustration.

Stupid to waste my energy in such a pointless exercise. I dropped onto the bunk, seething with helpless rage. Eventually, I rolled onto my side and sought the comfort of oblivion.

I lost track of time, drifting in a restless sleep, then waking to a silence and a darkness so oppressive that they pinned me to the bunk.

What's past was past, and I'd never been one to waste time chewing over things I couldn't undo, but I found myself staring at the black ceiling, full of self-reproach. I should've rushed the deputy and risked a quick death from the shotgun blast. Should've made some move when locked in the back seat of the patrol car. Should've attacked while he was marching me to the jail cell. Anything would be better than dying slowly in this hole.

Quit whining and think.

My gumption finally asserted itself. I'd been assuming that the deputy was done with me, but maybe the compulsion to strike out at the Janissaries still rode him hard. Could be it wasn't enough to know that I was dying alone in the dark. Maybe he wanted to kill me himself, and if that was the case, he'd be back.

And I'd be ready.

I got up and drank a can of water, then put it under the faucet to fill again. After eating three corn nuts and one small bite of the candy bar, I felt the sugar hit my system and lend me a scrap of energy.

Sitting on the cement floor, I tried to slide my bound wrists under my ass, so I could wriggle through my arms and position my hands in front of my body. No luck. Maybe if I was a skinny gymnast I could do it, but the heavy muscles in my arms and shoulders got in the way.

I paced the dark cell, stretching my legs and keeping blood circulating to my limbs. Bending over and shimmying like a stripper—an image that made me smile in spite of the shitty circumstance—I shook the astronaut ice cream out of my pocket, picked it up with my teeth, and placed it under my pillow.

Sleep. Drink. Eat three corn nuts and a bite of candy bar. Stretch. Pace. I repeated the cycle several times, always keeping my ear cocked for the deputy's return.

I awoke to the distant sound of a door clanging. Turning my head, I gulped down the half-full can of water I'd wedged between the mattress and the wall. Footsteps approached my cell, accompanied by a lively whistled tune. With my teeth, I tore open the package of astronaut ice cream and wolfed it down. I'd saved the big gun, the calorie bomb, for the deputy's return.

"Thanks, Gus," I whispered.

The deputy dragged the barrel of his shotgun across the bars. "Wakey, wakey!"

I groaned, as if unable to drag myself into consciousness.

"Time to go, asshole," he announced.

The key rattled in the lock, and I smiled into the darkness. I wouldn't squander this opportunity by doing anything stupid. If it came to it, I'd always have the option to make a suicide attack, but survival was my goal, retrieving my bike and riding home to Mac and Miles.

The door slid open, and the deputy brandished his weapon. "On your feet, Janissary."

I mumbled an incoherent response, then sat up, swaying back and forth like a third-world office tower during an earthquake.

"I don't care if you have to crawl. Get your ass in gear."

Apparently, he bought my feeble act, so I hammed it up. Shoulders hunched, my head lolling to one side, I shambled ahead of him out of the jail, his shotgun prodding my back. I fell across the back seat of his patrol car, then clambered to a seated position.

Nothing to worry about, officer. I'm as helpless as a baby.

The deputy navigated the car to I-5 and drove north on the freeway for about half an hour before pulling over to the side of the road. He cut the engine and turned to face me.

"I had a baby sister once." His tone was conversational. "Sweet kid. Kelly was going to Rogue Community College, planning to study for a nursing degree. One Saturday night during spring break she met a man at a pizza parlor. A Janissary. He invited her to party at the clubhouse. Her friends told her not to go, but she said she was old enough to make up her own mind and wanted to have some fun."

He hopped out of the car and held open my passenger door, the shotgun tucked against his side. "Come on. I want to show you something."

Fuck. I knew where this story was going. Happened years ago, before I patched in, but Bulldog had filled me in on the details.

One of the Medford brothers had met a woman at a pizza restaurant and had invited her back to the clubhouse for a party. She said yes, but must've decided that the party was more than she bargained for. She told the brother that she was going outside for a smoke. Somebody saw her slip out the front gate and start walking toward town.

Last time any witnesses saw her alive.

I climbed out of the back seat and followed the deputy to the guardrail that bordered the freeway.

"See." He pointed to the body of water that ran under the freeway. "That's Evans Creek. Flows into the Rogue River not too far from here. See that rocky patch on the shoreline? That's where they found Kelly's body after your buddies killed her."

He was breathing hard now, his anger ramping up. "No charges were ever filed. No hard evidence pointed to the Janissaries. No witnesses came forward. The man she partied with alibied out. The coroner said the fall killed her, but I know one of you biker bastards threw her over the guardrail."

He smiled at me, and the menace in his expression pushed all my alarm bells.

"I'm going to give Kelly the justice the courts failed to give her. You're going to jump Janissary, and die the same way my sister did."

Before he could cock the shotgun and swing it in my direction, I sprang, barreling into the deputy and catching him off guard. He staggered backward, then wrapped his meaty arms around my torso and held tight. We danced on the edge of the overpass, a shambling two-step, tottering from side to side. Despite days of deprivation, I was still stronger than him and fitter, but he had the use of his arms while I could only shove at him.

The deputy tripped. When he tried to right himself, he lost his balance and toppled over the guardrail, taking me with him. One second my feet were planted firmly on the asphalt, the next they were cartwheeling through the air.

We splashed into the creek. The water and the deputy's beer belly cushioned my landing somewhat, but it was a hard fall, and I was in trouble.

Everything hurt. I was dinged up bad—probably cracked my ribs—but at least I was better off than the deputy. The fall broke his neck. If he was alive he would have coughed and sputtered against the water streaming over his face.

Ignoring the pain, I dug my boot heels into the creek bed. I had to make it to the shore before the current pushed me into the Rogue River. With my arms out of commission, I'd sink like a rock in deep water.

Something glinted at the deputy's waist. He'd clipped his keychain to his belt and nestled next to the key for his patrol car, I spied a handcuff key. That small metal item became the center of my universe. I had to get out of these damned cuffs.

Bracing my feet against the rocks, I rolled over and fumbled to squeeze the carabiner. Couldn't see what I was doing behind my back and the cold water numbed my fingers. Creek water tumbled across my face, and I twisted my head to the side to catch some air.

There. Finally, the carabiner opened. I grabbed the key chain and locked it in my fist while I pushed my battered body to the shore.

I heaved up onto the rocks. With the last of my strength, I shoved the keys into my back pocket, then collapsed, panting, against solid ground.

The world spun and dark spots clouded my vision.

"Mac. I'm trying..."

Shit. Was I dying? Had I ruptured something in the fall? Was I bleeding out inside?

I fought to stay conscious, but everything was slipping away. With a will of their own, my traitorous eyelids slammed shut.

FORTY

Ripper

They say your sins catch up with you sooner or later. I always figured that if the afterlife was a real thing, if we're judged for our actions, I'd eventually end up in hell. Grandma dragged me to Sunday school when I was a kid, and the lessons I learned there painted a vivid picture of eternal damnation. When I finally found myself in the fiery pit, I'd expect to hear the crackle of flames, the moans of the damned, and a demonic chortle or two.

What I didn't expect to hear was wind chimes and...was that a goat?

I frowned, stirring, as consciousness slowly returned.

"Dude, you thirsty?"

As soon as my mind processed the question, I felt parched, absolutely desperate for a drink of water. I pried my eyes open and squinted at the stranger.

He held a ceramic mug up to my mouth. I glanced inside, then recoiled when I saw the frothy white liquid.

"What is that?" I croaked.

"Kefir. Fermented goat's milk. It's really good for your digestive system."

My stomach lurched. "You got anything else?"

He poured something from a mason jar into a glass and offered it to me. I eyed the amber liquid studded with black dots.

"What's that?"

"Kombucha with chia seeds."

My brain was stuck in idle. I blinked and shook my head, trying to come to grips with what was going on.

If I was dead, hell must be customized for each sinner.

My imagination had failed me. I'd expected the devil to sport horns, a pointy beard, and a tail. Instead, this man had red hair twisted into dreadlocks that fell half-way down his back. He wore an orange and lime green tie-dyed T-shirt, camo board shorts, and a friendly smile.

I reached out to rub my eyes, and my hands flopped limply across my chest, lacking the strength and muscle coordination to touch my face.

The cuffs were off. He must have found the key in my back pocket. Hard on the heels of that happy realization came the knowledge that my hands weren't working right.

I glanced down at my chest, and my breath caught in my throat. My black tee had disappeared, and my Janissary cut was no where in sight. I was wearing a purple and yellow tie-dyed monstrosity. I wriggled. My jeans and boots were missing, too.

Fuck me. Fermented goat's milk. Kombucha with chia seeds. Tie-dye. I *was* in hell.

I groaned and closed my eyes.

"Um...Ripper?"

The devil knew my name. Of course, he did. Shouldn't be surprised we were on a first name basis.

"What?" I grunted.

"How about some water?"

I peered suspiciously through half-closed lids. Was he messing with me?

I nodded and waited for him to offer me a drink only to whisk it away at the last second. Instead, he held a glass of water to my lips. I gulped down half the glass. My head fell back against the pillow.

"Thanks." The water I'd managed to collect in my jail cell had kept me alive, but never satisfied my thirst. As the fluid hit my system, I began to feel better.

"Where's my cut?"

"Your what?"

"My leather vest."

He pointed across the room, and I saw it hanging from the back of a wooden chair.

I tried to sit up. Big mistake. Pain speared my head and my side, and my tenuous hold on reality slipped. I collapsed.

The stranger rolled me on my side when I began to vomit up the water I had just drunk. Footsteps told me that another person entered the room. I heard the word concussion before I lapsed back into unconsciousness.

Sometime later I awoke and cautiously opened my eyes. A young woman wearing a long skirt, her blond hair pulled back in a low braid, sat by my bedside reading a book. She must have sensed my eyes on her, because she put down the book and smiled at me.

"Welcome back," she said. She lifted a glass of water from the bedside table and turned the straw so I could drink.

Just in time, I remembered not to lift my head.

"Thanks." My voice sounded rusty and disused. "Name's Ripper."

"Yes, I know." She smiled. "It says so on your vest. My name's Serena. You met Dion a few days ago."

Days ago?

"How long have I been out of it?"

"Travis and Dion found you Friday afternoon. It's Monday morning now, so almost three days."

Three days. I tried to count how many days since I left Portland, but my brain was so foggy that mental calculations were beyond me. I was reduced to counting on my fingers like a first grader, but at least my fingers were cooperating. Meant I was regaining the use of my hands.

I left home on a Friday. I folded under the little finger on my left hand. Started searching for Sara on Saturday. I folded my ring finger down. Checked out the Medford chapter on day four. I bent my pointer finger. Day by day, and finger by finger, I tracked my journey. Tased on day six. Fell into the creek on day eight. Shit. Today was day eleven. Mac must be out of her head with worry.

"Where am I?"

"Elysian Fields." At my blank expression she continued. "It's a cooperative commune outside of Grants Pass. Our founder made a fortune in Silicon Valley. Ten years ago, he bought a thousand acres of land and started the commune. We grow vegetables and hemp, and we have—we had—a business brewing and selling our kombucha. Before the flu, forty seven people lived here."

"How many of you survived the flu?"

"Two. Dion and me."

Two out of forty-seven at the commune and two out of two hundred at the trailer park. The flu was a capricious bitch.

A tall, bearded, young man stuck his head in the door. "I thought I heard voices. Glad to see you're awake." He crossed the room and extended his hand for a shake.

"Ripper, this is Travis," Serena said.

"Heard I have you and Dion to thank for pulling me out of the creek." I shook his hand.

"We went into town to hunt for some propane and saw the patrol car parked on the side of the freeway. When we looked over the guardrail, we thought we saw two bodies in the creek."

"I'm grateful you hauled me out." They found me handcuffed next to a dead cop. Could I have looked more suspicious? It's a wonder they took me in.

"We recognized Deputy Barker," Travis said. "He stopped by Elysian Fields a few times. He'd show up, throw his weight around, and demand that we give him some of our food. He said the community had to support him because he was the only surviving representative of law and order. Shook us down, then called us hippie freaks. The man was a piece of work."

"Suppose you're wondering why he had me in cuffs?"

"Well, yeah." Travis offered a small smile, but I could see the steel behind his friendly expression. I suspected that if he thought I posed a danger to his people, he'd take action. Gotta respect that. Nothing but the truth would do, especially since they'd saved my life.

"I'm a Janissary. I came down from Portland to check on some friends. The deputy got the jump on me in the parking lot of the Medford chapter. He blamed the Janissaries for his sister's death years ago. He put me in a cell. Tased me. It must have been Friday when he drove me to that overpass. Same overpass where his sister died. I jumped him before he could force me over the side. We struggled and both fell."

"You're saying the only reason he arrested you was because you're a Janissary?" Serena asked.

I met her gaze. "That's right."

Serena turned her eyes to Travis. "I believe him. That sounds like Deputy Barker."

"It's a plausible story," Travis agreed, but I could tell he wasn't entirely sold. I didn't hold it against him. I'd be cautious, too.

"Listen, I appreciate everything you've done for me. The only thing I want is to get back home to Portland. I got people waiting for me. Could one of you give me a ride back to Medford so I can get my bike?"

Serena frowned. "You have a concussion. Probably a cracked rib. You're seriously dehydrated, and I doubt you're had much to eat in the past week. You can't ride a motorcycle for hundreds of miles."

I pushed myself up on my elbows and opened my mouth to protest. The room spun, and I dropped like a rock back onto the pillow, swallowing hard against the nausea.

Fuck. If I couldn't lift my head without wanting to puke there was no way I could ride.

"I'll drive you to Medford as soon as you've healed," Travis promised.

"Yeah," I reluctantly conceded. "I'm in no shape to ride."

"Let's start building up your strength." Serena hopped to her feet, her long skirt swishing around her legs. "I'm going to bring you a bowl of beef and barley soup and some fresh strawberries."

Soup and strawberries. My mouth watered. I never wanted to see a corn nut or a candy bar again.

Travis took her place in the chair. He leaned forward, elbows on his knees. "Serena thinks the best of everybody. She's ready to take you at your word about why Barker was holding you. Now, I can't deny that the deputy was an asshole, but I'm not going to pretend that I'm not worried about having a Janissary under our roof. You need to know that I'm ready to do whatever is necessary to protect my people."

"I hear you." I recognized a kindred spirit. "Swear to God, I mean no harm to you or yours. All I want is to get home to *my* people."

"All right." He inclined his head. "As long as you understand where I'm coming from." He pointed at the tattoo on my right arm. "You were a Ranger?"

"Yeah."

His brows slanted. "Seems like a mighty big leap from Ranger to biker."

"You might be surprised. A lot of bikers are ex-military."

"Huh." He leaned back in his chair, brow furrowed while he wrestled with that thought. "Did you miss the camaraderie, the whole band of brothers thing?"

"That's part of it," I said. Travis seemed like a decent man, but I didn't want to talk about brotherhood and feelings and similar shit. I deflected. "You serve?"

"No. I was a paramedic before the flu."

"How'd you come to live on the commune?"

"I met Serena and Dion while scavenging for supplies in Grants Pass. We eventually met a guy named Adam, too. Adam taught chemistry at the high school. We figured out pretty quickly that we're all good folk trying to survive, and that's it's better to stick together. We've got each other's backs. We bring different skills to the mix." Travis shrugged and shook his head. "And with so many people dead, it's a cold and lonely world. You need to hear another human voice, you know? To know you matter to somebody. To feel connected."

"Yeah." Totally got that. Mac and Miles kept me going. Gave me purpose. Helped me retain my humanity. "So, the four of you live together at the commune," I said slowly. "One woman and three men. How's that working?" Tension between me and Kyle had almost torn apart my band of survivors. Couldn't help but wonder if simmering jealousy had been eating away at their group, too.

"I understand what you're getting at," Travis said. "Listen, I've been on the streets taking care of people since the epidemic started. Let me tell you, this virus is unlike anything we've seen before. It's brought us within spitting distance of an extinction event."

He paused and let his words sink in. "Most men who get the flu die, but a few get better. I haven't heard of a single woman who fell sick and recovered. Moving forward, the only women still alive will be that small handful who are asymptomatic carriers or who are naturally immune to the virus. We're facing a future with way more men than women."

"Unreal," I muttered. His stark words painted a bleak picture. Suddenly, I was desperate to be home, to make sure that Mac and everybody was all right. Anything could have happened in eleven days. If Mac got sick...

"God knows what it's going to be like to live in a world where men outnumber women," Travis continued. "How do you make it work? Could things break down to the point where some assholes start to treat women like a scarce commodity?"

"What are you saying?" I asked. "That men will start to fight over women? Or share them?" Impossible to wrap my head around that concept.

I shared women with my brothers when partying at the club, but I always knew that when I claimed an old lady, I'd break the hands of anybody who touched her. That's why I took care to set Kyle straight when he showed up at the compound.

"No clue what will happen," Travis said. "Could play out a lot of different ways. Probably will depend on local circumstances. Some places, men might treat women like commodities. In others, women might retain the power to choose how they live their lives and who—if anybody—they share it with. Maybe some women will choose to take multiple partners. Shit, there were several poly family groups in the commune, so the idea of multiple partners is nothing new to Serena and Dion."

"And you?" I asked. "You down with sharing?"

"Fuck, no," he said emphatically. "The world's changed, so I get why it might come down to that for some people, but I'm not wired to share. Fortunately, Dion is like Serena's little brother and Adam is gay. Serena and I—it's early days—but we're building something, and it's good."

"Glad for you, man," I said. "Not wired to share, either. Understand why it might make sense for some people, but it ain't happening."

Serena bustled into the room, carrying a tray. "Travis, can you get some pillows so we can help Ripper sit up?"

"Sure." He dropped a kiss on her cheek and left the room.

"Adam just came home with a big mess of rainbow trout. We'll have fresh fish for dinner," she said. "The protein will do you good."

Travis returned with a pile of pillows. Despite my protests that I could sit up on my own, he eased an extra pillow under my head, lifting it enough that I could swallow without choking.

Serena pulled the chair close to the bed and spooned soup into my mouth. I insisted on eating the fresh strawberries by myself and was relieved that my eye-hand coordination was returning. No more floppy hands. I hit my chin on my first try, but managed to get the rest directly into my mouth. After a week of nothing but processed crap, fresh food was great.

I fell asleep after the meal, waking only when Travis brought another tray of food. I spent the rest of Monday and most of Tuesday alternating between resting, eating, and drinking water.

The dizziness improved so much that by Tuesday afternoon I was able to swing my legs over the side of the bed and stand up. Couldn't walk a straight line to save my life, and my head throbbed like a son of a bitch, but I was on my feet.

On Wednesday morning, my balance began to return and my mind felt clearer. My hosts filled the bathtub with hot water and I took a long soak, washing for the first time in more than a week. Dressed again in my freshly laundered jeans, black tee, and cut, I began to feel more like myself. The bruises on my ribs were fading, although I felt a stitch in my side when I walked. Travis concluded that my ribs had been only badly bruised and not cracked.

Over dinner that night, I asked Travis if he could drive me to Medford the following morning.

"No problem."

"Got another favor to ask you." Felt like a dumb shit because this hadn't occurred to me before now.

Travis raised his brows. "Yeah? What?"

"I met another survivor when I came to town. A fourteen-year-old kid named Gus Dominguez. He lives in a trailer park down by the Rogue River. Great kid. Smart. Resourceful. Friendly. Wanted him to come back to Portland with me, but he refused. Said he's waiting for his dad to come home from California."

Travis and Serena exchanged a glance.

"Yeah. That's not gonna happen, but Gus isn't ready to give up hope. I could've dragged him with me, but I knew that as soon as I turned my back, he'd run away and try to get back home. He's got food and water to last a while, but the kid's a sitting duck."

"I'll check on him tomorrow on my way back from Medford," Travis said.

"We'll tell him you sent us so he knows we're friends," Serena added. "It's been more than a week since you parted ways. He might be getting lonely or scared. Even if he's not willing to go to Portland, he might be willing to come back to Elysian Fields with us. I'll tell him we can leave a sign inside his trailer, letting his father know where to find him."

"We'll take good care of him. I promise," Travis said.

"Appreciate it."

That promise took a load off my conscience. I'd rather Gus came home with me. Never thought much about having kids, but I liked the idea of watching Gus grow up, keeping him safe, teaching him what I know. Gonna be someone else's job, but at least he'd have a shot at a good life.

I shared a final meal with Serena and the men Thursday morning. Buckwheat pancakes, scrambled eggs, and berries. I broke down and tried a glass of Dion's kombucha—which tasted better than it looked—but I drew the line at fermented goat's milk.

Dion insisted on sending along one of his tie-dyed creations. I smiled and thanked him, imaging how cute Mac would look walking around my bedroom in it, her long legs peeking out below the pink and lavender swirls.

Travis and I stopped at the dead deputy's patrol car so I could retrieve my Colt from the glove box. Ten days after my disastrous encounter with Deputy Barker, I'd come full circle and arrived back at the parking lot of the Medford clubhouse.

Odds were nobody had come near my Shovelhead since the deputy ambushed me, but it was a relief to find it untouched. I filled the tank with fuel from the commune's supply, found my wallet, then turned to Travis. We shook hands.

"Thanks for everything."

He nodded. "Good luck getting back to your family."

"No luck required. Nothing is going to stop me this time."

I swung onto my bike and fired the engine. The familiar rumble felt like coming home. In a few hours, I'd be reunited with Mac and Miles and Kyle. I raised a hand in farewell to Travis and watched him drive away.

My bike ate up the miles between Medford and Portland. I stopped about halfway home to top off my gasoline and take a leak, then quickly resumed my trip.

Something more than a simple longing for home drove my haste. The closer I got to the city, the more I sensed that something was wrong.

I'd learned to trust my intuition, that insistent, irrational prickle on the back of my neck that warned me of trouble.

Fifty miles from Portland, I saw a haze in the northern sky and began to smell smoke. Twenty miles from Portland, the smoke grew heavier, and I spied a red glow on the horizon.

Fuck, no. Portland was burning.

FORTY-ONE

Kenzie

"Let's be on the road in one minute, guys," Kyle said.

I ran to my bedroom and slipped the leather pouch into my go bag, then hurried back to the kitchen to snatch up Hector's leash. Through the window, I saw Kyle climb into the front passenger seat of the jeep. Sahdev threw his bag and Kyle's into the open rear hatch. He dashed back across the yard toward the house and grabbed my pack.

I whistled for Hector, who was sleeping in the living room. When he trotted to my side, I clipped the leash to his collar.

Sahdev opened the kitchen door, took my bag, and jogged toward the jeep.

"We're going for a ride, Hector." I closed the kitchen door for the last time.

The dog seemed to sense our urgency. He strained at the leash. I scampered after him across the yard, hesitating only to glance one last time at Miles's grave.

I'm sorry to leave you behind. I love you, cousin.

When we neared the open passenger door, Hector bolted.

I'd loosened my grip on the leash, expecting the well-behaved dog to jump inside the jeep. Instead, he hurtled across the yard, rounding Ripper's garage.

I gave chase and saw the dog make a right turn out of the driveway, heading south before he disappeared into the murk. I sprinted after him, determined not to lose my last living connection with Ripper.

Please God make him stop.

I didn't dare spare the breath to pray aloud. Smoke stung my throat, and my eyes watered. I stumbled, found my footing again, and kept going. The jeep trailed somewhere behind me, and Kyle's voice called out.

Up ahead, a round light pierced the smoky haze, appearing to float at waist height above the ground. Gasping for breath, I pushed on. Hector barked, and the sound propelled me forward.

I staggered to a stop when I neared the glowing circle. Hector danced on his hind legs, excitedly pawing at the chest of the dark-haired man who'd halted his motorcycle in the middle of the street.

I stared slack-jawed as Ripper cut the engine, toed down the kick stand, and swung off his bike. Three long strides and I was in his arms.

Clutching at his chest, I buried my face in his throat. My tongue darted out, and I licked his skin and moaned, tasting the salt and road grime.

He laughed softly. "I missed you too, darlin'."

Only then did I know that he was real, that my oxygen-deprived mind hadn't conjured him up to ease the way while the smoke stole my consciousness. I seized his head, pulling his face down for a kiss.

After we broke apart, he tugged on the two chains dangling from my neck. "My dog tags?"

I nodded. "Wearing them made me feel closer to you."

His fingers found my platinum pendant necklace, and he stroked the padlock charm. "Sorry I wasn't here for your birthday. I tried."

"You're here now. That means everything."

The jeep rolled to a stop behind us. I turned in Ripper's arms as Kyle and Sahdev climbed out.

"Ripper, this is Sahdev. He's a doctor and good friend who's been staying with us at the compound."

Sahdev stepped forward and extended his hand. "How do you do."

"Good to meet you." Ripper glanced at Kyle. "You look like shit, man."

Kyle shrugged. "The flu kicked my ass, but I'm getting better, thanks to Sahdev."

Ripper glanced into the jeep, frowning. "Where's Miles?"

Heart sinking, I twisted back to face him. "Miles is gone. He got the flu, and he didn't make it."

"Fuck. No." Ripper hunched forward, as if someone had punched him in the gut.

Because I was holding onto him, I felt his slight tremor as he processed the news. He straightened up, his face a mask. He'd lost too many people to break down over one more death, but I knew he loved Miles like a brother and would grieve his loss deeply.

He glanced at my face, his eyes softening. "I'm sorry, Mac. You all right?"

"I'll miss him forever, but I'm better now that you're here."

"The fire has spread to this side of the river," Kyle said. "Maybe it was Caleb, maybe the wind blowing embers. We'll never know, but we need to get moving. We have a destination, an isolated ranch in central Oregon. You want to lead the way to I-84 east?"

"Yeah. Mac, you with me?"

"Are you kidding? I'm not letting you out of my sight for the next week."

"Gonna go to my place first and grab a helmet for Mac outta my garage," Ripper called to Kyle.

Kyle nodded, then whistled, and this time Hector obediently leapt into the jeep. Sahdev took his place in the driver's seat and waited for Ripper to start his engine. If he was shocked to see me in the arms of a leather-clad, outlaw biker, he was too polite to let it show. It didn't matter, not in the long run. Once Sahdev got to know Ripper, he'd see beyond the cut to the loyal and brave man I loved.

I climbed on the bike behind Ripper and wrapped my arms around his waist. It took less than two minutes to retrieve a helmet from his garage. Without a backward glance, Ripper rode away from his home.

He dropped a hand to my leg, his fingers curling into my calf. From the moment we met, I'd been enthralled by his hands, by the promise of strength and protection they held.

I wanted to be loved and safe, the same things my mother wanted, but that didn't mean I was weak or that I'd repeat her mistakes. It had taken me too damned long to figure that out. Loving Ripper made me stronger. With him at my side, I could have and be everything I wanted.

I closed my eyes and pressed my cheek against his cut as the bike accelerated.

Heartbreaking loss and confounding change had reshaped our world. We faced an uncertain future, yet I looked forward with renewed optimism. Hope, as tenacious as a weed, had taken root in my heart. My man had come back to me. Good men stood by our side.

Whatever came next, we'd face it together.

Ripper and Kenzie's story continues in *Maelstrom*, book two of the World Fallen series.

ACKNOWLEDGMENTS

The publication of Pandemonium marks the fulfillment of a lifelong dream. I'm grateful to the many people whose advice and assistance made it possible.

Becca Syme helped me to discover the writing system that works best for both my brain and my inherent strengths. With that knowledge, I crushed the roadblocks that had hindered my progress. Within six months of working with Becca, I went from wannabe author to real life novelist.

Once I completed the first draft of my first novel, I screwed up my courage and sent the manuscript off to my favorite author's developmental editor, Christina Trevaskis. Was I intimidated? Yes, but only at first. Tina's enthusiasm and goodwill quickly put me at ease. She has a positive genius for identifying a story's strengths and weaknesses. Her knowledge and skills are unmatched. She is patient, astute, and wise. She taught me to write fearlessly and from the heart. Hiring Christina Trevaskis was one of the smartest things I've ever done.

I'm indebted to my critique partner, Raven Dark, a gifted author, for the many hours that she spent brainstorming with me. Raven is a pillar of support and the first person to read every chapter. Her encouragement and advice mean the world to me.

A big shout-out to my dear friend, Debbie Morley, plot-whisperer extraordinaire. When I need to bounce plot ideas off someone, Debbie is my go-to person. Her wild imagination and gleeful exuberance make the process a joy.

Brittany Meyer-Strom and Sharon Shook brought their impressive proofreading skills to the manuscript, combing through it, discovering typos and errors that made me blush. I called my male protagonist Ripple instead of Ripper? How the heck did that slip by me? If you think you don't need a proofreader, guess again.

Shree Aier generously agreed to be a sensitivity reader, helping me to avoid cultural inaccuracies, stereotypes, and problematic language in my depiction of a character whose family immigrated from North India. I love the character and want to do right by him. I very much appreciate her guidance.

I was lucky enough to secure the services of my favorite cover designer, Lori Jackson. Lori was endlessly patient with a first-time author and went above and beyond offering advice and assistance. Working with an image from the brilliant photographer Wander Aguiar, Lori designed a cover so perfect that I smile every time I see it.

To Korrie Noelle, who's beautiful both inside and out, many thanks for her unwavering encouragement, support and friendship.

Thanks to Cat Porter, whose work inspires me to be better every day.

Hugs and kisses to my sister-in-law, Kathy Bahr—a writer herself—who was one of the first people to read Pandemonium. Her suggestions helped me to craft a better story, and her enthusiastic support bolstered my confidence.

I lucked out when it comes to my brothers-in-law. Pete Dominguez and Kurt Bahr encouraged me every step of the way. Harry Shook shared his knowledge of both Harley motorcycles and firearms with me. When I asked Bill Hoefer what types of weapons a wild-eyed survivalist might stockpile, he spent hours patiently answering all my questions.

Thanks to Dion Williams for explaining the workings of ham radios to an absolute Luddite.

A final thank you to my husband, John Hoefer, who always encourages me to follow my dreams. Every time I tell him what I need, his response is, "Go for it." Quit my job so I have more time to write? Buy a new laptop? Sign up for a workshop? John always tells me to go for it. The man cheerfully listens to me ramble on about characters and plot points. He never complains when I ask him to spend one of his days off driving around the state with me, tracing the routes taken by my characters. He's my tech guy. I couldn't ask for a better, more supportive partner.